Wia

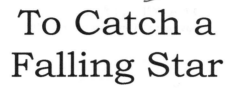

C000160787

To Catch a Falling Star

The sequel to *Twice Nightly*
Tales from the Great Yarmouth Series

– TONY GARETH SMITH –

An environmentally friendly book printed and bound in England by
www.printondemand-worldwide.com

Mixed Sources
Product group from well-managed
forests, and other controlled sources
www.fsc.org Cert no. TT-COC-002641
© 1996 Forest Stewardship Council
FSC

PEFC
PEFC/16-33-415

PEFC Certified
This product is
from sustainably
managed forests
and controlled
sources
www.pefc.org

This book is made entirely of chain-of-custody materials

www.fast-print.net/store.php

TO CATCH A FALLING STAR
Copyright © Tony Gareth Smith 2014

A catalogue record for this book is available from the British Library

ISBN 978-178035-713-3

First published 2014 by
FASTPRINT PUBLISHING
Peterborough, England.

For Audrey with my love

and also to my special friend Dee

Author's Note

When I wrote *Twice Nightly* it had not been my intention to write a sequel. However, such was the positive feedback I had from readers who were keen to know what happened to certain characters, here it is - *To Catch a Falling Star*. I hope you will enjoy it every bit as much as I have enjoyed writing it.

Tony Gareth Smith

Overture

T he reflection in the mirror looked back at her and her mind wandered for a few moments to the memories that now tricked her train of thought. Everything had been for a reason; everything that happened had been mapped out. Her elbow knocked the glass of water causing it to spill over and she came back to reality. The lights around the mirror lit her face and, looking at the array of make-up that lay on the dressing room table, she leaned forward and studied her complexion carefully. Taking the foundation container in her left hand she applied the base with her right in firm sweeping strokes. With a deft hand and attention to detail she applied her eyeshadow with the soft brush that had been with her from the start of her career. The brush was one she treasured; it was of fine hair and had been a gift from her great aunt for succeeding where she had failed. The wand of mascara provided the lift that her eyelashes needed and the black eyeliner made her eyes appear wider. She then picked up the false eyelashes and applied a thin streak of glue to each and laid them to one side in order that they would become tacky. Adding more colour to the base foundation made her face come alive as if it had been kissed by rays of Mediterranean sunshine, the rouge highlighted her strong cheekbones and her face began to create the other persona. Carefully applying the thick top false eyelashes and the slightly less heavy bottom ones gave her eyes the look needed for the strong stage lights that would flood them. Her lipstick was the final touch of colour to the collage and the thin black pencil outlined her lips with definition. She sat back from the mirror to view the end product. Her fingernails were freshly painted and all that remained would be for her to clip the diamond earrings to her ears, fasten the matching necklace about her neck, slip into the stage gown, place her feet firmly in the silver stilettos and prepare to face her public.

Her teeth dazzled as she smiled at her reflection, her transformation was complete. A voice behind her suddenly invaded her tranquillity.

"Are you ready now?"

She turned and looked at the person who stood in the doorway and nodded. She got up from the dressing room table and, after the handcuffs were applied to her wrists, she was led away in complete silence.

▪▪▪

Chapter One   *Winter Wood*

December 1969

J im Donnell picked up the post from the doormat and yawned. It had been a very late night at *Sparkles Night Club* where he and his best friend David Grant had been run off their feet. Party season had a lot to answer for, especially getting people out of the place when time was called. During the summer months Jim worked at *The Golden Sands Theatre* on the South Pier and Dave at *The Wellington Pier Theatre* further along the promenade. When the season was finished they both took up their winter jobs at the nightclub owned by Dave's cousin. The money was good but the hours were long and with every passing year Jim had been considering looking for something else.

With his daughter Debbie and son-in-law Peter now living in Norwich and a baby on the way, life had taken an upturn since his wife Karen had died and he hoped he would be able to spend more time with them as a family.

His mate Dave had settled down with Dan Forester, a young guy from Preston, and they were living in the flat above a gift shop that was owned by Enid Smith the sister of Maud Bennett who ran the box office during the summer season at the *Sands*. Jim missed his wife, and the chair that stood near the small fireplace was a constant reminder that Karen was no longer with him. He had never sat in the chair since her death, in his head it had become a shrine to the woman he had loved since childhood. He knew that he really should try to move on with his life and make some changes to the house, but his heart told him a different story and so things remained as they had been when Karen was alive.

He poured himself a cup of tea and sat down to open the mail. Among the bills and *Reader's Digest* offer for yet another set of long-playing records featuring artistes of yesteryear, there was a letter from Rita Ricer, the wife of comedian Ted. Rita mentioned that Ted had been busy touring the nightclub circuit and she had been doing a few engagements around the country in various showcases. Jim smiled as he continued to read Rita's news and he could hear Rita speaking to him as if she were in the room. He really liked Rita and, over the years they had known each other, her and Ted had been good friends. He smiled to himself as he remembered how Rita would busy herself around old Ted like she was his mother. Any wardrobe malfunction was dealt with, a new joke sheet sorted out, and as for dealing with any theatrical producer or director she was second to none. Many years previously Rita had done an act in her own right as Moira Clarence, but had given up the business to nurture and look after her husband as he toured the country with his stand-up comedy routine. An unexpected turn of events earlier that year had seen Rita once more return to the stage as Moira Clarence and a new career for her had begun.

He put the letter down and wondered what the next summer season would bring. Bernard Delfont was sure to be bringing a big television star to *The Golden Sands Theatre* and, unlike the summer season just gone, there would be no pre-season summer show. The memory of that was still foremost in his mind.

He lit a cigarette and inhaled deeply. He was annoyed with himself, only a couple of weeks before he had promised himself that he would give them up. Pouring a second cup of tea he tore open the *Reader's Digest* envelope, noting immediately that he was already in the third stage of their latest prize draw. He, like many others, wondered if anyone had ever won the top prize. Perhaps he would order the sixty golden greats on offer, there were some tracks on there that he and Karen had enjoyed. He looked for a pen — perhaps he would order two sets, old Maud and Enid might enjoy the set over the Christmas holidays and he was never quite sure what to buy them. If Karen were still around, she would have known what to get them both, but now those decisions were left to him.

Christmas could be a lonely time and although Debbie and Peter had moved to Norwich he was unsure of their plans. Peter may well want to spend Christmas at his parents. He had thought of inviting Dave and Dan over for Christmas Day, but as this would be their first Christmas together they may have other plans. Then there was Maud and Enid to consider. With Karen at the helm they had often joined the Christmas celebrations in the Donnell household. Maud was always good for a laugh and once you had given Enid a second sherry, she began to loosen up. Enid had been known to protest at being offered the demon drink, but that didn't seem to stop her helping herself to a third sherry before lunch when she thought no one else was looking. Still, now that they had both moved in together at Maud's, perhaps they would invite him over for the day. Why was Christmas so complicated and how had Karen made it look so easy?

He looked at the clock, it was nearly midday and he really should take some flowers to the grave. The last few mornings had been so cold and he had felt so tired that he hadn't made the effort. He cleared the table, put a stamp on the *Reader's Digest* envelope, remembering to include all the entry papers for the prize draw, deciding he would rather have the money than a new car, and grabbed his coat. Picking up his keys from the hall table he headed out of the front door.

The cemetery was relatively quiet as Jim walked along the path between the many gravestones. A chill in the air made him pull his scarf tighter and his gloveless hands took the brunt as they held the flowers he had purchased. He hoped that Debbie and Peter would be able to visit, even if they didn't come for the Christmas holidays. He knew how much it meant to his daughter that her mother's memory was kept alive. Kneeling down on the damp grass, Jim removed the dead flowers from the urn and wrapped them in the folded newspaper from his jacket pocket. He went to the stand pump and filled the urn with water and began to arrange the floral offering as best he could. He read the inscription on the headstone as he always did and spoke a silent prayer in his head. He reflected on many things and, not for the first time, wished his beloved wife was still here with him. As he moved away from the grave he heard a voice he recognised call his name.

"Hello Lilly. My goodness it has been a while since I saw you, how are you?"

Lilly Brocket smiled at Jim and touched his arm. "No need to ask where you have been."

"Or you," Jim replied, remembering the words he had read in the article Lilly had given on the publication of her first novel, a baby boy taken too soon and a husband she had loved dearly. "Are you planning on returning to the *Sands* next summer?"

Lilly shook her head. "I don't think so Jim. I've been offered a book deal and with the royalties from my first, I'll have no need to continue cleaning. I'm afraid Bob Scott will have to find someone else. I've continued to do a few days at the hospital, but that will end come January."

Jim looked at Lilly and couldn't quite believe she was the same person. Until a few short months ago, Lilly had worked as a cleaner at the *Sands Theatre*. She looked different and sounded different, not put upon as she used to. There was a confidence that had never been there before and Jim felt happy for her.

"Have you time for cup of tea?"

Lilly nodded. "That would be most welcome Jim."

Jim led the way to his car which was parked just outside the gates and decided that tea and toast in *Palmers* coffee shop would fit the bill nicely.

* * *

Maud Bennett had left her sister Enid to run the gift shop, it wasn't particularly busy at that moment and she felt in need of some fresh air. There was a definite chill in the air that morning; she hurried along the row and on to the market place. There were one or two people with shopping baskets and the fruit and veg stalls were festooned with coloured lights and baubles. The twenty-foot Christmas tree took centre stage just in front of the chip stalls and was a blaze of twinkling lights. Christmas, it seemed to Maud, got earlier every year and she sighed heavily at the thought. Father Christmas had taken up residence in both *Palmers* and *Arnold's* department stores. This year *Arnold's* had Father Christmas in an underwater cavern, while *Palmers* had a traditional sleigh and reindeer set in a wooded glade together with a toyshop. She headed across the road and was just in time to catch the bus to Gorleston High Street where she had some business to attend to. She nodded to a few people she knew and settled herself down at the back of the double-decker in the hope of some time to herself. Since Enid had moved in with her, peace was something that was in short supply. Although they both had their own living quarters, Enid seemed to prefer to sit in Maud's living room every night. Maud liked to busy herself and Enid was a distraction. Enid didn't have any hobbies and liked nothing more than chatting with her sister.

Opening her handbag, Maud took a *Mint Imperial* from a paper bag and popped it in her mouth. The bus set off on its journey and Maud rubbed the condensation from the glass and looked out of the window in the hope that no one came and disturbed her.

* * *

"Morning Maud," called Marjorie.

The wool shop was buzzing with customers and Marjorie and her sister Ethel were rushed off their feet. Maud busied herself looking at the latest patterns as one by one the shop began to empty leaving her a clear run at the counter.

"You are busy in here this morning," said Maud, sitting herself down in the chair at the side of the counter, reserved for the more discerning customer.

"More two-ply in mauve?" asked Marjorie, clearing the counter of unwanted samples.

"Want to get a move on and finish the cardigan I have planned for Barbara's Christmas present and then I can make a start on a pullover for Jim. Enid says if my needles click any faster I will need a bucket of water beside my chair to dip them in to. Says she wouldn't be surprised to see smoke coming off them."

"How are things with you and Enid now she has moved in with you?"

"Well, we both have our own living areas since the boys helped convert the house and she does have the rent from the flat above the shop coming in which helps the coffers," Maud replied, with one of her customary sighs. "But I have to say living with one's sister isn't an easy thing and no mistake. Enid has never married as you know, though, strange to relate looking at her now, there were several offers of marriage. I think she would have turned out a happier person if she had had a man in her life."

Marjorie nodded her head in agreement and looked at her sister who was sorting out some stock that had arrived. "I know what you mean Maud. Now, how many balls of the mauve did you want?"

* * *

Freda Boggis came puffing along the road carrying her Christmas shopping just as her neighbour Muriel Evans was coming out of her front garden gate.

"Its taters today," said Freda, putting her shopping down in the hope of a bit of a chat. She hadn't seen Muriel in a week and wondered if something was amiss. She noticed that Muriel was wearing yet another new coat; she hadn't seen that one before. In fact, her neighbour seemed to have more coats than *C&A*.

Muriel, who was in a rush but didn't wish to be rude, smiled at Freda. "Hello Freda, been shopping I can see. I am just off to get a few bits in. Barry and I have been over to visit his sister who has been taken very poorly."

"Is she at death's door?" asked Freda, who was well known for saying the wrong thing.

Muriel raised her eyebrows. "No, she isn't thank goodness. Chloe is Barry's only remaining flesh and blood and he is very fond of her."

Freda coughed out of embarrassment. "I saw your Barry with some ladders the other week, has he started a new job?"

"He is repainting some of the bedrooms ready for next season. You would be advised to do likewise Freda Boggis. Get that husband of yours out of the *Legion* doing something useful for a change."

"You know my Dick, won't do a hand's turn around the house, but is more than willing to help them down at that club. Anyway, there is nothing wrong with my bedrooms, I never get any complaints."

"And never any visitors coming back," Muriel said knowingly and went on her way.

* * *

Lucinda Haines was also in the throes of having some work done in her guest house. Since having Ted and Rita Ricer to stay she had realised she needed to smarten things up a bit. Lucinda, who had been quite smitten by Ted, had overheard the couple talking about the threadbare carpets and the worn out eiderdowns.

Lucinda, who had always played her cards very close to her chest and had squirreled away money for that rainy day, had also come in to money some years before. Alice, a friend from way back, had left her a considerable sum, providing that Lucinda didn't touch the inheritance until five years after she had passed. It seemed rather a strange clause to have in a will but the solicitor had been quite firm about the details. As it turned out, five years down the line the initial sum was worth more, thanks to some investment that Alice had made. It was with this money that Lucinda felt that some worthwhile improvements to the guest house could be made. She, like others in the same business, knew that she couldn't go on working for ever and would someday have to sell up and move to a smaller, more manageable home.

So, taking some advice from a local carpenter-cum-plumber, she was going to have washing facilities put in every bedroom, new beds and wardrobes, some much-needed bed linen, and carpet laid throughout. The dining room would have some tables and chairs that she had picked up as a job lot from an auction that would far outshine the ones she currently had. And a new, larger cooker would mean that she could consider offering an evening meal on a more regular basis. The ground floor at the back of the property was going to be turned into a self-contained living area that would have its own door leading in off the back garden as well as a communicating door from the main house. A small bedroom, bathroom and kitchen-dining area would mean that in the winter months Lucinda could save on fuel bills. Her guests during this time were usually workmen from the oil rigs and all they required was bed and breakfast. They came highly recommended by the companies they worked for so Lucinda had little worry that any harm would come to her property.

This was a big step for Lucinda who had always been frugal, but after the goings-on during the season of 1969, she felt that she should embrace change. Besides, she had heard on the grapevine that Muriel Evans was having her guest house interior repainted and she had no intention of one of her rivals coming out on top. When her home was fully refurbished she would invite Muriel and that neighbour of hers, Freda, for tea and give them a guided tour, if only to see the look of envy on Muriel's face. There was no doubt about it, Lucinda Haines was moving up in the world.

* * *

Jim and Lilly found themselves a corner table in the coffee shop and Lilly told him of her plans. She had decided that the time had come to move away from the house which for so many years had held painful reminders. She had her eye on a small cottage on the outskirts of Gorleston and hoped that everything would be settled by the New Year. Jim expressed his concerns that moving away from the area where all her friends were might not be such a good idea.

"I know what you mean," said Lilly, taking a sip of tea. "I have never had very much in my life and now this book publishing has given me a new lease of life. I know I shall never be able to live like a queen, but at least I will be able to see out my years in some kind of comfort. I have nothing to lose Jim, and if it all goes wrong, I can still pick up a scrubbing brush and find work."

Jim looked at the lady whom he had known for many years and could see that a transformation had taken place. Gone was the worried look that clouded her face, her eyes now twinkled and she had a smile that would have lightened the hardest of hearts. "You really have thought this through haven't you? I have to applaud your bravery. I don't know that I could make such a change."

Lilly remained quiet for a few moments and then continued. "For you Jim, everything is still raw. For me, the ghosts have gone, though the memories are always with me." She reached out and touched his hand. "Maybe one day Jim you too will be able to move on when the time is right."

Jim smiled and nodded in acknowledgement but in his heart he was afraid that that day would never come.

* * *

In Hull the Ricer household was in chaos, Ted was sorting through his theatrical wardrobe to find something suitable for his next set of gigs. Rita his wife stood and watched in horror. "Now my old lover, I hope you're not expecting me to put that lot back when you've quite finished emptying everything out of that blessed wardrobe?"

The spare bedroom had always been used to house theatrical regalia and now that Rita was also back in the business, it had spilled over into the third bedroom of the small terrace, to which some of Ted's gear had mysteriously found its way.

Ted was holding up two jackets as he turned to face his wife. "Rita I can't find my blue jacket, the one I like with the braided lapel."

"You left it in Grimsby at the *Dockers' Working Men's Club* so that you didn't have to keep packing it. You play there so often it seemed to make sense."

"Oh, don't say that," said Ted, feeling agitated, "I really wanted to wear that tonight, it's my lucky jacket."

"Lucky jacket indeed!" Rita exclaimed "The only time that jacket was ever lucky was when Mystic Brian's doves missed it by inches and deposited a nasty mess all over that Dean Sister's wig at the *Sands* in Great Yarmouth last summer."

"Fancy you remembering that," said Ted, picking up a red jacket that had seen better days. "I wonder where they are now."

"Touring in some European circus I expect, if all went to plan. Brian is doing Christmas in Bristol this year, it was in this week's *Stage*."

"Any chance of a bacon buttie my little love?" asked Ted, looking hopefully at Rita as she stood arms folded in the doorway.

"I will make you a bacon buttie my old lover if you make sure you leave this room tidy. I have my own wardrobe to sort out later I will have you know. The *Empire* is hardly my favourite venue, but at least it's work and I have to look good if nothing else."

"You always look good my darling," said Ted, playing his trump card in flattery.

"And you can cut out the flannel Ted Ricer, and don't look at me with those doe eyes. You remind me of Bambi's mother and we all know what happened to her."

"Oh Reet!"

* * *

Meanwhile, in Norwich Debbie was debating how she was going to tell her father that this Christmas she and Peter would be spending the holiday with his parents. With a baby on the way in the New Year, Debbie knew that the only place she really wanted to be was with her dad. But realising it was not fair on her husband she had agreed with Peter that this year it was his mum and dad's turn. She didn't like to think of her dad on his own in the house where she had grown up, but it would have to happen sooner or later. And maybe this way it would ease the pain when the next Christmas she and Peter would want to spend it in their own home with their first-born. She looked down at her bump and felt a flush of excitement. This time last year a baby would have been the last thing on her mind. She hoped it would be a girl, but knew that Peter had his heart set on a boy as he had often talked about playing football with his son. One thing was certain, it would be one or the other and disappointment would be someone's fate. She picked up her shopping basket and went off in search of the bus into the city centre.

* * *

"And where have you been?" asked Enid, as Maud entered the shop carrying her wool supply.

"I had to go over to Marjorie's for some more wool," replied Maud, laying the package down on the counter. "Why, has something happened that I need to know about?"

"Contrary to some people's belief it has been quite busy in here this morning and an extra pair of hands would have been most welcome. I had that Mrs Jary in from the convenience store and she had me turn the shop upside down. She wanted some of those candle holders with the robins on we had last year."

"Well, you wouldn't have found any," said Maud, noting her sister's curtness. She must have got out of the wrong side of the bed and no mistake. "We sold the last of those in the sale last January and you said you weren't going to get any more as they were what you termed 'slow burners' which, given the fact they held candles, I thought was rather funny at the time. Now, are you going to stand there with a face like a smacked arse all day, or shall I put the kettle on and make you a nice cup of *Camp* coffee with a cream horn I picked up from *Matthes* on the way?"

Enid knew when she was beaten and half-smiled at her sister. "That would be very nice Maud dear, and then you can help me price the boxes of crackers that arrived this morning," she said, pointing to the large parcel in the corner of the shop.

Maud sighed and took off her coat. "And what delights will they have in them this year I wonder? Honestly, the price of them they should at least have something decent beneath all that coloured paper toilet roll."

Enid clicked her tongue. "I will have you know they are this year's deluxe range."

"Oh fantastic!" said Maud, warming to her theme. "There will at least be one tea caddy spoon in one of them. The customers will be cock–a-hoop!"

"That's enough of your sarcasm Maud Bennett. Now, are you making that drink or not, I'm fair parched."

No sooner had Maud placed a cup of coffee in front of her sister than the shop suddenly became full of eager shoppers. Maud could not remember the shop being this busy last year, and not for the first time did it cross her mind that there was money to be made in tat and knick-knacks and it really would be worthwhile expanding the business to Regent Road during the summer months. But somehow she couldn't imagine Enid shifting on that, her sister wasn't one for change as the sharing of her home had proven.

* * *

Above the shop and out of earshot of their landlady Enid, Dave and Dan were enjoying a late breakfast. Dan had a day off and intended to make the most of it and get a few things in for Christmas. He needed to go and visit his family in Preston and take some presents to them but limited time off at this busy time of the year was proving to be a stumbling block. It wasn't the same, parcelling up presents and putting them in the post, besides he liked to see his mum and dad. He was hoping he could persuade Dave to go to Preston with him to meet the family; they seemed to be getting on well and he thought the time had come to tell his parents about his new found boyfriend. He knew his mother wouldn't have a problem with it, his father on the other hand could be quite old-fashioned where these kind of things were concerned. Though both knew about their son's preferences.

Dave buttered some toast and took a slurp of his coffee. "Something on your mind?" he enquired, noting Dan's thoughtful expression.

"I was just wondering when I would get the chance to take some presents up to the family," Dan replied, whacking the top of his boiled egg. "I don't think I can get any extra time off. Ken has told Stella and me it's all hands to the pump and, as Stella said, it's unlikely that any extra staff will be taken on to help out."

Dave knew how important family was to his friend; in the few months that they had known each other that much had been evident. "I don't know if Ken would agree to this, but how about if I were to offer to do your shifts for a couple of days so that you could go up to Preston. I've worked bars before and I think I could get old Jim to pitch in a few hours."

That was one of the things that Dan loved about Dave, he always thought of others, never putting his own needs first. "But you have your nightclub shifts, you couldn't possibly do mine as well."

Dave smiled. "Look, it would only be for a couple of days. I could do the evening shift and Jim could cover for me at the club until I got there. The door is hardly busy at ten, it's after eleven when most of the punters start pouring in, all after their late night drinks. Jim could manage a lunchtime I'm sure and that way Stella wouldn't be left holding the fort. Look, put it to Ken and see how he feels about it. I'll have a word with Jim; you never know, we might even be able to rope in Maud as an extra pair of hands."

Dan gave Dave a broad smile. "Thanks mate, I'll mention it to Ken tomorrow." He would broach the subject of Dave visiting Preston another time.

*   *   *

Enid had just gone to get some lunch when Jim came into the shop. Maud looked at her old friend and smiled. "Hello young Jim, what brings you into this trove of treasures and curios?"

Jim leant over the counter and gave Maud a kiss on the cheek. "Just had elevenses with Lilly, did you know she was thinking of moving to a cottage over Gorleston way?"

"Do you know, I haven't actually seen much of Lilly since the launch of that book of hers. It's a bit like you and I, once the summer season comes to an end we all go to our winter work. I mean, how often do you walk in here? Never the twain shall meet, as my old mother used to say." Maud sighed, as only Maud could. "I never thought our Lilly would want to move from that house of hers, not after all that has gone before, memories and that."

"I think it's because of the memories that she does want to move," said Jim, recounting the conversation that had taken place. "Lilly was quite animated, like she wanted to get everything off her chest. She seems different now. I remember how she turned up at the *Sands* every summer, always wearing that same outfit, how she beavered away at her cleaning, dropped the odd Lilly comment which always made me laugh. I will miss that."

"So she won't be returning to the *Sands* next summer?" Maud replied. "I had my doubts about that but you can't blame her. Whenever I see Lilly in my mind's eye I can see her red hands, too many years spent dousing cleaning cloths into *Flash*. She's had a hard life and not one I would wish on anyone. Who could begrudge her a change of pace now?"

"You will hear no complaints from this quarter," said Jim, "though what old Scott will do when he learns she isn't coming back I don't know. He will be hard pressed to find anyone as hard-working or as loyal as Lilly has been all these years. She told me that she is still working a few hours at the hospital until the end of January. Said it would help her ease her way out of cleaning work."

Maud smiled in acknowledgement. "Our Lilly Brockett, who would have thought it? Whereabouts is this cottage anyway?"

"I don't have all the ins and outs but she did say that we would all be invited to see it when she had settled in."

A lump came to Maud's throat. "Good on you Lilly," she said and turned away from Jim to hide her tears.

* * *

When choreographer Jenny Benjamin had reluctantly decided to take the advice of others and retire she had entrusted her dancing school to the more than capable hands of two former pupils, Jill Sanderson and Doreen Turner. The agreement was that the name of Jenny Benjamin would live on and Jill and Doreen would inject some much needed change of style and pace. Jenny tried to stay in the background as much as possible and would take herself off on trips out of Great Yarmouth so that Jill and Doreen could get on with the business. The dancers had some bookings left to see them through to the end of year, with pantomime the final outing of 1969. It was at this time of pantomime rehearsal when Jenny heard that the pair were planning a name change for the dancers. She immediately called a meeting, hurt that she hadn't been consulted.

Jill was the first to speak, "Jenny, firstly I would like to apologise on behalf of Doreen and me that you got to hear about our plans from someone other than us. I can assure you that nothing is set in concrete and that we had every intention of discussing it with you first. Someone obviously overheard us talking before knowing the full facts."

Jenny played nervously with her beads, a gift from Rita Ricer at the end of last season's summer show. "I thought we had agreed that the name Jenny Benjamin would live on. I have, as you know, built a strong reputation within the business and I thought I had put that reputation in very safe hands."

"And you have," Doreen interrupted before Jill could intervene. "We were merely looking at alternatives. With the likes of dancers like the GoJos and The Young Generation we thought a name change would bring us bang up to date."

"So, The Jenny Benjamin Dancers is now deemed old-fashioned?" questioned Jenny, tapping the table with her ballpoint. "What about The Pamela Devis Dancers, The Caroline Haig Dancers or indeed The Lionel Blair Dancers — are they old-fashioned too?"

It was obvious that Jenny was upset and Jill and Doreen knew they would have to reach some kind of compromise before the meeting concluded.

"While I appreciate that I've given you carte blanche to come up with new dance routines and styles, I did not give you permission to change the name of my troupe. Perhaps you would like to tell me the names you were considering."

Jill and Doreen looked at each other and replied in unison "The JB Showtime Dancers."

"We thought it had a ring to it," Jill added. "We thought it would look great on the posters."

"And, of course," Doreen added, "it would mention your name in the programme. We really weren't trying to push you out of the picture, that never was or ever has been our intention."

Jenny put down her pen and smiled. "Well, when you say it like that, The JB Showtime Dancers does sound rather good. I had visions of you calling them Jilly's Girls or Doreen's Dolls!"

Both Jill and Doreen burst out laughing and as relief swept over Jenny's face she joined in.

"We might as well mention that we had had another idea we wanted to run by you." Doreen gave Jill a quizzical glance and shook her head, but not without Jenny noticing the interaction. Jill continued unabashed, "We thought we might introduce boys into the troupe."

Jenny arched her eyebrow as her eyes narrowed. "Boys!"

Jill looked to her companion for support. "Doreen and I discussed this at some length. Male dancers are the in thing Jenny, you only have to look at what is happening on the television shows. A couple of male dancers would bring a new angle to the routines."

Jenny did not seem impressed. "And no doubt reduce the line-up you currently have to accommodate the BOYS."

Doreen shook her head. "No Jenny, we thought they would be extra to the line-up."

Jenny laid her hands on the table and looked at the pair directly. "And you will, of course, have done your sums on that I trust. The girls currently work on the *Equity* minimum rate with an annual bonus paid to them if the work rolls in. Introducing extra dancers would put up the costs and the kind of seasons they have played over the years you may not be able to afford the extra dancers, boys or otherwise."

Jill and Doreen looked at each other feeling rather small; they had not taken cost into the equation. The Jenny Benjamin Dancers were usually a troupe of six and no less than four, depending on the venue and the contract. Two troupes were sent out during the busy summer seasons and Jenny had, over the years, lent a hand providing choreography to other dance troupes who did not have a regular choreographer, ensuring that money was always coming in to the dancing school. Her own troupes always had a head girl who would ensure, during the seasonal runs, that the dancers were kept in line and rehearsed when necessary, giving Jenny the freedom to visit the various venues and source more work. In the signed agreement she had made with Doreen and Jill all of these details were in notes she had drawn up for the pair. From her bag Jenny pulled out the documentation and laid it in front of Doreen and Jill.

"I strongly suggest that you both sit down and very carefully read the documents I gave you. I was under the impression you had already done this, but I can tell by our little discussion that you have done nothing of the sort. There is a clause within the contract that allows me to regain full control of the dancing school at any time; perhaps I may need to act on that before my dancing school disappears in a sea of debt."

Jill and Doreen felt very uncomfortable. They had not thought that taking on the dancing school was going to be easy and now they were hearing Jenny as the astute businesswoman she really was. Jenny wasn't just that muddled-headed leader who got things wrong from time to time; she had had to have her eyes on so many other things all at once and did not have the luxury of a partner who would help lighten the load.

Jenny could see that her outburst had hit a nerve. "Perhaps we should have another drink and carefully go over the plans you have in mind. I am not opposed to male dancers, but you both have to realise that not only will it incur cost, it may also bring with it concerns that perhaps neither of you have thought of."

Jill got up. "I'll go and organise some more drinks and something to eat. I think this may be a longer meeting than we first thought."

Doreen looked sheepishly at Jenny. "I think I speak for both of us when I say how very sorry we both are. We have let you down."

Jenny softened her tone. "You are full of enthusiasm and much younger than I am. I do understand that. Maybe you need some help in how to grasp the business side of things."

Doreen nodded. "And would you be able to help us with that?"

Jenny smiled. "Nothing would give me greater pleasure. Now tell me a little bit more about how you will fit boys into the routines."

Chapter Two   *Deck the Halls*

"**D**ick Boggis, you could get off that chair and help me put these trimmings up; we have to be a bit Christmassy even if it is only going to be you and me at the dinner table."

Dick watched his wife as she balanced precariously on the wooden steps from the garden shed and reluctantly got to his feet.

"Don't know why you want to bother with this tinsel stuff; it's not as if the Queen will be paying us a visit."

"And if she did she would expect to find us trimmed-up," said Freda, applying another drawing pin to the crepe paper twist she had made. "I was hoping that Muriel might invite us in this year but I think she and Barry are going to see his sister, she's been very poorly."

"Perhaps your mate Lilly might have us over now she seems to be doing all right from that book of hers."

"I have never once set foot over her doorstep, so that is not very likely. Anyway, she is more a friend of Muriel's than she is mine," replied Freda, with a hint of jealousy in her voice. "No Dick, it looks like it will be just you and me and a bottle of stout apiece."

"We could always go down the *Legion* for Christmas lunch and it would mean being with other people. You might even have a bit of fun Freda me old darling."

"The last time I had any fun was when Larry Barnes took me on the galloping horses at the Pleasure Beach. Ever since then my life has been nothing but hard work trying to keep a roof over our heads. Besides, you spend far too much time down that *Legion*. What about me, when do I get taken out? An odd evening at bingo is my only pleasure these days Dick Boggis."

Dick could feel his Christmas at the *Legion* slipping through his fingers and tried another approach. "Let me finish putting these trimmings up old girl then I'll make you a nice cup of tea. There's a good film on at the *Regent*, perhaps we could go to that tonight, what do you say?"

Freda gently eased herself down the wooden steps. "Well, coming from you Dick Boggis, I would say that was a date. What's the film anyway?"

"Boris Karloff, *Bride of Frankenstein*," Dick replied, climbing the steps.

"It bloody would be," said Freda, falling into the armchair with a huff.

* * *

Dave was as good as his word and Dan had managed to get a couple of days off so that he could go to see his family in Preston. Ken had agreed with Jim and Dave covering Dan's shifts and Stella was more than happy to have either of them on board. Jim had once ill-judged Stella but Dave had soon put him straight on that. Working alongside her he saw a very different side to her. Stella managed the bar with a fine art. She always acknowledged the customers as they arrived and was never in any doubt as to who was next in line to be served. Which, as Jim witnessed, saved many an argument on the busy lunchtime shift when workers were coming in for their pre-Christmas tipple.

Dan had gone on his way with a clear conscience and a bag packed with presents. He intended to tell his parents about Dave in the hope that it would result in an invitation, His brother Gary would not be a problem, he was in the Navy, and as for his younger sister Kate she would just be glad to see her big brother happy at last.

As Jim was helping Stella clear the bar she mentioned how good it was to see Dan and Dave together and wondered if Jim had ever thought he might settle down again when the time was right. Jim was used to being asked this question and he answered it as honestly as he could.

"They say you should move on with your life. But I have never really seriously thought about another woman since Karen. That isn't to say I don't find other women attractive, because I do. I think it would be too soon for me to start entertaining those kinds of thoughts, especially now my Debbie is expecting her first. It may be difficult for her to accept seeing someone else in her mother's place. Besides, the house she grew up in holds so many memories for us both, it would be disrespectful to everything Karen and I shared together."

Stella handed Jim a glass cloth. "That's the problem with houses, they always hold memories. But that's all they are, memories, and you can take them any place you care to dwell. Have you never thought of moving house?"

"When Karen died I thought I would go crazy in that house on my own, especially with Debbie being newlywed and them moving away from the area. But in a strange way the house gave me great comfort, it still does."

Stella observed Jim carefully. "It isn't my place to say this, but don't become a prisoner to your memories. My old mum did that when dad died and she became a person so wrapped up in the past that she never saw the beauty of the world around her. You get one chance in this life and you have to grab it with everything you've got. All those times you spent with Karen will never leave you Jim and I feel sure that she wouldn't want you living on a memory for the rest of your days."

"You sound like old Maud, she has often said the same," said Jim, putting the polished beer glasses on the shelf. "Maybe it is time for me to move on as they say, but I will wait to see my grandchild, that's my first priority. I can wait a little."

Stella smiled and nodded and prepared to put on her coat, looking forward to having a sit down before she returned for the evening stint.

* * *

When Dan got off the train at Preston station he heard a familiar female voice calling his name. Coming towards him with her arms outstretched was his old friend Josie. Dressed in her trademark leather jacket, *Levis* and *Doc Marten* boots, she grinned broadly as Dan got nearer. Dropping his bag Dan threw his arms about her and gave her a big cuddle.

"Josie, how lovely to see you, how did you know I was coming?"

Josie held her friend at arm's length. "As much as I hate to disappoint you old mate, I had no idea you were coming home, I was just seeing Madge off to her parents."

It was good to know that his two favourite lesbians were still together. They had met one night when Dan and Josie were at *The Flying Handbag* in Blackpool and had been together ever since, that was six years ago now.

"Not bad news from home I hope."

Josie shook her head. "Oh no, nothing like that. Madge thought she would go down before Christmas as this year we are going to be staying with my parents for a change. Got time for a coffee, the café is open?"

Dan looked at his watch. "Yeah, of course I have, I can get a cab to mum and dad's. I've missed the next bus anyway."

"No need," said Josie, picking up her mate's luggage and throwing a bag over her shoulder, "I've got my little runabout outside, I can drop you off."

"You're runabout?" Dan queried, following Josie as she headed towards the café.

"Yeah, it's got no bleeding floor in it."

Dan chuckled, same old Josie, always one for a good laugh and a joke.

"So, what's the news then Danny boy? I was surprised when you didn't return at the end of the summer season. How was Great Yarmouth, not as lively as Blackpool I'll bet?"

Dan stirred his coffee and grinned. "Great Yarmouth was great. In fact, I would say Great Yarmouth was the greatest thing that has happened to me in a long time."

"You've met someone haven't you?" said Josie, with a delighted yelp. "Well you old son of a gun, it's about blooming time. So where is he, what's his name, how old is he, is he good looking, is he good in bed?"

People in the café were beginning to take an interest in the conversation. Dan blushed., "Keep it down Jose, people are looking."

"Let them look," said Josie, glaring around at the onlookers. "Come on, I want to hear all about it."

Dan told her his news and when he got to the bit about introducing Dave to his parents, Josie whistled. "Wow, this is serious stuff old mate. How do you think your dad will react?"

"That's the bit I'm dreading, that and telling Dave I want him to come and meet them."

"Hang on a minute, you've lost me. You mean to sit there and tell me that you haven't even mentioned it to your boyfriend?"

Dan nodded and took another sip of his coffee. "I thought I had better sound out mum and dad first, no point worrying him with it if it's a no go up here."

"I see your point," said Josie, reaching in to her jacket pocket for her cigarettes and offering Dan one. "We had a similar problem with Madge's parents, but funnily enough it was her mother that wasn't comfortable with it. Her dad is a doll, he didn't seem to care as long as Madge was happy. Her mum came round eventually, though I have to admit there were a few frosty teatimes to be got through first. The turning point was when we were all out in her mum's car one afternoon and it broke down. You know me Danny boy, I like nothing better than getting my nose under the bonnet of a car. Sorted it in minutes and Madge's mum was thrilled, said it was more than her old man could do and we laughed about it. Now when I go over, if there is anything that needs fixing she leaves it to me. Josie Jobs she calls me, yeah we get along really well now."

Dan smiled "I'm really pleased for you Josie." He stubbed out his cigarette. "Shouldn't really be smoking, Dave and I promised his mate Jim that we would try and give it up. You'd like Jim, salt of the earth and made me feel like family. He lost his wife a couple of years ago. His daughter Debs is expecting her first in March and we are all excited about it."

Josie looked astounded. "There must be something in the air at Great Yarmouth. You went away last April without a by-your-leave and you come back here a totally different person. I can't tell you how great it is to see you looking so happy mate. Come on, I'd better take you home, you've got a lot of explaining to do." She noted the look of concern on her friend's face as he got up from the table. "Don't worry, I think it's going to be all right. If you approach your parents with this new found confidence of yours, you will nail it my boy. You will have them eating out of your hand and, let's face it, it will save on the washing-up."

Dan laughed out loud, once again his best mate had made everything right again.

* * *

Much to his relief, Dan's parents were okay with their son's news. In fact his dad surpassed himself; he picked up on a couple of details about Dave and found that they may share some of the same interests.

Dan was much relieved that everything went so well and his sister Kate pestered him about when he would bring Dave to meet them all. Over a drink later that same evening, Dan discussed with Josie how he would best tackle Dave. *The Bulldog Arms* was their local and Josie was well known as she and Madge ran the local darts team.

"I don't think it will be meeting your parents that will be the biggest problem," said Josie, taking a mouthful of her bitter. "It will be convincing him that you want him to move North with you. Blackpool is a very different beast to Great Yarmouth; the latter by your description sounds almost gentle. You have to also remember that you will be asking Dave to give up his friends. He and this Jim character sound as if they are joined at the hip, at least they were until you came along. What will you do if he says he won't move?"

Dan looked at Josie sitting opposite him and lowered his eyes to the table. "I don't know Jose; I don't want to think about it."

* * *

Derinda Daniels sat on the floor of her living room; she wore no makeup and was in jeans and ballet pumps, far removed from the glittering gowns and outfits she wore in her cabaret and theatre appearances. Beside her on the fur rug was a large cardboard box surrounded by many prettily-wrapped presents with red and pink bows attached. Writing the last gift tag, *To Jeanie with love Mama*, she fastened it to the largest of the packages. Every other Christmas over the last eight she had performed this ritual. Placing the parcels into the large box, she sealed it with parcel tape and looked at it. Then she stood up, wiping away tears with the back of her hand, and moved the box to the corner of the room ready for it to be picked up by Sasha the following day. She checked her diary to make sure that she had the right date.

The clock on the glass cabinet told her that she should be getting ready to be collected by the band for their gig later that evening at *The Talk of Norwich*. Her body felt heavy and she felt no more like singing for her supper than flying to the moon, as Neil Armstrong had done earlier that year. She hovered by the drinks cabinet, but thought better of it and went to the kitchen, prepared a sandwich and poured herself a coffee from the filter jug that was warming on the hotplate. The house always seemed so empty and a reminder of the happy life she had once had. She longed for her London apartment by the river where she felt more at ease and peace with herself. But this Christmas season there were no London bookings to take her away from Norwich and the festivities would be spent with her friends from the business who were either appearing in panto at the *Theatre Royal* Norwich or, like her, doing the odd gig in the local area to tide them over, what some termed as just resting. There would be plenty of laughter and the exchange of ridiculous gifts. A lunch prepared and cooked by Susie and her boyfriend Dennis. Cynthia, Shamus, Hilary and a few people she didn't know would fill Susie's house with good cheer but there would be no sound of Jeanie's laughter, the sound she longed to hear above all others. She ran up the stairs and flung open the bedroom door. The room where once there had been love seemed cold and uninviting. She wandered to the next bedroom and there, set out on the dressing table, were a few of Jeanie's things that she kept, though the child rarely came to the house and only then under the blanket of night. She went over to the bed where a large teddy bear sat on the pillows; she picked the bear up and cuddled him, deeply inhaling the scent in the hope that a little bit of Jeanie had been left to help her through another Christmas.

The shrill ring of the telephone brought her back to reality and she ran to answer it.

"Hello Baz. No, nine will be fine, I'll be ready. Oh Baz, can you remind Jeff that we will need a couple of seasonal favourites tonight." She paused, listening to the voice at the other end of the telephone shouting out the request. "*White Christmas* and *Have Yourself a Merry Little Christmas* will be fine. Thanks Baz."

She replaced the receiver and looked out of the window. She could just make out the frost on the front lawn and shivered at the thought of turning out into the night air to entertain a bunch of people who would be so full of Christmas cheer that she might as well sing *Summer Holiday* for all the attention she and the boys would draw.

At nine on the dot, the toot of a horn announced that the van had arrived to collect her. The blue and white vehicle was painted with the names of Derinda Daniels and her band on the side and, though it was perfectly serviceable, it was a far cry from the Rolls Royce Derinda had dreamt of when she had first gone into show business. She climbed into the front seat, called out hello to Baz, Jeff, Will and Freddie and they set off down the road.

The doorman at *The Talk of Norwich* greeted the party like long lost friends and Derinda and the boys made their way down a side corridor to the dressing room area. The boys bundled in to one and Derinda took the dressing room which indicated it was for the top of the bill. On the opposite side was another dressing room for the support act. Tonight it would be Bernie Duggan a comedian from Lowestoft whose jokes left a lot to be desired. Derinda had worked with him many times and his routine never changed, the jokes were older than he was. He was heading toward seventy-five with no get-out clause.

Baz knocked on the door and entered carrying two gowns covered in heavy polythene for Derinda along with her song list. There would be two sets tonight, one at 11:00 and the second at 12:30. *The Talk of Norwich* was licensed until 2am and Derinda's second set would be twenty minutes in total and she planned to finish with the two Christmas numbers selected earlier.

The reflection in the dressing room mirror looked back at her and the lights illuminated her face. She looked at the array of makeup that lay on the dressing room table, set out before her in her usual fashion, and she leaned forward to study her complexion carefully. Taking the foundation container in her left hand she applied the base with her right in firm sweeping strokes. With a deft hand and attention to detail she applied her eyeshadow with the soft brush, it was of fine hair and one she treasured for sentimental reasons. The wand of mascara provided the lift that her eyelashes needed, the black eyeliner enhanced her eyes further and she picked up the false eyelashes and applied a thin streak of glue to each and laid them to one side. She then applied more colour to the base foundation, rouged her cheekbones and began to create her other persona. Carefully applying the thick top false eyelashes and the slightly less heavy bottom ones she sat back and smiled at herself. Any drag queen would die to be wearing these little beauties. Her lipstick and thin black pencil outlined her lips, which she blotted with a tissue. Her fingernails were painted in her trademark red and all that remained would be for her to clip the diamond earrings to her ears, fasten the matching necklace about her neck, slip into the stage gown, place her feet firmly in the stilettos and prepare to face her public. A voice from the doorway suddenly invaded her tranquillity; she turned and smiled at Baz.

"Going to get the boys a drink from the bar, fancy one?"

"I could murder a gin and tonic, but make sure there's plenty of ice in it. Thanks Baz, you're an angel."

The spotlight hit the cabaret floor and the MC announced the wonderful Derinda Daniels as her band played *The Lady is a Tramp*. The strong voice of Derinda filled the venue as she walked down the staircase onto the floor, her purple gown sparkling in the lights. She smiled at her audience, who were surprisingly sober, but then, being the first show, perhaps the drink hadn't taken hold of them yet. As she said good evening before going in to the second number she caught sight of someone she knew. The boys played the opening bars of *This is a Lovely Way to Spend an Evening* and for a moment Derinda was distracted and nearly missed her cue. It couldn't be? The lady sitting alone at the table at the right-hand side of the floor was June Ashby or someone who looked very much like her. Derinda avoided looking again until she was about to begin the third number, but when she did the lady was gone.

She returned to her dressing room after muted applause had greeted her at the end of the set. The alcohol had obviously taken hold on the audience and she thought she should cut her losses and not bother with the second show. But as her contract stipulated she had to perform two, she would have to ride it out.

Baz came in to her dressing room. "Well, they were hard to please," he stated, laying down the next order of songs that had been agreed. "It was like pulling teeth. I hope the audience will be a bit more receptive tomorrow. It's my birthday and I hate having to work on my birthday."

Derinda, who had just pulled on her silk dressing gown, walked out from behind the screen that she always insisted on having with her. Sometimes she felt like she was changing in a field.

"I'm sorry about your birthday Baz, but perhaps we can do something tomorrow after the show. Ask your wife to come along."

Baz acknowledged the gesture. "We won't have to worry about her, she left months ago."

Derinda sat down at the dressing table and looked at Baz who was looking crestfallen. "I'm so sorry Baz, I didn't know." That was one of the problems with this business; you worked closely with people but never really knew them.

She thought back to June Ashby; who knew what had really gone on there and why she might be in Norwich? Baz continued to ramble on, but her thoughts were elsewhere. She wondered if Rita would know anything, she was the person June had turned to earlier that year when things had happened. She would give Don Stevens a call and see if he would give her Rita's number. There was always the possibility that Rita, like herself, would be out on the road, but her mind wouldn't rest until she had made that call.

* * *

The following day Derinda awoke with a start. She looked at the bedside clock, it was ten. She leaped out of bed and headed for the bathroom. She had to be ready for when Sasha arrived, he didn't like to be kept waiting and she knew how quickly his temper could flare at the least little thing. She showered quickly and dried her hair, leaving it loose. She put on the minimum of makeup she thought Sasha would find acceptable and decided to wear his favourite skirt and top, anything to make the visit more pleasant. Breakfast was a hurried affair of coffee and a couple of biscuits. She ran up the stairs, quickly made the bed and brushed her teeth, taking one final look at her reflection in the mirror. Drat, she had smudged her lipstick. She had just finished correcting it when she heard the front door open; Sasha still had keys to the house. Taking a deep breath to calm herself she walked slowly down the staircase and saw Sasha standing in the hallway.

"Good morning Sasha, I hope you had a pleasant journey. It's lovely to see you, how's Jeanie?"

Sasha half-smiled at her and in his strong French accent demanded to know if there was any coffee. He strode purposefully into the kitchen and Derinda followed, feeling like Cinderella. She poured him some coffee, hoping that it was hot enough and placed it in front of him.

He had sat in his usual place at the table and lit a *Gitane*. "You have the Christmas packages ready I hope," he said, gazing around the kitchen. "I do not like those curtains, English rubbish. Where are the blinds my mother bought us from Paris, they were much better?" His eyes clouded over, his shoulders were hunched and the handsome features that had first attracted Derinda to him were screwed up in an angry and pained expression. The flight had obviously not been a good one; he wasn't usually this bad on arrival.

Derinda ignored the comment about the curtains and sat down at the opposite side of the table and did her best to conceal the fear she felt. How could this beautiful man, the one who had swept her off her feet ten years ago in a whirlwind romance, have changed. Did he really hate her that much? When Jeanie had been born she had played the dutiful wife and mother for the first few months, but the call of the greasepaint was never far from her mind. And when she decided to return to the world she loved, her marriage began to crumble. The house had been part of the divorce settlement; the flat in London was hers alone and the only place she felt really at ease. Jeanie had been born in France at the family chateau where Sasha's mother ruled with an iron fist. Jeanie's birth certificate stated she was French and during the painful proceedings that followed it had been the judge's ruling Jeanie would spent six weeks every summer with her mother and Christmas every alternate year.

But that wasn't the complete story; Sasha had been deeply wounded by his wife's lack of respect for family life. He loved his daughter with all his heart and still secretly carried a torch for Derinda whom, from the day they had met, he had worshipped. But he concealed these feelings lest he be rejected. Jeanie had only been to Norwich a couple of times when she was a baby. Derinda preferred to have her stay in London, away from the prying eyes of the neighbours and friends who knew nothing about the daughter she had given birth to. The very person who did so much for children's charities had chosen her career above all else and Sasha was never going to let her forget it. It had been remarkable that it had been kept a secret for so long.

Sasha's mother refused to have anything more to do with her daughter-in-law, and her own mother, never the best role model, didn't seem to mind that she rarely saw her granddaughter. Her father said nothing, and he had never been very vocal, even when Derinda was growing up. Derinda had often felt she had inherited her mother's ways, but with every passing year, the painfulness of never seeing her daughter grow up haunted her very being and Sasha knew how to play on those emotions. She topped up his coffee and went to the kitchen drawer, took out a sealed envelope and laid it in front of him.

"It's all there; you don't have to count it."

Sasha slid the envelope to the side of the table and placed it in his jacket pocket without acknowledging it. "So what delights have you given your daughter this year, not another one of your records? My mother cannot stand them. They are so sickly and full of that national sentiment you British are so fond of. Didn't anyone ever tell you that the war ended in 1945."

His cruel words hit a nerve and Derinda turned to face the window so that he shouldn't see that she was still intimidated by him. She felt tortured inside, she wanted to tell him how much she still loved him, but she knew that would be a folly on her part. Sasha would push her away and tell her what a bad mother and wife she had been and that if the payments didn't keep coming he would reveal her story to the press and then her career would be finished for good.

"We have to decide the weeks you want to see Jeanie in the summer," said Sasha, draining his coffee cup and lighting another cigarette. "You know your work schedule I hope."

Derinda turned back to face him. "I'm sorry Sasha but at the moment there is only cabaret work lined up for next year which means I will be working late. I'm trying to free up some time to spend with Jeanie in London. If you didn't want so much money from me I could actually turn down some of the work I've been offered."

"You're not trying to go back on our little arrangement I hope," Sasha replied. "Why don't you sell this house, it's too big for one person. You could get yourself a little home somewhere on the Norfolk Broads, perhaps a houseboat, you'd like that I am sure."

"The thought had crossed my mind," Derinda replied, noting the rise in volume of Sasha's voice. He was getting angry. "I'll let you know what I decide."

Sasha got up from the table. "You love your work, I am surprised you are not working now. Don't they do lunchtime shows somewhere? I have to get something from the car, I won't be a moment. Please make me some fresh coffee, that last one was terrible. In France we know how to make good coffee." When he returned he placed three small packages on the table and one envelope. "From Jeanie to her mama, would you like me to put them under your Christmas tree?"

"You know where it is. I am going to make a sandwich I didn't have time for breakfast would you like one?"

Sasha turned in the kitchen doorway. "You English and your sandwiches. I do not want to eat such rubbish."

Derinda took a knife from the drawer and held it firmly in her hand. "Dam you," she said to herself and stabbed the knife into the chopping board where it stood proudly.

Sasha left an hour later and Derinda went upstairs to her bedroom, picked up the telephone and dialled the number of Don Stevens's office. The call was answered by Elsie his wife and after a few pleasantries Derinda had the number she required.

"Hello Derinda," said the jolly voice of Rita, "how nice to hear from you." Rita listened with great interest to what Derinda had to tell her. "How strange, I had a Christmas card from June only yesterday; she didn't mention visiting England at all." Rita racked her brains for a moment. "I last spoke to June on the telephone, oh let me see, it must been the end of October. I remember because we talked about Halloween. No wait a minute, she called again after that, around about the second week of November. She told me that Wally Barrett, you remember him, June's old flame, anyway she and Wally had parted. Sad really, I thought Wally would make June happy after that sorry business with Lorna Bright last summer." She paused for breath. "I don't know about you but this travelling around the country doing one-nighters fair wears me out, I had forgotten what it was like. I keep hoping for a more residential engagement, or at least one that will keep me in one place for several months of the year."

"I thought your career had really taken off again," said Derinda, being drawn into Rita's monologue.

"That's what the papers would have people believe," said Rita, knowingly. "Admittedly, when I made that comeback of sorts a few months ago the papers were full of it and so was old Don, but the places I used to play have fallen by the wayside and I'm not keen about returning to cruise liners or working abroad. I have Ted to think about and, as near as damn it, I do try to see that we work together as much as possible. In fact, some news came through to me only a few weeks ago of something in the pipeline but I'm sworn to secrecy on that so I can't say any more."

"I am sorry Rita, I really thought that Moira Clarence had taken off in a big way."

Rita sighed. "Let's just say the bookings tick over, but it's hardly the same as a season at the *London Palladium*. Anyway enough of that, we were talking about June. I can't think of any reason she would have to be in Norfolk and certainly not at *The Talk of Norwich*. If it was her, and I am not saying it wasn't, I'm surprised she didn't come along and say hello. After all, it isn't as if you two are strangers, you did meet her last May or whenever it was. See, my mind is playing tricks again. Sorry, can you hold a minute, Ted is calling out." Rita covered the mouthpiece but Derinda could still hear her dulcet tones. "No me old lover they are in the top drawer. Honestly Ted, you're getting right forgetful in your old age." Rita returned her attention to Derinda. "Sorry about that love. Men! Who would have one? If I hear anything Derinda I'll let you know. Truth is I don't phone her because it costs so much and old Ted gets annoyed if we get a big bill. Says it's less he has to spend on a night out. Now, a night out, that would be something! When you spend all your time entertaining folk who are drunk, you don't really want to have a night out do you?"

* * *

Ted found what he was looking for and headed for the stairs. He stopped halfway down, feeling the pain across his chest. "Bloody indigestion," he muttered to himself. "Reet, are you ever coming off that phone? I fancy a cup of tea."

Chapter Three   *Should Old Acquaintance*

M aud was just about to step through the doors of *Palmers* department store as Lilly was just coming out. Maud smiled at her old friend. "Hello Lilly, how lovely to see you. Where have you been hiding?"

"I've been run off my little benders," said Lilly, with feeling. "I'm going to move house and I can't tell you the run-around these secret agents give you. Papers to sign, measurements, it's enough to make me go daft."

"Jim did mention something of the sort to me a few days ago. A place over Gorleston way somewhere?"

Lilly nodded. "I thought it would be nice to have a change of scenery. I expect he told you that I won't be returning to the *Sands* next summer. I'm still helping out at the General until the end of January, by then the cottage I'm moving into should be mine. Seems funny saying something like that, I've never owned anything in my life."

Maud studied her old friend and there could be no denying that there was a definite change in her. "Have you time for a cuppa? I'm just going in to get some last minute gifts for Enid's stocking."

"I've just tried to get a seat in the coffee shop. I tell you Maud, it's like sod 'em in Glamorgan in there."

Maud smiled to herself, Lilly may have changed but her way with words hadn't.

"Why don't we go in to *Arnolds*, they do a nice pot in there, it may not be as busy as *Palmers*? I can come back and pick up my bits after."

The two friends linked arms and headed off.

* * *

Muriel and Freda were also out Christmas shopping, and were at that moment chatting over a coffee and a toasted teacake in *Arnold's*.

"I am telling you," said Freda, pushing her teacake to one side, "if that was fresh in this morning then I am married to Roger Moore."

A more unlikely scenario Muriel couldn't imagine but she said nothing. "What are you buying your Dick?"

"Well, I picked up a nice sweater on the market last week and I thought I might buy him some of that *Brut* aftershave. But have you seen the price of it? Scandalous, that's what I call it."

"My Barry is very fussy about aftershaves, says they make a man smell girly. However, he has taken to *Cossack* men's hairspray like a duck to water. He says he prefers it to plastering his head with *Brylcreem*."

"Funny how things are changing," said Freda, making another stab at her teacake and picking out a couple of currants. "Who would have thought that men would start using hairspray? Funny old world."

Who'd have thought Dick would be using aftershave, thought Muriel, it was indeed a funny old world. "Now Freda Boggis, are you going to eat that teacake or can we make a move and go into *Woolworths*. I want to get some pick 'n' mix to take to Barry's sister for Christmas."

Freda huffed; she pushed the plate away again and picked up her shopping bags. "Come on then. I bet *Woolies* will have the heating on full blast as usual; I'll be blowing down my blouse just to cool down. Why do they want the heating on so high? It brings on my flushes and you knows how I get when I have one of those."

And no doubt so does the rest of *Arnolds* snack bar, thought Muriel, getting up to follow her neighbour.

* * *

Without the coloured lights and the music from the adjacent funfair, the South Pier looked drab and lifeless. There was a blast of cold wind blowing from the North Sea as Jim pulled his scarf tighter in an effort to keep warm. The remains of a poster advertising last season's summer show hung in the window of Maud's box office like a swing tag from an item of fashion in *Palmers* department store. Resisting the temptation to light a cigarette, he walked purposefully on, watching as the waves crashed over the side of the pier making rivulets of water. Everything was shuttered along the pier and presented a ghostly appearance against the greying clouds that hung low in the winter sky. Apart from three anglers who were chancing their luck, Jim was the only other person present. As *The Golden Sands Theatre* came into view it set a scene of an abandoned and unloved building. The entrance to the theatre looked uninviting as if it were rejecting all comers. Tatters of posters hung from the hoardings on either side of the entrance, stripped of the paste that had once held them securely. A fierce gust of wind suddenly brought forth some abandoned fliers carelessly left in a box on the theatre steps. One flier adhered itself to Jim's body and his gloved hand grabbed the piece of paper which he looked at in wonder. *Summer Frolics* it read, *a pre-season summer show presented by Don Stevens. Twice Nightly at 6:10 and 8:45.* Jim stood motionless; even now the events of that show unfolded in his mind like the turning pages of a novel. The name June Ashby was for ever etched on his brain along with her sisters Lorna and Veronica. All that had happened seemed incredible now.

Catching his breath, Jim moved to the side of the theatre and at the stage door he could once again hear Jack, the stage doorkeeper, uttering the words, "Noises off young Jim. The so-called star has arrived and from all accounts she isn't very happy," as if it were yesterday. Mystic Brian and his beloved doves, the Dean Sisters on their glittering roller balls, Maurice Beeney and his orchestra tuning up, the Jenny Benjamin Dancers tap-dancing across the stage and Ted Ricer cracking his well-known jokes; they came to him like the Ghosts of Christmas Past. What now of the Ghosts of Christmas yet to come?

* * *

Sauntering along Marine Parade at the same time was Dave who, like Jim, was trying to resist lighting a cigarette, though his nerves could use one right now. Dan had returned from visiting his parents and quite out of the blue had suggested that Dave meet them. Dave wasn't too sure how he felt about meeting Dan's parents, but Dan had assured him that they had been okay about everything and that his sister Kate was itching to meet him. Dan had also mentioned Josie and Madge, who he said Dave would like and that they were both a good laugh. So if it got too much at his parents they could always escape and go and see the girls. This was all new ground to Dave. He had never met anyone's parents, his relationships in the past had been short-lived, but this one seemed to be moving on in leaps and bounds. The thought of sleeping under the same roof as Dan's parents while sharing their son's bed didn't sit well with him and he needed the advice of his best friend Jim. And just as he reached the South Pier who appeared but Jim like the answer to a prayer.

Jim waved at his buddy and walked over to greet him. "See you had the same idea as me. Needed to get some fresh air in my lungs, this stopping smoking is bloody torture. I can't tell you how fed up I am chewing *Wrigley's*, I feel like a cow chewing the cud."

Dave laughed. "I keep sucking mints, I got through four packets yesterday. At this rate all my teeth are going to fall out."

"Made any plans for Christmas Day yet, you said you were going to have a word with Dan about it? I can still do some lunch, Maud and Enid are going to join us and I asked Lilly along as well."

"Sorry mate, I forget to tell you, Dan and I will be pleased to come over for Christmas Day on the understanding that you join us both in *Henry's* on Boxing Day. They're laying on a free buffet at lunchtime and it might be a bit of a hoot. Dan will only have to do the first hour, they're getting in a couple of casuals so that he and Stella can come round our side of the bar for a change."

"It's a deal," said Jim, with a smile. "At least that bloody nightclub won't be open again until New Year's."

"Yeah, funny that," said Dave, taking a packet of *Polos* from his pocket and offering Jim one. "Last year we were open on Boxing Day night weren't we. Apart from a few of the girls from *Docwra* we were the only other buggers there."

"I just wished that Peter and Debs would come home for Christmas, but I have to understand that his parents want to see them too."

"That's a tough one and no mistake. Never mind mate, you'll have us lot to keep you on your toes. Besides, the baby is due in the New Year and that will be something to look forward to."

Jim nodded. "I can't wait. To think, this time next year I will be a granddad." He felt a lump come to his throat as Karen came in to his mind's eye. What a great grandmother she would have made. "How did Dan's visit back home go?"

"I'm glad you mentioned that. His parents want to meet me."

"Blooming heck Dave! That will be a big step for you, how do you feel about it?"

"I'm a bit worried if you must know Jim. I can't imagine actually meeting the parents of the bloke I'm sleeping with."

"Come on mate, it's a bit more than that isn't it? You're in an affair now, a good one, or so it seems to us on the outside. If Dan's parents are willing to shake you by the hand and welcome you into their home, then the least you can do is meet them. I bet it will mean the world to young Dan and you will be part of a proper family, that's got to be worth the sacrifice."

Dave grabbed his friend in his arms and hugged him. "Thanks for that Jim, it's what I needed to hear. You really are a great friend to have."

Jim grinned. "You're not so bad yourself. Come on, let's get a wriggle on, the *Barking Smack* will be opening its doors in a few minutes, we'll have a couple of jars before we have to head off to work. I might even stretch to a pork pie."

Dave laughed and together they headed back along the seafront where the welcoming lights of the *Barking Smack* beckoned.

* * *

Muriel handed Freda a glass of sherry. "I thought it would be neighbourly to have a glass of Christmas cheer before Barry and I set off."

"Very nice of you, I'm sure," Freda replied, making herself comfortable on the settee and taking in yet another dress that Muriel was sporting. "Where is Barry, isn't he going to join us?"

Muriel sipped her sherry and sat down. "No, Barry is sorting out some last minute problem with the car. Gone down to see Manny Hobbs about it."

Freda nodded. "Yes, I've heard Manny is very capable with an engine. Sorted out Dick's big end in no time at all."

"Really?" said Muriel, in mock surprise. "Manny has sorted many a big end, well that's what I've heard."

Freda took a mouthful of sherry. "Oh this is nice. Is this the one in the bargain bin at the *Coop?*" "*Harvey's Bristol*," said Muriel, with a sniff and a look of distain. "I don't entertain any other at Christmas; *Palmers* stock a lovely selection. I always say if you are going to have a sherry at Christmas, have the best one."

"Dick isn't too fond of sherry and it's hardly worth getting a bottle in just for me."

"That's your trouble Freda Boggis, you never treat yourself. I bet Dick doesn't go without his beer over the holidays."

"He's got a crate in out the back; the *Legion* did him a discount for helping out."

Muriel raised her eyebrows at the mention of the *Legion* and was so glad that Barry had never wanted to join. "Help yourself to a sausage roll Freda, freshly made this morning. And I thought, as I'd invited Lilly over, it would be nice to have a little something "

Freda eyed the plate of sausage rolls feeling peckish, though if truth be known she had eaten a couple of cream slices earlier with a cup of *Camp* coffee.

"They do look lovely Muriel. I'm surprised you had time to make pastry, what with all the packing and getting everything ready for the off. Is it tomorrow you go?" Freda took a side plate and helped herself to two of the largest sausage rolls. "And they're still warm, scrummy; I do like a warm sausage."

"Have you got all your Christmas shopping sorted Freda?" Muriel, asked handing Freda a linen napkin that she had got out especially and noting the crumbs that were tumbling down Freda's floral frock. Which looked remarkably like the one she had worn for the summer show and there was a distinct smell of mothballs and lavender smacking the air.

Freda took another bite from her sausage roll and rolled her eyes. "Well, I've got him a couple of shirts for work, some socks and some lovely men's aftershave off the market."

"Oh, really, which one? My Barry likes *Old Spice* or *Burley*."

"It's called *Torment*, comes in a lovely blue box and it had a free handkerchief with it. I decided against the *Brut*."

"Expensive was it?"

"Four and nine, it was on offer."

I bet that will smell lovely, Muriel thought. as she looked at her watch. "I wonder what's keeping Lilly, she should have been here by now."

"I expect she's still packing to move to that new house of hers. Can't imagine why she wants to go over Gorleston way, she's lived in the town all her life."

"Well, maybe she fancied a change Freda. I've heard she's giving up her job at the hospital next month and she won't be returning to the *Sands* in the summer. I remember her telling me that her house was very cold and not easy to heat and there was a time when she had mice."

"Did she ever get a cat?"

"Oh no, Lilly was never one for pets, not since that incident with the tortoise." Before Muriel could elaborate further, the doorbell rang, much to Freda's annoyance.

Lilly came into the lounge wearing a red coat and matching hat and smiled. "Hello Freda, Merry Christmas." She handed Freda a small package gaily wrapped in pretty paper and with a large red bow on it. "And this is for you Muriel."

"Thank you very much Lilly, very kind of you," Freda replied, feeling slightly embarrassed that she had nothing to offer in return. Lilly sat down opposite Freda and beamed.

"You really shouldn't have bought us presents," said Muriel, pouring Lilly a sherry and offering her a sausage roll, just as Freda was about to help herself to two more "I have a little something for you both under the tree."

Freda felt herself go bright red in the face. Now she would have to find something to give Lilly. She had something for Muriel, some bath salts that she had been given for her birthday and wasn't fond of. There were also some embroidered handkerchiefs lying in her bedroom drawer that she had won at a Christmas Bazaar. They were a bit yellow but none the worse for that. She could wrap those and pop them through Lilly's door with the card she had written.

Muriel sat herself down again and looked at a very changed Lilly Brockett. Everything that had once been dowdy had suddenly become alive. An air of confidence now surrounded her old friend and Muriel felt extremely happy for her, knowing only too well what had gone before.

"How are the book sales going?"

Lilly smiled. "Oh the sales are going very well indeed Muriel, thank you for asking. I'm going to do another signing in *Jarrold's*, but this time the Norwich store, they've been promoting me as a Christmas must-have. It's all very exciting and they are sending a car to take me all the way there."

Freda, who was just about to take a bite, stopped midway. "My goodness, that's going to cost a pretty penny, a car all the way to Norwich. Fancy!"

"Muriel, your tree looks lovely," said Lilly, choosing not to answer, as she put her glass down beside her. "I haven't bothered with one for myself this year. The house is all cluttered with boxes at the moment."

"You must feel very excited about moving," said Muriel. "I expect you will find it all a bit strange at first."

Lilly sat back in the armchair and reflected for a moment. "I've had some good times in that house and some sad ones, but I mustn't worry about those now. After all, it is only bricks and mortar."

Freda was about to say something when she choked on a piece of pastry and Muriel rushed to pat her on the back. Recovering her composure, Freda commented, "That pastry is very short, lovely, but short."

"Barry says I have a light touch when it comes to pastry."

"Fancy," replied Freda, looking at her empty glass and hoping a refill would be offered. That *Harvey's Bristol Cream* was going down a treat. "What are you doing on Christmas Day Lilly? You would be most welcome to join Dick and me."

It was Muriel's turn to look surprised. In all the years that Muriel had known Freda she had never once known her to open her doors to guests. It was usually Freda going to someone else.

"How kind of you to offer Freda, but I am quite sorted, Jim has invited me over for the day. I understand there is going to quite a gathering."

Freda huffed as she thought of spending the whole day with Dick who would no doubt be asleep before the Queen made her speech on the television. "Fancy."

Muriel poured more sherry in Freda's glass and offered more to Lilly who protested, "Oh no, thank you Muriel, one glass at lunchtime is quite sufficient for me," as she eyed Freda who had downed hers in two gulps. "I was invited to a writer's convention last week to talk about my novel and if they had had their way I would have been three blankets to the wind."

"Sheets Lilly, it's three *sheets* to the wind," corrected Muriel, smiling as she turned and looked at her neighbour. "Freda, I'm sorry I forgot to top you up."

Lilly had a quiet smile to herself, as Freda held out her glass to Muriel.

* * *

Great Yarmouth Town Centre became ever busier with Christmas shoppers. The market place displayed its finest wares and the Christmas tree came alive with the sound of the *Salvation Army Band* playing Christmas carols. The cold winter air added to the feeling of the season and friends waved and acknowledged each other as they hurried about their business in the hope of finding that elusive present for their loved ones. *Palmers'* doors swung open and shut as the hordes rushed in to buy perfumes, clothing and all manner of other items to fill their Christmas stockings. Children clutching their mother's hand queued to see Father Christmas and his reindeer and the coffee shop boomed with Christmas music while customers relieved their aching feet for a ten minute breather before heading back out on the never-ending shopping trip.

Arnolds painted a similar scene with shop assistants taking money from anxious-looking shoppers who were trying desperately to remember whether auntie was a size 4 or 5 in a slipper. The gaily-wrapped confection caught the shop lights and added a sparkle to the proceedings.

Jarrold's book department was heaving; people were collecting their books ordered weeks before and juggling bags with purses and wallets. *Woolworths* had queues at the pick 'n' mix and toys were flying off the shelves quicker than the staff could fill them. Children who were tired grizzled at having to stand around while their mothers browsed what was on offer, grandparents in tow made their own secret purchases and the newlyweds and soon-to-be-engaged couples giggled and entered the Christmas throng. Floor managers and store managers across the town rubbed their hands in glee as the money poured into the tills. Bus conductors had to stop too many passengers boarding to prevent overcrowding.

The weather played its usual game, very cold one day, freezing the next and then, just to lull everyone into a false sense of security, rays of sunshine would filter through the clouds and give hope of brighter days to come. The boats at the quayside bobbed up and down tugging at their moorings and the summer cruise boats were wrapped in their tarpaulins for the winter. Taxi ranks outside the town hall were busy as shoppers who couldn't face the local transport decided to dig deep and treat themselves to a taxi ride home. Fathers and sons dragged real fir trees from the market stalls and carried them home to erect them in the chosen spot, safe in the knowledge that they were doing their bit for the Christmas season. Old seadogs filled the public houses alongside shoppers enjoying a glass of Christmas cheer and filled the air with pipe smoke. The bar staff smiled and served their customers with pints of beer, schooners of sherry and glasses of *Babycham* with a cherry on a stick. Plates of sandwiches came out of the kitchens and bags of *Smiths* crisps passed over the counters to eager waiting hands and hungry mouths. The chip stalls on the market place were busier than ever, with no one on the market passing the opportunity to put something warm into their bellies.

Carollers came a-carolling in the evening and many a household demanded the full carol in return for a sixpence or shilling. The churches prepared for the school carol concerts and the ever-popular midnight mass on Christmas Eve. The seafronts of Gorleston and Great Yarmouth went into hibernation as only a small number of locals ventured on the promenades and beaches walking their dogs. Posters and hoardings of shows and attractions long past were still on display. The funfairs and amusement arcades were shrouded in darkness, awaiting the return of the summer when they would once more come alive. The once glittering summer season promenade lights had long been turned off and apart from the odd light shining from a pub doorway the scene was a bleak one. The hearts of many people were filled with a mixture of anticipation for what Christmas and the New Year would bring. But among the joy and frivolity were the old and forgotten, the poor and the less-well-off who would scurry invisible among others who were oblivious to their plight. And so Christmas had come once more.

Christmas Morning

With a cup of coffee at his side, Jim tore open the present from Debbie and Peter. It was a shirt, much like the one Karen would have bought him and he smiled to himself. There was also some talc and aftershave, the obligatory socks and a book about Norwich that Jim had been considering buying. Debbie had obviously been speaking to his old friend Maud. The gentle sound of music from the radio lulled him in to a thoughtful mood and he remembered the many Christmas mornings that had gone before.

The ringing of the telephone interrupted his memories and he was pleased to hear Debbie's voice down the line. "Merry Christmas Dad, thanks ever so for the scarf, just what I need on these cold winter mornings, and Peter really liked the pullover. We will open the other presents later."

"I remember when you were at home that your presents were opened at the crack of dawn. Thanks for mine by the way, I'm really pleased with the book."

"Auntie Maud said you would be."

"I'll be seeing her later along with Enid and Lilly. Dave and Dan are also coming along. I've been quite busy in the kitchen."

"Sorry we can't be there Dad, but you know how it is."

"Of course I do love. How are things there, Peter's mum and Dad okay?"

"Yes thanks. Mum is in the kitchen doing something with sprouts and chestnuts and dad is in the garden trying out his new spade that he was allowed to unwrap this morning.

Different rules here Dad, we all select one present we would like to open and we have the others after the Queen's speech."

Jim raised his eyebrows. That would never have suited Karen. Christmas presents were for you to have at the bottom of your bed or round the tree on Christmas morning, and he just hoped that when his grandchild arrived he or she wouldn't be subjected to the same rules.

"Dad, Peter wants a word. Have a lovely day and we will see you in the New Year."

Jim and Peter exchanged greetings and as he put the receiver down the front door bell rang heralding the arrival of the cavalry. Dave and Dan had offered to get things ready for dinner and by all accounts Dan was a dab hand at table arrangements. The boys came bounding in as Jim opened the door; Dan was carrying a crate of beer and Dave a sack that would have made Father Christmas groan.

"I've some other stuff in the car," said Dave, dropping the red sack under the Christmas tree. "Dan, put the beer out the back and come and give us a hand."

"I thought you didn't have a car any more" said Jim, feeling the icy chill from the open door.

"Present from Dan's mum and dad, they sent him some money to buy one and I put the rest towards it. It's second-hand but it goes."

Jim grinned to himself. "You two really are the perfect couple aren't you. What next, matching jumpers?"

Both the boys turned to face Jim before heading out of the doorway, unzipped their jackets and showed off their new knitwear. "Present from my sister Katie," said Dan, laughing at the look on Jim's face. "If you look closely they have our names on as well."

"It's worse than I thought," said Jim. "Come on, I'll help you. Whatever have you got in that boot, there's enough stuff to feed an army?"

"Hope you don't mind Jim, but Stella might pop in later this afternoon. She's on her own since her latest walked out on her, " Dave replied, lifting out another box of goodies from the boot.

"Give her a call and invite her round to lunch, there will be plenty of room. I can grab another dining chair from the shed."

"Thanks mate, I know she would like that. She was meant to be going to her sister's but there was some kind of family problem going on with her sister's eldest so it all got a bit, you know..."

Jim nodded. "Families eh? Come on, let's get this lot inside and get the kettle on."

"Kettle?" said Dan, looking at the two. "I'm ready for a glass of Christmas cake."

"Don't start before the girls get here," said Dave, knowing what his other half would be like if he began drinking on an empty stomach. "We'll have a brew first, you can give Stella a call and then we'll give Jim boy here a hand with the vegetables."

"No need," said Jim, "they are all prepared, sprouts, potatoes, carrots, parsnips, cabbage and a turkey big enough to keep us going to the New Year."

"Have you made chestnut stuffing?" asked Dan, taking the last of the bags from the boot and following the other two into the warmth of the lounge.

"Sorry mate, I've got a packet of *Paxo* to make up later and mix with sausage meat. Karen never stuffed the bird; she said it took longer to cook. Oh, and I've some little sausages wrapped with bacon that Debbie said everyone would like."

"Just as well I brought some fresh chestnuts from the market then," Dan said, diving into one of the bags and retrieving his goodies. "I can make the stuffing; mum gave me the recipe. It won't take long to do, if you don't mind me taking over the kitchen for a while."

"Be my guest, and while you're about it you can make us all a brew. I'll give Dave a hand with this lot and let you get started."

Dan headed towards the kitchen leaving the two best friends together.

"Merry Christmas mate," said Dave, giving Jim a hug. "This is really going to be a great Christmas."

A flurry of activity ensued. The table was laid, the box of deluxe Christmas crackers from Enid's emporium were opened and laid at the side of the cutlery, the Christmas tree lights were switched on and another log placed on the open fire and everything was ready to welcome the other guests.

Maud and Enid were the first to arrive, Maud carrying a bag of presents and Enid with a five-year-old Christmas pudding that was one of her specialities. Glasses of sherry were poured for the ladies while Dave and Dan opened bottles of *Lacons Encore* ale. Jim joined Maud and Enid with a sherry.

"Do you need a hand in the kitchen?" asked Maud, sitting down on the settee. "I'll just have this and pop out and give you a hand."

"No need," said Jim, "I think Dan is taking care of things out there for a while."

"You would never have caught our father in the kitchen," said Enid, taking a sip of the dark golden liquid and pulling a face. "Funny how things change."

The conversation turned to the subject of chefs in hotels and then the arrival of Lilly brought another buzz to the proceedings. Wearing a new powder-blue coat she had purchased in *Palmers* and a neat new hairstyle, Lilly beamed round at the gathering. "Oh this is lovely," she said, "I cannot remember ever being at such a bunk up."

"Knees up," said Maud, giving Jim a wink, "and it's hardly that yet. We are all enjoying a tipple before lunch, are you going to join us Lilly?"

Lilly handed her coat to Jim, revealing a blue skirt and white blouse with a smart waistcoat that hugged her petite figure. "I don't know if I should, I had one at Muriel's the other day."

Jim laughed and handed Lilly a sherry. "Come on Lilly it's Christmas, let your hair down, you're among friends here."

Lilly took the glass and raised it. "Yes, I am aren't I. Merry Christmas and, as Tiny Tom said in a *Christmas Carol.* 'God Bless Us Everyone'."

"God Bless Tiny Tom," said Dan, who got a kick from Dave.

Lilly sat herself down and surveyed the company. "I see you boys are drinking beer, my father and my husband always liked their beer in a tanker."

Everyone chatted and Jim took the opportunity to nip up the stairs. He found a box of ladies' handkerchiefs and chocolates that he had in reserve. Debbie had given him the tip and it was something that Karen had always done, kept a few things to one side in case an unexpected guest turned up. He wrapped the offerings and wrote a couple of labels. There, Stella would not feel left out when the friends exchanged presents later on.

When Maud learned of Stella's invitation she changed a label from one of the gifts meant for Enid, a chiffon scarf that would do nicely. Stella arrived an hour later and everyone was chatting and laughing. "This really is very kind of you Jim," she said, and handed Jim a bottle of port and some chocolate brazil nuts. "I feel quite embarrassed to be gatecrashing like this, but I am most grateful."

Jim put a reassuring arm around Stella's shoulder. "You are more than welcome Stella, now get yourself in there before Enid finishes off that bottle of sherry. That's her third to my reckoning."

The conversation flowed with reminiscences of festivities past and a few stories recalling some of their aunts and uncles and their strange gifts. Maud recalled being given a monkey wrench one year and Stella recalled the time that she had received a set of coasters that had obviously been taken from a hotel. Talk then turned to the end of the *Coliseum* cinema. January would see it closing its doors for the last time with demolition of the site later in the year to make way for a shopping arcade. It was yet another nail in the coffin of entertainment, what with the *Little Theatre* closing after the last summer season. Talks about turning it over to a cinema were met with mixed feelings.

Christmas lunch was a rousing celebration with Perry Como crooning out of the record player with *It's beginning to look a lot like Christmas*.

Lilly sipped her ginger wine and sighed, "I always liked Nina and Frederick's *Little Donkey*."

"We've got that," said Jim. "Dan, look in that pile of 45s, green label, *Little Donkey*."

"I like Bing," said Enid, who was trying to focus. "You can't beat a Bing at Christmas time. My old mum, God rest her soul, always liked a bit of Bing. Maud, I said mum always liked a bit of Bing."

Maud looked at her sister across the table and giggled. "How much have you had Enid? And put that paper hat on straight, you're all at sea."

"I saw Muriel, Freda and Lucinda exchanging pleasantries the other day on the market," said Lilly. "Unusual really, because Lucinda really doesn't get along with the other two."

"I spotted them too," said Dave, "when I was out buying some oranges and lemons. Put me in the mind of a scene from *Macbeth.*"

"Oh Dave that's cruel, and at Christmas time too," said Maud, trying her best to look disapprovingly at him. But then she burst out laughing. "I say it, and shouldn't, but I can't help agreeing with you."

"Right, who's for Christmas pudding?" asked Dan, as he turned his attention away from the record player as *Little Donkey* began to blare out. Everyone's hand shot up with Enid's just visible above the tablecloth as she began to slide to the floor. Stella went to the rescue and pulled her back up again.

"Who said that?" said Enid, screwing her eyes up.

"Who said what?" asked Maud, getting up to give Dan a hand in the kitchen. Enid nodded her head and began to sing the refrain of *White Christmas*. "It will be a cab home tonight. She was like this at our Cousin Rene's eightieth, talk about knocking it back. Tomorrow morning she will be telling me all about the evils of drink. Jim, please pour me another there's a love, if you can't beat 'em, join 'em, that's what I say."

"I love a Bing," said Enid and slid to the floor.

* * *

The cold spell of December made way for the freezing days of January as the New Year rang in across the town. The River Yare iced over and many thought that if it got any worse it would be possible to walk across the frozen water from Great Yarmouth to Gorleston. Something that hadn't been done since the days of the trawlers that had docked side by side making it a pathway from one boat to another. Those were the days when the air had been filled with the voices of the women who came down from Scotland to gut the herring in what was then a thriving fishing industry for the port.

Children loved the snowy conditions, while the older ones in the community cursed the white stuff for making walking to the shops almost impossible. The easterly wind gained strength and the townsfolk were wrapped in their winter best with the home-knitted scarves, that they had found in their Christmas stocking from grandmothers or great aunts, coming in more than useful. The local transport crawled along behind cars whose engines failed causing a hold up. The colourful displays of the festive season gave way to the January Sales with customers once more in the shops and stores that had not long since served them with Christmas fare. Bargains were sought by many an eagle-eyed shopper and rails of clothing that had filled backrooms made their way once more to the shop floor at greatly reduced prices.

The local amateur dramatic societies staged their annual pantomimes. One group performed at the *ABC Regal* theatre at the beginning of the month and another group at *The Pavilion* theatre in Gorleston at the end of January, giving people the chance to enjoy this traditional entertainment twice.

Lowestoft had its own local amateur pantomime so you really were spoilt for choice, providing you didn't mind travelling. The professional pantomime staged at the Norwich *Theatre Royal* attracted its own followers with coach parties descending upon its doors from local towns and villages. And with the promise of a star name headlining this was a must-see attraction.

Queues had formed at the *Coliseum* cinema to view its last showing and as the usherettes showed people to their seats, it reminded them of when the cinema had been busier. Customers reminisced about their courting days in what they lovingly called the flea pit and as the curtains closed for the final time and the National Anthem was played, there were one or two tears shed. One usherette who had worked there since leaving school and had clocked up over thirty years cried openly as the manager locked the main doors. It was the end of an era, left to memories to recall another day.

Tony Gareth Smith

Chapter Four

Open a New Window

I t was on the same day in March when the news came of the safe arrival of Jim's baby granddaughter, who was to be called Karen Louise, that Don Stevens took a call from Bob Scott at *The Golden Sands Theatre* in Great Yarmouth.

"It's most unusual and I can't get to the bottom of it," said Bob Scott, with some agitation in his voice. "The *Delfont Organisation* have been presenting summer shows here for years. I know they have Leslie Crowther lined up for the *Wellington* because there was a small piece in the *Mercury* last week. I've never been in this situation before because it's always a done deal. You can guess why I've called you."

Don tried not to allow the happiness he suddenly felt sound in his voice when he replied. "You want me to pull something out of the bag for the season. How many weeks are we talking about?"

"11ᵗʰ June until at least 12ᵗʰ September, that's what we had pencilled in for Delfont. But I warn you Don, we will be up against stiff competition. Peter Noone is lined up for the *Regal* so we need a really strong variety theme. I know you don't handle many television stars but do you think you would be able to come up with a good bill?"

"I have one or two ideas up my sleeve," said Don, trying to sound more confident than he was actually feeling. Elsie, who had been listening in from another extension, was going through the files on who they could possibly line up for what would be a long season. "Is this going to be twice nightly?"

"It has to be," said Bob, tapping the side of his coffee cup to attract the attention of his secretary, Beverley, in the hope of getting another. "You know as well as I do that to pay the kind of money stars want these days it's the only way we can meet the cost. Although the first house is usually less well attended than the second and that's to do with the way the guest houses serve their evening meals. Some visitors don't have full board so they come to the first house. Then we have the villages to consider. Groups come on days out to the resort; an early evening show is just right and gets them home in plenty of time for going to bed at their usual time. If you can come back to me as quickly as you can with the kind of line-up you have in mind I shall sleep easier in my bed. See if you can get that Ted fellah back and what's his wife's name, Sonia Clarence?"

"Moira Clarence. I can certainly sound her out, Bob. Look, don't worry, we will see what can be done."

"Thanks Don, I know you will do your best."

"Well," said Don, replacing the receiver and looking at Elsie, "that was a turn up for the books and no mistake. We have got to come up with something."

Elsie laid down the files she had been looking at on her desk. "I don't think you will get Rita to do it, she was really down after she and Ted heard that the musical they hoped to be in had been shelved. She told me that her voice suffers, playing in the smoky clubs."

Don looked thoughtfully at his wife. "That's a bummer, they really liked Moira last year, but I will still try to persuade her. Have we got Ted booked into anything for the season?"

"He was going to play four weeks in Clacton, but we could pull him from that and replace him with Dickey Durant, no contract has been signed."

"That's something at least. I would prefer Ted to be my lead comedian and Bob Scott asked for him particularly; I don't want to risk any of the others. We will need a good speciality act, can you think of anyone off the top of your head?"

Elsie pulled a file from the pile in front of her. "What about The Olanzos, they haven't anything lined up for the season?"

"A plate spinning act with singing. Do you really think they would be up to the mark for the *Sands*?" said Don, with some doubt.

"You're forgetting," said Elsie, "they come with the added bonus that she does a black theatre puppet act as well; two for the price of one."

"Can we see them work first, I haven't seen them in action for a while and I would like to be certain."

Elsie nodded. "We can catch them next week in Brighton."

"What are the chances of us getting Mrs Mills. Now she really *is* popular?"

"Gladys Mills is under contract to the lot that present the *ABC* circuit and has been for years. If you want a piano player you couldn't do better that Ricky Drew."

"The Scot's fellah with the dog, is he still on our books?"

"He better be, otherwise we've been taking ten per cent under false pretences. You really should get to grips with who is and who isn't on our books Don."

"That's what I had Gwen for," he replied, not looking Elsie in the eye.

"Then it's just as well that I'm here now," said Elsie, not wishing to pursue the subject further. "Now, you track down Rita and Ted, I'll see how the land lies with Ricky and we will also need dancers. I'll get on to the Jenny Benjamin lot, Doreen and Jill, I've heard that they are doing better things with that dance troupe so it won't be the same old routines this time round." Elsie looked at her husband who appeared to be somewhere else. "Are you listening to me Don Stevens? You will find Rita's number in the address book in your top drawer, now get to it, we have a show to put together."

* * *

Coming in from the garden, where she had been raking over the soil of her newly-planted vegetable patch, Rita answered the phone. "Oh, hello Don, how are you, is Elsie well?" Don explained the reason for his call. "I see," said Rita, "Well Elsie is right, I have been having problems with my voice and to be honest Don, the thought of playing a fourteen-week season twice nightly is not what I had in mind."

"But Rita, Moira is so popular with the punters, your old recordings did really well when they were re-released, and the men at *Decca* were elated."

"I am sure they were," said Rita, "but Don, my old lover, I am not as young as I was back then when those recordings were made. Yes, I don't deny that it was great being back on stage at the *Sands* and the *Wellington*, but it didn't lead to anything else. I am really upset that the musical we were hoping for has been put to one side. There were two great parts in that for Ted and me. I am sorry Don, but you will have to look elsewhere for your top of the bill. Ted will do the show, I know that, he wasn't looking forward to four weeks in Clacton."

Don sighed. "Rita, my darling, are you sure you won't reconsider, sleep on it?"

"Don Stevens, I think you know me pretty well and when my mind is made up, wild horses wouldn't make me change it."

"But what will you do all season with Ted in Great Yarmouth?"

"The same as I always do, pop down every now and then to make sure he's not up to his old tricks. Besides, I do have a couple of engagements in Norfolk during the summer which I must honour, so it won't be all pleasure. Who else have you got in mind for the show?"

"Elsie is looking at that now, she had one or two ideas," replied Don, wishing there was some way he could persuade Rita to change her mind. And then he had a thought, and he wondered why he hadn't thought of it sooner. "Rita can I put a proposition to you, it's an idea I've had." There was a pause and then he continued. "How would you feel about directing the show?"

Rita was taken aback. "Well, I don't know where that idea came from me old lover, can you elaborate? I have never directed anything in my life and anyway you always sort that out for yourself."

Don knew that he had Rita's full attention and continued. "You are wrong about never having directed, you do it all the time with Ted. And look at what you did at the *Sands* last year, you were always suggesting and feeding ideas to the company. It was you who made Jenny Benjamin sit up and take notice. Besides, I will need someone on the spot all the time keeping an eye on things. I can't be there; I have to go around the country looking at my other shows, making sure they are ticking over. Rita, you would be brilliant, what do you say?"

Rita felt a shiver go down her spine, the idea appealed to her. "We would have to discuss terms and I would need to see the acts first. They would have to be ready to do two rehearsals at the *Sands*. I can't work with that rehearsing lark you went through last year, it was a complete farce. In fact, I'm sure Brian Rix would have liked to have appeared in it."

"I take it the answer is yes," said Don, with great relief, dismissing the comments that cut him to the quick and giving Elsie the thumbs up. "You will have a list of acts by the end of next week. You can see them all work first and then we can agree on a running order for the programme."

"Correction Mr Stevens," said Rita, taking command of the situation, "*I* will work on the running order of the programme."

And those words told Don Steven that he had Rita on board and he smiled the biggest smile he had in many a year, much to the surprise of his wife.

* * *

The *Audrey Audley Agency* for variety acts and variety extraordinaire was in a side street adjacent to the market place in Norwich, situated above a dry cleaners. Entry was gained via a strong, panelled, ebony door that displayed a named brass plaque, a large lion head door knocker and, for convenience, a push button on the left-hand side that rang a bell one floor up to the chimes of Big Ben. The office was large and roomy and gave the impression of having many others leading from it because of the many doors that were dotted about. Apart from the separate reception entrance, where visitors waited to be called, in truth there was one toilet facility with handbasin and a small kitchenette housing a sink, a two-ring burner and a fridge. The other doors hid cupboard facilities, with one being large enough to house a baby elephant should one be required. But, as this was windowless, hardly practical and Audrey used it as a walk-in wardrobe to keep a rail of blouses, skirts, jackets, coats, wig extensions and shoes and boots of varying colour and height. Audrey was in her early fifties, but her peachy, unlined complexion denied this could be so. She stood five feet two when in the low-heeled court shoes she favoured for the office, her figure was of medium size but she had a bosom that could withstand two pot plants with room to spare. Audrey's chestnut hair, with a hint of mauve running through it, was swept upon her head in a bun or pleat when working, often supplemented by the use of various hairpieces to give it volume and the stature of one who was taller. A trick she had learned from one of her clients who had been a *Tiller* girl. Her emerald eyes were always shaded by a subtle green eyeshadow with fine false eyelashes, to enhance her own thinning ones, and her lightly powdered, rouged cheeks gave her natural pallor life. The added bonus of a beauty spot, a tip from watching Margaret Lockwood films, was applied every morning. But, because of her short-sightedness, could appear anywhere on her face depending on where her black eyebrow pencil happened to be aimed at the time. Her spectacles were of a framed, winged style much favoured by agony aunts and gave her the look of a bird of prey. Something highlighted further by her talon-like fingernails. She always wore a strong lipstick and matched her nail varnish whenever possible from a range of cosmetics she liked in *Woolworths*. She wore blouses and skirts whilst in the office but favoured the more flower power look of the fading sixties when relaxing at home or with friends and never missed the opportunity of wearing a gaily coloured headband securing the shaggy, loose-curled wig she wore with dark glasses whilst listening to what she described as the 'in music'. When working she kept jewellery to a minimum. Her only ring, a large emerald in a gold claw setting, had been given to her by her parents at her graduation ceremony from university.

Audrey drove to Norwich every day in her red Mini from home on the outskirts of Ipswich where her business persona went undetected and she was able to be the free spirit she felt within. A small cottage with picket-fenced garden encapsulated her world and garish silks and cottons adorned every freestanding chair, with tinkling bells hanging from the wooden beams. The cottage was a cluttered affair, unlike the orderly fashion of her business world. Her bedroom was festooned in drapes, a large feather bed and patchwork blankets which her cat Thomas could often be found hiding among, when he wasn't in the garden chasing wildlife. The furniture had been purchased from auction sales and had an old, battered, worn look she liked, hating anything that looked as if it had been purpose-made. Chairs with uneven legs, drawers that stuck when you opened them, a bath tub with clawed feet, brass taps that dripped into Victorian Belfast sinks. The clouded mirrors with their black aging spots would not look out of place in Miss Haversham's mansion in *Great Expectations*.

Audrey had no one in particular in her life; an array of like-minded souls with whom she shared her world would drift by unannounced and take up refuge in the spare bedroom securing entry with the key kept under the doormat at the rear of the cottage. Sometimes a stranger would come in to her life and if the fancy took her, she would think nothing of hopping into bed with him and having some fun. She didn't want the confines of marriage or relationships; she much preferred to drift and float and to take love where she found it, something that would horrify her mother if she ever discovered her daughter's dalliances. Her mother resided in Tunbridge Wells, in the manor house where Audrey had been born, and imagined her daughter to be the pivot of the variety world, something that at first she had frowned upon. But, as time had passed, she had embraced it, boasting to her friends about the magical and wonderful settings her daughter moved within. Because of her own whirl of social activity, her mother never made a trip to visit her daughter and had only seen the cottage once when it had first been purchased by her late husband as a base for their much-loved daughter.

There were a few select acts on the books of the *Audrey Audley Agency*, handpicked and managed with the love and care that only a bosom as large as Audrey's could nurture.

Before anyone was deemed good enough, she would see them working first, something she was aware that some of her fellow agents didn't adhere to. Her relationship with other agencies was a reasonably good one. There were times when she or they had to call in favours and through this civil way of working everything was kept at a harmonious level. She charged the usual ten per cent and kept her relationships within the business on a purely universal level. Keeping strict office hours of 9:00 to 5:00 she was able to be at her desk most days, answering the telephone in all manner of voices to fool the caller into thinking that her agency was not a one-woman operation. She had Julie the Liverpudlian and several other voices she could do at the drop of a hat, but one of her personal favourites was the Brummie tones of Margaret from Solihull. Audrey loved nothing better than acting over the telephone and putting her vocal talents to use in the way she had heard Beryl Reid do on the wireless endless times. She asked the person to hold the line whilst she enquired whether or not Miss Audley was available to take a call. This proved difficult if she had to be out on the road and reluctantly she would have to engage the services of a temporary member of staff from the *All Saints Employment Forum* two streets away. Whenever possible they would always send the same girl who knew the workings of the office. When this wasn't possible the person was told to take messages only, saying that Audrey and her staff were on a trip to look at new acts. The only person truly employed was the cleaner, Gladys, who came to the office every evening to give it the once-over, as she called it, and ensure that if a temporary had been in place that everything was locked away as it should be. Gladys was a trustworthy and hardworking woman in her late fifties who serviced several other offices in the area but the agency was her priority. She liked looking at the framed photographs of the variety acts, past and present, that hung on every inch of the wall space covering the floral wallpaper. Audrey paid her well for her services with a bonus every Christmas and a bottle of sherry.

On the rare occasion that her regular clients visited the office, by appointment only, Audrey would cover the fact that Julie, Margaret or any of her other staff were either off sick, on holiday or tied up in another office dealing with all manner of important things. She told her visitors that she much preferred to be the one who greeted them in the small reception area, as it was she they had come to see, and the secret was maintained.

One or two of her regular acts would send chocolates at Christmas to share with her staff; these were distributed to local children's home where Audrey thought they would do most good and her waistline the least harm. Always with a smile in her voice, she gave the all-round persona of one who loved her work and respected her clientele, ensuring they were given only what she considered to be the best bookings the business could offer. Audrey Audley was at one with her world.

"Good morning, the *Audrey Audley Agency,*" said the Brummie tones of Margaret, whom Audrey thought would be her member of staff for that day.

"Hello Margaret." Don Stevens recognised the voice instantly. "Is Audrey available please, this is Don Stevens."

"Hello Mr Stevens, lovely to hear your voice. I will just see if Miss Audley is free, she was on the other line."

"Hello Don, how the devil are you and what can I do for you this bright and cheerful morning?" Audrey was feeling vibrant and alive, following a weekend with friends at a concert and, although the Monday morning blues sometimes caught her out, she was on top of the world. What fun it had been listening to Joe and his guitar singing the folk songs that she had grown to love over the years.

"I was wondering if Derinda Daniels might be available for the summer season."

"I am sorry Don but Derinda is playing three night clubs, Norwich, Lowestoft and Ipswich with the boys."

"Three, how is she managing that?" asked Don, somewhat surprised.

"She will work alternate nights over the week with no cabaret show on a Sunday. Derinda specified that she wanted to stay local this season as no London engagements have been on offer. I think she is tired of travelling around the country. I was very lucky to fix this up. She will be on at midnight most nights and that gives her the whole day free. Why, what had you in mind, perhaps I can offer you someone else?"

"Well, something fell in my lap quite unexpectedly. The *Delfont Organisation* will not be presenting a summer show at the *Golden Sands* this year and I was asked to come up with a bill. I had thought that Moira Clarence, along with her husband Ted, would bite my hand off and although Ted is game, Moira has made it clear she isn't interested. However, she has agreed to direct the show." There was a pause as he awaited some kind of reaction to his announcement, but when there was none he continued, "Derinda was such a great help to me last year."

Audrey tapped her pencil, feeling slightly peeved. Moira Clarence directing indeed, what next, Kathy Kirby running the box office. "I am surprised, Don, that you didn't consider Derinda first. She is, after all, a well-established name in the business and much sought after."

Don knew this was how Audrey would react. "I am sorry Audrey. Naturally I would have thought of coming to you in the first instance, but Ted Ricer has been on my books for years as you know and when Rita, sorry Moira, made her comeback it was natural that I approached her."

"Forgive me Don, but if Moira was doing as well as we are led to believe, then why was she available to play the *Sands* in the first place? Surely work would have already been lined up for her?"

Don groaned. "Artistes, who can fathom the way their minds work? Ted wanted to work alongside his wife, though I suspect it was the other way round. The interest in Moira has been good, but she is very selective about what she takes on. They had hoped to be doing a West End musical, but that all fell through. The *Sands* becoming available was an answer to a prayer, but now catastrophe has struck."

Audrey allowed herself a smile to herself. "I bet the musical was *When the Boys Come Home*."

"How did you know that, Audrey, I thought it was all very hush, hush?"

"It was offered to Derinda, who would never touch a musical with a bargepole, though she has often been asked. I'm surprised that Moira would have even been considered, a bit out of her league wouldn't you agree? I read the script; there was definitely a part in it for Ted."

Don was slightly perturbed, he hadn't been offered the script, but such was the way of these things in show business. "Is there no way that Derinda could do the *Sands?*" he continued, getting himself back on track. "It would be twice nightly and I'm sure we can come to some arrangement concerning the fee."

Audrey thought for a moment., Derinda's London season wasn't going to happen and she had her ten per cent to think of. "I would have to talk to Derinda first but I warn you Don, she is very likely to say no. Imagine, two shows on the end of a pier and then rushing off to fulfil a cabaret engagement, that would make it thrice nightly. And, of course, there are her boys in the band to consider."

"Ah yes, I had forgotten about them," said Don, looking over at Elsie who was working her way through the names of support acts. "I couldn't employ the band; it would mean Derinda working with Maurice Beeney and his orchestra. We will be pretty full-on company-wise, I have to put as much variety into the show as possible."

"Look Don, I'll have a word with Derinda and see what she says. I do have other artistes on my books you know; I'm surprised you haven't another of Derinda's calibre on your own."

"If you could see how the land lies I would be most grateful," Don replied, wiping a bead of sweat from his forehead. "Look, I am coming down to Norwich in the next few days, I'll pop in and see you."

"Best to call first," said Audrey, "I'm often out and about."

"I can always leave a message with Margaret or Julie if you're not there."

"Yes, of course," said Audrey, blushing.

"Did she give you a hard time?" Elsie asked, looking at Don's ashen face.

"She loves to rub my nose in it that I don't have someone like Derinda on my books," said Don, clearly put out by the conversation that had taken place and reaching for the comfort of a cigar.

"Next time you speak to her, ask her how Ted Rogers is getting on."

Don took a long puff on his cigar. "Why would I do that?"

"Guess who could have been his agent?"

"No, I don't believe it."

Elsie gave her husband a knowing look and dialled the number of the *Jenny Benjamin Dancing School*. "Hello, is that

Jill? It's Elsie Stevens here, I have some work to put your way."

* * *

A few days later, and after calling her office and speaking to Margaret, Don sat across the desk from Audrey Audley. "I like this office," he said, making small talk, "you feel as if you have space to breath. I love all these framed photographs you have on the walls. I didn't realise you were representing so many artistes and if my eyes don't deceive me that is a photograph of The Dean Sisters."

Audrey touched her hair in a gesture she often used when she was taking command of a meeting. "The Dean Sisters, yes indeed. I manage one or two circus acts and the girls are doing very well. They have dropped all that singing nonsense and now do a fully-fledged circus act that is second to none. You should pop over to Europe someday and catch them in action. Can I offer you a coffee or perhaps tea if you'd prefer?"

Don nodded, choosing to ignore Audrey's swank. "Coffee would be lovely, thank you."

Audrey picked up her telephone. "Margaret, could you make two coffees please and perhaps a plate of assorted biscuits for Mr Stevens. Don't worry Margaret, pop it on a tray and I'll come through shortly. No, don't apologise my dear, I know you are a bit stretched in there at the moment with Julie indisposed. Give the temp agency a call and get someone in to help." Audrey replaced the receiver and returned her attention to Don. "Sorry about that, a bit of sickness in the office and Margaret is desperately trying to catch up on some outstanding work. Coffee won't be long."

"So, have you had a chance to speak to Derinda?"

Audrey played with her necklace, not taking her eyes off Don, and then picking up her pen she leaned forward. "I have indeed spoken to Miss Daniels. Quite a busy little bee she is too and sometimes difficult to pin down."

"But you managed to pin her down?" Don asked, watching Audrey with some amusement.

"Oh yes Don, pin her down I did. I put your proposition to her and..." reaching just under her desk, but not moving back from her position, Audrey pressed a button and a buzzer sounded in the office. "Oh, that will be the coffee. I'll just pop through and get it; Margaret is so busy, just rushed off her feet with all the work we have coming in. I won't be a moment." She got up from behind her desk and walked to a door at the back of the office to the right. Once safely inside the cupboard Audrey poured two coffees from the filter machine, placed a jug of milk and a sugar bowl on the tray, with the plate of biscuits she had prepared earlier, and carried it back to her desk. "That girl is a treasure; I shall never find another like her. Help yourself to milk and sugar. I prefer to take mine black, my doctor says too much dairy is not good for me, though I just adore yoo-gurt."

Don was totally mesmerised by what he was witnessing. "You said you had spoken with Derinda," he said, trying to get the conversation back on track.

Audrey took a sip of her coffee, sat back in her chair and placed her hands to her temples. "Yes Derinda. She was quite surprised by your proposition but not dismissive of it. At first she took a bit of persuading about not having the band with her." Audrey paused again and took another sip from her cup. "As you will know having worked with her briefly last year, the boys go everywhere with her. It's rather like The Beverley Sisters, one performing without the other two wouldn't be the..."

"Beverley Sisters," Don put in, not quite sure which planet Audrey was on, but she clearly didn't seem to be on the same one as him.

"Yes, quite," said Audrey. "She thought the idea of Moira, or Rita as she prefers to call her, directing the show was a bit off the wall. But as Derinda comes with her own act it really wouldn't be a problem."

"Well, they all come with their own acts," said Don, suddenly feeling exasperated "Rita would only be ensuring that the programme was evenly balanced and that timings were kept to, and she does know Derinda."

"Yes quite, timings, that was something Derinda mentioned. She said she was happy to do an opening number but didn't want to appear again until her final set as she needs to save her voice, what with doing cabaret appearances on top."

"Well, that will be something that Moira, sorry Rita, would need to decide."

Audrey leaned forward on the desk again, her ample bosom resting on the desk top, and looked Don straight in the eye. "Rita, Moira, whoever. May I remind you Don that Derinda calls the tune on this, you need her more than she needs you." Audrey knew that this wasn't true at all, Derinda had practically bitten her hand off when the job was offered. Derinda needed to make up the money she would be losing from the lack of London engagements.

Don wasn't going to be bullied. "If Derinda doesn't wish to go along with what my director wants then it doesn't matter. Elsie has been in touch with The Bachelors and they would be able to do part of the season and we could have Ted Rogers for the remainder. Be quite a catch for the *Sands*."

At the mention of these household names Audrey bristled. "I didn't know you were going to be in touch with other acts."

"Elsie's idea, always on the ball is my Elsie. She realised that Miss Daniels might be too busy to accept the offer, as she always plays a London season, and made other enquiries. I have to get an answer to the *Sands* within the next few days, so time really is not on my side. Of course, I fully understand the position that Miss Daniels is in. Please thank Margaret for the coffee Audrey, and give Julie my best for a speedy recovery, and thank you for your time." Don stood up to leave.

Audrey jumped to her feet and hurried round to the other side of the desk. She grabbed hold of Don's arm. "Don, please don't go yet, I'm sure that I can work out something with Derinda. You know how temperamental these artists can be."

Just then the telephone rang and Audrey quickly picked it up. "The *Audrey Audley Agency*," she said, rather too hastily in the voice of Margaret. And then realising her mistake quickly tried to cover her tracks. "Sorry, this is Audrey Audley, to whom am I speaking?"

Don wasn't quite sure what he had just witnessed but he was sure that Audrey had just impersonated one of her staff.

"Oh hello Elsie, yes he is here with me now, did you wish to speak to him?" Audrey offered the receiver to Don. "It's Mrs Stevens for you."

"Hello Elsie love, no I was just about to leave." There was a long pause. "That's marvellous and you are sure that Ted can do the whole season?"

Elsie chuckled at the end of the line. "Yes Don, Ted Ricer has agreed to do the whole season."

Don looked at Audrey. "Ted Rogers can do the whole season. Elsie, love, I'll have to call you back, Miss Audley appears to have fainted."

* * *

Two weeks later the *Great Yarmouth Mercury* carried an advertisement with an article:

Surprises all round this summer season as Bernard Delfont pulls the plug on his regular summer show at The Golden Sands Theatre. Stepping up to the challenge, Don Stevens has pulled together a wealth of talent that promises to deliver variety entertainment at its best. Bob Scott, the theatre manager, said, "It will be the highlight of the Great Yarmouth summer season. This will bring a wealth of variety to the venue and make it a must-see family show. I am delighted to say that Derinda Daniels will be headlining and the ever popular Ted Ricer will be making a welcome return to the Sands. Don has been fortunate enough to engage the pianist everyone is talking about, Ricky Drew. I am always pleased to encourage local talent and magician Jonny Adams will experience his first summer season here at the Sands. Following in the variety tradition of The Dean Sisters, seen here last year, the big surprise on the bill is The Olanzos; I don't think the resort will have ever seen an act like them before."

Don Stevens proudly presents for the Summer Season

The Incredible Voice of

DERINDA DANIELS

in

"SUMMERTIME SUNSHINE"

Opening Thursday 11th June for the summer
season at 8pm and thereafter

Twice Nightly 6:10 & 8:45 (except Sundays)

Ted Ricer A Laugh a Minute	**The JB Showtime Dancers** with choreography by Jill Sanderson and Doreen Turner
Melodies for You **Ricky Drew**	"Pulling Strings" Petra's Puppets
Introducing the Magic of local talent **Jonny Adams** Making his summer season show debut	The All Rounders Orchestra under the direction of **Maurice Beeney**
Direct from their sell-out tour of the UK The Fabulous **OLANZOS** *"Singing while Spinning"*	
Produced by Don Stevens and Directed by Moira Clarence	
Seats Bookable in Advance from the Theatre Box Office 12/6, 10/6 and 8/6	

* * *

Over a pint of *Lacons Affinity*, Jim and Dave had discussed the news.

"I just hope Don can pull it off. Some of the acts I've never heard of," said Jim. "I'm rather surprised that Rita didn't phone me with the news. Bob never said anything when I went in to the office the other day to discuss advertising for a new cleaner."

"Don't take it to heart mate," said Dave, resisting the urge to go and buy some cigarettes. "I expect they all had to keep quiet about it until it was official. You know Rita really well. She wouldn't have deliberately not said anything, especially after the lovely present she sent Debbie for the baby that you told me about. Old Scottie wouldn't say anything until he was dead certain, it's the same with my lot at the *Wellington*, I always read in the paper who will be topping the bill for the summer season. Anyway, changing the subject, how are Debbie and the little one?"

Jim smiled. "Doing well by all accounts. Baby Karen is a lovely little thing and she does have the look of my Karen about her. You'll see for yourself soon enough. I don't like to keep going over there, Debbie and Peter need time to adjust and I think Peter's mother more than makes up for me. Debbie says she drives her mad with her interfering. It would have been a different story if Karen were still alive, but there you are, different people, different ways."

"You are doing the right thing mate," said Dave, draining his glass. "Fancy another?"

Jim nodded. "Shouldn't really, but what the heck. Let's have another and then you can tell me about the visit to meet Dan's family."

Dave picked up the glasses and raised his eyebrows. "I'm dreading it."

"You'll be fine mate," said Jim, reassuringly. "You will knock 'em out with that charm of yours, you'll see."

* * *

Mona Buckle marg'ed another round of toast and poured herself a cup of tea. Her husband Bertie watched as she put a dollop of marmalade on top and smacked her lips in her usual fashion as she munched her way through what was, to his reckoning, her sixth. Bertie was a quiet man; he worked hard at the electronics factory in Great Yarmouth and always handed over his weekly wage packet to the eager hands of his wife. Quite a catch in his day, Bertie could have had his pick of the ladies, but somehow Mona Brown, as she was then, had fluttered her eyelashes and spun him round the dance floors of local venues and, before he knew it, he had proposed marriage. His mother, who had watched from the sidelines and from whom he had often sought advice, had said of the union, "Marry in haste my boy, repent at your leisure," and those words had often come back to haunt Bertie over the years. Looking at his wife now he could not believe that the once slender girl he had courted had turned into the lump of lard before him. The mere sight of her overweight body, forever encased in crossover pinafores of dubious colours, did nothing to make her alluring. Bertie was glad when the clock on the mantelpiece chimed seven-thirty so that he could pick up his packed lunch and head off to be with his workmates.

The kids had long since left home in search of a life far removed from the confines of the seaside town. William had joined the Royal Navy; Gordon the Merchant Navy, and Wilma (named after Bertie's late mother) had run off with a travelling salesman from Leeds never to be heard of again. The odd card from Gordon and William told of foreign shores, but the boys never returned to the house where they had been born. Bertie pined for his sons and daughter; Mona on the other hand had been glad to see the back of them. Never of maternal stock, like her mother before her, children were like a stone around her neck and she never mentioned their names, much to Bertie's distress.

The marital bed had long since been abandoned and Bertie slept in the back bedroom of the three-bedroomed terrace, surrounded by photographs of his family, and which Mona had been forbidden to enter. Bertie had had to stand firm on that, and it had taken several large whiskies to show his overbearing spouse that he meant business.

The sound of the newspaper boy pushing the *Great Yarmouth Mercury* through the letterbox brought Bertie back to life.

Mona slurped her tea from the saucer, a habit that made Bertie wince. "That will be the *Mercury*."

Bertie got up from his chair and went to the front door and laid the paper on the table. The clock on the mantelpiece chimed seven-thirty. He picked up the brown paper bag containing his fish paste sandwiches and an apple, dutifully pecked Mona on the cheek then wiped his hand across his lips and headed for the haven of the factory.

Mona, who had never grunted a 'goodbye' or a 'see you tonight' in over thirty years of marriage picked up the local weekly and looked at the front page. Some nonsense about the buses terminating earlier in the winter months didn't hold her interest. She turned to the obituaries and was pleased to see that her old form teacher had finally gone to meet her maker. The vacancies page was another favourite of Mona's, though it was true to say that work and Mona had never really gone hand in hand. But she had, in her youth, worked in a shoe shop, a chemist, the hat and glove department of *Arnolds*, a fish and chip shop and in the latter years had done the odd bit of cleaning for the big houses on Marine Parade in Gorleston. Mona was often dismissed or left jobs on a whim, thinking that her family would send money home to their mother for at least giving them a shelter over their heads whilst they were growing up. Unbeknown to Mona, her two sons sent their father a little something every month but this was paid into an account that the boys had set up so that their mother would know nothing of it.

Mona's last period of employment at a small guest house had ended quite suddenly when the owner had missed several pieces of glassware from a display cabinet and, though nothing had been proved, Mona had been given her marching orders.

Mona's eye caught sight of the unpaid gas bill at the side of the mantle clock and she sighed. She glanced at the vacancy list and her attention was drawn to the advert for a cleaner at *The Golden Sands Theatre*:

Cleaner required – The Golden Sands Theatre – for the summer season. Apply in writing to Bob Scott. Good rates of pay.

Mona, who knew of Lilly Brockett's reputation but didn't know Lilly personally, felt that there was no reason on God's Earth why she should not inherit the title. She heaved her bulk out of the chair and went in search of a pen and paper.

* * *

Rita sat down with a glass of milk and looked again at the acts that were engaged to grace the *Golden Sands* stage. She knew a little about them as they were on Don's books, but she had never worked with any of them. Elsie had been able to fill her in on some of the finer detail and it had been arranged that all the acts would be seen at a studio in London. Rita would then be able to judge the timing of each act and then say what needed to be cut to fit into what would be a packed programme.

Don had told her about Derinda Daniels following his visit to Audrey Audley but this cut no mustard with Rita. She would expect Derinda to follow the regular format, an opening number, a speciality number halfway through the first half and a closing set before the finale. Once she had sounded out Ricky Drew, Rita thought that it would be a good idea for Ricky to play for Derinda in her final spot, thus cutting out the need for extra players in the orchestra. She put pen to paper and began making a rough draft of how she thought the running order would look.

Ted was away for three days doing a stint in Durham and she had the house to herself with no distractions. There was a lot to organise, Rita took her responsibilities seriously and intended to ensure that everything ran according to plan. She made herself a note to call Jim later that day and also to give Lucinda Haines a call and enquire whether she would be prepared to house her and Ted for sixteen weeks. The summer season of 1970 was going to be a hectic one and Rita was looking forward to it with relish.

* * *

Coming from Scotland Ricky Drew had shown promise at an early age for his piano playing. Often the butt of jokes from his school friends, Ricky's mother had seen a talent in her son that his father discarded as 'that racket' and found him a piano teacher. Winning several talent contests, Ricky soon found himself in demand at clubs and parties. One evening while he was hammering out some good old Scottish tunes intertwined with the more classical pieces he was fond of, he was spotted by Don Stevens and his wife Elsie who were on a quiet break away from the hustle and bustle world of show business. And so for the last twenty years Ricky Drew had been represented by Don and found himself playing summer seasons and several of the London clubs where he mingled with Tommy Trinder, Danny La Rue, Barbara Windsor, Max Wall and the like.

Ricky was somewhere in his early fifties but for the purposes of his show business persona claimed to be late thirties. He had looked after himself well and had maintained his youthful looks by careful diet and exercise. He topped up his tan whenever the British sunshine allowed and the one or two trips that he secured abroad to Malta or on cruise ships ensured he never went back to his Scottish pallor. He was short, which gave him a schoolboy charm, but what he lacked in height he made up for in personality. His twinkling blue eyes, sparkling white teeth and well-groomed hair made him popular with the ladies, especially those who wanted to mother him.

He had often thought of settling down and although he had twice nearly made it down the aisle the fiancées in question had got cold feet about a man who was going to be on the road and never at home. So Ricky had taken solace in the company of his little dog Bingo and found the warmth of a woman's bosom whenever the opportunity presented itself, which was one of the reasons he steered clear of Scotland as much as possible. Affairs with other men's wives had seen him on the receiving end of many a black eye, meaning he had to play his sets whilst wearing dark glasses. And with the arrival of Roy Orbison in the sixties, Ricky felt he didn't need the competition.

His act was a mix of tunes giving Ricky the tag line of 'Ricky Drew – melodies for you'. Playing several seasons for Don Stevens he had learnt to take part in sketches that sometimes the top of the bill would be involved in. This in turn led to him being offered a part in pantomime, usually as the Court Jester or Silly Billy character of the story.

Ricky always took a two weeks break a year and retreated to his small cottage in the Suffolk countryside. He had obtained the cottage for a song from a farmer who was keen for the property to be let. Ricky purchased the cottage and the small piece of land that it stood on and for several weeks of the year it was let by an agency as a holiday home, meaning that there was always money trickling into his bank account if the work dried up.

He was thrilled to be asked to play the summer season in Great Yarmouth and he was very much looking forward to meeting Rita and Ted Ricer, whom he had often heard of, but had never met. Elsie had enlightened him on the line-up for the show and when he had been sent the advertisement that had appeared in the paper he was beside himself with excitement; he had been placed further up the bill than usual, it could only be a good omen.

* * *

Petra and Mario Olanzo were an Italian plate-spinning act with a difference. Mario sang opera as they spun two dozen plates spaced out in bars of six across the stage. There was no doubt about it, Mario could sing and managed to bring the house down at every performance. Petra provided the glamour but also joined Mario in the act by juggling with balls and clubs, proving that she was not just false eyelashes, lipstick and legs. They both spoke with a slight Italian accent; Petra did most of the talking, Mario appeared to be rather quiet and was often referred to as sullen when not performing on stage.

It seemed clear that Italian blood ran through their veins, at least that was the impression that they gave people. Petra could often be heard shouting in Italian, but the hint of a Brummie accent crept in more often than not. Mario was pure Italian when it came to singing, but in the privacy of their home Pam and Mike Denham were more English than fish and chips.

They had started off in the business with a poodle act and had played circus in and around Europe. It was there they picked up their Italian habits. The act had been known as Denham's Performing Poodles, and although they were well known in Germany, France, Holland and Italy, they were unheard of on British shores. They had both decided not to perform in England as they had developed a taste for the Continent. The act folded when one of the poodles – Dodgy, a crossbreed of dubious parentage - bit Pam several times during the run of their Hamburg season. The other poodles had reacted badly when Mike had returned from an errand minus Dodgy, who was never to be seen again. The remaining poodles refused to perform to order and all manner of erratic behaviour suddenly made its debut in their well-honed performances. Pam and Mike left their circus season short of four weeks and went away to rethink the business they both loved.

In those days Mike was more vocal where the act was concerned but the sudden demise of his prized pets sent him in to depression. Some months later, and completely poodle-less, Pam had been doing some hardline thinking. There had to be something else they could turn their hands to in the profession. She had thought of juggling acts, magic acts and even at one point a knife-throwing act, but as Mike had sunk further into his depression, drink had taken a hold and his hands were not as steady as they once had been. But one thing did transpire that gave Pam hope, when he was drunk, Mike sang and he sang well. The problem was, could he sing when he was sober? Seeking help, Mike eventually came to terms with his drink dependency and with it came the silences, but as soon as he heard music on the wireless he would burst in to song. He had always loved opera and in particular the voice of Mario Lanza.

A year had passed since Denham's Performing Poodles had bitten the dust and Pam, with a sudden brainwave, suggested to her husband that singing would be the way forward, and perhaps she could supply the harmony. Because of his insecurities Mike didn't like the idea of standing on a stage singing, he was better when he was busy, as he had been with the dogs. Pam's idea finally came one day while they were washing up the dinner plates in their Italian villa. Mike, who was wiping, lost grip of what he was doing and one of the plates flew in to an air spin and came crashing down on the stone-tiled kitchen floor.

"Plate spinning," said Pam, pulling off her rubber gloves to reveal her well-manicured nails. "Singing and spinning, we can do a plate spinning act and you can sing opera. Don't you see Mike, it will be a novelty, no one has ever done that before." She watched as she could visualise the cogs in Mike's head turning. He smiled, then he laughed and then he burst into an Italian love song as he smashed several pieces of crockery, grabbing his wife in the process and showering her with kisses. The Olanzos were born,

They thought it best to avoid the circus circuit and headed back to Blighty to launch their unique act as a variety turn. Keeping their Birmingham roots firmly under cover, Petra and Mario Olanzo registered with agent Don Stevens. When they had received the news about their summer season engagement, Petra was slightly concerned. She knew of Rita's reputation as Moira Clarence and she worried that it wouldn't take long for Rita to work out that The Olanzos were not all they first appeared to be.

* * *

Derinda hesitated as she dialled the number. This was a call that filled her with dread.

"Hello Sasha, it's Derinda."

"To what do I owe this unexpected pleasure *ma chérie?*" The sarcasm oozed from his voice and Derinda knew she was going to be treading on eggshells.

"There has been a change to my scheduled summer season."

"You want to have Jeanie earlier than usual; it can be arranged," Sasha replied. "It is no problem, she will be on holiday for six weeks."

Derinda swallowed hard. "It won't be possible for me to have Jeanie this summer; I won't be doing my usual London season." This announcement was greeted with silence; she waited for a few seconds and continued, "You see, Sasha, I've been asked to do a summer season in Great Yarmouth and because of the money I'm unable to turn it down. I'm also going to be working local night clubs."

"You are breaking the agreement, you do realise that? Custody was agreed in the courts. If you miss one of the arrangements, then you forfeit your rights to see Jeanie again unsupervised. I will ask the courts for sole custody." There was an edge to Sasha's voice that gave Derinda cause for concern.

"But Sasha, it cannot be helped. It will not be possible for me to have Jeanie with me in Great Yarmouth, you know that."

"You make me very angry Miss Daniels. Have you asked yourself why you have no London work? Perhaps London is tired of you, perhaps the great Derinda Daniels is losing the hold of top star status to others who are more talented."

"Why do you have to be so cruel? You have to understand Sasha that without regular income I cannot give you the money. I'm devastated that I cannot play London this year. Do you really think I don't wish to see my daughter? You know how much I love her. If you hadn't been so unreasonable from the beginning we would still be a family."

"Unreasonable am I? I will tell you what is unreasonable, that a mother who claims how much she loves her child places her stardom and ambition above all else. If you do not see Jeanie this summer, I will see to it that you never see her again. The courts will come down on my side."

"But think of what that will do to Jeanie, Sasha. There has to be another solution, you cannot take away my rights to see Jeanie, she is all I have now. Please don't let the authorities know, please, just this once, I beg you."

"I wish I could see you on your hands and knees to me. I am not an unreasonable man, despite everything you say. It will cost you, another two hundred a month."

"But that is too much Sasha I cannot afford extra, I am already paying you a lot of money now."

Sasha raised his voice. "You will find the money Derinda."

"Sasha please, I beg you, don't do this to me." Derinda began to sob.

"Then you will do what I ask and make no mistake. Remember the photographs I have." The phone line went dead.

Sasha Boureme felt a comforting hand on his shoulder. "Don't worry my angel, Derinda will find no work in the lucrative clubs she has played in London; I will put paid to that. They are more interested in your new star now."

Sasha turned and looked up. "But how can you be so certain?"

Lorna Bright smiled. "But my darling, that singing coach June lined up for me has been brilliant. I won't fail again. Besides I am more comfortable singing in French, it seems more natural to me. I shall be the new Edith Piaf."

"I am not so sure. My family have high stakes in those clubs, they trust me," said Sasha, pulling her closer and kissing her neck. "What if it all goes wrong?"

And in a perfectly pitched French accent Lorna replied.

* * *

Muriel and Freda were duly invited to take tea with Lucinda. Muriel wore another new outfit, whilst Freda turned up in her 'old faithful', the faded rose creation with the hint of lavender water mixed with the unwashed smell that hadn't quite left it. Lucinda opened a window in her newly refurbished lounge, despite the weather having turned again to a very cold spell.

Muriel looked about her. "My word Lucinda, you really have gone to town haven't you?"

Lucinda smiled. "Wait until I show you what I've had done upstairs," she replied, moving as far away from Freda and her frock as possible. "Washbasins in every room and the two rooms at the top of the house will be let out to Ted and Rita Ricer for a whole sixteen weeks. You will have seen the announcement in the paper. They enjoyed their stay with me last year and wanted to return."

The look on Muriel and Freda's faces said everything.

"I've had a bit of decorating done," said Muriel, running her hand over the soft fabric of the armchair and avoiding saying anything about the booking that had been secured. "I thought I needed to update a bit. Barry has been very busy with his brushes and it really does look brighter."

"And have you had anything done Freda?" Lucinda asked, as she noted Freda's silence since her arrival.

Freda blushed. "Dick and I have talked about doing something," she said, "but he really has been quite busy down at the *Legion* of late."

"I had someone in to do mine," said Lucinda, enjoying the moment.

"It must have cost a fortune," said Muriel, admiring the new curtains that hung in the bay window.

"Money in fair words, as my old mother used to say," she replied. "Now ladies follow me upstairs and I'll show you the changes there, and then I think we will have a pot of tea and some cake I got in special."

Freda pulled herself up from her chair and followed Muriel, totally in awe of the many changes that caught her eye. She would be having words with Dick and no mistake. After all she had won a raffle prize at the landladies' convention at the end of the last summer season and there was no reason why she shouldn't win the coveted trophy and wear the blue sash with pride. It would show Lucinda Haines what she was made of.

Lucinda had been thinking along the same lines, she was determined more than ever to be top guest house landlady. For too long Shirley Llewellyn the Chair of the *Great Yarmouth and Gorleston Guesthouse Association*, known as GAGGA, had favoured others. It was her turn now and she would pull out all the stops to prove it.

On their way home Freda could not help herself commenting on what she had heard. "Can you tell me, Muriel Evans, that Ted Ricer and Lucinda are not having a bit of how's your father? Bold as brass and under the same roof as his wife. Mark my words, there will be more flowers and chocolates to come," and with a sniff she added, "and heartache. What can they be thinking of?"

Muriel chose to say nothing, but was thinking along the same lines as her neighbour. If Lilly Brockett ever needed ideas for another story, there were plenty of pickings to be had and no mistake.

* * *

Before things got busy, Dan and Dave agreed on having a few days away so that Dave could finally meet Dan's parents. Arriving at Preston station, Josie and Madge met them from the train and after introductions and a quick chat over a coffee, drove them both to Dan's home. Dave felt his stomach churn; he hadn't felt this nervous in years. However, the welcome he received from Mary and John Forrester couldn't have been more surprising. While Mary fussed around them both asking if they had a good journey and busied herself laying the table for a meal she had prepared, John grabbed hold of his 'new son' and ushered him outside to his shed to show him a coffee table he had been making.

"They seem to be getting on okay then," said Kate, as she came into the lounge to welcome her brother. "I just heard them talking in the shed as I came in the back gate." She dropped the shopping bag on the floor and hugged her big brother. "I told you everything would be okay. Besides, dad has been doing a bit of thinking, well according to mum he has. Turns out some bloke he used to know at school is having a 'relationship', as dad chooses to call it. He found out a few weeks ago and he seems quite all right about things and has met his mate's friend, Patrick and Dean. Dad calls them Pearl and Dean."

Dan looked at his sister. Mature for her early years, she was always such a comfort to him and a fountain of knowledge about all that was going on around her. "Heard anything from our Gary?"

"Mum had a letter last week, he knows about you and Dave, mum wrote and told him. Gary says he is really happy for you and is looking forward to meeting his new brother when he is next home on leave. Says he might even go down to Great Yarmouth to see you both."

Mary Forester came in to the room with a tray of tea. "Katie love, go and tell Dave and your father that there's a pot of tea here. I'm not running a delivery service."

Dan smiled at his mother. "Thanks for making Dave feel so welcome Mum. He was really nervous about meeting you both."

"That's okay me old love, if first impressions are anything to go by, then I would say he is going to fit in really well. I expect Kate has told you about Pearl and Dean."

"Patrick and Dean. Yes she mentioned it. I bet dad was surprised."

"Surprised yes, horrified no. Once you get past his funny little ways, your dad is more worldly-wise than people give him credit for. There's a letter on the sideboard from Gary, have a read of it while I go and take a look at how the hotpot is coming along."

* * *

The following day Dave and Dan accepted an invitation from Josie and Madge to go over to Blackpool for the day. Although there was a chill in the air, the sun bravely shone turning the day into a brighter one than had been forecast. Things were beginning to awaken along the Blackpool promenade and signs that the summer season was not far off became evident. After a bracing walk along the North Pier and a stroll down the prom, they had lunch in a small café beneath the shadow of Blackpool Tower. Dave took in all that went on around him and compared it to the scene in Great Yarmouth; Blackpool was bigger and brasher than the Norfolk resort. He loved watching the trams go up and down the promenade and after they had finished their meal he persuaded everyone to take a ride on one.

"Let's go to Lytham St Annes," said Madge. "There's a lovely teashop over there and the local shops are very twee."

Taking seats on the top deck, the tram rumbled on its way passing the infamous piers and the Blackpool Pleasure Beach.

"I like your mum and dad," said Dave, while the girls' interests were distracted by something going on on the beach. "You never told me that your dad was a carpenter. That coffee table he's making is very impressive."

"It's a hobby really," Dan replied, with a smile, happy knowing that things had got off to a good start. "All manner of

things come out of that shed. The coffee table is a birthday present for mum, at least that's what Katie told me."

Josie interrupted their conversation. "You two, get a load of them silly buggers having a paddle, the water must be bloody freezing."

They arrived at St Annes and wandered down the parade of shops that were on both sides of the wide road. It was a far cry from Blackpool and a pleasant surprise. After a stroll on the pier and along the seawall they made their way to the tearooms that Madge had been so keen they visit. The panelled walls and the prettily gingham-table-clothed tables were like taking a step back in time. Waitresses in black outfits, white aprons and hats welcomed them as they entered. Dave excused himself to go to the gents and it was on his way back that he spotted a familiar face. There sitting at a table with a pot of tea and a scone was Marie Jenner. Marie had run the gift shop at the entrance to the *Wellington Pier* but issues with her husband Alf, her wayward daughter Sara and the arrival of an old flame, Graham Pettingale, had forced her hand to move away and start afresh.

"Hello Marie, fancy seeing you here."

Marie Jenner looked up and a big smile lit up her face. "Dave, my goodness, oh how lovely to see you." She stood up and threw her arms around Dave's neck, giving him a warm hug. "Oh this is a lovely surprise, what brings you to these parts? I wish Graham was here, he's gone to have the car serviced."

Dave went over to the others and explained the situation and they agreed that he join his old friend and catch up. Marie was clearly as pleased to see Dave as he was to see her. He gave Marie a brief outline of what had been happening and she smiled at him and acknowledged his happiness.

"I'm so pleased you're settling down at last, you're too nice to be left on your own. I'd guessed that Dan was your beau when I saw you together a few times along the prom."

"And how are things with you and Graham?"

"Couldn't be better, we have a nice home here in St Annes. He has been such a breath of fresh air to me I can't tell you. He is everything that Alf never was or, as I see it now, could ever be. I haven't been as happy as this in many a year."

"Are you in touch with your husband?"

Marie's faced clouded over, but only for a brief moment. "I did telephone him a couple of times to let him know I was okay and to find out how Sara was. I haven't given him any indication where I live and I hope that once the ball starts rolling divorce proceedings will commence."

"Did you want me to take a message home for you?"

Marie shook her head. "Always thinking of others," she said, touching the back of Dave's hand. "That's a fine quality in a man and something I have always admired about you. Look, I've kept you long enough from your friends." She reached in to her handbag for some paper and a pen. "Look, here is my address and telephone number. I know I can trust you not to disclose them to anyone else. Let me know when you are next up here and you and Dan must come over for lunch. I know Graham would like to meet you, I always talk about you."

The friends hugged as Marie got up to take her leave. She stopped and addressed Dan, "You are a very lucky young man, take care of Dave, he's one in a million. Be happy together and I hope that in the not too distant future we can get to know each other a little better." She waved her hand and was gone.

"What a lovely lady," said Dan, as Dave sat back down opposite him, and Dave's heart agreed in spades.

On their way back to Preston later that evening Josie asked Dan if he would ever consider moving back up North. Knowing this was the opening for a discussion between him and Dave he worded his reply carefully. "I don't know Josie. I have Dave to consider now and, besides, we have just got ourselves set up in the flat."

"But you could get yourself a little house up here for next to nothing; they don't ask those fancy prices they do down south."

Madge who was driving and with Dave sitting up front with her interrupted. "Leave the boy alone Josie, he and Dave have just got settled. They need to get to know each other better first before they start playing happy families."

"Hark at you madam," said Josie, jokingly. "Who was it that went on and on until we got a little place of our own, and I had known you how long?"

"That was different," said Madge, changing gear and checking on an oncoming motorbike, "we were both the same age. Besides, girls are a bit different to boys. No offence Dave, but there's a good ten years between the boys and anyway it's too soon in my opinion for them to start thinking too far ahead."

Dave listened but made no comment. "Besides," continued Madge, warming to her theme, "what about jobs? Dave, from what I gather, is well set up work-wise."

"There's plenty of work up here," said Josie, quietly squeezing Dan's hand. "Blackpool is full of it, remember it's a longer season than Great Yarmouth. There are the lights for one thing, those illuminations bring in loads of people, and it's like the summer season all over again."

Dan decided to speak up. "If I were to move back up North, it wouldn't be without Dave. I love him too much; he means the world to me."

Dave took a quick look out of the window and caught Dan's face in the wing mirror. "And you mean the world to me Dan," he said, with a big smile.

Chapter Five   *Putting It Together*

A udrey was perturbed, why was it that the London club circuit was refusing to entertain Derinda as their headliner for the summer season? They were all telling her the same thing; they had a bigger name taking over from July and would not reveal who it was. Forgetting that she was the sole occupier of the office Audrey called out to Julie to make her a coffee. She busied herself with some post that had come earlier and when she realised that a beverage would not be making its way to her desk anytime soon, she reluctantly got up and headed for the cupboard. As she made her way back to her desk the telephone rang. "Good morning this is Audrey Audley to whom am I speaking?"

"Hello Audrey this is Rita Ricer, perhaps you know me as Moira Clarence, and I am directing the show at the *Golden Sands*."

"Yes, so I have been told," said Audrey, stirring her coffee and wishing she had remembered to buy some more biscuits on the way in. Those joints over the weekend had made her ravenous.

"Just a question really, Derinda does know about the call meeting in London tomorrow to meet with the other artistes?"

"Yes, of course she does, and from what I gather she is travelling to London today and staying overnight so that she won't be late."

"Another question if you don't mind," said Rita. Audrey raised her eyebrows wishing she could be left alone. "Has June Ashby been in touch with you?"

"Why would June Ashby be in touch with me, I have never represented her."

"Some months ago Derinda said she thought she had spotted her in the audience at one of her cabaret shows. I have been trying to get hold of June ever since, but have had no luck. She isn't answering my letters."

"And this is my concern because...?" said Audrey, impatiently. "Look Rita, Moira or whatever name you are calling yourself these days, I really cannot help you so would you please get off the line and stop wasting my time." She replaced the receiver. It was too early for lunch, the pubs wouldn't be open yet, but she did have a little roll-up in her handbag, surely a couple of puffs wouldn't hurt.

Ted looked at his wife. "Everything okay Reet?"

"That was Audrey Audley, Don has always told me what a charming and lovely person she is, if a bit eccentric, but she was downright rude."

Ted got up from the chair in the bay window of their hotel overlooking Kensington Gardens. "I'll get room service to bring up some sandwiches and a pot of coffee; you've been at it since the crack of dawn. Everything is going to be fine, you'll see."

"Thanks me old lover," said Rita, with a half-smile. "I still don't understand why June hasn't been in touch. Even Wally doesn't know her whereabouts; mind you, he said that they had not split on the best of terms. Sad really because I thought they made a lovely couple."

"Try talking to that Robin Preston or Lorna her sister."

"They appear to have vanished as well," said Rita, tapping her pencil on the pad.

Ted picked up the telephone receiver and dialled room service. "Maybe they have all gone on holiday." He felt his chest tighten and a sharp pain. Squeezing his eyes shut, he held his breath for a moment not wishing to alert his wife.

Rita walked across the room and picked up her handbag and coat. "Perhaps you're right. I'm going for a walk in the park, are you coming, I need to think?"

Ted cancelled his call and dutifully grabbed his jacket and slowly followed Rita out of the room.

* * *

Audrey paced the office. Derinda had always done well on the London club circuit and, in fact, for some years now there had been a battle between venues to secure her services. Derinda was versatile and could deliver any song that hit the popular charts along with the favourite ones that kept the older audience members happy. Why were the managers of these venues refusing to speak to her and who exactly was this mysterious star they had lined up? Audrey sat back down behind her desk and pulled open a drawer. Taking from it a blue book, she thumbed her way through the leaves until she found the telephone number of Rueben Roberts, a great friend of hers and one who was in the know about what was happening in the world of entertainment. She dialled the number and waited to hear the rich baritone of her old friend.

"Rueben, darling, it's Audrey, how are you?"

"Audrey, baby shoes, how lovely to hear your voice. I am absolutely fine and what can I do for my favourite girl?"

Typical Rueben, straight to the chase, thought Audrey, he must be very busy. "Darling, would you have heard of any new talent on the club scene recently? I have not been unable to secure Derinda with her bookings this summer and it is a cause of some concern as I am sure you will appreciate. London without Derinda Daniels is like Brighton without the pebbles."

"Well, strange to relate," said Rueben, stroking his goatee beard, "there was some talk a few months ago that someone, I am not sure who, had bought large shares in several of the venues. My source told me that at least four of the clubs were joining forces, setting up some kind of cooperative, if you have ever heard of anything quite so daft. These venues have been sole entities for as long as I can remember, why would they want to join at the hip unless, of course, as my source suggested, there had been cash flow problems. The trouble with them has always been that they run a select members policy. I am surprised that they have turned their backs on Derinda, she was always a dead cert when it came to filling up the venues."

"Did your source ever mention who had a vested interest?"

"My dear, you must understand that I hear about these things quite by accident. For some reason people like to chat to me, they trust me."

"I can see that," said Audrey. "Is there any way you can find out who this so-called new star is, for instance? Because whoever he or she is, they are taking work from one of my most valued artistes."

"Audrey my sweet one, why don't you come up to town for a couple of days and we can do the club circuit together. Are you known at the venues Derinda normally plays?"

"One or two," said Audrey, replacing the blue book in the drawer. "But that is easily remedied, I can wear one of my hippie wigs."

"I haven't seen you in one of those for ages, are you still hitting the party scene?"

"Whenever I can," said Audrey, with a giggle in her voice. "Anything to escape the nine-to-five existence. You must come down to the cottage the next time we are having a bash."

"I'm making a mental note of it right now," said Rueben. "Now, how about coming down here for a few days and living a little? One of your girls can take care of the office whilst you are away. I've just had the spare room redecorated; I think you will like it, crushed raspberry and apricot."

Audrey winced, Rueben's decorative attempts left a lot to be desired. "Rueben, I shall pack a bag tonight and catch a train tomorrow morning. I won't risk the drive, besides it will do me good to unwind."

When the call ended Audrey phoned the *All Saints Temporary Agency* to put in place her regular. Besides, in her mind, Margaret and Julie were on annual leave!

* * *

The following day Rita and Ted arrived at the *Studio Eight* in Earls Court, which Don had booked, to find Derinda already there going through a song. A bark from a little dog sitting at the side of the piano revealed that Ricky Drew was playing. As Rita took off her coat The JB Dancers walked in in their leotards followed by two young men, in equally skimpy attire, with Jill and Doreen chatting.

Rita clapped her hands together. "Good morning everyone, glad you could make it. For those of you that don't know me I am Rita Ricer and this is my husband Ted. I am reliably informed that The Olanzos are on their way, held up in a bit of traffic I'm afraid on their way back from last night's gig in Watford, which Ted and I were able to catch. A very unusual act as you will all see. Jonny Adams, Don's up-and-coming magician from Norfolk, you will meet at the theatre where we will be joined by Maurice and his orchestra."

A loud bang was heard, and then a crash of what sounded like breaking crockery as Petra and Mario of Olanzo fame walked in.

"So sorry we're late," said Petra in her high, squeaky Italian accent and doing her best to balance on the rather high heels she was wearing whilst trying to adjust the tight pencil skirt that was riding up her skinny thighs. "Hello everyone,

I'm Petra and this is my husband Mario." Mario nodded and said nothing. He was dressed in a pair of smart black trousers, white shirt and black jacket with Italian crocodile shoes adorning his feet. "It's so lovely to be here with you all and I can't tell you how excited we both are to know that we will be sharing the stage with all you talented artistes at *The Golden Sands Theatre*. Isn't that right Mario?" He nodded. "You'll have to excuse my husband, what he doesn't say in words he more than makes up for in singing, isn't that right Mario?" Again he nodded. "We are so excited to be here, so much in fact that I had to give my neighbour a call back in Italy to let her know we were going to be working with the cream of variety, isn't that right Mario?" He duly nodded.

Ricky Drew stood up from his piano stool and whispered to Derinda, "Do ye ken that hen, it's Sooty and Sweep, they've booked Sooty and bloody Sweep."

Derinda tried her best not to laugh and moved forward to welcome them both. "Hello, I am Derinda Daniels, I am very pleased to make your acquaintance."

Petra took Derinda's hand and shook it warmly. "This is Derinda, Mario, isn't it marvellous that we are all going to be working together?" Mario nodded and, with a sudden movement which made Derinda jump, he grabbed her hand and kissed it. "Miss Daniels, my husband Mario."

Rita clapped her hands in the hope of regaining some kind of control over the proceedings. "I think we should all have a quick cup of something and perhaps a friendly chat, then we can get down to the serious business about how I see the show coming together." Rita walked purposefully over to Derinda and smiled. "I am so pleased you took up my suggestion of working with Ricky in your final spot, from what I heard when I came through the door it's coming together nicely."

The company moved to the back of the studio where refreshments had been laid out and a general hubbub of noise ensued.

Ricky Drew sidled up to Ted. "At last I get to meet the famous Ted Ricer. I understand we have played some of the same venues over the years."

"Inevitable in this business," said Ted ,eyeing Ricky with some interest. "And that over there must be the famous Bingo I have heard so much about."

"Aye it is," replied Ricky. "Bingo goes everywhere wi' me, he's a bonny little fellah and no mistake. He keeps me on my toes."

"I see we have acquired some male dancers," said Derinda, acknowledging the pair as they walked by chatting to Jill.

"Oh yes," said Rita, "an idea that Jill and Doreen had. I believe Jenny took a bit of persuading but she seems to have come round to the idea that we must move with the times. I think they will add a little something, at least that's what my Ted says."

"They certainly have a way about them," said Derinda. "I can't wait to see them in action."

With everyone having made their own introductions, Rita finally called the group to attention and presented them with the running order of the show. "I am aware from seeing your acts individually that you all have your own schedules but as you will see from my running sheet," she proceeded to hand round the papers she had prepared, "there will have to be certain adjustments made. I am sure that many of you are already familiar with this format."

One of the male dancers stood up. "Hi Rita I'm Bill. Pete and I were wondering why this couldn't have been done at the theatre, we had to travel on the milk train to get here this morning."

"Hello Bill, yes I am sorry about that, but Petra and Mario are playing over in Watford, Ricky is down at Eastbourne, Ted is appearing in Hendon tonight and with Don Stevens based in central London and expected to drop in on us today, London seemed the best solution all round. When we get to the theatre in a couple of weeks we will only have two days before we open. I thought that spending time together now we could sort out some of the teething problems we might otherwise experience."

"So why isn't the musical director here, how are we going to perform without our music?"

Reluctant to mention that Maurice had just undergone a hernia operation, Rita said with a smile, "That's where our Ricky comes in; he has very kindly agreed to accompany you on the piano."

"With the promise of a wee dram," Ricky called out and Bingo woofed in agreement and everybody laughed.

Bill sat down again and allowed Rita to continue.

"Now, if you will take a couple of minutes to glance over this we will commence. Jill, Doreen a quick word if you please."

* * *

Later that day Rita and Ted met with Don and Elsie over a drink. Don was keen to hear how the initial rehearsal meeting had gone and was disappointed that he and Elsie had been unable to attend.

"I was pleasantly surprised," Rita began, as she settled herself down on the leather sofa in the hotel bar. "I think what impressed me most was the way the company came together. For instance, Ricky and Derinda got on like a house on fire and seemed very comfortable with each other."

Don smiled, feeling somewhat relieved. "One always takes a risk bringing these acts together and it's important that they all get on well. Derinda is a professional as past experience has told us. All in all I think we have a good company and with your direction Rita I think we could have a winning formula. Taking the summer season at the *Sands* is not going to be an easy ride, we have no real big star name to draw the crowds in, but Elsie has been busy behind the scenes and has secured several press interviews for Derinda and some other members of the company.

"Yes," said Elsie. "The *Mercury* and *Eastern Daily Press* are going to run with several articles over a period of time and *Anglia Television* have expressed particular interest in an interview with Maurice Beeney and another with Jenny Benjamin. Both are well known throughout Norfolk, and Jenny standing aside to allow Doreen and Jill to take the helm, bringing with them male dancers into the mix, is most newsworthy."

"I have also had reports from the box office that advance bookings are doing well," said Don, with a grin on his face. "That will keep old Maud busy."

Ted, who had listened carefully, spoke up, "As you say Don, we have no big star name to pull in the punters and that may yet be our downfall. I am the first to admit that I am not mainstream and I don't have the pulling power of someone like Arthur Askey or Leslie Crowther. Derinda Daniels is a first-rate entertainer and no one can doubt that, but she is not Kathy Kirby."

Don leaned forward and looked directly at Ted. "I think you are missing the point Ted. The fact is that you and Derinda are known throughout East Anglia and beyond. You may not be on the telly, but that can work in your favour, people don't necessarily want to see an act that they have seen in their living room. If that were the case then the Old Time Music Hall would never have survived at the *Gorleston Pavilion* all these years. I admit our biggest risk is, unlike the

Pavilion, we are playing twice nightly and the *Sands* is a large venue to fill, but with some clever advertising we can pull it off."

"Don is right me old lover," said Rita, giving Ted's hand a gentle squeeze. "Once word gets around about the sheer variety we have on offer I believe the holidaymakers will flock to see us."

Ted looked at his wife, acknowledging her enthusiasm. If anyone knew anything about the business, Reet most certainly did.

* * *

Back in Great Yarmouth Jim Donnell was whistling as he cleared his breakfast things away. The weather looked promising and he was looking forward to getting things underway at the *Golden Sands*. Maud, who had been suffering from a heavy cold, would be back at the helm and Barbara, who came in when things were busy, would once more be there to help. The box office had been open a week and the ticket sales were looking healthy enough but were not on the same level as the show at *The Wellington Pier Theatre* where Dave had told Jim that the bookings had been coming in thick and fast for Leslie Crowther and his company.

It would also be the first day for new cleaner, Mona Buckle, and Jim had yet to meet her. After years of working alongside Lilly, he was unsure how he would adjust to a new person working for him. Lilly had always been reliable and left to get on with her work. He just hoped that Bob Scott's new employee would cut the mustard.

The weekend had been a very pleasant one with the company of Dave and Dan, and Peter and Debbie had been down to Great Yarmouth for the day. Baby Karen was still a tiny little thing, but the lungs on her made her presence known when she was hungry for a feed. Debbie was taking motherhood in her stride and Peter was basking in the glory of being a dad. The trio epitomised the perfect family and Jim recalled how all those years ago he and Karen had been much the same.

As he sauntered down Regent Road he said good morning to one or two of the shop owners who were setting up their shop fronts. As he reached Marine Parade he looked across the road at the South Pier entrance and noted the publicity material now firmly in place advertising the show. The large face of Derinda Daniels smiled down along with smaller ones of Ted Ricer, Ricky Drew and The Olanzos. Maud Bennett, who had arrived earlier than usual to ensure that everything was just as she liked it, came out of the box office and waved as Jim walked across the road.

"Are you feeling better?" Jim asked his old friend and gave her a quick hug.

"I'm much better," said Maud ,with a smile. "Enid has it now and is feeling very sorry for herself, but she insists on opening the shop even though Barbara offered to stand in for her."

"Give her my love," said Jim. "It's good to see you up and about. Sorry you missed Debs and Peter, they send their love and told me they would be down again soon and would see you then. Well, I had better get on, the new cleaner arrives today, I hope she's every bit as good as old Lilly."

Maud, who had been hearing one or two tales about the new member of staff, decided to keep quiet. No doubt things would iron themselves out, often these things did. And besides, you couldn't believe everything people told you.

Jim greeted Jack the stage door keeper who looked up from his *Daily Sketch* with a cheery smile. "Morning Jim, there's a woman to see you sitting out front, says she is the new cleaner. She arrived with a mop and bucket."

Jim laughed. "Why on earth would anyone arrive with their own mop and bucket?"

"It's one of those galvanised ones," said Jack, taking up his paper. "By my reckoning they make a bit of noise when moved about."

Jim found the larger-than-life Mona Buckle sitting in the front row of the auditorium and right at her side stood one bucket with mop. "Hello you must be Mrs Buckle, I'm Jim Donnell." He held out his hand in greeting.

Mona, never one for anything so gracious, ignored the gesture and instead looked him up and down. Her left eye watered as if she had something in it but she made no attempt to deal with the problem. She heaved her bulk out of the seat and looked Jim firmly in the eye. "Pleased to meet you I'm sure Mr Donnell. Mr Scott said I was to report to you, but the front door wasn't open so I had to come round the side. The man at the backdoor there said I should wait for you, are you late?"

"I think you are a little early, I wasn't expecting you till nine."

"I didn't want to be late on my first day, like to make a good impression," Mona replied, with a huff.

"Come with me and I'll show you where you hang your coat and hat, then I'll show you round the theatre and explain what your duties are."

"I'll keep my hat on if you don't mind Mr Donnell; I never take my hat off when I'm working."

She followed Jim through to the front theatre entrance.

"This will be your cupboard Mona."

"I prefer to be called Mrs Buckle if you don't mind Mr Donnell, keeps it business-like."

"Yes, of course Mrs Buckle, forgive me. You can call me Jim, everyone does."

"You will be Mr Donnell to me," said Mona, taking off her coat and revealing her crossover pinafore in red gingham check.

"This is where all the cleaning material is kept and you can hang your coat in the kitchenette at the side there. I see you have a bucket and mop with you."

"I like to use my own bucket and mop, you know where you are with your own."

Jim showed Mona the front theatre entrance and the offices, explaining what would need to be done. Mona huffed in reply at each point. They went back into the auditorium and Jim pointed out the brass railing that ran behind the back of the last row of seats. "The brass will need doing every day; Bob Scott likes to see it shine."

Mona looked at the brass rail. "You want me to do that?"

Jim looked at Mona, not quite knowing where the conversation was going. "Yes please Mrs Buckle, Lilly Brockett always did it as part of her daily routine."

Mona huffed again and followed Jim down the theatre aisles as he pointed out the various other things that would need her attention. They then made their way backstage where Jim showed her round the dressing rooms and the Green Room.

"There has been sadness here," said Mona, looking around her, "I can feel it. Can you feel it Mr Donnell? There are restless spirits, the place is full of them."

"I can't say I have ever noticed," said Jim ,trying not to laugh; he could see that Mona was very serious indeed.

"I see things Mr Donnell, not many have the gift. I have the gift, I am a medium. All around me I feel the presence of those tortured souls, gone to the great beyond." Her voice rose with the dead as if saying it loudly made it more believable. "There is unrest here, you mark my words, and this place is a bed of unrest."

"If I can draw your attention to the floor back here Mrs Buckle," said Jim, trying to get things back on track. "As the artistes' freeway to the stage area, the floor must not be highly polished as there is a chance they could slip. A bucket of hot soapy water should suffice and it must be thoroughly dried. Lilly used to do it first thing in the morning."

Mona, who appeared to have drifted off somewhere, came back to the here and now. "You want me to do that?"

Jim nodded, Mona huffed.

"Just about to make a brew," Jack called out as the two got nearer the stage door entrance. "Can I get you both one?"

"That would be great," said Jim, looking for some relief from his first encounter with the new cleaner. "I am sure Mrs Buckle here would welcome a cup of tea."

Mona Buckle shook her head. "I never stop for tea until the allotted hour of eleven. All tea breaks should be at eleven, it keeps the mind and soul together. Drinking tea out of the allotted time would upset my aura, and I won't have my aura upset Mr Donnell. But you go ahead if you would like to have a cup now."

Jim threw a quizzical look at Jack who hurried back behind the safety of his glass window barrier and turned the kettle on. Jim wasn't quite sure how to progress further, but Mona Buckle had plenty to say.

"I must make a start Mr Donnell; I shall fill my bucket and mop that floor to within an inch of its life. I will then tend to the offices and the front steps of the theatre, leaving the dressing rooms to last if you don't mind. I will be happier working in them when the sun is higher in the heavens."

"And the brass rail?" asked Jim, for want of something to say.

"The brass rail will receive my extra attention, you have the word of Mona Buckle. I will see you at eleven for that cup of tea Mr Donnell and maybe a biscuit or two. I must go to my task; the devil makes work for idle hands." And with no further word, Mona Buckle waddled away.

* * *

Maud enquired how the new member of staff was settling in when Jim called by the box office later that morning and Jim explained his strange encounter with the lady. "We've got a right one there and no mistake. I don't know what the company will make of her," he said, with his hands firmly in his pockets. "She claims she's a medium and can contact the spirits."

Maud sighed. "Medium is it?" She paused and then chuckled. "I would say she is more of an extra-large from what I saw of her earlier."

Jim grinned. He wondered what Lilly would have made of her replacement, and she would have had plenty to say no doubt.

"Well, I best get on; the boys are unloading some of the sets."

Just then two people appeared at the box office window and Maud greeted them with a smile.

Jim left Maud to it and walked back up the pier. The sea looked calm and one or two people were walking along the beach enjoying the unexpected sunshine. He pulled out from his pocket the letter he had received earlier and read it again. He sighed and put it back in his pocket. Just as he reached the front of the theatre Bob Scott came out of the door.

"Morning Jim, how is our new cleaner getting on? I hear from Jack she came with her own mop and bucket."

Jim filled Bob in on his findings.

"Best keep an eye on that one, we don't want anything to go wrong this season, there's a lot riding on it."

"I'll do my best," said Jim, and as Bob walked away he looked at his watch. It was eleven, Mona would be expecting that cup of tea, best not disappoint her on her first day, though what he was going to talk about he had no idea. Perhaps he could mention his granddaughter, that always got the conversation flowing. Women liked babies.

* * *

Lucinda Haines was getting ready for the season. Already her bookings were up on last year and with the added bonus of having Ted and Rita Ricer to stay for the whole season, things couldn't be better. Her new living quarters had been completed and she had decided that now was as good a time as any to move in to them. The bedroom was serviceable if small, but then Lucinda wasn't one to need lots of room. She kept her wardrobe to a minimum and when she purchased a new item would send an older one to the jumble. She had debated on whether or not to offer the self-contained accommodation to Ted and Rita, but she realised that the space was just large enough for one person. And as it was at the rear of the house on the ground floor, the view from the windows may not be acceptable to her paying guests. She had negotiated a fair price on the two rooms at the top of the three-storey house which offered privacy plus a decent view of the sea beyond. She tapped the top of the newly delivered chest freezer, picked up her shopping bag and went off in search of frozen produce that would help her through what was looking like a demanding summer season.

* * *

Muriel Evans was doing a final check on the newly decorated bedrooms and putting the finishing touches to the excellent job Barry had done on them. The paintwork had given the rooms a fresh look and the carpets, which had been cleaned thoroughly with the use of a hired machine from the laundrette, set off the new bed linen and curtains a treat. She had written to her regulars informing them that the tariff had been increased by a guinea a week. This was in order to help repay the money she had removed from the joint bank account. She knew that she would hear no complaints from them, her regulars had become friends over the years and they obviously enjoyed staying at her guest house otherwise they would have gone elsewhere.

* * *

On the other side of the wall Freda Boggis was surveying her bedrooms with all the enthusiasm of someone who had just been told that they had been chosen to ride in the Donkey Derby. The bedspreads were looking tired and worn, the carpets had seen better days and the furniture was so dark that Dracula would have had no problem occupying a room, even with the curtains open. The nets that were hanging at the windows hadn't been washed since the beginning of two summer seasons previous and the ray of sunlight that had been trying to penetrate them, like Freda, had given up. It wasn't that Freda couldn't see what needed doing; it was the effort of doing it. Dick rarely helped her and she found that some of her paying guests were usually of the non-paying kind. After one night they did a flit and left her a food bill to pay and no means by which to pay it. She sat on the edge of one of the beds and the springs groaned under her weight. She looked around her again and taking a hanky from her apron pocket she howled in despair. The wailing was so loud that Muriel could hear her through the wall and decided to go and investigate.

After ringing the doorbell for what seemed an age, Freda finally opened it looking red-eyed and visibly upset. Muriel, who had often criticised her neighbour, felt a pang of sorrow. "Freda love, whatever is the matter?" she said, stepping inside and putting a comforting hand to Freda's ample shoulder.

Freda blubbered for a further few minutes and as Muriel led her through to the lounge she did her best to suppress her tears. Muriel made her sit down and went through to the kitchen to switch the kettle on. When she returned Freda was wiping her eyes, but her bottom lip was quivering.

"Come on Freda, tell me what the matter is. Has Dick been in an accident, are you feeling unwell? Whatever it is you can tell me."

Freda calmed herself and began to tell Muriel about the bedrooms and how Dick wouldn't help her and that she didn't have the energy to do it all herself, that her guests didn't always pay their bills and she felt like she was beneath the likes of Lucinda. Muriel handed Freda a cup of tea and sat down. As much as she knew that Freda was lazy and that she didn't always do her best, she really did feel dreadfully sorry for. When Barry's sister Chloe had passed away shortly after Christmas, Freda had been the first at their door with a card and flowers; in moments like that Freda could not be faulted. Muriel looked at the sad woman in front of her and decided she would do something to help her.

"When do you expect your first guests Freda?"

Freda slurped her tea, spilling some down her pinafore front. "Week after next, the Harrisons are coming with that blessed dog of theirs."

"Look Freda, this is the deal. I will give you the bed linen that I've replaced, together with some new packets of sheets that Barry's sister had. I will ask Barry if he will give Dick a hand to put a lick of fresh paint round the bedrooms. I will help you take the nets down and put them through the machine. You can have the curtains I no longer need now I have the new ones, but they will need dry cleaning. I still have the carpet machine I hired, it will have extra to pay on it, but it will be less expensive than getting someone in to do it for you. Do you think Dick will be willing to tackle the carpets?"

Freda nodded. "He might take some persuading."

Muriel stood up. "Right, when Dick comes in you tell him that Muriel wants to see him urgently. You will have your carpets cleaned or my name's not Muriel Evans."

Just then the front door opened and Dick walked in. "Oh, just in time for a cup of tea," he said. "Hello Muriel, unusual to see you in here at this time of day."

Muriel, who was not in the mood for taking prisoners, jabbed Dick in the chest. "Never mind cups of tea you good-for-nothing. Come with me, I've a little job for you my boy and there won't be any tea until you've made a start on it."

Dick looked at Freda and then meekly followed Muriel. Freda's lips began to quiver and she put down her cup and saucer and began to howl even louder than before.

* * *

Audrey's trip to London had borne little fruit. Wearing one of her best wigs and some cleverly applied makeup, Audrey had accompanied Rueben to four of the clubs where Derinda would normally be engaged. Each of the clubs had an act on and these varied considerably, especially on the talent scale. A magician whose rabbit refused to materialise from a top hat, a comedian who was so drunk he couldn't remember his tag lines, and some most unmemorable vocalists were among the mix on offer. One barman, with whom Audrey and Rueben got in conversation, was more forthcoming and said he had heard that they were expecting a French vocalist for the summer, but the name escaped him. He thought it was Laura Doom or something along those lines.

"Who on earth would call themselves Laura Doom?" said Audrey, helping herself to some peanuts on offer at the bar.

"Who indeed baby shoes," said Rueben, knocking back a brandy and ordering another. "We seem to have hit a wall of silence."

"Maybe they really don't know anything," said Audrey, "though I do find it hard to believe that we have seen no posters advertising forthcoming attractions. And by the look of some of the acts we have witnessed over the last few evenings you would have thought that a talent like Derinda would be their port in a storm."

"Someone must know something," said Rueben, "you will have to leave it with me. Now, how about a dance, I feel like letting it all hang out."

Audrey laughed and grabbed Rueben by the arm. "Come on then let's show these people how it's done."

Chapter Six   *Lipstick and Lashes*

Thursday 4ᵗʰ June

As Maud Bennett walked down Regent Road, in the distance she could see the large transporter trucks that were lined up at the entrance to the South Pier. More sets and costumes had arrived. She knew that Jim had been keen to get them in place before the arrival of the company, expected the following week, and he had thought things were being cut a bit fine. Maud arrived at the box office just as the first pallets were being loaded onto a small truck that would travel down the pier to the rear entrance of the theatre. She opened the door of her box office and began to set her stall out. It was unusual not to see Jim supervising the delivery but she had noticed that Roger, his second in command, appeared to have things in hand. Just then she heard a tap on the door, it was Mona Buckle looking none too pleased going by the look on her face

"Haven't time to stop and gossip Mrs Bennett, I've work to do. I was wondering if you had seen Mr Donnell this morning only he isn't at his post and I need some more *Brasso*. I like to get myself sorted out first thing; I haven't got time to go chasing people. If he had given me a proper supply of cleaning materials from the off then I wouldn't be having this run-around now."

"Have you asked Jack, he usually sees Jim before anyone else?"

Mona shook her head. "He hasn't seen him."

"Well I'm sure he will be here soon enough. Is there something you could get on with until he arrives, leave the *Brasso* job until later perhaps?"

Mona huffed, her eye watered and she scowled. "I can always find something to do Mrs Bennett." She looked around the box office and looked Maud straight in the eye. "There has been grief in this office, I can feel it, and the spirits never lie. I can see things Mrs Bennett, it's a gift I have. All around me, the eyes are watching."

"Everything okay Mrs Buckle? Morning Maud."

"Morning Jim," said Maud, with some relief. "Mrs Buckle was after some more *Brasso*."

The Golden Sands Theatre backstage area became a hive of activity as various components were put into place. Backdrops were secured to their heavy steel poles and hoisted into the fly tower using the various pulleys that secured them. Interchangeable wings were erected and three pairs of curtains were put in place to provide a variety of colour during set changes. The main curtain, which flew up into the tower, was heavy red brocade which during the interval would have the white safety curtain lowered in front of it and onto it would be projected local advertisements. There were two staircases, one for the opening that curved from the right-hand corner of the stage, and a second that stretched the full length of the stage at the back providing a wide walk-down for the entire company. These were wheeled into place on trucks and secured out of sight backstage when not in use. A grand piano was housed at the side of the stage ready for Ricky Drew and his own act and later to accompany Derinda Daniels in her cocktail set of songs. The plate-spinning units and the black theatre puppet set would arrive with The Olanzos. Rails of costumes for the dancers arrived and were deposited in the large below-stage area for the wardrobe mistress to attend to. Blocks with wigs arrived; boxes of spangled tights and makeup were distributed to the various dressing rooms. The stage floor was swept and Jim, following the set plan, marked it out with the various coloured tapes to ensure that when the scenery flew in or a truck was wheeled on, it would hit the spot it was meant to.

At eleven o'clock sharp, the feet of Mona Buckle appeared in his sight line as he was applying white tape where the piano would eventually stand.

"Time for tea Mr Donnell," said Mona, in a commanding voice.

Jim looked up and smiled. "I won't have time this morning Mrs Buckle, I have a busy day ahead and I am behind now."

Mona looked at Jim with her steely look. "Mr Donnell, you will work better with a cup of tea inside you. Besides, I have bought some bourbons in special. I heard that you were partial to a bourbon." She made no attempt to move and continued to stare at Jim.

Jim thought for a moment, checked his watch and got up from his task. "Perhaps you are right Mrs Buckle, I haven't stopped since breakfast."

Mona smiled, which Jim found quite unnerving, as she led the way to the Green Room, much to the amusement of the other stagehands who watched. It was going to be an interesting summer season.

* * *

Rita and Ted Ricer arrived to a very warm welcome from Lucinda Haines and were very impressed with all the changes that had been made to the guest house since they had stayed there the previous year. Lucinda glowed with pride as Rita complimented her on the décor and, although she tried to hide it, she couldn't stop herself giving a girlish giggle whenever Ted was close by. Rita smiled to herself and could see that

Lucinda was as smitten with her husband as she had been all those months ago.

Settling themselves into their newly refurbished surroundings, Rita duly unpacked the suitcases and Ted poked and prodded his way around the room.

"Look here, new beds Reet and a new carpet. Are we in the same place? That dining area was something else. If I didn't know better I would say Lucinda has a sugar daddy tucked away somewhere."

Rita laughed. "The only man she has tucked away my old lover is you. She carries a torch for you which is so bright I'm surprised the lighthouse is still in use."

Ted blushed. "Yeah, I'd forgotten about that. I'm going to have to watch myself."

Just then the voice of Lucinda could be heard from outside on the landing.

"When you are ready, I have tea laid out for you in the lounge. It's your favourite Ted and some nice cherry cake for Rita."

Ted looked at Rita, who was doing her best not to laugh too loudly or Lucinda would hear her. "Sardines on toast Ted. Oh you really are in her clutches me old lover." And Ted blushed even more.

* * *

"How are things going?" asked Dave when he bumped into Jim later. "I saw more trucks there this morning."

"Everything has gone very smoothly thanks, and how are things at the Wellie?"

"Our sets arrived yesterday and Leslie Crowther is here already with Sheila Bernette, they were looking the stage area over. They both seem very nice." Dave studied his best friend's face. "Is everything okay Jim, you look like you have something on your mind?"

"I had to see the doctor this morning," said Jim, as his face drained of colour. "I didn't want to say anything to the others; you know how Maud gets upset."

"Jim, you are worrying me," said Dave. "What's wrong mate."

Jim motioned for them to sit down on a bench and Dave suddenly felt a cold chill run through his body. He had experienced it before, when Jim had found out about Karen's illness.

"I've been having some tests done at the Norfolk and Norwich" said Jim slowly. "That's why I haven't been around much; I got the results this morning."

Dave looked at Jim's ashen face, he gripped his best friend's arm and not another word passed between them.

* * *

Maud arrived home to find Enid preparing the evening meal. "I thought we were going to have fish and chips," she said, putting her bag down and taking off her coat.

"I fancied some liver and bacon, hope you don't mind," said Enid, switching on the kettle. "I closed the shop early today and went for a walk around town. It's been very quiet in there today."

Maud looked at her sister and wondered if she should broach the subject again. "Enid, I told you there's a unit going begging at the Wellington, the one Marie Jenner had, it's still standing empty. I think you would do good business."

"Maud dear, we have had this conversation before. If business was that great then Marie Jenner wouldn't haven't have given it up. Besides, I can't keep two units going, how would I staff it?"

"There are plenty of people who would be grateful for a' summer job. Barbara's daughter for instance is at a loose end, I could mention it to her."

"I'm not keen," said Enid, checking the frying pan.

"Two lots of stock, someone else's wages to find, and then there's the break problem. Marie Jenner rarely had a minute to spend a penny. It's a big commitment."

Maud knew when she was beaten and decided to let the matter rest and poured herself a cup of tea.

"That liver smells lovely, did you go to *Jary's?*"

Enid nodded. "I meant to tell you, on my way in this morning I saw old Jim coming out of the doctor's surgery, is he okay?"

"Funny thing, he was late this morning. Mona Buckle was in a right state when she couldn't find him. He never said anything, he looked fine. I know he has his blood pressure checked regularly, I expect it was that. He would say if anything was wrong, you know how close we are. Now, where is that dinner, I'm starving, being in that box office all day gives me an appetite."

* * *

Dave walked into *Henry's* bar, Stella was serving, and Dan was nowhere to be seen. "Hello Stella," said Dave, "pint please, where's the boy?"

Stella poured the pint of bitter. "Out the back sorting the barrels. Ken was meant to do it this morning, but you know Ken. You okay Dave, you look like you have something on your mind?"

Dave put on his best smile. "Been a hectic day at the Wellie, a few things to sort out, always something going on. You're quite busy in here tonight, bit early for a rush. I can remember when this place used to be empty."

"A coach party from Sheringham," said Stella, wiping the bar with a cloth. "I think they are booked to see the circus. They came in here as soon as the doors opened; it was a job to hold them back. Talk about all hands to the pump. They looked pretty busy over at the *Sands* this morning, no end of trucks outside. Bet Jim was pleased, he was saying the other day that the sets were late arriving."

"You know Jim, likes everything just so," said Dave, sipping his pint. "Oh look here's Dan. Got a minute mate, I've something I need to talk to you about?"

Stella smiled at them both and made her way to the back of the bar to find some boxes of crisps. The Sheringham party seemed to be working their way through every flavour they stocked.

"What's up mate?" said Dan, looking at Dave with concern. "What's happened?"

* * *

Rita and Ted took a walk along the seafront; the place was alive with gaily coloured lights and the sounds of the amusement arcades became background noise. Early holidaymakers were making their way to the circus which had opened in May and there were one or two people playing crazy golf. The ponies that had been giving rides to the eager toddlers during the day were being hitched up behind the Wells Fargo Wagon and the smaller cart rides as their owners were getting ready to walk them back through the town and over the bridge to their stables in Cobham.

They walked further along the promenade and passed the *South Pier* where the poster hoardings advertised the summer season show at the Golden Sands and Rita felt a sense of pride and achievement when she read that the show was being directed by Moira Clarence. And Ted squeezed her hand as he too acknowledged the announcement. Rita had decided not to use her own name but go with her stage name as she felt that people who had witnessed her return the season before would readily recognise it.

The chance to direct the summer season show had come as a big surprise and one she had embraced; she intended to prove to everyone that Moira Clarence was not a one-trick pony. Working with the company and seeing what they could do had given her food for thought. She was eager to begin the two-day rehearsal and couldn't wait for the full company to arrive. She was slightly concerned about the two male dancers, feeling that they seemed set on becoming the focal point of the dancing troupe and she knew that that wasn't what Jenny Benjamin would want. She would have to ensure that Jill and Doreen's routines, two of which she had seen, were in keeping with what she envisaged.

It was a comfort to know that her top of the bill came with no baggage and that she appeared to have taken well to working with Ricky. The Olanzos were a new entity and, though she had seen their act, she was concerned that Mario's lack of communication other than when singing, would cause problems. Petra's black theatre puppet act seemed quite delightful and would fill a five-minute gap in the show providing more variety to the bill. Then there was Maurice Beeney and his All Rounders, still the same faces and all getting a little bit long in the tooth. But their orchestrations could not be faulted and under the direction of Maurice she knew she was in safe hands. Of course, her own husband Ted would have the audience eating out of his hand. She had sourced new material for him and he had had a couple of new outfits made courtesy of his friend in Carnaby Street. Unlike the pre-season show she had been involved with before, she knew that the success of this show rested on her shoulders.

The walk took them to the entrance of the *Waterways* where the boats were moored and ready to transport holidaymakers around the narrow water themed gardens. Each boat had the head of an animal on its prow, a bull, a horse, a ram. The gardens, which had been well kept, were lit from illuminated boxes placed at intervals around the mossy banks and hidden from view. The small islands contained gnomes, fairies and pixies and there were larger, flat, cut-out hoardings of nursery rhyme characters lit by bulbs around them adding to the fairy tale feel. Rita and Ted walked hand in hand around the pathways, over the various wooden bridges connecting each part of the islands, enjoying the summer air and each lost in their own thoughts of the season ahead.

* * *

"Dave has been putting them back a bit," said Stella, as she dried some glasses. "You best get him home to bed Dan, I can finish off here. Call me if you need anything."

"Thanks Stella," said Dan, grabbing his jacket. "Come on Dave let's get you home, you need to sleep this lot off before the morning otherwise you are going to be in trouble."

Dave said something totally inaudible as Dan helped him to his feet. With a good deal of muster he got Dave through the saloon door and into the fresh air.

The smell of hotdogs and chips frying hit Dave's nostrils and he retched.

"Come on Dave, get your arse in gear we have to walk you round the block and I am not having you throwing up on me."

Stella locked the doors and switched off the lights. Ken was in the back office and she bid him goodnight and headed out on to Marine Parade. She had been watching Dave all evening and she knew that something was up, but whatever it was no one was saying. She just hoped that the two of them weren't thinking of parting. They had come a long way since they had met and Dave and Dan were now seen as a couple by those that knew them. She lit a cigarette, took a long drag, collected her thoughts and began her walk home.

Sunday 7*th* June

"Hello Dad," said Debbie, as she walked into the kitchen where her father was busy at the sink. "We're not too early are we? Peter is just getting the things out of the car. Karen is asleep in her carrycot."

Jim dried his hands and embraced his daughter. "Pleased you could come over, you know what it's like when the season gets going, I won't have much time to call my own."

Peter came in carrying Karen, who now seemed to have awoken from her slumber and was crying for her feed. "I'll just get her settled Dad and then we can have a good old natter," said Debbie, busying herself with her bag.

"Hi Peter, good to see you, hope the little lady isn't keeping you awake at nights."

Peter shook hands with Jim and handed over baby Karen to Debbie. "She's pretty good as a rule," said Peter, "and we take it in turns to get up to her if she does cry in the night."

"Debbie was no trouble when she was a baby," said Jim, looking lovingly at mother and baby. "It was when she got older that the trouble started." He laughed and Debbie threw her eyes to the ceiling in mock surprise.

When Karen was fed, Jim held her for a moment and he could see his late wife looking back him, the same eyes and the same peachy complexion. Karen fell asleep and the three settled down to a roast Sunday lunch and chatted about how Peter's job was going and how the show was shaping up at the *Sands*.

Maud called in later that afternoon for a cup of tea and to see how her god-daughter was faring. She reported back to Enid that the little family were doing very well indeed.

On the drive back to Norwich, Debbie kept twisting her handkerchief round her index finger. Peter noticed and commented, "What's up Debs, I know something is 'cause you're playing with your handkerchief the way you do."

"I don't know Pete," said Debbie, looking out of the window. "Dad was very quiet today. Not like him, didn't you notice anything different about him?"

"Can't say I did," he replied, avoiding a rabbit that had decided to hop across the Acle Straight. "He was probably tired. He has a lot on when that show goes up, you know how it is."

But Debbie wasn't so sure.

Monday 8*th* June

As Jim entered the auditorium he could hear the Sally Army tones of Mona Buckle singing *The Old Rugged Cross*. Her metal bucket clanked as she kicked it along the aisle, mopping as she did so. He walked by waving his hand and went out through the door at the back of the theatre. He was checking to see that the lights were working and the bulbs he had told his men to replace had been done. He headed out onto the pier and walked along in the warm sunshine. He reached the box office where he was pleased to see a queue had formed and looked up at the hoardings. He was joined by Rita and Ted who had just arrived to begin rehearsals.

"Looks good doesn't it?" said Rita, with a smile.

"It does indeed Rita, morning Ted," replied Jim with his usual cheery smile. "I expect you can't wait to get started. Is Don expected at all?"

"Not until the dress on Thursday," said Rita, adjusting her bag which had fallen off her shoulder. "I thought there should be a complete run through before we open at eight, so I've told the company I expect a full dress rehearsal at four, which will give them plenty of time to have a rest."

"The boys have all been briefed," said Jim, "they want to go through the lighting cues with you when you have a moment."

Rita looked at Jim in surprise. "Aren't you doing that? You usually do."

"I'm letting Roger get his hands dirty for once, I thought the experience would do him good," said Jim. "Can't stop, I have to go and see someone." And with that Jim waved his hand and headed across Marine Parade to Regent Road.

"He seemed in a bit of a hurry," said Ted, taking Rita's arm. "Looked like a man on a mission." Rita smiled at her husband and said nothing as they headed towards the theatre, but she had seen that look before.

* * *

Dinah and George Sergeant duly arrived on schedule and Lucinda Haines welcomed them. They had been staying with her for many years and made the trip down from Newcastle every year for the same two weeks of the season. Always in time to witness the opening of many of the shows on offer and to be one of the first to go and see them. They would regale anyone who would listen with their findings and in their own way were a source of free advertising. Lucinda showed them into the lounge and offered them both a cup of tea after their long drive. Dinah was impressed by the new décor and George agreed in his usual way by acknowledging everything his wife said. Lucinda sat down, as she always did for a few moments with her guests to make them feel welcome.

"I think you will be taken with the bedroom Mrs Sergeant," she said, offering a plate of biscuits. "I decided that it needed to have a change"

"It all looks very nice, doesn't it George?" said Dinah, sitting herself down on the new settee.

"Very nice indeed Dinah," said George, taking a sip of his tea.

"Did you have a pleasant journey?" asked Lucinda, keeping a watchful eye on the time."

"We stopped off at our usual café didn't we George?" said Dinah, helping herself to another biscuit. "Though I have to say Mrs Haines, they have put their prices up. I said to George, it's a rip-off, didn't I say that to you George?"

"You did Dinah," said George, agreeing and smiling at Lucinda.

"We had the chicken Mrs Haines and I'm not kidding you when I tell you it were chewy. They claim it was fresh from a local farm and it had been running round a field only a few days before. That chicken was tough weren't it George, and the only way that ever got round a field were on crutches."

Lucinda got up. "I just have to go and check something in the oven," she said. "When you are ready I will show you to your room. It's the same as always, at the front."

"You hear that George, we're at the front again, that's good ain't it, and we will be able to watch the world as it passes by. Now let's have a quick look at that *Mercury* and see what they've got on the piers this year. Don't really fancy that Peter Noone at the *ABC* and those New Seekers. It will be loud George, all that pop music, though I have to say I do like Ted Rogers, always makes me laugh."

Dinah paused for breath and then continued, "Oh look George, that Derinda Daniels is on at the *Sands* with that Ted Ricer, you like her. And oh look, Leslie Crowther is on at the Wellington with that Vince Hill. What's the bet he sings *Edelweiss*."

Dinah busied herself with the paper. "Have you seen the price they want at the *ABC Theatre*, it's a rip-off George, that's what it is, a rip-off."

* * *

Settling herself down in the middle of the fourth row centre, Rita looked at her running notes. She was keen to see what the young magician, Jonny Adams, had to offer and had called him in early so that he could set up his act on the stage. Jonny was a slim, good looking young man and, unlike some young men of his age, he showed no signs of acne, was clean-shaven and had a thick mop of blond hair that gave him the look of a young Alan Ladd. He was dressed in his stage outfit, a pair of black trousers, white shirt and red tuxedo. Maurice Beeney had agreed to come in and play the piano from the pit so that Rita could get a feel for the act proper.

Ted had made his way to the back of the auditorium in order that he too could see the act from the audience's point of view. He hoped that Jonny did not have doves in his act, recalling the antics of Mystic Brian's 'girls', as they had become known the previous year.

Jonny started off nervously, but as he got into his stride he produced satin handkerchiefs from empty tubes, made cards disappear, produced golf balls from his mouth and made his walking cane dance suspended in front of him. He moved with the grace of a ballet dancer, smiled throughout and ended his act by making his red tuxedo become a blaze of coloured sequins. Rita was pleasantly surprised and stood up and applauded him. "Well done Jonny," she called up to him, "I've seen more seasoned performers who haven't been as slick as you. You must have worked hard to achieve such perfection."

Jonny nodded.

"Well done my boy," said Ted, as he walked down the centre aisle to join his wife. "You could teach Mystic Brian a thing or two."

Jonny attempted to answer, but struggled to get his words out and stuttered badly.

Rita gripped Ted's hand and whispered, "Take him under your wing me old lover and introduce him to the others." She walked purposefully on to the stage and hugged Jonny. "You were brilliant son, I'm very proud to have you as part of my company."

And the young Jonny blushed happily.

* * *

The other acts began to arrive and were shown to their dressing rooms by Roger. Derinda was familiar with hers as she had been housed in it the year before. Next to her were The Olanzos. On the other side of the stage were Ted and Ricky Drew. Jonny Adams was in a smaller dressing room below the stage next to the larger one where The JB Dancers were. The male dancers had a dressing room to themselves on the opposite side. The Maurice Beeney Orchestra had a room at the rear of the floor next to the Green Room.

Derinda began laying out her makeup and brushes on the dressing table and could hear her neighbour Petra Olanzo instructing her husband Mario on where he was to put his costumes. Mario appeared not to reply but after a short time he burst into an aria at the top of his voice that filled Derinda's dressing room causing her to be unable to think what her next move was. She laid down a dress she had unpacked and walked across the stage to Ted's dressing room.

Ted was sorting out his gag sheets as she knocked on the door and entered. "Can you hear that?" she said, looking at Ted for some support. But with the dressing room door closed and the distance between Ted and The Olanzos' dressing room, all was quiet. "I won't be able to think if he carries on like that throughout the season."

Ted looked at Derinda and smiled. "I suppose we could get them moved to the floor below. Maybe they will settle down once we are under way. I had a trombone act next to me a couple of years ago, they were practising all the time, it was like being next to the elephant house. The funny thing was they were in tune when they were rehearsing, it was on the stage that it all fell apart. The audiences booed, some laughed and the local press had a field day."

Ted watched as Derinda's face relaxed in to a smile. Old Ted had done it again, poured oil on troubled waters.

Tuesday 9th June

Rehearsals were in full swing with the acts taking advantage of the stage whenever they could. Maurice and his boys were doing a sterling job and The JB Dancers were on cracking form. Jill and Doreen had worked hard on up-to-date routines and with the added mix of the two boys they really had improved from Jenny's day. A top hat and cane routine was particularly effective and the two boys could tap-dance for England.

Jenny had looked in to see how things were progressing and standing at the back of theatre she had watched how Jill and Doreen worked together to ensure they got the best out of the troupe. Rita caught up with her and the two sat and watched the finale routine, and Rita gently squeezed Jenny's hand as she detected a moment of sorrow.

When the set had ended Jenny turned and smiled at Rita. "They have done well. I was right to let Jill and Doreen take over. I was concerned about having boys in the act, but even I can see that they do add some variety."

Rita walked Jenny to the theatre exit and promised to reserve a seat next to hers for the opening night. As Jenny walked down the pier she turned and looked back at the theatre feeling that she was saying goodbye to her past.

Rita went back in to the auditorium just as Jonny Adams was about to begin his routine for a second time that day. He had lost the top hat and tails and was now dressed in a pair of black trousers and red jacket; he had also lost the greased hair and now sported a more modern style thanks to some handy work by Pete, one of the dancers. Rita walked down to the front of the stage and watched Jonny closely. There was no doubt in her mind that the boy was talented. It seemed such a shame that he was only doing a short act. When he had finished she motioned for him to join her. With her arm around his shoulders she walked him to the back of the theatre and asked him to sit down.

The stage was now alive to the sounds of Ricky Drew going through his medley of tunes that would have the audience clapping in time to the music.

"Jonny I am very impressed with your act. I was wondering if you had more tricks you could use. I would like to give you a bigger spot if you think you could manage it."

Jonny nodded as he struggled to get his words out, but he told Rita that he had several more tricks that he had rehearsed.

Rita stood up. "Leave it with me young man, I will have a word backstage and see if I can't wangle you another five minutes." She left a rather surprised but excited Jonny to work out what he was going to add to his act.

Rita walked through the pass door to the back of the stage and found Ted is his dressing room brushing down one of his jackets.

"Ted me old lover, a word please," said Rita, sitting on the arm of the chair.

Ted smiled at his wife. "Am I in trouble, what have I supposed to have done now?"

"Listen me old lover," said Rita, "there is something you can do for me."

"Anything," said Ted, relieved that she hadn't found out about his latest dalliance.

"I want you to give up five minutes from one of your two spots so that I can let Jonny do a longer act. The boy is brilliant and he is just what this show needs, young vibrant talent. Look what a difference having two men in the dance line-up has made. Variety is changing and we need to change with it. Jonny has a modern twist on the regular magicians we've worked with, he is lively, the audiences will love him."

"So what's in it for me if I agree to shave five minutes off one of my routines?"

Rita smiled. "I say nothing about that bloke with the horses you've been seeing since we arrived."

Ted admitted defeat, Rita had rumbled him again.

Wednesday 10th June

Roger Norris had worked at the *Golden Sands* since leaving school. Under the watchful eye of Jim he had learned a lot about the backstage working of summer season shows and had recently become the second in command. Like Jim, during the winter months when the theatre was dark, Roger did another job and helped out Stan, his brother, who ran a garage in Caister, as a general help and taxi driver. Stan had a fleet of five cars under the banner of *Stan's Cars — door-to-door service with a smile*. It helped Roger bring in a wage, but like Jim he looked forward to getting back to the *Sands*.

Jim had called him to the Green Room and told him he would need him to take charge of things as he was going away for a few days. Jim had said very little to Roger and when people asked where Jim was Roger was able to answer truthfully that he really didn't know. Even when Maud approached Bob Scott about Jim's absence, Bob said nothing but knew all the same. Enid advised her to leave well alone and not to telephone Debbie with her concerns in case she too had been sworn to secrecy or didn't know anything. Maud had spoken briefly with Dave when she saw him walking along Regent Road, but he too seemed to be unable or unwilling to let on anything he might know.

Rita too was concerned about Jim's sudden disappearance; she had always been able to rely on him for a chat and knew that if there was anything amiss on the theatre front Jim would be able to deal with it. Roger made it known that he was around and in charge of things while Jim was away. Though a nice enough person, Rita didn't have the same rapport with him. Opening Night was the following day and she wanted to ensure that everything went off as smoothly as possible.

* * *

Muriel and Freda were chatting outside their front doors and Freda was particularly keen to let her neighbour know how many bookings she had had. Muriel was impressed. Freda usually attracted passing trade whereas Muriel had a regular clientele that booked the same weeks every season. Though often at odds with each other, Muriel was pleased for Freda.

"And I am asking them to pay up front," said Freda, folding her arms as she held court. "I have learned my lesson, none of this staying the night and then running off without paying."

"And how do your guests feel about paying before staying?" asked Muriel, who would never dream of asking her guests to pay first. Besides, she knew she could trust them.

"They don't seem to mind, and if they did I would send them packing," Freda replied, with one of her huffs and puffs. "At least I can sleep easy in my bed at night knowing there will be something for my trouble. The couple that left this morning said they might come back next year. They particularly liked the decoration and I've you to thank for that Muriel." Muriel smiled and knew that it had taken Freda a lot to admit that. "Even my Dick has been helping out a bit more since you had that chat with him. I'm thinking of giving the house a name; I quite liked the idea of *The Boggis Boarding House* or *Freda's Family Guest House*." Just then Dick came rushing out of the front door. "And what are you in such a hurry about Dick Boggis?"

"That couple that left this morning, they've taken that lovely brass bedside table lamp Muriel gave you."

* * *

Dave looked down in to the bottom of his empty glass and sighed.

"You won't find the answer in there my friend," said Stella, replacing the beer mats. "You best get yourself off home; Dan told me he was doing your favourite tonight." Dave looked up at Stella and nodded. "Go on, off you go otherwise you'll be in trouble."

Dave left the pub and walked slowly along the road deep in thought.

Thursday 11th June

The day of the opening night had finally arrived. Last minute alterations were being made to costumes. Sets and lighting checks were carried out and the ever-important sound checks. Roger had things pretty much in hand when Rita arrived at the theatre that morning. Mona Buckle's bucket could be heard clanking along the corridor backstage to the refrains of *He Who Would Valiant Be* which was remarkably in tune.

Rita collected some letters from Jack at the back door and placed them in the relevant dressing rooms, obviously good luck cards from well-wishers, family and friends. There was a particularly large pile for Ted;, it never failed to amaze Rita that Ted's fan base seemed to grow as the years went by.

There were several large envelopes for Derinda, one bearing a French postmark with a very interesting stamp on it. Ricky seemed to have quite a few from Scotland, Maurice and the boys had some from various clubs which bore their logos on the tops of the envelopes, for Jonny several bearing local postmarks and The JB Dancers had one that was definitely the trademark pen of Jenny Benjamin. Strangely there was not one card for the Olanzos.

As Rita tore open her own mail, she was delighted to receive one from Don and Elsie Stevens. There were several from friends in the business, and a rather lovely one from Ted. Lucinda Haines had also sent one, though there was no stamp on hers so she must have had it delivered by hand.

* * *

A full dress rehearsal had been called for eleven to give everyone the opportunity of a rest before the opening performance at eight that evening. An after-show party had been laid on by Don and Elsie in the theatre bar. All manner of local dignitaries had been invited to the opening along with members of the local press and the obligatory complimentary tickets for local landladies and businesses. Rita was feeling slightly nervous but very much excited.

She was distracted from her thoughts by the voice of Mona Buckle who seemed to appear from nowhere.

"Miss Clarence, there is a lady waiting for you in the auditorium, front row centre. Came through the main door she did. I said to her, 'You aren't supposed to come in that way', but she just brushed by me, knocking me mop to the floor and me with my bad leg. She is wearing quite a big hat and if you ask me she is trouble. I could feel it, I sense things Miss Clarence, it's a gift, I could see that her aura wasn't in line. You mark my words. Says her name is Orderly. Funny sort of name if you ask me, might be foreign. I met someone foreign once, didn't bother me, we made ourselves understood, looking for the circus he was, nice chap. He did an act with knives!" Mona Buckle carried on about her business and she left a bemused Rita to make her way to the auditorium.

Audrey Audley was indeed wearing a rather large hat and what appeared to be a fox fur round her neck despite the weather being warmer than it had been. She stood up as Rita approached and held out her lace-gloved hand.

"Am I addressing Moira Clarence or Rita Ricer," she said, with a hint of sarcasm in her voice.

Rita shook her hand gently. "Please call me Rita, we have spoken on the telephone."

"I believe you have had the pleasure," said Audrey, sitting herself down again and rustling what appeared to be the entire stock of ladies separates from *Palmers*. "I was on my way to visit a new act of mine and thought I would call in."

"How every kind of you," replied Rita, making no attempt to sit but choosing to stand so that she could observe the lady. "How can I help you Miss Audley?"

Audrey played with the clasp of her rather oversized bag. "You mentioned to me on the telephone something about June Ashby. Well, I have reason to believe that she is the person who is stealing the thunder from Derinda on the London club circuit. Of course, I have no sound proof of that as yet, the clubs are keeping very quiet about their new booking, but your phone call got me thinking."

Rita was puzzled. "I think I got to know June Ashby reasonably well but I never had the impression that she ever wanted to play clubs. Besides, as far as I am aware, June has given up on the business completely. When I called you it was because of something that Derinda had told me about, believing her to have been in the audience. I am surprised that Derinda never mentioned it to you herself. I had wondered whether June had been in touch, maybe to secure work for her sister Lorna Bright. June and I were in regular contact and naturally, as a friend so to speak, I was concerned for her whereabouts. And I still am, I've heard nothing for ages."

"Mmmh," said Audrey. "It all sounds very peculiar to me. Derinda Daniels has been topping the bill at selected clubs in London for some years and now suddenly they are telling me they are booking some new found talent."

"I am not sure how I can help you, but I will say that I am as intrigued by all of this as you are."

Audrey eyed Rita carefully. "I think I can trust you Rita and I wondered if you would help me find out more. You have lots of contacts in the business."

"In case you had forgotten, I have a show to put on," said Rita. "It opens tonight and one of your artistes is headlining it."

"Yes, of course," said Audrey, standing up and brushing some imaginary fluff from the sleeve of her jacket. "But I can tell you are as interested in this as I am. Derinda Daniels is a well-respected star and has never been treated in this way before and I want to know why. I am sure that once this show is underway you will want to help me; after all we are sisters in the business, so to speak. Derinda has left me a complimentary at the box office so I shall be attending your opening night. I am expecting to see great things Rita, and you are spoken of very highly. Now, if you'll forgive me, I must get back to the office, Margaret will have letters for me to sign. Think over what I have said, maybe you can help me solve this mystery. I am looking forward to the show so much – *ciao* for now." And with no further comment, Audrey Audley walked purposefully towards the back of the auditorium as Rita did her best not to laugh.

"Who was that?" asked Ted, as he came down the steps from the stage.

"Audrey Audley," said Rita, "Derinda's agent and if you ask me the woman is on drugs – she's as crazy as a broken cuckoo clock, you know the cuckoo is in there but the door is jammed."

Mona walked down the aisle just as Audrey walked up it. "There is something strange about that one," she said, kicking her bucket along the floor. "The spirits never lie."

Ted nudged Rita. "Come on Reet, let's escape while we can. Here comes the other cuckoo in the nest!"

* * *

Maud was on edge, something that Barbara picked up on when she arrived for work that morning. Bookings had certainly been going well and people were trying to get tickets for the opening night, which had sold out days before. Barbara knew that Maud was worried about Jim and, with no one saying what was going on, she shared her friend's anguish. A few times, Barbara had had to take over a booking as Maud's mind was elsewhere.

Postal bookings were on the up, as news began to spread of the show at the *Sands*. It was usual to receive such bookings, but the postbag seemed to be bursting at the seams and Barbara approached Bob Scott about getting another pair of hands in to help cope with the demand. With Maud the way she was at the moment she could visualise double bookings, refunds and all manner of problems. Bob rallied round in the absence of Jim and found a couple of staff who worked as usherettes in the evening and were glad of the extra money. Barbara took command of them and showed them what needed to be done. Maud was remarkably quiet about the situation which only confirmed the worry she was experiencing.

* * *

Elsie Stevens had been working hard behind the scenes to ensure that every opportunity to advertise her husband's season at the *Sands* was exploited to the full. Interviews with some of the acts had appeared in the local press and there had been mention of the summer show on the media. Not one for giving interviews, Elsie had persuaded Don to appear on *Look East*, the regional television news programme. He spoke with passion about the forthcoming attraction and said that the show would appeal to all the family. Local boy Jonny Adams was mentioned with a clip showing his act. Derinda Daniels always attracted attention, but Don played on the fact that he was presenting three acts never seen at the resort before, Jonny Adams, The Olanzos and Petra's Puppets.

Jenny Benjamin had been interviewed a couple of days before and asked about what it was like handing over her dance school to two former pupils. Jenny, who kept her emotions in check, spoke positively about the changes that Doreen and Jill had made. She enthused about having two male dancers join the line-up and said how much she was looking forward to seeing them perform on opening night. As she stated, quoting words long drummed in to her by Don and Rita, times had changed and it was great to see that her troupe was changing with them. Off camera, she broke down in tears and had to be comforted by one of the television crew.

* * *

Derinda sat quietly in her dressing room before preparing herself for the final dress rehearsal. She had heard about Audrey visiting the theatre from Mona who had told her the news when she came in to dust. Derinda, who had become used to her agent's unusual ways, was not upset that she hadn't come to see her. She only ever saw Audrey when there were new terms to be discussed about a contract or if she just happened to turn up at a venue to see how a show was going.

Communication was usually by telephone, which seemed to suit them both. Derinda began laying out her make-up and was checking the costumes she would be wearing when Rita knocked on the door.

"Hello Derinda, are you all set? Did you want to run through anything before we start the dress? The stage is free now and Maurice and the boys are more than happy to go through any last minute changes you may have."

"Thanks Rita, but I think I'm okay. Ricky and I ran through my final set yesterday. He really is a gem; I'm pleased you suggested we work together."

Rita smiled. "Yes, Ricky is one of the best. He never seems to get fazed by anything. As long as you're happy with your orchestrations I'll tell Maurice and the boys to take a break."

"Any news on Jim?" asked Derinda. "Only some of the cast have been talking about him."

Rita's mind had been so preoccupied with the show that she hadn't given Jim too much thought and she chided herself. "If I hear anything I will let you all know. Maud is usually a good source of information around here, but even she seems to be in the dark. I haven't seen Dave Grant around either, come to think of it. Perhaps if I get a moment I'll go along to the Wellie, but it will have to wait until tomorrow as there's still so much to do before we open tonight."

Rita left Derinda's dressing room and made her way to see Ricky.

"Bingo, will you give that back please, naughty dog. I shall not give you that bone I got from that nice lady in the butcher's this morning."

"Everything all right in there?" asked Rita, knocking on Ricky's door and trying to open it. The door had been bolted from the inside.

"Everything is fine," Ricky shouted back, as Bingo growled happily. "I am in a state of undress at the moment Rita."

"Oh, I see," said Rita. "Just checking everything was ready for the dress."

"Everything is tip-top Rita," said Ricky, trying his best to retrieve the item that Bingo was holding firmly in his jaws. "See you out there."

Rita moved across to The Olanzos' dressing room and could hear what sounded like an actress from the Midlands soap opera *Crossroads* giving orders in the motel kitchen.

"Morning Petra, morning Mario, just checking that everything is okay. Anything you need?"

A broken English-Italian accent replied, "Hello Rita, me and Mario is fine, thank you."

Deciding to leave them to it, a friend of theirs had probably turned up to wish them well for the rehearsal, Rita called in on Ted who was studying the racing paper. "Hello me old lover," she said, pulling up a chair. "I've been rushing around like a blue arse fly this morning. Roger is no Jim. I've been going through sound checks, checking this and that and I swear if that Mona Buckle comes near me with another one of her mournful observations I may well have to smack her. I have never come across anyone like her before."

"What you need my darling is a nice cup of tea and one of Lucinda's homemade scones."

"Well there won't be any of those knocking about," said Rita, looking down at the running order for the show she was holding.

"Well my darling that is where you are wrong," said Ted, retrieving a brown paper bag. "Lucinda made these special. She said to me, you take these along with you today I expect Rita and you will need a little sustenance to get you through that rehearsal. I'll put the kettle on."

"What an old darling," said Rita with a smile, "she's proving to be quite a friend."

* * *

Over in Southtown Dave knocked on Jim's front door. "Hello me old mate are you ready?" Jim handed Dave the overnight bag and followed his friend to the car. Debbie stood in the doorway supported by Peter as baby Karen cried in the background awaiting her next feed. Dave started the engine and drove away and Debbie turned to her husband for comfort, preparing for the dark days she knew lay ahead.

Chapter Seven The Good, the Bad and the Ugly

R ita and Ted walked hand in hand along the seafront after what had been a very good dress rehearsal indeed. Everything had run smoothly backstage and the acts were more than well prepared.

"I really liked Derinda singing with Ricky at the piano. It made a change from listening to a singer competing with an overloud orchestra," said Ted, enjoying the stroll back to the guest house. "The lighting is very effective; I loved the lampposts, your idea no doubt love."

"Actually it was Jim's. When I mentioned the idea of Derinda and Ricky doing the final spot together and calling it *The Cocktail Hour*, he said he knew where he could get some lampposts and with the black backdrop studded with stars it gives the set a cosy night-time feeling. My original idea was to have Derinda sat at a bar while Ricky played, but Jim said it would look too American."

"Jim is good like that," said Ted. "Any news on his whereabouts?"

"Everyone is keeping remarkably quiet on the subject," said Rita, "even old Maud hasn't heard anything. I was thinking of going along to the Wellie tomorrow and having a chat with Dave."

"You might be best leaving well alone, I'm sure we will hear something soon. It may be a very private family matter and we mustn't go poking our noses in."

"I guess you're right me old lover," said Rita, trying to dismiss the thought from her head. "I hope Lucinda has the kettle on. You have left her some comps at the box office haven't you Ted?"

"Of course I have, three in all. I thought she might like to bring that Dinah and George with her for company, they seem a good sort from what I've seen of them."

"She makes me laugh," said Rita, remembering her first encounter with the couple. "They've been staying with Lucinda for several summers now, so I expect they have all become quite friendly. Though if you had used friendly and Lucinda in the same sentence when we stayed there last year I would have questioned it!"

"She's not a bad old stick when you get to know her," said Ted, "and she can't half put away the drink when she wants to."

Lucinda greeted them both with a smile and brought a tea tray to the lounge where Dinah and George were also sat. They had just returned from a day trip to Reedham and Dinah began relating their experience. "No bigger than a scone that pasty were it George. I have never seen a pasty so small and the measly bit of salad with it wouldn't have fed a sparrow. It were a rip-off."

When she had finished her tea Rita went to have a lie down for half an hour and was woken by Ted when the cab arrived to take her to the hairdressers. She wanted to look her best for the opening night. The salon in the town centre where the wigs were dressed was fully booked and Maud had recommended Doris Banbury in Gorleston where she and Enid went once a month. It was a bit old-fashioned but Rita was told that Doris was an expert when it came to styling ladies hair and she wouldn't be disappointed with the results.

* * *

Doris Banbury had been a ladies hair stylist all of her life, learning her trade from her mother, whose salon she now owned, but had renamed T*he House of Doris*. Her mother had retired to Spain many years earlier with a man she had met on holiday. Doris's father had run away to sea and was thought to be drowned. For the sake of decency, Doris's mother had refused to live 'over the brush' and had insisted that Frank and she move away from the area leaving Doris to get on with things. Doris, who had never seen eye to eye with her mother, had been glad to see the back of her. As for her father, he had upped and left when Doris was in her teens so she really had got quite used to not having him around. Her brother Benjy had married and now lived somewhere in Stockport. They exchanged Christmas cards and the odd letter, and an occasional visit brought Benjy and his wife Christine down to Great Yarmouth once every other year.

The flat above the salon, a converted terrace, was a small, two-bedroomed affair with barely room to swing a cat. The downstairs was mainly salon with an out-the-back area where Doris kept her solutions and equipment. In the early days Benjy and Christine would stay with Doris above the salon. But this soon proved to be a disaster waiting to happen with Christine falling down the stairs and ending up headfirst in a pile of towels that were sitting on the bottom step awaiting the attention of the twin-tub washing machine out the back. So Benjy and Christine were now guests at Muriel's guest house which they much preferred to the smell of perming solution and hair lacquer.

Among her regular clients were Maud Bennett, blue rinse wash and set, Muriel who preferred a perm as required for her busy season schedule, and the sisters from the wool shop who always came in together and chatted constantly about their couture yarns and silks. The salon was divided into four curtained cubicles; Doris could manage four clients all at once if she put in place her foolproof Doris method. Client one for wash and set, client two a perm, client three a colour and cut, client four a trim and finger wave. Doris ran the salon with the precision of an army general. She insisted that clients were on time as anyone who turned up late would throw out her schedule. There were always plenty of magazines to offer her clients to read while they sat beneath the large domed hairdryers. The salon was open Monday to Saturday with a half-day closing on a Wednesday when Doris could take herself off to the market place, buy some fruit and vegetables, have a bag of chips and savour a coffee and a custard slice in *Palmers* coffee shop and catch up on the latest gossip with her friends from the WI. Returning home she would turn on her wireless, put her feet up and settle down with a *Woman's Own*.

* * *

Rita arrived at the bay-fronted house and walked in to the small waiting area. There was no receptionist to report to, so she made herself comfortable and flicked through one of the magazines that were lying on a small table. Doris, who had heard Rita arrive, appeared from behind some floral curtains and introduced herself. Doris was a tall, thin lady with a gentle face and warm eyes, but her sharp nose did nothing for her other than draw people's attention to it. She was dressed in a long white coat, her grey hair was permed and she wore little makeup apart from some face powder and a hint of red lipstick. Her soft handshake and warm voice made Rita feel welcomed.

"Won't be five minutes," said Doris, "just combing out Mrs Smith and I will be right with you. It hasn't been so busy today; if you had wanted to come in yesterday I would have turned you away.

A few minutes later Mrs Smith emerged from behind one of the curtained areas with more curls than Shirley Temple could have coped with. She smiled at Rita as she left the salon and Doris showed Rita to the end cubicle nearest the window.

Rita refused the offer of a cup of tea and told Doris how she liked her hair. Doris nodded and smiled. "Don't worry Mrs Ricer, you leave it to Doris. You'll look a picture when I've finished with you. It's your opening night at the *Golden Sands*, Maud was telling me all about it, and you will want to look your best for that."

Rita was slightly worried about the picture that Doris had in mind! She came out of the cubicle an hour later in a cloud of hairspray and what felt like a stiff neck. She wasn't sure whether the stiff neck had been caused by sitting under the dryer or whether the amount of lacquer on her hair had caused her neck to malfunction. However, she was surprised with what Doris had done and had tipped her generously. The cab had returned to take her back to Great Yarmouth and she sat in the back barely able to move her head. Later that evening she would hear the words, "You've been Banburyed," and know what was meant.

* * *

Bingo had been a faithful companion to Ricky for seven years. His boundless energy and mischievous personality made him popular with all those who met him. But if Bingo took a dislike to someone or some other dogs who might growl at him, he trotted up to them and cocked his leg. Bingo was cunning, he didn't do this when his master or others were around, he chose his moment carefully and when his target was on their own. Ricky knew of Bingo's little games, but when challenged by an irate or upset owner he would deny that Bingo could have done any wrong. Bingo would sit on his little rug looking up adoringly at Ricky, causing him to smile and forget his frustration with his little friend. As had happened earlier that day.

Ricky was once again trying to get Bingo to give back his ill-gotten gains. But Bingo was feeling very playful that afternoon and when Mona opened the dressing room door, Bingo made his escape. Ricky had a towel on his head looking none too pleased.

"Sorry, I didn't think anyone was in here, just came to put these on your table," said Mona, laying down a bunch of flowers. "That Jack at the stage door asked me to bring them up."

"Thank you Mrs Buckle," said Ricky, trying to contain his annoyance. "Perhaps you would kindly knock next time."

Mona huffed. "As I said Mr Drew, I didn't realise you were in here otherwise I would have. I've had something of a busy day and now they have asked me to stay behind to help with the party after the show. My feet are fair singing they are."

Ricky managed a smile. "Perhaps you should go and make yourself a cup of tea."

Mona looked at her watch. "Not six yet, I never have a cup of tea before six, it upsets my aura. My Bertie will tell you that."

"Can I offer ye something stronger, a wee dram perhaps?" said Ricky, desperate to bring this conversation to an end so he could go and find Bingo.

"Never touch the stuff," said Mona, folding her arms. "It brings unhappiness, oh yes. My Uncle Ernie was a drinker, was he happy, he was not. He led my poor aunt a merry dance and no mistake. I could read your palm if you would like me to Mr Drew, I can see things in people's hands, and teacups."

"Perhaps another time Mrs Buckle. Now if you will excuse me I have to prepare myself for tonight's show."

Mona huffed again and left the dressing room. She wandered down to the Green Room where she saw Bingo and what appeared to be a rat in his mouth. Not squeamish about such things, she went towards the little dog muttering words of encouragement for him to drop the offending creature.

Bingo trotted towards her, cocked his leg and ran off as fast as his little legs would carry him leaving a very unhappy cleaner in his wake shaking her leg.

* * *

Dave walked in to *Henry's*. Stella nodded and motioned for Dan to go and serve him. "Everything okay?" asked Dan, pulling Dave his pint of *Legacy*. "You got there okay?"

Dave nodded. "Everything's okay. Peter and Debbie are at the house, all we can do is wait and see."

"Perhaps you should go over and see the opening of the show tonight, take your mind off things a bit," said Dan, giving Dave his change. "Besides, Jim will want to know how things went, it will be something for you to talk about."

"I'm not in the mood to see a show," said Dave, wishing he had a cigarette for company. "Anyway, it would be no fun going on my own."

"Perhaps Stella will let me take the night off."

"No, you're all right mate. Besides, it will get busy in here later now that the season is kicking off. There have been lots of people on the prom today."

Dan watched as Dave went over to the corner table near the window and wanted to go and hug him. Stella put her hand on his. "Try not to let it get to you Dan. Dave will come through this okay. Lots of things are sent to test relationships, it's par for the course."

Dan looked at his friend in the corner and for a few fleeting moments wasn't feeling so sure.

* * *

Just after six the stage door was opening and closing as members of the company began to arrive. Jack watched them with interest from behind his glass panel. For many years now he had seen the comings and goings of the famous and the not so famous. This lot were somewhere between the two. Derinda arrived wearing dark glasses and her hair hidden under a turban; she waved to Jack as she went by. Petra and Mario Olanzo came in with Petra muttering something in Italian to her husband who seemed to be taking no notice at all. He was a strange one, Jack had thought on meeting him. He had never heard the man utter one word; it was probably a language thing, but his wife more than made up for it. Jonny Adams came in and in his own way tried to say good evening to Jack who nodded and wished the boy well. Jack had a brother with a speech impediment and it made him warm to young Jonny instantly. A few of the orchestra strolled in looking in no particular hurry to be anywhere, unlike their conductor who, despite his years, always seemed to be in a rush about something or other. The two male dancers arrived loudly chatting excitedly to each other; they were really looking forward to their first summer season. The regular line-up of girls that had once been under the direction of Jenny came through the door smiling at Jack, one of them handing him the evening paper. Their heavy false eyelashes were already in place and Jack often wondered how they managed to see out of them. Rita and Ted were the last to arrive and they both had a chat with Jack before going to Ted's dressing room. Jack looked about him, it was the same theatre, and yet it didn't feel the same. There was no Lilly Brockett this year bustling about the place with her dusters, and the linchpin of it all was missing, there was no Jim.

* * *

The theatre doors opened at seven-thirty and the usherettes tore tickets, showed the audience to their seats and sold programmes. The local dignitaries arrived with ten minutes to spare and were ushered to their reserved seats. Maud and Enid arrived together followed by Muriel and

Freda, the latter wearing what Muriel termed as Freda's old faithful. What was it about this hideous creation that Freda loved so much? Muriel had yet to fathom. The aroma of mothballs once again hit the air and was fighting with the very overpowering smell of Freda's latest buy *Love Comes Calling*. This quickly hit the nostrils of one or two of her neighbouring audience members who began to sneeze. Lucinda came in with George and Dinah, with Dinah bemoaning the price of a programme and letting the whole row know it was a rip-off. Rita, in a sparkling gown and white fur stole, took her seat and fumbled nervously with the programme. The audience were abuzz with chatter, boxes of chocolates were opened and passed along rows and some of the dignitaries played with their jewellery, bow ties and handbags.

Don and Elsie Stevens stopped by the office to have a word with Bob Scott before proceeding in to the auditorium. Both were pleasantly surprised by how full the theatre was.

"Hardly an empty seat to be had," said Elsie, adjusting her wrap. "I am so pleased for Rita, she must be terribly proud. You were right to let her run with this Don, I always knew she was something more than a singer."

"I think we will have to wait until the end of the show before we commit ourselves to that statement Elsie. It's great to see one of my shows so well attended. According to old Scott the bookings are very healthy for the rest of the season, even the first houses are selling fast."

Elsie took her husband's arm. "I think we had best get ourselves to our seats, we don't want to be going into a row once the lights go down. You know how I hate people disturbing me once I've settled."

Don glanced behind him. "Come on, let's get to our seats quickly, I think that might well be Audrey Audley buying a programme and I don't want to get into conversation with her before curtain-up."

Audrey Audley, who was somewhat toned down dress-wise from her earlier appearance at the theatre, busied herself with her purse and handed the coins to the rather attractive young man offering programmes for sale. She gave him one of her customary smiles and winks and hoped she might bump in to him later at the party. Walking slowly down the aisle she located her row, apologised to the people she had disturbed, sat down and opened the programme.

"SUMMERTIME SUNSHINE"

"We Wanna Say Hello" – The JB Showtime Dancers introduce Ted Ricer, Ricky Drew, Jonny Adams and The Olanzos.

The Star of the Show – DERINDA DANIELS
"With a Song in My Heart"

The East Coast's Favourite Comedian – TED RICER

Magic Fingers – welcome East Anglia's very own Jonny Adams

Melodies for You – RICKY DREW

Broadway Melody – Derinda Daniels and the JB Showtime Dancers

Interval

Discs a Go Go – The JB Showtime Dancers introduce

The Fabulous OLANZOS *"Singing While Spinning"*

TED RICER

Pulling Strings – Petra's Puppets

The Cocktail Hour – The JB Showtime Dancers introduce
DERINDA DANIELS with Ricky Drew at the Piano Forte

Fin! Finito! Finale! The Company say "Goodnight"

* * *

A small figure entered the back of the auditorium neatly dressed and sporting a new hairstyle. She was escorted by one of the usherettes and shown to a vacant seat beside Rita.

"Oh Lilly, how lovely to see you, I'm so pleased you could make it."

Lilly beamed. "Wouldn't have missed it for the world, hasn't Jim arrived yet?"

Rita looked at the two empty seats on the other side of her and patted Lilly's hand. "He has a lot on just now," she said, "perhaps he will make it to the party afterwards."

"I do hope so," said Lilly, "it's been ages since I last saw him."

Hurrying down the aisle was Jenny Benjamin. Sitting down beside Rita she apologised for her lateness, said a quick hello to Lilly and then settled herself and looked expectantly at the stage.

The lights began to dim and Maurice, who had taken his place in the orchestra pit, turned to face the audience as a spotlight hit him. He raised his baton and the orchestra struck up the overture.

* * *

At the interval, Audrey made her way to the bar where she had a large gin and tonic waiting for her. She turned to Don and Elsie who were nearby.

"Quite a good show you have here."

Don smiled and introduced Elsie to Audrey; Elsie looked at Audrey carefully and immediately took a dislike to the woman. Bloody agents, she thought to herself, nothing but trouble. Agents had certainly given Elsie the run-around over the years when, during its infancy, she had worked at the office on a regular basis.

Audrey was none too struck on Elsie either. What a dowdy-looking woman, she thought to herself, no wonder

Don had an affair with that secretary of his, now lying in some grave somewhere.

"We have Rita to thank for this," said Don. "I gave her full command of this ship and if the first half is anything to go by I think we are in for a treat with the second half."

"And where is the delectable Rita?" said Audrey, looking around her. "I would have expected her to be mingling with the good and great." Audrey then caught sight of Muriel and Freda and added, "And the not so great."

"I expect she is rallying the troops backstage," Elsie interjected. "Rita is too much of a professional to be seen at the bar during the interval. Now, if you'll excuse me, I want to go and have a word with Jenny."

"What's got up her nose?" asked Audrey, knocking back her gin and pondering whether to have another.

Don was too much a gentleman to tell her.

* * *

Rita knocked on Derinda's door and went in. "It's all going very well, that opening number worked really well." She paused for a moment noting the look on Derinda's face. "Are you okay Derinda? I thought you looked a little strained at rehearsal."

"I'm a bit anxious about playing the cabaret stints I'm contracted to do. It wasn't until we did the full dress today that I realised how much it might impact on my voice." She looked about her, collecting her thoughts. "Doing three shows a night is a lot, even for a seasoned professional. The problem is I go on quite late at these venues. The band will collect me every night from here and take me to whatever club I'm booked to appear at. I've cancelled my appearance tonight in Norwich as I wanted to be here for the party with the others. Audrey won't be too pleased when she hears about it but I've got a sub I know to fill in for me. I'll have to pay her of course."

"I see," said Rita. "In that case I'm surprised you agreed to do this show. Don hadn't filled me in on all the details, just that he was mighty pleased to have booked you. There's no doubt in my mind who the public pay to see."

"Normally I would be playing a season in London and getting paid a lot more than the clubs around here can afford. I took this on for no other reason than the extra cash it would bring in."

"Look, if you need anything or you want me to change something for you, do feel that you're able to come to me. I'm sure we can work something out."

Roger's voice came over the tannoy system, "This is your five-minute call ladies and gentlemen, five minutes."

"I'll leave you to it," said Rita, "see you afterwards, and remember what I said."

* * *

When the curtain came down the audience showed their appreciation with clapping and wolf-whistling, the likes of which had never been heard at an opening night for a summer season. Reporters had been busy writing their pieces that would be read over the breakfast table the following morning. Congratulations were made, glasses raised in toasts and a generally good time was had by all. Ted hugged his wife and whispered something in her ear and she smiled. He excused himself and went to the gents. Splashing some cold water on his face he looked at himself in the mirror, steadying himself on the washbasin.

Audrey was making herself known to anyone who would give her the time of day and the landladies made free with the nibbles and drink. Derinda, who was in conversation with Ricky, felt a tap on her shoulder. She turned and her smile froze.

"What are you doing here?"

"That is no way to speak to your friend. We need to talk."

"Is everything okay hen?" asked Ricky. The man had arrogance about him that Ricky had seen before, especially in the husbands who came baying for his own blood when they found out he had been having it away with their wives.

"It's all fine," said Derinda, doing her best to sound reassuring.

But Ricky wasn't assured and he followed the pair as they left the bar, keeping just far enough behind so as not to be noticed.

Chapter Eight   *Come to the Cabaret*

Friday 12ᵗʰ June

Lucinda Haines was practically beside herself with excitement and was waiting for Ted and Rita to come down to breakfast. Dinah and George had just finished their own when the pair walked in to the dining room.

"I said to you didn't I George that was the best show we had seen in ages." George nodded, about to make his own contribution but his wife continued, "You couldn't have seen a better show if you had been in one of those fancy theatres up London, didn't I say that George. The people sitting beside me were falling about laughing at your jokes Mr Ricer and those dancers were great. It's the first time I've seen two men kicking their legs in the air, you never see that Lionel Blair do that on the telly. What a clever little chap that Jonny person is, all those tricks, and as for them Olanzos, singing like Mario Lanza and spinning plates, now that takes some doing. That bloke on the joanna, he could bang them out, George liked that bit, didn't you George?"

"And Derinda Daniels?" said Rita, daring to interrupt Dinah's flow.

"Oh she were good, reminded me of Kathy Kay off the *Billy Cotton Band Show*, I could listen to her all day."

Lucinda came in carrying two plates of breakfast. "Congratulations, congratulations," she said, her face flushed with excitement. "you wait till you read what the papers made of it all. I'm so happy for you both."

And coming from Lucinda that was more than Ted or Rita could have hoped for.

* * *

Muriel was at Mrs Jary's grocery shop when Freda came in.

"You missed a treat last night Mrs Jary," Muriel was telling her, as she cut some ham. "Morning Freda, I was just telling Mrs Jary what a good night we had."

"I heard you," said Freda quietly; her head was banging from drinking too much free sherry. "When you're ready Mrs Jary I'll have some bacon and a couple of tins of baked beans."

"Saw your Dick this morning, unusual to see him up at the crack of dawn," said Muriel, selecting a couple of packets of biscuits from the shelf. "Has he started working again?"

Freda, who wasn't really in the mood for chatting, answered her friend as politely as she could, "I took your advice Muriel. I told him, either he found himself some regular work or he could help around the house. I wasn't feeling too clever this morning so he had to cook the breakfasts"

Muriel nearly dropped the packets of biscuits in surprise and Mrs Jary smiled to herself as she began to slice the bacon.

"Come to think of it my Barry said he thought he saw smoke coming out of your kitchen window."

Even Freda couldn't hide a chuckle as she recalled the scene. "Honestly, men! My Dick is useless when it comes to anything domestic, silly beggar turned the toaster up full and wondered why he was surrounded by black smoke. What my visitors must have thought I don't know. Anyway, by the time I got downstairs he had managed to serve everyone. He'll learn, I'm not standing for any more of his nonsense."

Muriel looked at her neighbour with renewed respect and then thought of Dick Boggis and hoped the change in him would last and that Freda wouldn't find her purse light as a consequence.

* * *

Maud couldn't help herself. She telephoned Barbara and asked her to cover the box office for her and despite protests from Enid she put on her jacket and headed out to Southtown. She rang the doorbell and was taken by surprise when Debbie opened the door.

"Hello old love, I was after your dad, haven't seen him at the *Sands* for the last few days."

Debbie half-smiled at her visitor. "You best come in Auntie Maud, I'll make some tea."

Maud left Jim's house an hour later feeling quite shaken. She walked over Haven Bridge and cut through the passageway that led her to the back of *Palmer's* car park. She leant against a wall out of sight of customer's parking their cars and began to cry. After a few minutes she wiped her eyes and, using her compact mirror, she checked her face and put some powder on her nose. Taking some sunglasses from her bag she held her head high and walked with purpose across the market place and down Regent Road.

Barbara was busy at the box office window, but noticed Maud going by on to the pier. Presenting herself at Bob Scott's office Maud banged on the door and, without waiting to be invited, entered. Bob looked up from behind his desk.

"Maud, what can I do for you?"

Maud sank into a nearby chair. "Why didn't you tell me about Jim, why did you keep it from me?"

Bob laid down his pen and looked at Maud who was clearly distraught. "I'm sorry Maud but I had to follow his wishes. You know Jim, he wouldn't want a fuss."

"But I'm family too. I've been beside him through everything, when Karen died, when Debbie had the baby.

Maud has always been there, they are like my own, and someone should have told me." Maud began to sob loudly, wringing her hands.

Bob came out from behind his desk and handed her a hanky. "He might come through this Maud; we just have to wait and see." He picked up the telephone receiver. "Beverley, can you bring in some tea and biscuits for two please, and hold all calls for the time being, thank you."

* * *

Rita had arrived at the theatre much earlier than she had needed to but, as she had said to Ted, she needed to make sure everything was in order. And without the reliability of Jim she had to be on top of things. Though Roger was a very pleasant chap, she didn't find his work to be on a par with Jim's.

It was about five when she wandered down to have a chat with Jack. "Jack me old lover, have Petra and Mario had any visitors backstage today?"

Jack shook his head. "I never allow anyone through the stage door unless they are part of the company, those are the rules. Any visitors are usually asked to wait at the front of the theatre. Why, is there a problem?"

Rita looked puzzled. "I went by the Olanzos' dressing room earlier and just like last night I heard a woman talking Brummie. I was going to knock but Roger called out to me, he wanted to run something by me. I never saw anyone with them at the party last night. It may be nothing, perhaps they had the radio on."

"I'll let you know if I see anyone Rita," said Jack. "Wouldn't have happened if Jim were here, he was in the place day and night, whereas Roger, he comes and goes as he pleases."

Rita couldn't have agreed more. She thanked Jack and went to check with wardrobe that Derinda's costumes had been prepared as per her instructions. One of the hems had come undone and she didn't want any accidents.

* * *

The stage door once again became a hive of activity. The topic of conversation was the write-up in the papers and everyone seemed to be looking forward to repeating the success for the next audience, only this time twice. Jack had seen and heard it all before, give it a few weeks and they would all be so tired they wouldn't know which performance they were on. And as for that Derinda Daniels appearing in clubs after the final curtain came down, she would be a shadow of her former self and no mistake. To Jack's mind she needed a decent meal inside her or she would waste away.

Thursday 18th June

Ted sauntered along the corridor and knocked on Ricky's dressing room door. "Have you got a minute Ricky?"

There appeared to be some activity on the other side of the door which included a lot of banging, dog barking and the frantic voice of Ricky calling for something to be returned.

"Are you okay in there?" shouted Ted through the door.

The harassed voice of Ricky called out, "Give me a minute Ted and you can come in. Bingo is playing up." After a few minutes Ricky opened the door and smiled at Ted. "Sorry about that Ted, do come in."

Ted entered the dressing room where a panting Bingo, sat on his rug, looked up and barked a friendly greeting. "Have a seat, Ted, Bingo has been misbehaving. He does that when he gets fed up. These twice-nightly affairs don't allow me to exercise him between shows. I don't like going out on the pier with stage makeup on."

Ted sat himself down. "You could ask one of the lads backstage if they could exercise him for you."

"I thought of that but they are so busy taking down the finale set and setting up the opening. I may ask Jack at the stage door, it would be a once round the theatre. Bingo likes to cock his leg and have a good sniff. He gets a big crazy when he's shut up in the dressing room for long periods."

"I'll have a word with my Rita, when things settle down a bit I'm sure she would oblige."

"Thanks Ted, I appreciate that. Now what was it you wanted to see me about?"

"I've been trying out some new material and that joke about the grocer doesn't seem to be hitting the laughter button with the first house audiences and we've been at it a week now. I'm thinking of taking it out altogether."

"I've heard the joke Ted and it makes me giggle. Take my advice and leave it in, it always goes better second hoose," said Ricky, offering Ted a small Scotch. "You can't always judge the first house; they have either had nothing to eat before they come in here or have stuffed themselves with chips. The second audience are always more receptive. I have the same problem with my singalong medley. The first house audience hardly utter a note, whereas the second lot are out to have a good time. You listen tomorrow night and you you'll see what I mean."

"You seem to be getting along well with Derinda, that spot you do with her at the end of the show is really great. Rita was a bit concerned when she was asked to direct this show, having never done it before."

"Well, you would never know it," said Ricky, taking a sip of his Scotch. "She had everything mapped out beautifully and I have to say it's the first time in many a year that I've been part of such a smooth operation Ted. Whatever knowledge your lady wife has she certainly knows how to get the best out of people."

Ted welcomed the comment. "That's nice of you to say Ricky. She's a great gal is my Reet. She really could have been something if I hadn't come along."

Roger's voice over the tannoy interrupted their conversation. "This is your five-minute call, overture and beginners please to the stage."

"Best get back to my dressing room, thanks for the chat Ricky; perhaps we can go for a drink one night after the show?"

"Would be a pleasure Ted," replied Ricky, taking the empty glass from Ted, and Bingo woofed in agreement.

* * *

Rita was enjoying a few moments of peace on the pier, before going back inside for the start of the second show. Her thoughts were interrupted by the sound of a man and a woman speaking in very Brummie accents.

"I tell you Si, I would know Pam anywhere. What was that boyfriend of hers called, he was a friend of John? Come on Si, you must remember."

Rita continued to listen with interest.

"Denham," said the woman, "Mike Denham. He and Pam got married on the QT, broke her mother's heart that did. They lived in Solihull. Pam used to knock about with the girls from *Spenser's Garments*, and then they vanished off the face of the earth. Pam Smith. Who would have thought it, up there on a stage spinning plates and Mike singing in Italian. I bet it was her doing the puppets as well."

"Says here Doreen," said Simon, looking at the programme, "their names are Petra and Mario Olanzo. They were a brilliant act, you have to give them that."

Doreen nodded. "It will be their stage name. I've a good mind to go round that stage door and ask for their autograph. Imagine the look on her face if she saw me standing there. I can't get over it, Pam and Mike Denham; you wait till I tell Rose when we get back to Brum."

"We haven't time for you to go autograph hunting," said Simon, rolling up the programme and putting it in his jacket pocket. "We were off to get some fish and chips. Besides, people are going in for the second show and I doubt Pam would be able to come to the stage door."

Doreen conceded defeat, linked her husband's arm and they sauntered off down the pier. Rita smiled to herself and went back in to the theatre, this was one nugget of information she would do best to keep to herself.

* * *

Derinda stood in the wings ready to make her entrance; she was feeling very tired and the first show had taken it out of her. She had been late finishing at the *Trawlers Rest* in Lowestoft the night before and then the van had broken down. She and the band had not got home until the early hours. Performing three shows a night was taking away the pleasure of singing, but she knew in order to keep her husband quiet she had to make the extra money.

Ricky had been keeping a watchful eye on her. He hadn't told her that he had overheard the conversation on opening night and was still trying to work out who exactly the Frenchman was. He was debating whether or not to have a quiet word with Rita, she seemed trustworthy enough if all he had heard about her was true, and maybe she could help. One thing was certain in Ricky's mind, whoever that man was he was trouble and he was upsetting Derinda.

Wednesday 1ˢᵗ July

Palmers' coffee shop was heaving, it was market day in the town and Rita wasn't sure she would ever find a table.

"Over here Rita," said the booming voice of Audrey Audley. "I was rather early." She motioned for Rita to sit down. "I'll get another pot, coffee okay for you?" Rita nodded. "And I bet you could go a cream horn, or are you an Eccles kind of girl?"

Rita settled for an Eccles and asked Audrey why she had been summoned to this meeting. "Like I said the other day, we are sisters as such and sisters have to stick together in this business. I've heard some news concerning this so-called new star for the London club circuit. Apparently she opens next week. I know it's a she because when I spoke to Kenny at the *Brunswick* he let it slip. Still won't reveal exactly who it is or who represents her and that's where you come in."

"Audrey, I have a summer show to oversee, I haven't got time to go poking my nose in places it ought not to be. Why me anyway? We hardly know each other and if our last encounters are anything to go by we hardly like each other very much."

Audrey bristled. "We just got off to a bad start darling, that's all. Let's put that behind us, join forces and do it for the sisterhood."

"Have you been drinking," asked Rita, having a stab at her Eccles which seemed determined not to be broken in to, thanks to the sugary crust.

"We could go for a snifter in that nice little pub down the road, *The Growler*. They have a quiet back bar, we could chat more freely."

"I know *The Growler* very well; the company used to go there last year." But though tempting, Rita shook her head.

"Sorry Audrey but I do have other things to do, so cut to the quick and tell me exactly what it is you want me to do."

"I knew you would help me. I'm quite well known around the club scene in the Smoke so I really need someone who wouldn't draw attention to themselves."

Remembering the outfit she had seen Audrey in that day at the theatre Rita understood where she was coming from. "It would be no good me going in any of the clubs. In case you'd forgotten, my face was plastered all over London last year, not to mention the telly. Anyway, exactly what is it we are supposed to be looking for?"

"I need to know who this new artiste is and who is behind her appearing in all of the top clubs, and why Derinda has been dropped like a sack of potatoes. The club circuit contract was worth a lot of dosh, more than Derinda can make in summer shows and clubs in Norfolk, it kept her solvent. Besides, I've seen my percentage drop and I'm not in this business for the fun of it."

"That much is obvious," said Rita, eyeing the expensive two-piece suit her nemesis was wearing.

Audrey chose to ignore the remark and continued, "I was thinking you could persuade that wife of Don Stevens to sniff out the information."

Rita laughed. "Elsie! You have to be joking, Elsie wouldn't be seen in a club unless she was on the arm of her husband. And besides, I know she would say no to the idea. However, I do have a contact of my own that might be willing to undertake a little job for me, but it would cost you."

"We can talk money later," said Audrey.

"No Audrey, we will talk money now," said Rita standing up. "Come on then, a quick snifter in *The Growler*, there may not be so many listening ears."

* * *

"I wonder what that was all about?" said Freda, pushing the sugar container to Muriel who was trying to retrieve her purse from an over-laden bag of shopping. "Now if Lilly was still working down at the *Sands* she would know. One thing is certain; you wouldn't get anything out of that Mona Buckle, according to what I've heard it would upset her Ariel."

Muriel raised her eyebrows. It was like having Lilly right there, Freda was getting just as bad at mixing her words up. "You mean it would upset her Aurora. Now for goodness sake Freda, do something with that cake, you've been staring at it for ages. And don't tell me you're on a diet because if you are it certainly isn't working."

* * *

"I'm pleased to tell you your father's condition has improved. All being well you will be able to take him home tomorrow but, as I have already told him, he has to take things easy. He cannot return to work for the moment and when, if he does, it will have to be light duties. He will not be able to lift things and dash about the way he has done before. The situation could change at any time and he mustn't take any risks." Debbie listened and nodded. The doctor continued. "I will ask the Sister to prepare his medication and discharge papers for tomorrow. You will have to see that he takes his tablets regularly and if there are any problems you are to call an ambulance immediately." Noting her worried look, he continued more gently, "He will feel better being in his own home. Perhaps after a few days someone could drive him down to the theatre and let him walk along the pier, the exercise will do him good, as long as he takes things steady."

Debbie smiled gratefully at the doctor. This was better news than she could have hoped for and she knew that Auntie Maud, Dave and the gang would rally round to help her. What her father needed was looking after, something he had been without since her mother had died. She couldn't wait to call Peter and tell him the news. Things were looking up.

* * *

The following day Jim found himself sitting in his own armchair with a newspaper on his lap, feeling tired but grateful to be home. Peter had made up a single bed for him in the lounge so that he didn't have the trouble of the stairs until he was feeling better. Baby Karen had gone to stay with her grandparents to allow Jim the peace and quiet he needed for his recovery.

Dave was the first person to visit, followed by Maud who arrived with a fruit basket that Enid had helped her prepare. There were cards from well-wishers, including one signed by all the cast and crew at the *Sands*, with a lovely message from Rita and Ted that made Jim smile.

For the first few days, Jim dozed at irregular intervals and took his medicine when told to. He had lost his appetite and ate only a few mouthfuls of the food that his daughter lovingly prepared for him. After a week of rest, Jim felt ready to face the world and so, with Dave driving him and Debbie beside him in the back of the car, Jim went to see his friends at the *Sands*. But not before he visited the cemetery to lay flowers on Karen's grave and to tell her he was okay.

Walking gingerly along the pier he was greeted by Roger and the backstage boys and a very happy Maud, pleased to see her old friend up and about again. Over a cup of tea, Bob Scott chatted about Jim's possible return to work and explained that he would let Jim help Jack at the stage door. Jim wasn't happy to hear the news, but put on a brave face and accepted it with the good grace in which it had been offered. However, that was a few weeks away yet and he needed to get back in to some kind of shape first. He bumped into Mona just as he was leaving and thought he detected some kind of smile.

"It is very nice to see you again Mr Donnell," she said. "I have been thinking of you and the spirits told me you would come back again, they never lie you know."

Jim felt humbled and knew that he was much loved and cared about.

"Come on dad, let's get you back home," said Karen, walking towards him. "Dave is going to drive us along the seafront and back over the river., I've got some liver for dinner. The doctor said you needed plenty of iron to build you up again."

Sitting in the car, Jim looked at the photograph of Karen he kept in his wallet and smiled.

Friday 10*th* July

Having had no luck with her contact, Rita decided to take the bull by the horns and go to London herself. She had booked an early train from Vauxhall station and was checking in to her hotel by lunchtime. Don and Elsie met her in the bar and over a pot of coffee and sandwiches she explained further about the mission she had undertaken for Audrey Audley. Don was surprised, but Elsie remembered how Rita had worked in the past and said that she would willingly accompany her to every club in town if it helped. Elsie was not known for staying out late at night and Don was beginning to see a new side to his wife. Elsie produced the *Evening News* from the night before and in it was a listing of who was appearing where, but strangely where an artiste's name should have been under a club heading it said only *See the New French Singing Sensation on stage tonight at Midnight*. It seemed that the engagement was for a full week.

The club opened its door at 10:00 and the cabaret was on at midnight and again at 1:30. Elsie would meet Rita in the hotel bar at 9:00 and after a couple of drinks they would take a cab to the *Mayfair Club*. Elsie was quite excited about the whole thing and talked about it all the way home in the car to Don, who was thinking that maybe he should be at this club to keep an eye on things. But as he was a well-known face he thought better of it. Rita, on the other hand, had her own way of dealing with such matters.

* * *

Petra and Mario arrived at the theatre in their usual manner, Petra talking at Mario and Mario saying nothing. Jack motioned to her. "This came for you today," he said, handing Petra the envelope.

When they were in their dressing room, Petra looked at the envelope which was addressed to The Olanzos care of *The Golden Sands Theatre*. She pulled out the pretty card, read the note inside and then sank into the nearest chair. "Bloody hell!" she exclaimed. "It's from that bitch I went to school with, Doreen Warner. Says here she and her husband Simon came to see the show and how much they both enjoyed it. *Rose sends her best wishes and may come down to see the show for herself. Tell Mike he has a great singing voice, Love Doreen.* Oh shit, that's all we need Mike. I could have sworn we would be safe here, who would have thought the likes of Doreen would holiday in Great Yarmouth, her family was more the Skegness type. I've done everything I can to get away from my roots, changed my hair, my accent. She must have good eyesight to have spotted who I was. I mean to say, I'm running round that bloody stage like a mad thing spinning those plates. I hardly stand still long enough for anyone to clock me. Perhaps after the dogs we should have done a clown act, no bugger on earth could detect who was under that makeup."

Mario smiled at his wife and as usual said nothing. Petra flung the card across the room and sighed heavily.

* * *

Dave walked into *Henry's* and ordered a pint of *Lacons Encore.*

"Hello Dave," said Stella, with a smile. "I was so pleased to hear the news from Dan about Jim; it's good that he's back at home. I bet his daughter is mighty relieved."

"We all are," said Dave. "It was touch and go there for a while. The operation seems to have been a success and providing he follows doctor's orders there's every chance that he will return to work at some point. Though there is some doubt about him going back to the club."

Dan, who had just finished serving, added, "And doubt about whether you will either."

Dave frowned at Dan but he just laughed. "It's okay Dave; I let Stella in on our news."

"No disrespect Stella," said Dave, taking a sip from his pint, "but we don't want anything getting out. I haven't even mentioned it to Jim yet."

"Don't worry Dave, "said Stella, handing him his change, "I won't breathe a word to anyone. Besides, from what Dan has told me, it's only an idea, nothing concrete."

"I have to be certain in my own mind that it's the right thing to do and, besides, I don't want to leave Jim. I need to know that my old mate is really going to be okay first."

And neither Dan nor Stella would challenge him on that point.

* * *

"Where is the lovely Rita this evening?" asked Ricky, as he walked in to Ted's dressing room with Bingo trotting behind.

Ted looked up from his evening paper. "Oh, she's gone on some talent hunt in London for a few days. I think Don has asked her to look at some acts for him."

"Mind if I help myself to one of your apples?" asked Ricky, eyeing the bowl of fruit.

"Please do me old mate, some punter sent them backstage after seeing the show the other night. It's very nice of them, but I wish they would send something to drink instead."

Ricky laughed and bit into an apple.

* * *

"This is your thirty-minute call. Thirty minutes ladies and gentleman."

Derinda hurried in through the stage door carrying a dress on a hanger. "Good evening Jack. Running a bit late, I hope I make it to the opening number, otherwise Rita will have my guts for garters."

"No need to worry about Rita, she's in London for a few days visiting the clubs. From what Ted told me she's on the lookout for some new talent."

Derinda went into her dressing room feeling slightly puzzled. Why would Rita be talent scouting for Don in London with a summer show to run, surely he would do that himself? She hung the frock on the rail and went back to the stage door. "Jack, can I use the telephone please. I need to make a call to my agent." She dialled the office number but there was no reply, so she tried calling Audrey's private number, nothing.

"This is your fifteen-minute call, your fifteen-minute call ladies and gentleman."

Derinda thanked Jack and ran back to her dressing room to get ready. "Damn and blast," she muttered, why was that woman never available when she needed her, and where were those so-called assistants of hers? Sloped off no doubt while the boss was out. It really was time she considered getting herself another agent, at least one who could ensure she had a decent living coming in. She glanced at the letter she had received from Sasha and felt her blood run cold. She knew that she would not be able to meet his demands, but what to do about it she hadn't a clue. A voice from the doorway distracted her.

"You okay hen?" asked Ricky. "You're cutting it fine."

"I had another late night at the club last night and it does take it out of me. I'm not playing Ipswich dates any more, it's too far away," said Derinda, smiling at her friend. "Oh blast, I forgot to bring my new eyeliner." She brushed past Ricky. "I'll just go and see if Petra has a spare one she can lend me, I can't go on without my eyes done properly."

The letter fluttered off the dressing room table and on to the floor. Ricky went over and picked it up, probably some fan mail. Always interested in such matters he read the letter and gasped. He put the letter back on the table and went back to his own dressing room. Derinda was in big trouble and he had to find a way of helping her.

* * *

When the curtain fell on the second house, Ricky grabbed Derinda's arm as she was leaving the stage. "I wondered if you mind me tagging along to the club in Lowestoft tonight," he said, smiling. "I would like to catch the show and also have a look at the *Trawlers Rest* for myself."

"Of course, you can Ricky. If you don't mind getting in the back of the van with the boys we can give you a lift. I don't go on until after midnight, only one show tonight, so if you hang around afterwards we can give you lift back here."

* * *

The *Trawlers Rest* was quite small. There was a long bar and a seated table area where customers could order chicken in the basket. A small dance floor was at the front of a stage that was no bigger than a postage stamp and there was taped music playing in the background. The club was quite busy and Ricky fought his way to the bar to get himself a drink. The boys were setting up their equipment on the stage as he made his way backstage to Derinda's dressing room.

"Not exactly *The Talk of Norwich* is it?" he said, pulling up a nearby chair. "Why on earth did your agent book you in here?"

"Beggars can't be choosers," said Derinda. "This and Norwich would have been my only source of income this season if the *Sands* hadn't come along when it did. It's a bit of a strain on me playing thrice nightly, but it pays the bills so I must be grateful."

Derinda stripped to her underwear and pulled on her red evening gown. Ricky didn't bat an eyelid, when you had shared dressing rooms with dancers who stripped off completely, nothing fazed you.

"You must have been gutted about losing your London bookings," he said, studying Derinda's reaction carefully. "I bet they pay a lot more than this place does."

Derinda adjusted her shoulder straps. "Be a love and zip me up. I was upset and no mistake. I have been playing four clubs in London on a regular basis for the last few summer seasons and suddenly they announce they don't want me any more and no one will tell me why. The clubs are quite select and the usual punters got to know me quite well. It's bound to be down to cost, they have probably engaged someone who is cheaper."

"And probably not as talented," said Ricky. "Surely they owe you some kind of explanation?"

"Audrey negotiates those contracts at the beginning of every year and every year the fee is raised, not by much, but I have to cover my own costs, not to mention Audrey's ten per cent. I was always liked and welcomed back, but then, like us all, I was only the hired hand. I'll have to find other work or it's panto horse for me."

Ricky noted a waver in her voice and watched as he could see her fighting back tears. He went over to her and put his arm around her. "Who is Sasha?" he asked gently. "You can trust me Derinda, I would never tell anyone. I want to help you."

* * *

Rita and Elsie settled themselves down at a table at the back of the *Mayfair Club* not wishing to be too near the cabaret floor. It was a world away from the venue that Derinda was appearing in that evening. Elsie had phoned well ahead of their arrival and explained that she was connected to the business; the secretary who had answered her call said that there would be complimentary tickets at the door for her, knowing full well that no one attending that evening was a paying guest. Elsie and Rita were surprised that the club wasn't busier. The framed posters at the club entrance stated a new French discovery would be appearing that evening and the photograph only showed the artiste in silhouette.

Elsie sipped her gin and lime. "You would think they were ashamed of this new act," she said. "Strange that they're withholding the name."

"That may account for the fact that there are not many people here, you would have expected a club of this calibre to be heaving on a Friday evening," Rita replied, looking around her. "They certainly have spared no expense on the décor. That wall covering is a work of art and the bar looks like something out of a sci-fi movie. I wonder how much they pay the pianist."

The pianist, who was dressed in a very striking velvet evening suit, was playing standards from the forties and helped create a calming ambience. Several ladies were in full evening splendour with their spouses suitably attired. There was a small group who were definitely following the fashion of the day but they were the minority.

"Time for a chat with one of the flunkies I think," said Rita, getting up. "I won't be long Elsie." Rita approached the bar with a smile and was rewarded by a wide grin from one of the barmen. "Good evening," said Rita, "this really is a charming venue. I'm sorry that I haven't come here before, does one have to be a member?"

The barman placed a bowl of salted peanuts in front of Rita and smiled. "It is a member's only club as a rule, but the new proprietors have relaxed the rules for a few evenings as they are launching a new act here."

"I thought Jackie Morrison ran this particular venue," said Rita, helping herself to a nut. "I knew Jackie back in the days when he owned the *New Hampshire*."

"Mr Morrison sold up a few months ago and retired. He was a nice man, always very good to the staff."

"That sounds like Jackie. Out of interest, are the new owners Peter and Clara Jewson by any chance? I heard they were moving away from the Northern scene."

"Our new owners are French madam. The Boureme family have taken over this and three other clubs in London. The son, Sasha, is presenting the act here tonight. I've heard she is very good."

"So you haven't had a sneak preview of the act then?"

"No madam, none of the staff have met the artiste, that's what makes it all the more exciting for us."

"I'm surprised that the club isn't busier," said Rita, fumbling for her purse. "Isn't this where Derinda Daniels has appeared?"

"Ah, the lovely Miss Daniels," said the barman, enjoying this chance to chat. "What a singer, the members loved her. It's sad that she is too busy to appear here any more. Quite a few of the regular customers have stayed away this evening, despite the opportunity of seeing a new star."

Rita ordered two more drinks, thanked the barman, whom she now knew as Alex, and went to re-join Elsie.

"French family, Boureme, ever heard of them?"

Elsie shook her head. "No, but there just might be someone who has. Jenny Benjamin used to work for Miss Bluebell, she may have come across the name. I'll call her tomorrow, there's no point trying her now; she's probably tucked up in bed with a *Horlicks*."

The club lights dimmed and a spotlight hit the small stage where an accordion player now stood. He was softly playing *La Vie En Rose* as a voice announced, "Ladies and gentleman please welcome France's new singing sensation Laure Dupree."

* * *

Back in Lowestoft Derinda Daniels walked onto the small stage and with her eyes firmly on Ricky she sang, *As Long As He Needs Me* to rapturous applause. Ricky watched her as she played the audience. She had them in the palm of her hand. He had worked with many a pro who couldn't work an audience the way Derinda did. She went through a repertoire of songs that ranged from the classic to pop and then rock 'n' roll to country and western. Her audience lapped it up. When she finally took her bows to calls from the appreciative crowd for more, she smiled and thanked them. Ricky was spellbound; this lady was pure magic, why oh why hadn't the London club scene kept her on their books? This was a totally different act to the one he had seen her perform every night at the *Sands*; she had one persona for stage and another for club appearances. Ricky, like the audience around him, was hooked.

Saturday 11ᵗʰ July

Rita had a lie-in the next morning. She had planned to meet Elsie at Don's office at noon and then the two were going out for lunch. There was a message at the front desk from Elsie informing her that a car would collect her. She found Elsie in a very excited mood when she entered the office suite.

"I knew old Jenny would come up trumps," said Elsie, handing Rita a cup of coffee. "Philippe and Marcella Boureme are known to be very wealthy business people. According to Jenny they help fund some of the floor shows in and around Paris. He was an architect by trade and she came from a very rich family. Jenny believes Philippe is now dead, but Marcella still has her fingers in lots of business ventures."

"So how on earth did Lorna Bright worm her way in there?" asked Rita. "I have to admit that the person I saw perform last night was a far cry from the one I saw last year. She has certainly mastered French ballad singing and the new look actually suits her. That dark cropped hair gave the appearance of a little wave and the black dress screamed of Edith Piaf. Did you notice how the name Lorna had become Laure? Another name for the list; that girl has had more names than the royal family."

"The little sparrow," said Elsie. "Perhaps they will find a tag name for Lorna."

"Well, on a scale of ten, I would say she merited the little budgie status. Hasn't quite mastered the sparrow yet, though time will tell."

Elsie was convinced that Lorna's sister June Ashby was behind it all, but Rita wasn't so sure. This didn't have the June touch; where Lorna was concerned there had to be a man involved.

"Did Jenny mention if there was a son?" Elsie shook her head. "We will have to make a return call to that club and see if we can't find out some more."

"Oh Rita are you sure?" said Elsie, still trying to get over the night before when they hadn't left the club until two in the morning, way past her bedtime.

"Afraid so, me old lover," said Rita, draining her coffee cup. "You best make a call to the club and see if you can't wangle some more complimentary tickets. It might be a bit tricky with it being a Saturday night. I must grab a paper when we head out to lunch in case there's any mention of Lorna's opening night. Where are we having lunch by the way?"

"We are to meet Don at the *Cumberland*, he's treating us," said Elsie, glancing at the clock. "And we best make a move, he doesn't like to be kept waiting."

They found Don in the restaurant and he was smiling broadly. "Hello my love, Rita. I have some exciting news for you. I've taken the liberty of ordering us all a glass of something sparkly."

Elsie eyed her husband suspiciously and pecked him on the cheek before sitting down; he was like a cat on heat. "What is it?" she said, putting her handbag down. "It has to be something if you've ordered the sparkly stuff and I'm guessing it wasn't lemonade. Though knowing your wallet the way I do I wouldn't put it past you."

"What is it Don, you look fit to bursting?" Rita joined in; she had rarely seen Don so fired-up.

"I received a call this morning at the office. Bit unusual for a Saturday morning but just as well I was there. Elsie, we must see about getting a new secretary at some point, it isn't good to have the office unmanned. That Audrey Audley manages it."

"Sorry to disillusion you, old lover," said Rita. "I tried phoning her and she may well have two office assistants but it would seem they are never there when Audrey isn't, which to my way of thinking is a total waste of time. The woman must have money to burn."

"That's as maybe," said Don, interrupting and trying to get the conversation back on track. "Delfont's office called, they want *Summertime Sunshine* to play the North Pier in Blackpool for the illumination season."

Elsie's mouth fell open and Rita looked at Don in utter astonishment. "First Bernard Delfont pulls out of his season at the *Sands* and now you are telling me he wants us to step in at his other stronghold for the illumination season in Blackpool? I take it someone from his organisation has seen the show."

"Yes Rita they have, they sent two people from his office and both attended separate shows on different nights and they say it would be just right for Blackpool."

"So what are we going to be paying Mr Delfont for the privilege?" asked Elsie, who always looked a gift horse in the mouth.

"That's the joy my love," said Don, who was quite beside himself, "I am doing him a favour. Me, Don Stevens, doing Bernard Delfont a favour."

The waiter arrived with the glasses of champagne and Elsie downed hers in one. Rita, ever the level-headed one, sipped hers and smiled at Don. "This is wonderful news but the problem we have is whether or not the entire company will want to play the season. What are we looking at here, October and part of November if my memory serves me right? You will have to check when his summer show closes at the North Pier. I will have to have a chat with the troops. If Delfont's people want the show as seen we may have a big problem, they won't want us changing the bill and putting in subs."

Don came down to earth with a bump. "I hadn't thought of that, I was so caught up in the excitement of it all. Elsie, you will have details of any other bookings we have accepted. The show at the North Pier closes the same day as ours, so we would want to open as soon as we could and there would be a lot to organise beforehand, posters, sets and costumes."

"Nothing that hasn't been done a hundred times before," said Rita, reassuringly. "I will have to call a meeting with everyone. I wasn't planning on going back until Monday but I may have to return tomorrow."

"Oh no Rita," said Elsie, "you must stay and come over to lunch at our house tomorrow, mustn't she Don. We can all go out for a walk along the river, the weather is looking good. Besides, we are going back to the club tonight and you won't want to get up too early tomorrow."

"What's this, you two out on the town again tonight?" said Don, in mock surprise. "Whatever next? Now let's order something to eat and then you can tell me what you both got up to last night, I have never known Elsie to come in so late."

Later Rita made a call to the theatre and asked Jack to ensure that every member of the company was made aware that she wanted them at the theatre on Monday, assembled in the auditorium by four and no later. She had important news to tell them. It was at times like this that she really missed good old dependable Jim and she made a mental note to go and visit him as soon as time allowed. Using her belts and braces approach she phoned Lucinda who called Ted to the telephone just as he was about to set out to the theatre and told him what she had told Jack. Not stopping to explain further to Ted she replaced the receiver and thought about what she could wear on her second evening out with Elsie. Grabbing her bag she headed out to see what she could possibly add to her limited London wardrobe.

* * *

Backstage at *The Golden Sands Theatre* the rumours were buzzing around. Petra was convinced they were going to pull the show, Ricky was of the opinion that Rita was going to announce she was making changes to the running order, Derinda was so tired that she really didn't care what was going to happen and young Jonny was so excited to be part of a summer season, he just wanted to carry on. The JB Dancers, on the other hand, had been here before; last minute changes to routines had been the order of the day when Jenny had been in charge. Doreen and Jill were already making plans for a couple of new routines they were keen to get started on for any forthcoming bookings so would be well prepared for whatever Rita might have to say to them all. It was Ted and Maurice, who chatted together about what Rita might have up her sleeve, who were nearest to the truth.

"Knowing your lady wife," said Maurice, accepting the offer of a small whisky in Ted's dressing room, "she has probably secured another seasonal booking for this show and maybe, who knows, in London. The press were lavish in their praise and you have to agree Ted that Rita runs this show like a tight ship. No chopping and changing her mind like we had last year with old Don running things and poor Jenny never knowing whether she was doing a finale or the opening number to a pantomime. Rita is a great director and you must be very proud of her Ted." Maurice patted Ted on the shoulder and went to get ready for the first show.

Ted was immensely proud of his wife; she always knew what to do and how to do it. He put down his empty glass and felt a sudden pain across his chest, it was the second time he had experienced the dull ache in a fortnight. He sat down and looked at himself in the mirror. Too many fried breakfasts and afternoon teas at Lucinda's, that was his problem, a case of acid indigestion. He went along to the stage door.

"Hello Jack, have you got any *Rennie* or some *Andrews* to hand, got a bit of indigestion."

Jack smiled and handed Ted some *Rennie*, it was always wise to keep such things to hand, especially with this theatre lot, always ailing with something.

Monday 13*th* July

When Rita arrived back at the guest house, Lucinda made some tea and put it in the lounge for her. Ted was out for a walk. Rita handed Lucinda a small gift she had bought for her in London which delighted her. The crystal penguin would be put in her glass display cabinet where it could be admired. Asking to use the telephone, Rita called Audrey's office and was surprised when Audrey answered.

"Hello Audrey, Rita here. I'm just back from London and have uncovered some of the details about the club bookings. Do you know of the Boureme family? I didn't think so. It would appear that these French business people have taken over a majority control of the four clubs that were so lucrative for you in the past. The so-called new talent that has taken Derinda's place is none other than Lorna Bright under the new guise of French singer Laure Dupree. Lorna, you will recall, is June Ashby's infamous younger sister who impersonated June in last year's show at the *Sands*. Elsie was convinced that June was behind this, but I didn't think so and I was proven right. I produced one of Don's cards at the bar and asked to speak to the manager, or whether it was possible for them to put me in touch with Lorna's agent. Sasha Boureme was the name I was given, it turns out he is one of the sons of the Boureme family, there is also a daughter."

Audrey gasped. "How did you find out this information?"

"I ask the right questions," said Rita, pleased that she had at least made Audrey sit up and pay attention. "I also took a wig with me and with a selected outfit and some other accessories I looked nothing like I did the night before. Elsie played her cards right and introduced me at the door as an agent. The rest was made up as I went along."

Audrey was stunned. "I have to take my hat off to you Rita, thank you so much. But where do we go from here?"

"Well," said Rita, "I suggest you don't say anything to Derinda at this stage. I need to do some more digging around. I didn't make myself known to Lorna and I don't think Lorna would remember Elsie; the poor kid was in such a state when she was here last season that she had trouble remembering what day it was. We were quite a way from the cabaret floor and it was very busy in there last night. Incidentally, Lorna seems to have mastered the French vocals but she still lacks presence and is no Edith Piaf. I rather got the impression that the audience was not all that taken with her. Perhaps you could ask your friend Rueben Roberts to put some feelers out; maybe they have heard of these Bouremes. I have to go Audrey, I am expected at the theatre in an hour and Ted has just come back from his walk. If you get any news from Rueben, please leave a message either here or at the stage door with Jack. Not a word to Derinda."

Audrey replaced her receiver. There was no doubt about it, Rita had done her homework, even dropping Rueben's name in to the conversation. Was there anything that Rita didn't know?

Rita's next call was to Jenny who had spoken with Elsie earlier that day. "Yes I remember the Boureme family. Philippe married in to a wealthy family, his wife's name is Marcella. I believe they became involved as backers for some of the Parisian clubs. He moved in very elite circles, using his wife's money to get what he wanted. I recall Miss Bluebell was quite taken by his charm. Through old contacts I was kept informed of what went on in Paris when I left. One of the *Bluebells* became romantically involved with one of his son's, Stefan I believe it was, but Marcella didn't approve and threatened to cut him off without a penny if he pursued the dalliance. Cornelia had a strong personality and tried to fight it for a while, but Stefan obeyed his mother. Cornelia went on to marry a French banker and lives in Lyon now and has five children. Somehow I never imagined Cornelia as the motherly type, but she seems very happy."

"Fancy you remembering all of that," said Rita, much impressed. "I suppose Elsie told you who is masquerading as a French singer."

Jenny laughed. "I didn't dare believe it when she told me. Honestly, is there nothing those sisters won't try. I wouldn't want to be around when Derinda Daniels finds out who is stealing her thunder, I should imagine she can be quite fiery that one."

"You've been a great help Jenny, thank you very much."

Rita was so wrapped up in all that had been happening she failed to spot that Ted was very much out of breath and not his usual chipper self. Gathering her thoughts together she motioned Ted to the car, deciding that she would drive the short distance. Ted was unusually quiet but Rita, concentrating on how she was going to deliver the good news to the company, didn't notice. She waved to Maud as Ted slowly followed her to the theatre. She was pleased to see that the entire company had gathered in the auditorium and was even more surprised to see that Jim, flanked by Roger, was also there. Standing centre stage, Rita told the company about the proposal. Jonny Adams was shaking with excitement; he had no firm bookings after *Summertime Sunshine* closed. Doreen and Jill spoke on behalf of the dancers that they hoped to be able to take the assembled troupe with them. They were rewarded by nodding heads. Ricky had made plans to go abroad for a few weeks rest, but he could shelve that. Derinda, not wild about spending more time at the end of a pier, especially one off the Irish Sea in what would be winter, raised no objection as she knew her diary was empty apart from a few bookings at *The Talk of Norwich* that she could rearrange with Audrey's help.

Petra Olanzo stood up and spoke. "I don't think Mario and I will be able to come with you," she said, in an Italian accent that would have fooled even Sophia Loren. "I am afraid you will have to go without us."

"That's disappointing," said Rita, "your act is proving to be one of the highlights of this season. I need to have a speciality act in the line-up and the *Delfont Organisation* was most complimentary about yours. Everyone says how original it is and, besides, you come with the added bonus of the delightful puppet show. You will indeed be a hard act to follow. I know you are on Don's books, perhaps you should discuss it with him before you commit either way."

Petra seemed unmoved by the compliments and continued. "Mario and I have plans to go to Australia." This was certainly news to her husband who looked at her in surprise. "I know how unique our act is and I think it should be seen worldwide and not be confined to the shores of England. I will be discussing it with Don."

Rita nodded. "Well, perhaps you will think it over Petra. Thank you for being so honest with me. In the meantime I will have to see if I can procure another act, time is of the essence." Petra nodded and sat down.

Jim found his voice. "Rita, I know it's none of my business but will you be taking any of the backstage crew with you? I know they are strictly the *Sands* staff during the season but they do know the ropes so to speak."

Rita smiled. "Lovely to have you with us Jim and of course it's your business. I hope that, with permission, I will be able to ask Roger and at least some of the boys to join us. But that largely depends on the arrangements the Blackpool North Pier have in place. I do know from my own experience that the backstage crew are usually employed on a show-by-show basis; like here, the venue is not open all year round. I will let you all know as soon as I have any more details; it would be good for the company to have familiar faces working behind the scenes with them."

Just then the voice of Mona Buckle was heard coming from the pass door. "Mrs Ricer, I think you best come quickly, Mr Ricer has collapsed back here and he isn't looking very well. I've said before there was great sadness here."

* * *

The show went ahead without Ted that night and the news of his absence from the bill was delivered at the beginning of each show by a very nervous Roger who, unlike Jim, was not used to standing in front of tabs speaking to an audience. A very worried Rita sat beside her husband's hospital bed praying that he would be all right.

Tony Gareth Smith

Chapter Nine   *Let's Go on with the Show*

T he following day it was business as usual. The *Golden Sands* box office opened with a notice that stated, due to the indisposition of Ted Ricer, Bernie Duggan – Lowestoft's very own comedian - would be appearing. It was news that was met with a certain amount of criticism from those who had seen Bernie perform.

The pier was busy with holidaymakers enjoying the bright morning. The promenade was alive with the noise from the numerous arcades of slot machines being played, children were enjoying pony rides and the crazy golf course was doing some good business. The smell of hotdogs, hamburgers and candy floss soon filled the warm air. A group of fishermen were heading on to the jetty to chance their luck and Bertie, Mona's husband, was with them enjoying a well-earned day off from his usual labours. The group of friends tried to get together as often as possible, weather permitting, and with a packed lunch to hand they enjoyed just chatting about things that were of interest to them.

* * *

Ricky was walking Bingo along the beach taking in the sea air while Bingo made play with the tide. His brief conversation with Derinda had worried him, but she hadn't opened up as much as he had hoped and he was still in the dark about who Sasha was. Maybe in time she would tell him, all he could do for now was keep an eye on her. She had looked tired most evenings and that had to be down to the fact that she was working the clubs after curtain. A couple of times she seemed to be sleepwalking through their act together, with Ricky prompting her from the piano about what song came next. The audiences didn't appear to notice and applauded all the same. But several of the backstage boys had watched her from the wings and commented that she wasn't as on the ball as she had been when the show had first opened.

* * *

Rita, who had spent most of the night lying awake worrying about Ted, was trying to get some fresh air in her lungs. At the Sister's instruction she had left Ted sleeping the night before and was told she could call in after the doctor's rounds. Lucinda had been kindness itself and she too was concerned about Ted.

On hearing the news it was Elsie who had engaged the services of Bernie Duggan after some negotiation. As Rita walked along through the town centre she knew that right at that very minute Bernie was going through his routine under the watchful eye of Maurice Beeney who was also timing the act so that it fitted in to the vacant slots. Jenny Benjamin had shown up at the *Sands* to lend her support, which was a great comfort to Rita. Pulling her shoulders back and walking with some purpose, Rita decided to make her way to the General in the hope that Ted had had a comfortable night. Phoning had not put her mind at ease and she needed to see Ted for herself and no amount of 'he had a comfortable night' was going to stop her.

* * *

"Quite a to-do," said Freda, folding her arms over her ample bosom as Muriel came out of her front door. "That Ted Ricer has taken ill by all accounts according to my Dick, he came home full of it last night. At death's door he said. I have to say I didn't think he looked too clever when I spotted him in *Palmers* one lunchtime. It will be the drink of course, it always is with that sort."

"And that is something your Dick would know nothing about Freda?" said Muriel. "I heard him come home last night, banging your back gate and singing at the top of his voice and you wonder why guests don't come back to you year in year out. I'm telling you, if he carries on, Ted Ricer won't be the only one in hospital. If he disturbs my guests again I may very well put him in there myself."

Freda watched as her neighbour walked down the road. Someone had obviously got out of the bed the wrong side that morning.

* * *

Maud and Barbara were also chatting about Ted's collapse.

"He does work hard with that act, no one can say otherwise," said Maud, passing a packet of custard creams to Barbara. "It can't be easy coming up with a fresh routine that has the audience rolling in the aisles night after night." Barbara nodded in agreement. "He has the love and support of a good woman behind him," Maud continued, picking up her knitting and settling down for a ten minute break from the window. "Poor Rita must be beside herself with worry. I'll get her some flowers when I go up town lunchtime and drop them off at Lucinda's." She looked at her pattern and continued to knit in silence while Barbara ate the last of the custard creams.

* * *

"Hello Rueben, it's only me," said Audrey, playing with the love beads she had forgotten to remove from around her neck before coming in to the office that morning. "Have you ever heard of a French family called Boureme?" Audrey listened carefully. "Really darling, how interesting, pray continue." Audrey made a few notes on her pad. "That's great, you are an absolute angel my darling. This weekend? Well no, I hadn't anything planned. Oh Rueben how divine, of course I'll come, it would be great fun. I might have to go and buy myself another little outfit; I have to look the part. Oh no darling, I'll have to wear one of my wigs, in case anyone is there that might know me. Rueben, you are too naughty for words! Thanks again for your help, *ciao* for now." Audrey replaced the receiver and picked up her handbag. "Margaret darling, I am just popping out to do some clothes shopping, hold the fort till I come back, there's a love."

* * *

Dan had had a lie-in that morning and was awoken by Dave coming in with some fresh rolls and pastries. "You are awake then," said Dave, popping his head round the bedroom door. "I'll make some tea."

Dan wandered through to the kitchen with his dressing gown hanging loosely and sat down at the table.

"We had a letter from Josie," said Dave, handing the envelope to Dan. "Says she and Madge have been looking over properties for us. It sounds as if they've found one or two that might be worth a look."

Dan unfolded the letter and began to read it. "They're all in Blackpool, nothing in Preston."

"I thought we discussed that Blackpool would be best for the kind of work I would be looking for, and you would have the run of the bars there."

When the subject had first been broached, Dave hadn't been so keen on the idea of moving, but now he knew that Jim was out of hospital, he seemed to be warming to the idea.

"You are sure about this aren't you?" Dan asked. "Because if you are, I'll arrange some time off work and we can go and look at some places with the girls. Mum and dad will be disappointed that they aren't looking in Preston, but Blackpool is hardly on the other side of the world."

Dave poured some tea and passed a cup to Dan. "I'll try and arrange some time off from the Wellie; though it won't be easy, even with the season up and running, but I'll do my best. Have a word with Stella when you go in tonight."

Dan smiled at Dave and nodded, this wasn't what he had expected at all.

* * *

Ted opened his eyes and half-smiled at Rita who was holding his hand.

"Hello me old lover, you gave me a fright. The doctors say you are going to have to stay here a couple of days while they run some tests. They believe you've had a mild heart attack." Rita squeezed his hand.

"Sorry Reet," he whispered, "didn't mean to frighten you. Felt a bit off-colour the last few days. Didn't think anything of it, thought it was acid indigestion. I sometimes get that."

"You're going to have to take things much slower for a while. I don't think you'll be back on stage any day soon. Lucinda said she could make you a bed on the ground floor in the back parlour so you won't have to climb any stairs."

"I'll be okay Reet, you'll see. I will be back on that stage making them laugh in next to no time. How are you coping without me?"

"On a personal level I'm not coping me old lover; on the theatre front we have had to put someone in your place for the time being. Bernie Duggan." She knew as soon as she had said his name Ted would react and wished she'd kept quiet.

"You have got to get rid of him Reet, he's box office poison. He does a rubbish act, people will be staying away in droves when word gets around. You have to find someone else."

"He was all Elsie could get at short notice," said Rita. "Now calm yourself or you'll bring on another attack."

"Do me a favour," said Ted, "give Tommy Trent a call; you'll find his number in my little book at the lodgings. Old Tommy is a pro and I bet he could do with some work. Old Tom has been down on his luck a bit lately since he lost his Alice. He only lives the other side of Norwich; promise me you'll phone him."

Rita nodded. "I'll give him a call when I get back to Lucinda's. But if he says yes I don't know what I'm going to tell Bernie."

"You'll think of something," said Ted, beginning to drift back to sleep, "my Reet always thinks of something."

"Mrs Ricer, the doctor would like a private word with you," said the Sister, who appeared at the bedside, "please follow me."

Rita left the hospital and walked back to the guest house. Lucinda was waiting for news and Rita told her what had been said to her. After checking with Don she made the phone call to Tommy Trent and asked him if he would be able to audition for her. Tommy agreed to drive over to see her at the theatre later that day. If Tommy was more the business she would give Bernie his marching orders. There had been several unfavourable comments about his act from those who had seen him perform before and she didn't want to see all the hard work that had gone in to the show ruined. Once word got around this business it spread quickly.

Several things played on her mind and it seemed to her that if one problem came along, more followed. Trying to convince Ted to give up smoking and cut down on the whisky seemed the least of her worries. He would just have to buckle down and do what the doctor had wanted or face the consequences.

Friday 17th July

Ted arrived back at Lucinda's with the welcome mat well and truly rolled out. True to her word Lucinda had placed a bed in the small room she rarely used on the ground floor and had made it as homely as she could. Ted tried to fight and say he would be okay going up the stairs, but Lucinda was having none of it and so his fate was sealed. Rita was pleased to have her husband back with her and she knew that while she went about her business, Lucinda would kill him with kindness, which was something that Ted was secretly worried about.

Get well cards and flowers arrived from the company and a special one from his old friend Tommy Trent who, after a successful audition, had replaced Bernie Duggan in the line-up two nights ago, much to the relief of the company who were sick and tired of Bernie's distasteful behaviour both on and off the stage. Bernie was paid a week's money for his trouble.

Tommy had been given an interview in the local press which helped build his confidence and gave extra publicity to the show. He mentioned his old pal Ted and how they had worked together when they were both starting out in the business. Bob Scott was more than happy with the advanced bookings and Don was wondering why he had never thought of handing the reins over to the more than capable Rita before; a sentiment echoed by Elsie.

* * *

Over in Southtown Debbie was packing the last of her daughter's clothes. She was still uncertain that she should return to her home in Norwich, but Peter had said that the time was right and Jim wanted to get some of his independence back as he grew stronger with each passing day.

He reassured Debbie that if he needed anything he would call her and as Maud was coming in on a daily basis she would be keeping an eye on him.

Jim was more than pleased to have a visit from Lilly Brockett later that day; she happened to be in town doing some shopping and thought she would call in on the off chance. She told Jim about her latest book and how much she was enjoying living in her new home. They reminisced about the old days at the theatre and how, over the years, things had changed. Jim told Lilly some of the stories he had heard about her replacement, Mona, and it made her laugh. She left Jim after an hour, noting that her friend was looking tired, with the promise of calling in again when she was next in Great Yarmouth.

* * *

Derinda arrived at the theatre early and was pleased to hear Ricky's voice coming from his dressing room. "Bad boy Bingo, you give that back to me right now."

Derinda tapped on the door and called out, "Hi Ricky, everything okay in there?"

A very flustered Ricky opened the door, he had a towel on his head, and Bingo took advantage of the situation and ran out of the dressing room and scampered on to the stage. "That dog will be the death of me," he said, doing his best not to laugh. "Come in, I was just about to make a cuppa if you fancy one."

Derinda smiled and went in. "Washing your hair I see," she said, sitting herself down.

Ricky smiled. "Something like that," he said, pulling the towel tighter to make a turban and busying himself with some cups. "You're here early hen, anything up?"

"Couldn't stand being in the house a minute longer," she said. "Turned up at *The Talk* last night, only to find they had double-booked and my services were not required. I must have a word with Audrey, that's if I can ever track her down. She isn't pleased that I've given up the Ipswich bookings, but she will just have to get on with it. I called in her offices on the way here, but as usual she was not there and neither were her assistants. I sometimes think that the only way of contacting an agent is by a séance, I'm convinced that half of them are either dead or of another world."

"I heard Ted was allowed home today," said Ricky. "I bet Rita is pleased. He's nice, old Ted, doesn't seem the same without him round the place."

"Tommy seems to be settling in okay though. I remember seeing him some years ago working at *Butlins*, the crowd loved him. He doesn't seem to have lost any of his stage presence. I'm very impressed with young Jonny too; he has a great act there. You should have been here last year with Mystic Brian and his doves, now there was something else. The few nights I stood in here, those birds of his were everywhere but in the right place. What a character!"

"That's the thing about this business," said Ricky, handing Derinda a cup of tea, "You do meet some folk. I don't know what I would have done if I hadn't come into this business. As soon as I walk out there, it's like 'pow', the spotlight hits me and it's show time."

And Derinda knew exactly what he meant.

* * *

Watching from the back of the auditorium, Rita sighed as the curtain came down on the first house and the audience began to exit. She was feeling very tired, it had been a long day and she wondered if she could miss the second house and go back to see how Ted was. All she wanted to do was kick off her shoes and relax in a chair. She put her head round the office door. "Bob, I'm going to call it day. Tommy has settled in well and everyone seems happy enough."

Bob nodded. "It's at times like this we really miss old Jim being round the place. Roger is good at what he does, but he's no Jim." And Rita couldn't have agreed more.

As she walked out of the stage door she noted the queue of people waiting to go in to the second house and felt a sense of pride. She reached the end of the pier and turned on to the prom and began to walk slowly, enjoying the night air and the buzz of the crowds. The prom was busy with families with young children who were excitedly running along, happy to be allowed out so late at night among the twinkling lights and smells of the seaside. Heaving a happy sigh she walked along looking forward to an evening chatting to Ted.

"Hello Lucinda, "she said, as she walked in the guest house "Just going to pop in and see how Ted is."

"He's been sleeping a lot," said Lucinda, who was busy dusting the hall table and mirror. "He ate his tea; he wanted to join the others in the dining room but I insisted he stay where he was and took him in a tray."

Rita smiled. "Thanks Lucinda, I really appreciate all you're doing. It's a great weight off my mind."

She walked in to the room and sure enough there was Ted propped up on the pillows, fast asleep. She put her bag down and went over to him and took his hand, kissing his forehead. "Hello me old lover." The words froze on her lips. She sat down on the bed still holding his hand. "You're full of surprises aren't you me old lover." She looked at his peaceful face and leaned over and kissed him again. "I love you, you old bugger," she whispered, feeling her world seemingly had come to an end.

* * *

Jim picked up his car keys and headed out of the front door. He hadn't driven since being out of hospital and took it slowly. He parked as near as he could to the *Golden Sands* and walked across the road.

Maud was just coming out of the box office. "Hello Jim, what brings you down here? I hope you haven't been driving." Jim grabbed Maud by the arm and asked her to accompany him to Bob's office. "Whatever is the matter?" Maud asked, feeling alarmed. "Jim, slow down, the doctor said you weren't to rush about."

Bob looked up from his desk. "You got here quickly."

Maud looked at Jim. "What's going on Jim, for goodness sake say something." Jim's face was ashen and Maud could see he was under strain, this wasn't good.

"I've got word to the company to stay behind after the show; they are to assemble backstage. I thought that was probably best. It will be more private."

"Will someone please tell me what this is all about," said Maud, getting agitated.

With as much composure as he could, Jim told Maud about his telephone call from Lucinda. She listened but couldn't quite take in what he was saying. "That can't be right; he was only just released from hospital. Lucinda has got it wrong. Oh my goodness, Rita! I must go to her, someone has to do something."

Jim gently held Maud's arm as she attempted to get up and she sat down again and stared in silence at the carpet.

* * *

Jack secured the stage door and went to join the others. When they saw Jim they were puzzled.

"I am sorry to be the bearer of sad news, but Ted Ricer died earlier this evening." There was a sharp intake of breath from the assembled company. "Rita is being taken care of by

Lucinda Haines and the doctor has sedated her so that she will get some sleep. As you can imagine, this has come as a dreadful shock, there was every indication that Ted would be okay. Obviously, neither Bob nor I can speak on behalf of Rita, but in the interim Jenny Benjamin has kindly agreed to stand in and will deal with day-to-day matters. Don and Elsie will be arriving here tomorrow and after the weekend we may have a clearer idea on things. The bar is open if anyone would like to go along for a drink and chat, Bob will take care of the tab. If I know Rita, and I think I do after all these years of association, she would want the show to go on as usual."

The group nodded and slowly began to break up. Derinda took Jonny's arm; he was visibly upset, Ted had been very kind to him and had shown him the ropes. He wanted Ted to know how grateful he was, but had been unable to express himself properly. Ricky guided a very shocked Tommy to the bar. He talked about Ted with great affection and how much he had helped him when he had lost his wife Alice. The rest of the company followed and Maurice organised drinks for everyone. Maud sat and looked at the brandy in front of her, then she stood up and raised the glass and shouted out, "To Ted!" And as everyone joined her in the toast tears welled up and fell.

Saturday 18th July

The sun shone brightly greeting the holidaymakers as they left their boarding houses and hotels; some were setting off to the beach, while others were heading back home after their summer holiday. Regent Street was busy with hordes of shoppers and some new arrivals enjoying their first taste of the days to come. Queues were forming at the chip stalls on the market place. Some had their chips with tripe, others with only salt and vinegar, but there was no doubt this was a popular choice for all those who came to Great Yarmouth. Children with their buckets and spades, heads covered with sunhats, were running towards to the beach to build sandcastles of enormous proportions, each with their own storybook in mind. A castle guarding a lost treasure, or a fortress to keep the good in and the evil out. Men with knotted handkerchiefs on their heads were fending off the sun while their wives and girlfriends sported large floppy sunhats with their faces covered in sun creams. The pink and pasty, the golden and tanned skins walked side by side along the prom or paddled in the sea.

The *Merrivale Model Village* welcomed young and old alike, the Pleasure Beach likewise, where its carousels, kiddies' rides, big wheels, helter-skelter and a roller coaster, not for the faint-hearted, were giving people the fun and relaxation they had saved up all year round for. The penny arcades and bingo stalls enticed people to try their luck; the open landaus with their well-groomed horses trotted along the Golden Mile carrying their passengers while others looked on. The beautiful flowerbed gardens, the waterways and the piers allowed those who had less energy to sit on the many benches and watch as the world went by while licking an ice cream cone or iced lolly.

Tickets were being booked for the circus and the many summer shows the town had to offer. The resort was alive, having long flung off its winter coat, and was embracing all those who came to visit whether for a few days or a fortnight. It was a typical Saturday in the summer season.

* * *

Rita had spent a quiet morning in her room and no attempts by Lucinda could entice her to eat breakfast. A tap at the door revealed that Elsie had arrived to offer moral support and to see that her friend had everything she needed. Rita accompanied her downstairs where Lucinda provided a light lunch for them both and Rita ate some but not all of her egg salad. She spoke about Ted, remembering the good times they had had together and the antics he had sometimes got up to. Elsie listened and waited. But there were no tears and when Rita looked at her watch and told Elsie that she really ought to get ready to go to the theatre, Elsie didn't try to stop her. Together they walked to the *Golden Sands* and Rita, as always, waved to Maud and as she went through the stage door she said good evening to Jack. Elsie followed her as she did her rounds of the dressing rooms as she did every night, ensuring that everyone was accounted for and that they all had what they needed.

Flanked by Elsie and Jenny, Rita watched as the first house audience came in to the theatre to take their seats. As the lights dimmed Rita took her usual seat at the back of theatre and watched. Elsie and Jenny waited. The dancers opened the show as they did at every performance; Derinda Daniels sang her first number and welcomed everyone to the show. Everything was as it should be, everything was normal. Then it came to the part of the programme when Ted was usually announced, but instead the name Tommy Trent came over the sound system. Rita began to shake and with the help of her friends was escorted back to Lucinda's where she had only memories to comfort her breaking heart.

* * *

The following morning, as the sun shone brightly, Rita pulled back the curtains and looked around her. Elsie had stayed over at Don's insistence and was in the adjacent room. She went over to the wardrobe and began to assemble her outfit for the day and then went to the bathroom to have a shower. Blow-drying her hair as she did every morning, she then applied some makeup and walked down to the dining room. A few of the other guests were already eating their breakfast and she smiled and said good morning. Lucinda came through carrying plates of bacon, eggs and mushrooms, pleased to see that Rita was up and about. Lucinda was wearing a black armband and Rita smiled to herself, Ted would be tickled pink. Rita was joined by Elsie, who had had a reasonably good night's rest.

"It's going to be a lovely day," said Rita, "the holidaymakers are very lucky with the weather."

Elsie relaxed and smiled. "Yes, it is a lovely morning. What would you like to do today?"

Rita buttered some toast. "There is so much that needs doing, but I think today, if you and Jenny are agreeable, I would like you both to come over to Gorleston with me and have lunch in the *Storm House Café*. Ted liked going over there. It's right opposite the pier and he liked to sit upstairs so that he could watch the ships coming in to the harbour. Ask Don to join us."

"Would you be okay if, after breakfast, I popped over to the hotel to have a word with Don?"

"Of course I'll be all right," said Rita. "I can sit quietly and write a list of what needs to be organised for the funeral and first thing tomorrow I can put the wheels in motion. But today is Sunday and Sundays are for being with family and friends and not worrying about the day-to-day things in life."

They finished their breakfast and Elsie headed off to see Don. Rita sat quietly in the dining room and Lucinda busied herself clearing tables. When the other guests had left the room, Lucinda sat opposite Rita and handed her an envelope from her trembling hand. "I found this while I was tidying up, it must have fallen down when the undertakers came to collect Ted last night."

Rita felt a cold shiver run down her spine, but composed herself as she took the envelope from Lucinda. It was Ted's writing.

"I'll leave you to read it, give me a call if you need anything."

Rita put on her glasses and began to read.

"My darling Rita, if you are reading this then I will have gone to that great comedy club we laughed about. I didn't want to leave you so soon. There are so many things I should have said. As I lie here I remember what a wonderful life we have had together. Not a conventional marriage, but it has always been an honest one. I loved you from the first moment I saw you; you have been the best wife a man could ever have wished for. I want you to know that if one day you meet someone and you love them, that you do so with my blessing.

A favour – look after old Tommy, see if you can't get him some bookings, and young Jonny Adams, I did as you asked and took him under my wing. I've been helping the boy with his act and also his speech. Remember in the old days when I used to get stage fright and I went to that man who helped me overcome my nerves with some breathing exercises? I tried them with the boy and he seems to be getting better.

Now for the practical – I would like to be cremated and some of my ashes scattered in each of the seaside towns I've played over the years, but I would like my final resting place to be in Great Yarmouth. We always liked it here.

Look after yourself Reet and when you see a bright star one night, it will be old Ted lighting up the heavens watching over you. Love, your old lover Ted xx"

* * *

Over in Norwich Ricky had joined Derinda for lunch at her house. She had taken a liking to Ricky and felt that she could trust him. It felt good to talk about things with someone who wasn't going to judge her. Ricky was a great comfort to her and when she explained about the photographs that Sasha had threatened to blackmail her with he almost laughed.

"Do you really think he would pull such a stunt?" he said, helping himself to more salad. "A friend of mine had a similar thing happen to her so she went straight to the press with the story, which of course was never published. That sort of thing doesn't just affect the victim it also drags in others. How would his mother deal with the publicity? How would he be able to face his own daughter and look her in the eye when she has grown up and say, 'Look, this is how I destroyed your mother'? Besides, the photographs you talk about sound tame to me, they are nothing you wouldn't find in some sleazy men's magazine or, for that matter, on page three of *The Sun*. I really think you're worrying about nothing there."

Derinda felt somewhat reassured. "Thanks Ricky, it does make sense when you put it like that. But you don't know Sasha. I know I was wrong to turn my back on my family life in order to pursue my dream, but Sasha bought into that dream too. I know his family thought that he married beneath him and his mother hates the sight of me."

"And there you have the answer to the problem, the mother. It's always the mother, perhaps her son wasn't turning out the way she would have liked him to. I don't know anything about the family set-up but his mother may be the bigger thorn in your side. Perhaps she is moulding your daughter in the way she couldn't with Sasha." He paused for a few moments and added, "And you, my friend, have been very silly. Why pretend you don't have a daughter, why try to hide her? Plenty of people in the business have children, why should you be any different?"

"I was ashamed," said Derinda. "You see..." she stopped and looked down at the tablecloth, afraid to meet Ricky's eyes, "my daughter isn't like other little girls." There was a cry in her voice and tears began to fall. "Jeanie is disabled and she cannot talk properly. I was ashamed, ashamed of my own flesh and blood and what others might think. I am a terrible mother, Sasha is right."

"I'm sure that isn't true hen," said Ricky. "Perhaps it would be an idea to prove it to yourself and gain custody of your daughter. Mebe you should consider giving up the business for the sake of Jeannie."

Derinda nodded. "I know you're right, but I've been out of Jeannie's life for so long. It may be too late now, but it does pain me not to see her. Looking back, I made the wrong decision. When she was born the doctors tried to convince me that she should be adopted. Sasha and I agreed we would stand together and be a proper family, but then I became resentful and started accepting engagements once or twice a month and then contracts that took me away from home. So you see, there are two sides to every story and I am the one in the wrong, not Sasha, he only wants what is best for his daughter."

Chapter Ten *Shadows*

Tuesday 28th July

Ted's funeral took place at the Gorleston crematorium, Rita had decided against a ceremony in Hull. Though it had been their base for many years, that was all it had been, a base, somewhere to hole up when the work wasn't coming in. The couple had spent most of their married life travelling.

There were few family members in attendance, a couple of distant cousins on Ted's side and a pair of elderly aunts and uncles. The chapel was filled with many faces from the show business world and one or two agents that Ted and Rita had worked with over the years. There had been cards and flowers from people who were unable to attend, including a rather funny wreath from Mystic Brian, the magician that Ted had worked with on many occasions – in the middle of the flower arrangement were three life-size doves depicting Caroline, Enid and Lottie, the birds that were part of his act and Brian's pride and joy. When she saw them Rita knew that Ted would have seen the funny side of the tribute.

The service consisted of two of Ted's favourite hymns, a reading from the Bible delivered by Don Stevens and a moving tribute to her husband from Rita that caused one or two sniffles among the congregation. Rita, who kept her composure throughout, spoke of the happy times that she and Ted had spent over the years and the many friends they had made within the business. She recited a few lines from a song that she and Ted had loved from the musical *The King and I* and finished with her own words, "Ted, my old lover, sleep well. You are and will always be my everything."

* * *

Don and Elsie had organised a buffet and drinks in the rear bar of *The Growler*, where many a happier evening had been spent. Lucinda would have liked to have tea at the house, but with the season in full swing and the number of people expected to attend she admitted defeat. Rita circulated and chatted with many people she hadn't seen for a long while and was comforted by the fact that there had been such a large attendance. Hovering in the background, Jim kept an eye on Rita, admiring the stoic approach she had taken.

"Any thoughts on what you might do?" Elsie asked as they walked back to Lucinda's, knowing that Rita preferred the direct approach.

"I will have to go to Hull at some point and sort out Ted's wardrobe and one or two other bits that will need my attention. Jenny will keep things ticking over as far as the show goes, so I think I will make the journey sooner rather than later. Besides, I want to be around to ensure that the transfer to Blackpool goes smoothly. I've asked Tommy to become part of the line-up, though I'm still unsure about the Olanzos, they still haven't confirmed whether they are coming or not. "

"Do you ever stop working in that head of yours? You really need to come to terms with Ted's death Rita. Otherwise you will make yourself ill."

Rita motioned for Elsie to sit down on a bench beside her. "I know what you are saying Elsie and I really am grateful for your concern. I have accepted my loss; Ted and I had often discussed what would happen if one of us went before the other. Once I have cleared the house of things I intend to sell it. The house is too big for me alone and it deserves to have a family living in it. If Ted was sitting here now and I had been the one who had died, he would say the same."

"You really do have all of this worked out don't you?"

"Ted and I discussed a lot of things during our time together and this is what we had both decided a long time ago. Of course I will miss the old beggar, and I expect there will be times when I will shed one or two tears when I'm alone, but I am a doer Elsie and it won't do me any good to sit around moping."

* * *

Jim opened the door and was surprised to see Dave. "Hello Dave, what brings you here at this time of the day? You have a show going up in an hour."

Dave followed Jim into the lounge. "I've wanted to have a chat with you Jim, but the time has never seemed right. I was coming over this morning but then I remembered you would probably be going to the funeral."

"What's on your mind, I can tell something is eating you up?"

"Dan and I are going to move up North to be nearer his family. We've been talking about it for some time and Josie and Madge have been looking at properties for us."

"Well that's great news," said Jim. "The change will do you good and, let's face it, Great Yarmouth is a bit small for both of you."

"Dan said you'd be okay about it. Sometimes I think he knows you better than I do after all these years."

"Have you told your bosses yet?"

"They have been one of the problems," said Dave. "I asked them for a few days off so that Dan and I could go and look at some houses in Blackpool and they refused me. So I told them where they could shove their job. After all the years I've worked for them, and the long hours I've put in, they count for nothing. Dan was none too pleased when I told him."

"You know your own mind," said Jim. "Guess I might have done the same thing."

"Dan has got time off from *Henry's* and we're driving up to Blackpool tomorrow morning early. We will be back by Sunday afternoon."

"What will you do about work until everything is settled? Finding a property and moving takes time, it won't happen overnight."

"I'll see if I can get some bar work, my cousin says I can work at the club till I move, but I'm not keen. It's bad enough working *Spangles* in the winter months. Now that's one place I won't be sorry to see the back of. Do you think you'll be going back Jim?"

Jim hesitated. "Between you and me Dave, I don't think I'm likely to be returning to any kind of work in the foreseeable future. Maybe next summer season, all being well. I've been told I need to rest and for once in my life I'm going to listen to the professionals." He noted the worried look on his friend's face and continued. "But it's not all doom and gloom, I'm going to be just fine. I've had a thought. You know I told you that the show at the *Sands* is going to play Blackpool from the end of September, why don't I put in a word for you with Don and Rita? I know Roger isn't keen on the idea of working up North. In fact, by the reports I've been getting he doesn't seem to like working at all. Even if you are in digs, a couple of months working at Blackpool's North Pier would put you in good stead for future work."

* * *

Rita drove to Hull the following morning. She hesitated as she put the key in the lock of the house, took a deep breath and went in. As usual, she found a pile of mail on the hall table that her neighbour had put there. If there had been anything important, it would have been sent on to her; Rita's arrangements with Sadie had been working well for some years. She had alerted Sadie she was coming back and there was milk, bread and a few groceries meaning she wouldn't have to go out to the shops.

Over the following couple of days Rita sorted through Ted's stage outfits and put aside six jackets that she thought Tommy would like, the rest would go to jumble. Sadie came in and gave her a hand as she sorted through her own wardrobe. There were dresses and outfits that she would never wear again and she gave her neighbour, who was roughly the same size, first refusal. Sadie, a pillar of the local church, was certain they would do well to swell the church funds at the next church hall jumble sale.

Not once during the two days did Rita allow herself any kind of sentiment, even as she sorted through albums of photographs in quiet moments in the evening. She was reminded of happier days and in her heart she knew that was how Ted would have liked it.

* * *

In Preston, Dan and Dave had been welcomed back and Josie and Madge had taken some holiday so that they could help the boys in their property search. Dave telephoned Marie Jenner and arranged that he and Dan visit her and Graham one evening. Marie was delighted that her friend would be moving up North and when Graham met them both for the first time, he was of the same opinion. Naturally Dan's parents, John and Mary, were disappointed that the boys were looking at properties in Blackpool, but understood the reasons why. Dan's sister Kate was quite excited that her brother wasn't going to be too far away and had already made her mind up to visit Blackpool more often when they were settled.

Dan was particularly happy and surprised when his brother Gary walked in to the kitchen; they hadn't seen each other for some time.

Gary hugged Dan and held out his hand to greet Dave. "So you are my new brother?" he said, with a broad grin on his face, his tall frame towering over everyone else. "Welcome to the family. We must have a couple of jars later."

"Not before you have all had something to eat," said Mary Forrester. "Don't you go overdoing it on your first few days home my boy or you'll be giving Dave the wrong impression."

Gary laughed and gave his mother a hug. "It's great to be home Mum." And Mary looked around at the assembled company and was once again reminded of how lucky she was to have been blessed with such a lovely family.

Monday 3rd August

Audrey parked her car and walked across the road to the *Storm House Café*, where she was meeting Rita for lunch. She found Rita upstairs at a table near the window looking out across the harbour.

"This was Ted's favourite view," said Rita, turning to face her guest. "He loved coming here."

Audrey sat herself down. "It is charming," she said, trying to sound positive. It really wasn't her kind of eatery, but it took all sorts. "I was sorry to hear about Ted, how are you coping?"

"Quite well, thank you," Rita replied. "But that isn't what we need to discuss. I understand Elsie has been in touch with you and filled you in on the Bouremes. I have also heard that their new artiste, who we know is Lorna Bright masquerading as some kind of French Torch Singer, with the emphasis on the torch, is not lighting many lamps."

"My, my, you are sharp today," said Audrey, noting Rita's tone. "Rueben was most helpful, he put a few feelers out but, of course, we are no further forward. It would seem that Sasha Boureme is quite elusive, no one knows, or will say, how to get hold of him."

"Has anyone approached Lorna and spoken to her?"

"Rueben's friend attended the club one evening, he said the place was virtually empty. What audience there was seemed totally disinterested in Lorna's performance. He tried to meet Lorna but was told that she didn't give interviews and left immediately after her show."

Rita thought for a moment. "I think I will have to meet with Lorna myself. Jenny has been making further enquiries while I've been away, she has contacts in France. I also think we need to tell Derinda what is going on."

Audrey wasn't so sure. "Perhaps we should wait until you have more to go on, I don't want Derinda upset. There have been one or two rumblings from the clubs in Norwich and Lowestoft, she hasn't been turning up for some of her performances and the band has been performing on their own when a stand-in hasn't been available. And she gave up her bookings in Ipswich without telling me first. Derinda seems to be all over the place and I'm getting a lot of flak because of it. If this carries on she will be losing her engagements here as well."

"Derinda is tired," said Rita, recalling her own experiences when she was treading the boards. "The *Sands* show is full-on and twice a night can take it out of the best of us. Performing thrice nightly is not a good idea and one that I admit I am not totally happy about."

"But she needs the money," said Audrey, coming in on the defence, "and before you say anything, it isn't all to do with my commission. Derinda agreed to do this; I didn't force her hand. The London season has always been a regular booking. There is more to this than meets the eye."

The arrival of a waitress temporarily brought the discussion to a halt while they both ordered. Rita removed her glasses and looked firmly at Audrey. "And I will get to the bottom of it," she said, "make no mistake about that."

* * *

When Lucinda went in to Mrs Jary's grocery store, Muriel and Freda were stocking up on a few items. Freda nudged Muriel when she saw Lucinda.

"Good afternoon Lucinda," said Freda. "I was sorry to hear about Ted Ricer, poor man, and dying in your very home. It must have been very upsetting for you."

Lucinda had been keeping her feelings in check, but in private moments she had wept for the man she had regarded as a friend and whom she had secretly loved dearly. She nodded at Freda and asked Mrs Jary for a half of best ham and a pound of cheddar.

"I expect Mrs Ricer is beside herself," Freda continued, letting her tongue run away with her. "I do hope it was nothing he'd eaten." Muriel gave Freda an ugly look; it was just like her to say the wrong thing.

Lucinda paid for her purchases and turned to face Freda. "Ted Ricer died from a heart attack, and for your further information he and his wife Rita have been very happy staying with me. I am sure that she would not want to hear any kind of gossip concerning her late husband so I will thank you to keep a civil tongue in your head Freda Boggis. Instead of standing around spouting about things that you know nothing about, I suggest that you put your own house in order because if what I hear is true, half of your home leaves with your guests. If you had half the brains you were born with, you might be considered dangerous." Lucinda smiled sweetly at Muriel, picked up her ham and cheese, thanked Mrs Jary and left the shop.

* * *

That evening Rita walked in to the theatre as usual and headed for the dressing room of Petra and Mario Olanzo. Petra opened the door and invited her in. Mario was quietly reading what looked to Rita like an old issue of *The Birmingham Mail*.

"I will come straight to the point," said Rita, accepting the offer of a chair. "I need to know whether you have made up your mind about joining us all in Blackpool. And I won't leave this dressing room until I have an answer. I have a show to organise and programmes and posters will need to be printed."

Petra, who had never seen the strong business side of Rita before, was taken aback. "Mario and I are still pondering what to do. We haven't had confirmation from Australia yet."

"I am sorry but that is not my problem," said Rita. "You are either in or out, now what is it to be?"

Mario put down his paper, looked at his wife and in a broad Brummie accent, which made his wife wince, said, "Well, what are we going to do Pam, shall we go to Blackpool? I don't really fancy Australia."

Rita did her best to keep a straight face. She was amazed by the fact that it was the first time she had heard Mario speak.

Totally unprepared for her husband's outburst, Petra blushed as she replied, also in a Brummie accent, "We will be coming to Blackpool Rita, I'm sorry to have messed you about."

Rita stood up. "Well I'm glad that's sorted. I will have the contracts drawn up. Thank you both." She left the room and smiled to herself as she heard Petra screaming in Italian at her husband. The crashing of several plates followed and she guessed they weren't being aimed at the floor.

Derinda was just coming out of her dressing room and heading towards Ricky's. She waved to Rita and knocked on the door and, without waiting to be invited, went in. Ricky turned on his chair in horror clutching his head.

"Sorry Ricky, I should have waited. Are you okay?"

Ricky let his hands slip and revealed his bald head. "Oh what the hell, I'm among friends," he said. "I'm bald Derinda and that little bugger Bingo has made off with one of my wigs again."

Derinda, who had seen it all before and probably worse, didn't bat an eyelid. "Big deal, so you haven't got a hair on your head. I have to say though, Ricks, that's a great wig you wear, I never detected it. You must let me know where you have them made."

Just then there was a knock at the door. Ricky quickly covered his head with a towel and Derinda answered it. There with Ricky's wig in her hand stood Mona. "I got this off your little dog Mr Drew. I am not supposed to be working tonight but one of the usherettes is sick. He was running up and down the theatre aisle he was, but I caught him quick enough, despite my leg," which she touched with a grimace of pain.

Derinda took the wig from Mona and smiled. "Many thanks Mrs Buckle. I've been hunting high and low for that, Bingo must have taken it from my room."

"Glad to be of service," said Mona. "And by the way Mr Drew, your dog has just cocked his leg on me, he needs training. These stockings were clean on this morning. I shall expect to be reconstituted."

When the door was closed, Ricky and Derinda burst out laughing. "Thanks for covering for me hen," said Ricky, giving Derinda a hug.

Derinda smiled back. "That's what friends are for," she said and hugged him again. "Besides, we don't want the whole world to know your secret, least of all Mona Buckle."

* * *

Rita called in on Jonny Adams, who she knew had been upset by Ted's sudden death. She found him at his dressing room table, looking sad and lost. "Hello me old lover," she said, pulling up a chair and sitting down beside him. "My Ted thought you were a very talented young magician and he wouldn't want you to be unhappy. When I was looking through his things back at the digs, I found this package addressed to you. Now if I know my Ted, it's something he was planning to give you when the company breaks up at the end of the season." She put the package down in front of Jonny. "Go on me old lover, open it, see what Ted bought you."

Jonny looked up at Rita, his eyes red from crying and he fumbled with the wrapping. It was a book of magic tricks with an inscription on the inside cover: *To Jonny wishing you good luck for the future, your pal Ted*. "I told Ted about this book, I had seen it in that book shop in town, but when I saved up enough to buy it, it had gone." He said all of this with no trace of a stutter.

Rita squeezed his hand. "Ted wanted you to have it. Over the years he has worked with many magic acts and he said that yours was one of the best he had seen in a long time. Dry your eyes me old lover. and when you go out there tonight, do this one for old Ted." She gave Jonny a hug and left him with his thoughts.

* * *

With Jenny at her side, Rita watched the first house from the back of the theatre. The show moved along at a cracking pace and she noted that Jonny seemed to have a spring in his step. When he reached the end of his act and took his bows, he took hold of the microphone. Maurice looked up from the pit and motioned for the orchestra to cut the play-off music.

"Ladies and gentlemen, thank you. I wanted you all to know that I am dedicating my performance to someone who helped me with my act. He was, and will be remembered as, one of best comedians ever, Mr Ted Ricer."

And as the audience acknowledged with applause, a feeling of pride swept over Rita.

* * *

Going backstage between the shows, Rita suddenly stopped in her tracks; going in to one of the dressing rooms was what looked to her like Ted.

"Rita are you okay?" asked Jenny, coming alongside her "You look as if you've seen a ghost."

"I'm sure I just saw old Ted going in to that dressing room, I must be tired, my mind is playing tricks."

Jenny took Rita by the arm. "It was Tommy you saw. From the back he does look a bit like Ted. He's wearing one of the jackets you gave him. Come on, I think you should call it a night. I can take care of things here. You get off home and have some rest; I'll get one of the backstage boys to walk with you."

Tuesday 4th August

Dave and Dan were taking advantage of waking early and walked along the deserted seafront drinking in the sea air. The sun was beginning to show signs of life as its rays flickered like dancing lights on the calm sea. This was the best time of the day and they both agreed that it was something they should do more often. Their thoughts turned to their proposed move to Blackpool and whether any of the properties they had seen were what they were looking for. The fact was, neither of them could agree exactly what it was they were looking for.

Dave thought a flat would suit them both, but Dan was more inclined to think that a house with a garden would be ideal. Some of the flats they had looked at were either above shops or within houses that had been made over to flats. The few they had managed to see were not appealing. One of the houses had proved more amenable.

Marie Jenner and her boyfriend Graham had been trying to convince the boys that they should consider looking at properties in Lytham. It was only a short distance from Blackpool where they expected to find work and away from the noises and smells of what was a busy seaside town. And as they both drove, transport would not be a problem. It was something that since returning to Great Yarmouth they were seriously considering and both were in agreement that they should return and take another look at what they could afford.

They walked as far as the Pleasure Beach and then Dave suggested that, instead of going back to the flat to cook breakfast, they ate at one of the cafés en route.

As they headed away from Marine Parade, a lone figure in the distance was also taking in the sea air and clearing her cluttered mind. Rita walked slowly along and watched as the gulls swooped above. One or two sparrows were hopping around in the hope of finding a few crumbs or an early worm in one of the many flowered beds that adorned the seafront. The sound of a dog barking in the distance drew her attention for a moment and if she wasn't mistaken that was Bingo with his master Ricky following on behind. Rita had often thought of having a dog, but Ted had been less keen on the idea. She thought that maybe in the days ahead she might consider getting herself one, after all there was nothing to stop her now. Her mind turned to the house in Hull and how she could best go about selling it. There were still a few more things that needed sorting and some of the furniture could go to an auction. If she was going to move, then she wanted to make a completely fresh start. There seemed little point moving the old to the new. Besides, she fathomed she would always have a few treasured things of Ted's, the photographs and, above all, the memories.

* * *

Sitting on the pier, Jim was looking out to sea. He loved this time of the morning and wished he had had the energy to come out more often to enjoy it. Things were changing, his best mate Dave was off up North any time soon, Roger had taken his place at the theatre and the uncertainty of whether he was truly over his ordeal was in the balance. He had continued to sleep downstairs at the house and had no desire to return to the bedroom that he and Karen had shared together. He found this thought alien to him, but inside he felt that now was the time to let go of the past and to try to make the most of the future. The house had not changed since Karen died and everywhere was a constant reminder of what had gone before. Maybe he should consider selling the house and moving to something more manageable, a bungalow perhaps, there were some nice ones in Caister. If anything happened to him everything would be left to his daughter, Debbie. There were her feelings to be taken into consideration, she may not want her father to sell up, and perhaps she and Peter would want to take the house on. He got up and began to walk slowly back to the pier entrance lost in thought and hoping that Karen would have understood the dilemma he was facing.

Maud Bennett was also taking advantage of an early morning walk. As she sauntered along Regent Road, she saw Jim walking towards her. Now, what was he doing out at this hour of the morning, she wondered to herself. Perhaps she could persuade him to join her for breakfast somewhere. It was a long time since she and Jim had a chat, and a morning free of her sister Enid's constant babble over tea and toast would do her a power of good.

Jim welcomed the distraction and the two settled themselves down in one of the cafés just off Regent Road. It was a well-known haunt for delivery drivers and although quite busy they managed to find a table. The two chatted about this and that and moved on to the more serious matters. Maud listened as Jim told her about the thoughts he had had, interjecting when she thought she should. Maud could see that her friend was at a crossroads in his life and he needed her advice. Casting aside her own cares, she went through each of Jim's ideas with a fine-tooth comb, ordering another pot of tea and some toast. It saddened her to learn that her friend might never be well enough to return to work full-time and the work he might do would be limited. Her heart went out to him and she did her best to conceal the worry and concern churning up inside her. It was unfortunate that Dave's move was definitely on the cards as he had often been the one Jim would turn to. Jim didn't need to see how upset she felt, what he needed was the support of someone strong and Maud intended to be that person.

* * *

When Rita returned to the guest house she found Elsie already in place at their table by the window. A couple of other guests were just leaving the dining room and a couple followed Rita in. She smiled at Elsie and sat down. "That walk did me a power of good," she said, dropping her bag under the table. "I could eat a horse."

"A walk can do that," said Elsie, pleased to see that Rita had a bit of colour in her cheeks. "Have you made any decisions, any plans, other than those we talked about the other day?"

"Oh loads," said Rita, tapping the side of her head. "All in here, I just need to put them in to some kind of order and act on them. One thing I have definitely decided on is I am going to sell the house in Hull and look for somewhere round these parts. Ted and I always enjoyed coming to Norfolk and the air agrees with me. I did think I might go back to the cabaret circuit. Which reminds me, I have an engagement to fulfil at Oulton Broad tonight. I've cancelled the others I had lined up, but the one in Oulton is a hangover from last year. I promised to appear at their fund-raising night for disabled children and I can't let them down. Just as well I remembered to bring a couple of frocks from home and some sheet music. If you fancy coming with me Elsie you'd be most welcome. Jenny is going to take care of the *Sands* again for me."

Elsie studied Rita and could see a spark that had been absent since Ted's illness. "You've taken to this directing lark like a duck to water, I think Don would be more than happy to put some more work your way if you were interested."

Lucinda interrupted with a pot of tea and some toast and took Rita and Elsie's order for a fried breakfast. Lucinda was pleased to see that Rita had got her appetite back and she had got some kidneys in special, she knew Rita was partial to them.

"Thank you, it's something worth considering," said Rita, stirring the tea and putting milk in the cups. "I don't like to be idle, and while I have a bit put by and with the sale of the house I could afford to live quite comfortably, that isn't my style, I like to be busy. What about you Elsie, when are you thinking of going up to London? I bet old Don is missing having you around the office."

"I'm pleased you mentioned that," said Elsie. "I was thinking of heading back the day after tomorrow but, of course, if you want me to stay on I will. Don can get a temp in to help him."

"I was thinking of going back to London, I think I need to pay Lorna Bright a surprise visit. I must get to the bottom of this Derinda saga. Audrey is of no use and I don't fancy accompanying her," Rita replied, pouring the tea. "What say you we travel up together? I would drive, but I would be happier on a train. When I went over to Hull, it was all I could do to remember where the gear stick was located; my mind was all over the place."

"That's sounds like a great plan Rita. I'll go over to Vauxhall station this morning and book us some tickets and leave you to get on with your plans. Any idea what day you'll be coming back?"

"I shall only be a couple of days; I don't want to lean on Jenny too much. She's been a brick doing what she has done so far. Bless her, she even cancelled a trip to the Isle of Wight; I found that out from Jack the other evening, she never said anything to me. I'll book myself in to the *Gardens* where I was before, it's very central for everything. Then, once I've sorted out that little problem, I shall set to and try and get Hull in motion before heading off to Blackpool. My neighbour will help me out. If I get a quick sale I may have to stay on here until I can find a little place of my own. Exciting isn't it, one door closes and another one opens? Now, where is that breakfast I'm starving to death."

* * *

Elsie wasn't the only familiar face in the audience at *The George Borrow* that evening; Lucinda had taken a taxi and met an old friend of hers from school who supported the charity that Rita was performing for free of charge. Rita did two sets, accompanied by a local pianist whom she had worked with before. Rita had chosen her repertoire carefully and her final number, *Hello Young Lovers* which she dedicated to her late husband, had Lucinda fighting back the tears. And Elsie, who did not consider herself to be a sentimental person, felt a lump in her throat. The evening was a great success and raised over five hundred pounds.

Someone else had watched the performance from the bar area with interest. He had seen Rita perform as Moira Clarence once before and then, like now, was too shy to go and introduce himself. He knew that he must do so sometime but not, he decided, tonight.

Thursday 6ᵗʰ August

Rita presented herself at the door of the *Mayfair Club*, taking money from her purse.

"You won't need to pay madam," said the young man at the desk, "it's free this evening."

"I am here to see Laure Dupree perform," said Rita, putting her purse back in her shoulder bag. "Isn't she appearing tonight?"

The young man smiled. "You will find Miss Dupree at the bar." He pointed to the poster behind him on the wall. "She gives her farewell performance on Saturday."

"I heard she was doing rather well," said Rita, "the new discovery from France."

"I am afraid our paying membership don't agree."

Rita walked into the club and found it to be even less busy than it had been when she had visited it with Elsie. She spotted Lorna perched on a stool at the bar. The barman had just given her a drink, which Lorna knocked back. Rita recalled the stories and remembered witnessing this behaviour before. It was true what they said, a leopard never changed its spots. She walked over and sat beside Lorna.

"Hello Lorna, do you remember me?"

Lorna turned and faced Rita. "You are Rita or Moira someone, that comedian's wife. What brings you in here? If you are looking for my sister June, I haven't a clue where she is. Just like the rest of them she sodded off and left me. Just like the bastard who promised me everything if I played his clubs, he wants rid now too. It's all down to that bitch, he still loves her."

Rita ordered herself a gin and tonic. "You had better put vodka in there for my friend," she said. "Is there somewhere private we can talk Lorna? I may be able to help you and you may be able to help me."

Lorna picked up her replenished glass and motioned for Rita to follow her through a side door and into her dressing room. She pulled out a chair and Rita sat down, shocked by the state the room was in. There were empty vodka bottles, costumes half-hanging from a dress rail, makeup strewn across the mirrored table and all matter of clutter on the floor. Rita listened as Lorna told her about how June had set her up with a singing coach in France in the hope of securing work for her at some stage. Lorna's one-time boyfriend, Robin, had flown the nest when he had fallen in with some girl working at a café he frequented and the two had headed back to England. When June had parted with Wally, she had gone travelling, leaving Lorna in the hands of her singing teacher who in turn had introduced her to Sasha Boureme, who seemed like the answer to her prayers.

"You said he was still in love with 'the bitch', I take it you mean that he has a wife?"

Lorna drained her glass. "I'll say he has a bloody, former, wife. But there is also some kid who is disabled. You probably know his ex-wife, Derinda Daniels. She stood in for me last year at that *Golden Sands* place."

Rita closed her eyes and tried to take it all in. She had thought that the ghosts of what had happened last year had long since been buried, but here they all were again. Now the jigsaw was beginning to make sense. Sasha had used Lorna to prevent his ex-wife Derinda appearing in London venues, but the plan had backfired. It must have been June Ashby that Derinda spotted at *The Talk of Norwich* that evening. She had probably been sounding out the management about getting Lorna some work. Rita couldn't understand why Audrey hadn't known about Sasha. Now it appeared there was a child involved. Things rarely remained a secret for long in this business.

She looked at the wrecked person beside her and put out her hand. This was one problem she really couldn't solve, but she could alert the clinic where Lorna was last treated in the hope they would take her back in for her own safety. She would then go back to Great Yarmouth and talk to Derinda about what she had found out. She helped Lorna into the little black dress she had seen her perform in before and hoped that Lorna would be sober enough to sing for her supper. She found a kettle and a jar of coffee, made a strong black one and told Lorna to drink it. The girl didn't put up a fight and did as she was told. Rita then made her another one and then another.

Lorna walked on to the cabaret floor as the spotlight hit her and began to sing. The small audience appeared not to be interested, but she carried on as the accordion player continued with the set. With no applause, other than from the bar staff and Rita, who was standing backstage, she took a bow and walked back to where Rita was waiting. Rita had never witnessed such a heartbreaking performance. The girl was obviously singing about the experiences she was having in this crazy world they called show business. Maybe, like Edith Piaf before her, Lorna had to experience the pain of life and loves to truly surrender it through her singing.

The following day, and with help from Elsie and a few phone calls, Lorna was readmitted to a clinic. At the flat where Lorna had been staying there were traces of a man's presence. In a wardrobe Rita and Elsie found clothes and costumes that did not belong to Lorna. It was obvious that Sasha had been using Derinda's flat. Elsie found medication in the bathroom cabinet belonging to Lorna and it became apparent that Lorna was far from over her health problems.

Lorna thought that Sasha was probably back in France. Rita left word with the *Mayfair Club* secretary who answered the telephone that Miss Dupree would not be well enough to fulfil her engagement and all further enquires were to be made via her solicitor, and she gave the name and contact number.

Don wiped his brow when Rita told him the sorry tale and Elsie looked at Rita with renewed admiration. It didn't seem to matter what the world threw at her, Rita always rose above it all and dealt with it. No wonder Ted had always admired his wife.

Rita decided she would go back to Great Yarmouth by the late train that evening so that she could speak with Derinda the following day. She felt that this was Derinda's business and however she wished to proceed with the matter was entirely in her own hands. Lorna was out of harm's way, that was the main thing, and Rita had her own life to sort out. Don and Elsie drove Rita to Liverpool Street station and waved her off. As she settled down in her seat, she drifted off in to a deep sleep and only awoke when the train reached Norwich, before pulling out on its final lap to Great Yarmouth Vauxhall.

Saturday 8ᵗʰ August

Rita was up and about early making plans. She waited until ten and dialled Derinda's home number. A sleepy-voiced Derinda answered and listened to what Rita had to say. "I can come over to Great Yarmouth if that makes things easier."

Rita thought for a minute. "I think it would be best if I came over to you. I have some business to do in Norwich and I would be killing two birds with one stone. As I explained, I want to go over the contract with you for Blackpool and some other things. I'd rather not do it at the theatre as I get too many interruptions."

When Rita arrived, Derinda showed her in to the lounge. "I hope you don't mind, but Ricky is here. He came to see me at *The Talk* last night and stayed over. He has just popped out to the shop to get some more milk and he should be back shortly."

Rita took the opportunity to tell Derinda as much as she could before Ricky returned.

Derinda sat down heavily on the armchair.

"I knew something was amiss. Nothing seemed to add up. I've been playing those clubs for years, they know me and above all they trust me. Sasha, and no doubt that bloody controlling mother of his, has been behind this, and to what end? There doesn't seem any sense to any of it, other than spite on her part. I knew she hated me, I didn't realise how much. What do they know about London clubs for goodness sake? If he was here right now I'd put a knife through him, so help me God."

Ricky walked in to the lounge at that moment, acknowledging Rita with a smile.

"You had better sit down Ricks," said Derinda, "and listen to what Rita has just told me. It's okay Rita, you can speak freely in front of Ricky I've told him everything."

Ricky listened and gripped his fists in anger. When Rita had finished he wrapped his arms around Derinda and gave her a big hug. "God hen, this is awful."

"Give over you sloppy thing," said Derinda, gently pushing him away. "I think we all need a cup of tea and when we've had that I'll fill you in on all the other details Rita. It will make *Coronation Street* look tame by comparison."

* * *

Phoning a friend in London who had a spare set of keys to her property in case of emergency, Derinda arranged for him to get the locks changed for her. It was going to cost her, but if she could get that done, it would be one less worry on her mind. The thought of involving the police at this stage wasn't one she wanted to entertain; she held on to the hope that by speaking to Sasha face to face she might be able to draw a line under everything. After listening to Ricky and Rita's thoughts on the matter, Derinda was no longer afraid to go to the papers with her story. Sasha's family would hate that, but Derinda had fire in her belly and no one was going to stop her now.

* * *

Rita drove back to Great Yarmouth confident that she had done what she had set out to do. Derinda's story hadn't been an easy one to listen to, especially with a disabled daughter being part of the equation. On reflection, Rita was certain that there were many such tales to be told across the country. She knew of unmarried mothers who had had their babies taken away from them and placed into children's homes for adoption. Many families had been driven apart because of the consequences. She hoped that Derinda's plight would have a happier ending, but that largely depended on Derinda and Sasha being able to come to an agreement away from the courts. Rita had been impressed by Derinda's level-headedness. Perhaps Ricky was the support she needed. It was also evident to Rita that Ricky was more than a little fond of Derinda, even if Derinda hadn't yet realised it herself. Life was certainly full of surprises and it wasn't over yet.

Chapter Eleven *Paying the Piper*

Wednesday 12th August

D ave leapt out of bed and hit the alarm button; he shook Dan and told him to get a wriggle on. They had an appointment with the bank manager to arrange a small mortgage and they had both fallen asleep again after resetting the clock. Dave and Dan had been out after hours the night before as Josie and Madge were in town for a few days and they had both had more than they should have to drink. The girls were staying at a small guest house and had promised to meet the boys near the town hall at ten-thirty. Then, following the appointment with the bank, they were all going to spend the day together and have some fun. The girl's favoured going to the Pleasure Beach and riding in an open landau along the parade, the boys wanted to take an evening trip on the Waterways. But they were all agreed on having a meal in the *Steak House* in Regent Road. And they had all vowed not to drink.

* * *

Rita was having lunch with Jim at the *Two Bears Hotel*, which was a short walk from where Jim lived in Southdown. The two friends were soon back on old ground and both said that they wished they had had more time to spend together. But life had taken them both on ways they hadn't bargained for. The talk naturally turned to how Rita was coping with the loss of Ted and Jim's recent health scare.

"I'm thinking of selling up and looking for a smaller place to live," said Jim, "though I haven't mentioned anything to Debs and Peter yet. I don't know how she will feel if I sell the family home."

"Maybe they might want to take it off your hands," said Rita. "It would mean you having them nearer to you."

Jim nodded. "I have thought about that, but it may not suit Peter, with his job being in Norwich. The house would go to Debs anyway if anything happened to me. But I feel I cannot go on living there. It's a family home and Karen and I were happy there, but that is in the past now and it's time I moved on."

"My feelings exactly," said Rita, "that's why I decided to sell the house in Hull. Ted and I used it as a base, but we were never at home long enough to call it home. Most of our lives we lived in digs. When I was sorting through some of the stuff we had amassed over the years. I found gowns from the old days that I would never wear again, let alone get in to again. Ted had loads of jackets, waistcoats and trousers for every conceivable occasion, including Jewish weddings and Masonic dinners. Don't let me mention the pairs of shoes, shirts, and all the paraphernalia that goes with them. I've given some of Ted's jackets to Tommy Trent and the rest of it is going to a local Am Dram."

"How is Tommy Trent measuring up?" asked Jim. "I keep meaning to come and catch his act. Bet he's not a patch on old Ted."

"Ted was the one that recommended him and I have to say that I had my doubts. He isn't the same as Ted, but he is nearly his equal. Tommy has a different style of delivery and the way he chats to the audience tells me he is used to playing the club scene. He gets on well with everyone, does what he is paid to do, and you won't find Tommy having a whisky like Ted used to. I am going to ask Don to put him on his books. I think he's an asset. Any night you want to come down and see the show let me know and I will join you."

When they were enjoying their coffee, Rita told Jim about Don's offer for her to direct some of his shows and Jim agreed it sounded like a great idea. She also mentioned that she was toying with the idea of setting herself up as a theatrical agent. After all, she knew what was expected and it might give her a new lease of life. But she didn't want to tread on anyone's toes, least of all Don and Elsie's who had been good to her and Ted over the years. The two friends agreed they both had a lot to think about and said their farewells.

* * *

Freda Boggis paid for her vegetables and headed along to the other end of the market to see what bed linen they had on offer. Two of the lovely bedspreads that Muriel had given her had been stolen. She wondered why she continued to take in paying guests when the ones she attracted seemed hell bent on robbing her in one way or another. As her neighbour Muriel had often remarked, she had a set of regular holidaymakers and she did not entertain walk-ins as Freda did. It dawned on Freda that maybe those that turned up on her doorstep were looking for a freebie they could get away with. She couldn't remember the last time someone had stayed a full week. Barry had been doing his bit to help, but it hadn't changed things. Now guests who paid up front for a one-night stay were taking things instead.

Freda looked over the wares that Willy Bragg had on offer at his stall and selected two sets of bed linen and one bedspread. She handed over the money and huffed and puffed her way across the market feeling far from happy. Maybe an evening at Bingo would cheer her up. So with that one small glimmer of hope in mind she soldiered on. The crowds of people heading toward Regent Road made the task of crossing the road a difficult one and she wished she had gone by a different route.

As she turned into her road, she saw a police car parked outside her house and feared the worse. Hurrying along as best she could she reached her front door and went inside. Dick was hoovering the lounge, much to her utter amazement, and there appeared to be no signs of any policeman. Dick switched off the Hoover and followed his wife in to the kitchen where she put down her shopping.

"Been a bit of a to-do next door," he said, feeling quite pleased that he was the one to have heard the news first. "Muriel and Barry have been burgled. That new colour television has gone, his brand new stereo and several other bits and some money. Seems it happened when they were both out this morning. No forced entry from what I've heard, so it had to be someone who was staying there."

Freda switched on the kettle. "Are you sure you've got that right Dick Boggis? Muriel always has the same visitors every year. She's always telling me about them. In fact, she was going on about some people she had in last week from Coventry, and they have been back the same week every year for the last ten."

Dick puffed out his chest. "Well not this time. Barry was telling me out the back earlier that a couple came to the door last night looking for a room and Muriel took them in. You had the *No Vacancies* sign in the window, otherwise she would have sent them here."

Freda smiled to herself. "So I did, I forgot to take it down. Well fancy that, our Muriel being burgled. I bet that has knocked the smile off her face. I think we'll treat ourselves to steak and onions tonight Dick Boggis and then you can take me down the *Legion* for a couple of drinks."

Dick looked at his wife with a quizzical eye but, with the promise of a night out at the *Legion*, thought better of making any comment.

* * *

Mona Buckle worked her way across the theatre aisle with her bucket and mop. Never had she come across such rubbish as people left behind. It was bad enough clearing up the ice cream cartons, but the sweet wrappers and discarded chewing gum were something else. She was out of *Brasso* again and no alerting that Roger Norris to the fact produced any. Now, if that nice Mr Donnell had been here it would have all been sorted. She cursed under her breath as her foot hit one of the iron seat legs. This cleaning lark was hard work and a theatre this size needed more than one cleaner, no wonder that Lilly Brockett had always looked so slim. Looking down at her own ample figure she wondered if, by the end of the season, she would be down a dress size or two. Picking up her bucket and mop Mona headed for her cleaning cupboard. She looked at her watch, three-thirty, now it must be time to stop for a cup of tea and the cream slices she had purchased on her way in. Now, if that nice Mr Donnell was still here, he would have made the tea for her. Resigning herself to her fate she went off to boil a kettle.

* * *

Lucinda Haines wiped her hands on her apron and went to answer the door. She wasn't expecting any arrivals and the gas man had called the day before to read the meter. She opened the door and came face to face with a man in his forties and almost died of shock. He was clean-shaven, smartly dressed and had neatly combed dark hair, and a face that she would have recognised anywhere. She swallowed hard and did her best to smile. "Hello, how can I help you? I am afraid I am fully booked this week if it was a room you were looking for."

The man smiled. "Oh no, I'm not looking for rooms, I was hoping I might be able to speak to Mrs Ricer if she was in please. The lady at the theatre said I might find her here."

Lucinda asked the man to step into the lounge and take a seat and she headed up to the top floor as fast as her shaking legs would allow.

"Rita," she said, when the door opened, "there's a man downstairs asking to see you, says his name is Ronald."

"Whatever is the matter Lucinda?" said Rita. "You look as if you've seen a ghost."

"He's back," said Lucinda, trembling, "you'll see."

Rita hurried down the stairs and in to the lounge closely followed by one very shaken-up Lucinda.

* * *

Riding along in the carriage, Josie and Madge were lapping up the good weather. Dave and Dan, both wearing kiss me-quick hats and sunglasses, were enjoying watching the world go by. Then, after paying for their trip, the four headed in to the Pleasure Beach and made headway for the carousel.

"Mum always rides this side-saddle," said Dan, climbing on to his steed. "Dad says she has something of the Queen about her."

The girls laughed.

"She's not the only one, sunshine. My mum wouldn't dare get on one of these," said Madge, pulling on the reins. "She fell off a ride as a kid, scarred her for life that did."

The carousel began to turn and the organ music continued to play. The gold statue of a lady in a glass case at the centre of the ride beat out the music on a bell and the sheet music of the organ could be seen running through the mechanism.

The ghost train was next on their list and they screamed as the train rammed its way through black swing doors into darkened caverns with wailing sounds.

Dan then paired off with Madge in one dodgem car as Dave and Josie rode another. Bumping into each other on the circuit they laughed and whooped like young kids, thoroughly enjoying themselves. Buying some tickets from a stall, Madge won a giant teddy bear, Dan and Dave played the shooting range, while Josie failed to knock down one single stack of tins for the chance of winning a yoyo.

With the large teddy bear squashed between them, Josie and Madge enjoyed the roller coaster while the boys went on the gentler tunnel of love ride on the large ducks that transported them through various scenes beneath the rocking roller coaster. Ice creams apiece, they walked happily along Marine Parade enjoying the vibrant atmosphere with all the other holidaymakers. It was a perfect day for all of them and made all the better knowing the boys had got a mortgage to buy a property in Blackpool.

* * *

Rita held out her hand. "Hello Ronald, I'm Rita Ricer. Lucinda, I would like you to meet Ted's son, Ronald." Lucinda's mouth fell open in amazement. "Perhaps a pot of tea and some biscuits please," Rita continued, "Ronald and I have a lot to talk about."

"How did you know who I was," asked Ronald, sitting down. "We have never met before."

"You have the look of your father for one thing," said Rita, "and your dad and I didn't have many secrets between us. I tried to get in touch with you when Ted passed away but the contact details I found in Ted's book were very old. I'm sorry we have to meet in such sad circumstances."

"I heard it on the radio, they were talking about seaside entertainment," said Ronald. "My wife said I should come. I came to the funeral, but I kept in the background. I didn't know how best to go about things. Mum died some years ago, but I know she did write to my dad from time to time to let him know how I was getting on, it was something she promised him she would do. I hope it didn't cause any problems. " He played nervously with his wristwatch and looked down at the carpet. "I don't want you to think that I came here with any ulterior motive. I just wanted to meet you to say how sorry I was that he had died and to give you this." He put his hand in his pocket and took out a small box and handed it to Rita. "It's a locket that mum wore, I thought you should have it now."

Rita opened the box and held the gold chain; the locket contained a photograph of a very young Ted. She looked at it quietly for some time and was only interrupted by Lucinda bringing in a tea tray. "It's lovely," she said, trying to hold back the tears she could feel welling up. "Are you sure you wouldn't like to keep it, you cannot have many photographs of your father?"

Ronald shook his head. "I would like you to have it. I have loads of photos of dad from all the press cuttings and the programmes I've accumulated over the years. I saw dad perform lots of time on stage. It was nice to see how much the audiences loved him, he was very funny. I was too late to see him in this show."

"Why didn't you make yourself known to him?" said Rita. "He would have been so pleased to see you."

"I felt it was wrong," said Ronald. "Besides, he had a new life and I had read that he didn't have children and I thought I might mess things up for him and you if I appeared unannounced. Mum said I should say hello to him, but Janice, my wife, agreed with me. When mum was unwell, I made a promise to come and see him, but I was too late. I should have been here in June, but had to change my holiday plans."

"I am so sorry," said Rita, her heart going out to the man before her. "You would have liked your father. He was great fun to be around and something of a character."

They talked some more over tea and biscuits and then Ronald made a move to take his leave.

"Please give me an address or telephone number where you can be contacted," said Rita. "If you would like any kind of mementos I'm sure there is something back at the house I can find for you. There's a lovely engraved silver cigarette lighter given to him on the anniversary of his thirty years in the business. Wait here, I have it upstairs."

Rita returned and handed Ronald the lighter; he looked at it with a grateful smile. "This is great Mrs Ricer, thank you very much; I shall take great care of it." He handed her a piece of paper with his details on.

"I expect you will be hearing from Ted's solicitors soon. I know he left something for you in his will. If there is anything you need, or you just want to talk about your dad some more, please don't be shy, you can always come to me." She handed him a business card. "If you can't get me on this number, try the one I've written on the back, they will know where to find me."

"You've been very kind Mrs Ricer," said Ronald. "I'm very pleased I worked up enough courage to come and see you."

Rita hugged him. "Thank you for coming to see me. It's good to finally put a name to a face and I'd have known yours anywhere, you are very much like him," she said. "And it's Rita."

"Goodbye Rita and thank you again," he said and, as she watched him from the doorway walking down the pathway, she felt a sense of happiness mixed with a great sadness come over her.

* * *

Maud dabbed some perfume behind her ears and turned to speak to Enid who was sorting out some stock. "I've told you Enid, it's no good burying your head in the sand, it's going to happen. The government have been banging on about it for long enough. The new money comes in next year and we are all, like it or not, going to have to get used to it."

Enid stopped what she was doing and looked at her sister. "But it doesn't make any sense Maud. How can twelve pennies become five new pence? And what's this half-penny lark? We did away with ha'pennies a long time ago. When I went to school there were two hundred and forty pennies to a pound, now they are saying there is only going to be a hundred."

"Well that's to make it simpler to work out," said Maud, putting her light jacket on and checking her watch. "You are going to have to get your head around it Enid or you will be left behind. All the pricing will need to be changed; some places are displaying the old and the new together and have been for some time."

"I don't think it will catch on," said Enid, who was resistant to any kind of change. "I was talking to a couple of the women on the market the other day and they agreed with me. It won't catch on."

Maud heaved a big sigh. "Enid, I am telling you, no matter what you and anyone else thinks decimalisation is coming and if you don't believe me go and have a chat with that bloke at the post office who is always giving you the come on."

Enid blushed. "Oh don't be so stupid Maud, just because he carried my shopping basket that time doesn't mean he's sweet on me."

"Really?" said Maud, picking up her bag and heading for the door. "It wasn't him that sent you flowers last Valentine's then? I read the label Enid, he's very keen and, let's face it love, none of us are getting any younger and we have to take our pleasures where we can find them. Now, make a start on the pricing, I'll check it for you later."

* * *

Bob Scott welcomed Rita in to the office. "I'm glad you popped in, I have something I want to discuss with you. But you first."

Rita sat down and looked at Bob across the desk. "I'm concerned about Jim. I was with him earlier and he was telling me that he may not be able to return full-time. I wanted to ask you Bob, if the *Sands* have any plan in place to help him if and when he does want to come back. Roger is not doing a good job, everywhere you turn you are made aware of the fact that he isn't as organised or as easygoing as Jim. I don't want to speak ill of the man, but things are not being kept on top of. The boys backstage lack supervision and if we aren't careful there could be an accident."

Bob frowned. "I hear what you're saying Rita and I promise I will deal with it. With regard to Jim, the best I can do for him is offer him light duties, either at the stage door or helping out in the box office, until he gets back on his feet. I would like him to go back to his old job here, but I dare not take the risk. You know our Jim, he would be rolling up his sleeves and doing things that his doctor has advised him against."

Rita nodded. "I hope you didn't mind me asking. Now you said you wanted to talk to me about something."

"Ah yes," said Bob, with a big smile on his face. "I've been given some money to tart this place up a bit. It's beginning to look a bit tatty and the first place to be given some treatment at the end of summer will be the bar and dressing room areas. The bar is big business here as you know and the dressing rooms could do with a bit of a lift. As general manager I've been given free rein to do what I like, within reason, and I would like the bar to be renamed. How would you feel Rita if we were to rename the bar *Ted's Bar?*"

Rita was stunned and for a few moments, lost for words. "Can I ask you why?"

Bob sat back in his chair. "Ted has played this theatre a lot over the years and he has always been a stalwart. I gave old Don a call the other day and we were discussing him at some length. This theatre is a palace of variety and Ted has been one of the best comedians we have had play here. I thought that, as he died in the town he so clearly loved, the least we could do was honour him."

Not for the first time that day, Rita felt tears pricking her eyelids. "It's a lovely idea. Oh I wish I had known about this earlier, there is someone who would have liked to hear this news. Ted would be so pleased." She paused for a moment to compose herself. "I wonder if you might call it *Ted's Variety Bar?*"

Bob laughed. "Now that has a ring to it, it sums this place up beautifully. I'll go through the plans with you when they have been drawn up. In the meantime, I wonder if you could find some suitable photographs of Ted we could use to put on the walls. I'm also going to find some shots of other artistes, perhaps with a bit of history written about them. Oh yes and by the way, I wanted to show you these, it's some idea I've had about a brass plaque honouring Ted. I thought it might look nice in the theatre foyer, but I would like you to agree on the wording. Take it away and come back to me when you've decided."

"I don't know what to say," said Rita, looking at the pad. "It's most generous of you. Thank you Bob, I really am most grateful and I know my husband would be too."

Sunday 16*th* August

Sasha Boureme was not a happy man. He had flown back urgently from Paris to find that club members had been voting with their feet. The *Mayfair Club* had been without any kind of entertainment and the other three clubs were unhappy with the calibre of acts they had installed. None of the acts that Sasha had engaged were well known. There was a conjuror that seemed totally out of his depth, a singing duo who couldn't harmonise and a comedian who struggled to remember the tag lines to his jokes and was more than a little bit under the influence of alcohol. The *Mayfair Club* now found they were without a star attraction and the lame imitation for one had disappeared with only a solicitor's name and address as a contact.

Sasha put his head in his hands. He had never been responsible for running any kind of business and only had his mother's guidance on how things should be done. He was clearly out of his depth and he hoped that he could find some way of sorting things out before his mother made an appearance, as he feared she most surely would once word reached her. Sitting back in the leather chair in the *Mayfair Club's* manager's office he looked at the figures for the past few nights. The bar takings were very much down. His visits to the other clubs told the same story. The club manager was beside him fearing for his job and Sasha prayed that things would only get better. But they were just about to get a whole lot worse.

Monday 17^h August

Jim watched as the tide rolled and furled on to the sandy shore creating a frothy foam. The noise of the pebbles and shingle filled his head as they gently washed up and then retracted with the moving water. It had been something that had fascinated him since his childhood days, when with his friends he had run along the beach chasing the waves, throwing sticks and pebbles and getting his shoes wet in to the bargain. He could hear the voices of his old school chums clearly in his head. They were calling for him to join them as they ran into the sea whooping and laughing. And then that terrible moment when the cries of joy had turned to cries of horror as young Jimmy Davidson had lost his footing and disappeared beneath the waves, the current too strong for his tiny frame to fight against. There had been warnings about playing on or near the Gorleston breakwater, especially when the sea was rough and angry, but he and his friends were superhuman like the characters they read about in their weekly comics. He remembered watching helplessly as George and Paul had dived into the sea to try to rescue Jimmy; he had been frozen to the spot unable to move. George and Paul, who were both strong swimmers, kept diving and every time one of them emerged from the choppy waters Jim hoped that Jimmy would be there too. But Jimmy didn't surface that day, or the next. It was several days before he was washed up on the beach further down the coast and the memory of that awful day and his feeling of helplessness had haunted him.

Jim continued to gaze at the spot, where today the sun dazzled and created mirrors of dancing light on the calm and gentle waves. Up on the promenade, Dave was watching his best friend and he knew why he was there. Resisting the temptation to go and hug him, Dave turned on his heels and walked slowly away.

* * *

Maud called in at the gift shop and was pleased to see that Enid had been busy double-pricing everything. She put the *Matthes* bag containing the sausage roll and doughnut on the counter. "Something for your elevenses," she said, smiling at her sister. "I'm just off to the *Sands*. Barbara has a dental appointment this morning and I promised her I would be there in plenty of time."

Enid looked up from her task. "I still don't understand how this all works," she said, looking at the chart that Maud had given her. "How do you price one guinea for example?"

Maud sighed as only Maud could. "Enid, when have we sold anything in here in guineas? This is not *Palmers* you know. Now I'm off, see you later tonight, I'll bring some fish and chips in so don't worry about cooking anything."

When Maud reached the end of Regent Road, she could see crowds of people at the box office window and there were cameras and photographers. She hastened across the road, pushed her way through several people who seemed reluctant to move aside and by the skin of her teeth managed to gain entry to the box office where Barbara was telling people that she had no idea what they were talking about and to please go away. Maud picked up the telephone and dialled Bob Scott's office. "Hello Beverley, can you get Bob down here quickly please, we appear to have television cameras and reporters. They're causing a bit of a problem. Do you have any idea what's going on?"

Taking her *Daily Mirror* from her basket, it soon became apparent to Maud what was going on. Derinda Daniels was front page news: *Singing Star Reveals All*. Maud sighed, knowing she wouldn't get any knitting done that day.

* * *

Rita, who had woken late that morning, was reading the headlines when Lucinda came in to the dining room with a pot of coffee and some toast. Asking to use the telephone, Rita called Don Stevens' office and was answered by Elsie. "Have you seen this morning's papers?"

Elsie, who had read every morning paper she could lay her hands on, concurred.

"She has certainly left no detail out," Rita continued, "Of course, I had no idea Derinda was going to be quite so candid about things. I thought she was going to tackle that ex of hers and sort it out quietly. I bet Don is hopping mad."

"On the contrary Rita, Don hasn't stopped smiling since breakfast. He says it's all publicity for the show. He was all for coming down there, but I told him to keep out of it. This is for Derinda to sort out, though it may cause one or two problems at the theatre. Have you spoken to Bob Scott?"

"I'm going to head down there once I've got my head together. Not much I can do, but it would do to show solidarity. I think I will give Derinda a call first, that's of course if she's at home. If her agent has given out her address, it will be curtains."

* * *

The article had been cleverly written. Derinda had simply outlined that she was being blackmailed with photographs that were taken of her before she made a name for herself and this in turn was being used against her both on a professional and personal level. Her message to her blackmailer was 'publish and be dammed, the payments stop now'. Asked about her professional life, she admitted that her fame had cost her dearly. She spoke of her disabled daughter who she rarely got to see and who, until now, she had kept secret from her fans. Knowing that her daughter was well cared for helped her and she hoped that one day she may be able to put things right.

When asked to elaborate further, Derinda had refused to name either her daughter or the father, thus keeping the Boureme name out of the press. She wasn't fool enough to think that a little digging around by a keen journalist wouldn't uncover the missing details. But for now she had been more than happy to speak with Gill, a sympathetic reporter who was roughly the same age as her and seemed to understand the plight she was in.

* * *

At last Derinda's number wasn't engaged. "What on earth is going on?" said a very exasperated Audrey Audley down the telephone. "As your agent you might have given me some warning that this was likely to happen. I cannot believe what I am reading, you of all people. I couldn't get in to my office this morning, there were reporters everywhere wanting to ask questions. I am actually calling you from a friend's office. Have you any idea how this will reflect on the agency?"

Derinda laughed. "Look Audrey dear, I have had my mother, Concerned of Tunbridge Wells, on the phone giving me earache about how well this is going to go down at the WI, so I don't need you giving me grief."

There was a sharp intake of breath. "Derinda really, I am your agent, your friend, your confidante."

"Forgive me while I throw up," said Derinda, who was beginning to enjoy herself. "You may take ten per cent of everything I earn, but I have never, and get this, NEVER regarded you as a friend and confidante. As an agent you stink, most of the work that I have done over the years has been through contacts of my own; you have sat back on that fat arse of yours and creamed off the bounty. This is my business and it has nothing whatever to do with you and that bloody so-called theatrical agency of yours. I am fed up being controlled at every given turn. I have lived my life in fear that one day my past was going to come back and haunt me. Well, I decided to take a stand and tell the whole world that, as well as being a singing star, I too have had a life and not all of it has been rosy. And another thing, I shall be looking for a new agent Audrey dear, so put that in the spliffs you enjoy so much and smoke it."

Audrey trembled, where had Derinda heard about her dalliances in drugs? She had been very careful to keep that side of her life out of view. Someone had grassed her up, surely not Rueben? Feeling more paranoid than usual she groaned and replaced the receiver vowing never to trust anyone again. Grabbing her handbag and checking her watch, she hoped that *The George* would offer her sanctuary from the cruel world she found herself in.

* * *

Ricky handed Derinda a mug of coffee. "Well, you certainly gave it to her with both barrels," he said, making himself comfortable next to Bingo who was lying on the sofa. "Are you happy that you've done the right thing?"

Derinda nodded. "Oh yes Ricks I am. It's out in the open and I feel that I can tackle Sasha and his family now without the fear and worry that has hung over me for so long. I know I may never get my daughter back, and perhaps she really is best left in the world she knows. All I want is to be able to see her from time to time and for her to at least grow up knowing that her mother is and has always been there when she needed her." Bingo cocked his ears and looked up and gave a couple of woofs. "You see, even Bingo agrees with me."

Chapter Twelve *Every Picture Tells a Story*

S tella handed the paper to Dan. "Have you seen this? It's all about Derinda Daniels at the *Sands*. Poor love is being blackmailed over some shady photographs. I bet there is many a young woman who has fallen prey to underhand goings on and all in the name of art. It mentions something about there being a disabled daughter. Well that will get the tongues wagging, you know how some of them love a good gossip."

Dan looked at the article leisurely. "Well, she obviously wanted the world to know, or she wouldn't have told the press. I couldn't believe how many reporters and TV cameras were outside the *Sands* this morning. Are they all stupid enough to believe that Derinda Daniels is somewhere in the theatre?"

"They barricaded poor Maud and Barbara in the box office all morning. Those reporters have no shame," said Stella, wiping a couple of glasses. "Do you remember all that stuff about Christine Keeler and that bloke in the government? The reporters hounded those people; let's hope the same doesn't happen at the theatre or Maud will never get that bed jacket finished, a present for an elderly lady she knows in Caister. Do people still wear bed jackets?" She was distracted by the arrival of a group of young men and went to serve them.

Dan put the newspaper to one side and went to change a barrel. Bed jackets, it was another world.

* * *

In Mrs Jary's grocery the friendly chatter soon turned to the news in the paper and not the great guest house robbery, which was a relief to Muriel.

"That *Sands Theatre* always has something going on," said Muriel Evans, looking for her purse. "Last year we had all that trouble with that June Ashby and now here we go again. I mean to say, it must be having that Stevens bloke bringing his shady shows to the *Sands*, we never got that with Bernard Delfont."

Mrs Jary, never one to become involved in such matters, waited patiently to be paid.

Freda shrugged her shoulders. "I don't know I'm sure," she said, picking up two tins of butter beans and a box of *Oxo* cubes. "Those theatre folk live a different life to the likes of you and me. I'm surprised that Lucinda has them staying with her. That poor comedian Ted Ricer died there. It might have been something he'd eaten. They said in the papers that it was a heart attack, but I'm not so sure."

"I expect the doctor knew what he was talking about," said Muriel, finally retrieving a five pound note from her purse and handing it to Mrs Jary. "Lucinda was very upset by all accounts."

"And there's another thing," said Freda, getting into her stride. "You can't tell me that there wasn't anything going on there. She's had her eye on him since last year when they stayed. Why do you think they were back there this year? It's probably what killed him. Lucinda's craving passions probably pushed him over the edge."

The shop doorbell jangled and Lucinda walked in. She nodded at the ladies and Freda blushed, hoping Lucinda hadn't overheard. Mrs Jary was always pleased to see Lucinda Haines. She was a good customer and did a lot of grocery shopping with her, unlike some of the landladies who went off to cash and carry establishments or the supermarkets. Lucinda handed Mrs Jary a list of groceries.

"I will collect them later Mrs Jary. I have some business to do in town."

Mrs Jary smiled. "No problem Mrs Haines, I will send the boy round with them later. About five-thirty all right with you?"

Lucinda nodded. "Thank you Mrs Jary, that would be lovely." As she headed for the door she turned. "I was sorry to hear about your burglary Muriel; it must have been very upsetting for you. I hope the police catch whoever did it."

Muriel smiled and thanked her. She was still secretly cursing her neighbour for not displaying her vacancies sign and glared at Freda, much to Mrs Jary's amusement.

* * *

Mona was waddling along the pier away from the theatre just as Maud was heading towards it. "I hope all those reporter people have gone," she said, changing her basket from one arm to the other. "I don't want my face all over the television news."

Maud smiled to herself. And neither would the viewers, she thought. "You will be quite safe Mrs Buckle, there are only one or two there now, they are hoping to catch Miss Daniels."

"I always said there was sadness in that dressing room of hers. When I met her I got the feeling. The spirits never lie Mrs Bennett, oh no, they never lie. When I first set eyes on her I said to myself, Mona Daphnia Buckle, this lady has great sadness."

"An unusual name," said Maud, trying not to laugh. "Daphnia."

Mona's eye watered as she looked straight into Maud's eyes. "She was a cousin on my mother's side Mrs Bennett,

Daphnia Petunia. It's where I get my gift from. She could see things Mrs Bennett. All around her she felt the spirits. Her aura glowed and she would tell you as true as I am standing here, that the spirits never lie."

"What did she do for a living?" asked Maud, thinking she should at least try to add something to the conversation.

"She was a pub landlady."

Mona appeared to go in to a trance for a few moments and Maud didn't know whether to walk away or wait. Just as she was about to put one foot in front of the other, Mona spoke again. "Never be afraid of the spirits Mrs Bennett, they can guide you in life. It was the spirits that brought me here, that very day when I picked up a pen and paper to apply for this job, it was their doing."

"Well, if you'll excuse me Mrs Buckle, I must get along to see Mr Scott, he is waiting for me."

Mona raised her hand in farewell and continued on her way.

Tuesday 18th August

Still the reporters hung around the pier entrance in the hope of catching a glimpse of Derinda Daniels and getting further comment from her, intrigued to know where her daughter was and who the father was. Maud felt sorry for them as the weather that morning had turned. The clouds were dark and the rain battered down, it was hardly the day to be standing around. She was almost tempted to make them all a cup of tea and offer them some gingerbread that Barbara had brought in the day before.

* * *

Bob Scott ensured he was in the office early, not having Jim to rely upon and knowing that Roger was not the best person when it came to dealing with other people. As he hung up his wet raincoat, Beverley came in to the office with some coffee and the morning papers.

"There are still a few lines in there about Miss Daniels," she said, putting the paper on the desk. "I expect some of the local press will be interested in getting a story. Remember all that hullabaloo we had last year with those Ashby sisters?"

Bob thanked Beverley for the coffee and paper. "I do indeed Beverley. Don Stevens has made it quite clear that he is keeping away from this one and I can't say I blame him. It is, after all, Miss Daniels' private business. I'm surprised that her agent hasn't showed up, did you meet her at the first night? Audrey something or other, a strangely-dressed woman to my reckoning. I couldn't quite get the measure of her."

Beverley nodded. "Yes, that was my opinion of her too. She was very chatty. It was all I could do to get away from her." Picking up some notes from the desk, Beverley headed for the door. "I'll get these typed then Mr Scott and leave you to it."

* * *

Audrey Audley had abandoned her office, placing a note on the door that, due to illness, the office was closed. She was more shaken-up by Derinda's comments than she cared to admit and had phoned Rueben Roberts and poured out her heart to him the night before. Rueben had assured her that he had had nothing to do with informing Derinda about anything and that she must have heard it from another source. He reminded Audrey that the kind of parties they attended attracted many people they had never met before and as most of the party-goers where blown out of their mind on grass and drink it was very likely that she had come into contact with someone who knew Derinda. Audrey had taken some comfort from that, but when the phone kept ringing she thought she was going to go mad.

She had left the office at midday on the Monday, leaving a note on her desk for her cleaner. When she arrived home she had made herself something to eat and poured a very large vodka. Just when she thought she could relax, the phone began ringing, it had been her mother demanding to know what on earth was going on as she had recognised the name of Derinda as the artiste her daughter represented and who she had been telling all of her friends to go and see whenever they were in the Great Yarmouth area. What on earth was she going to say when they began to ask questions? Audrey tried to get through to her mother that the agency hadn't actually been mentioned in the article so, as yet, her name was not in any way involved. It was then that her mother dropped the bombshell that the local evening paper had taken up the story mentioning the *Audrey Audley Agency* and saying that Miss Daniels' agent had not been available for comment.

Looking out of the window on that Tuesday morning, the rain beating down on the windows with a drummer's rhythm, only made Audrey's hangover feel even worse. It was at times like this when she wished she had followed her uncle's advice and opened a music shop. She groaned, curled up on the sofa and did her best to shut out the world.

* * *

Petra Olanzo had read the articles with interest. It was good to know that she and her husband were not the only ones hiding secrets from the world. She had since received more cards from long-forgotten friends all saying that if they were in Great Yarmouth they would definitely come along and see the show. Remembering how hard she had fought to keep any kind of act going and helping Mario through his dark days when the poodle act had folded, she decided that at least she had done something different with her life. Unlike all of those people she knew back in Birmingham, she hadn't been condemned to foundries, factories, the high-rise buildings and humdrum dreariness. She had seen parts of Europe that others hadn't and had met some very interesting and entertaining people in the circus world.

So what if her husband sang opera while they were spinning plates twice nightly? At least it was a lot more fun than working on a production line or behind a shop counter. She made herself a promise, that she would stop being afraid of who she was and where she came from. To the audiences that came to see the show, she was Italian Petra Olanzo and her husband was Mario. Pam and Mike Denham belonged to another time and place.

* * *

Rita settled herself down in Lucinda's lounge and was joined by Jenny, Jill and Doreen. "Thanks for coming along this morning," said Rita. "There are one or two things I want to run by you all. Firstly, I would like to thank you all for the support you have given me since Ted died and to say how grateful I am to you all. Secondly, I have decided to move down here on a more permanent basis. The house back in Hull is too big for me now and I would like to have a change of scenery."

Jenny smiled. "That's wonderful news. Have you any plans on what you might do, where you might live?"

"I've decided to set myself up as an agent, but also to direct some of Don's shows for him. We have discussed it at some length and Don has offered me, with their consent, a few of his acts. For instance, Jonny Adams is not represented and Tommy Trent hasn't had an agent for some time. I was wondering how you all felt about me taking the JB Dancers onto my books, once I get things up and running?"

Doreen and Jill nodded and looked to Jenny for her reaction. "That sounds like a great idea Rita. I always found it quite difficult dealing with agents who were not on my doorstep and, with much of the work being local, it would make sense to have someone on our side here," said Jenny. "The girls are keen to expand on having more male dancers in the line-up and having seen what they have achieved so far, I would like it expanded on."

Jill and Doreen looked at each other and grinned.

"That's good to hear," said Rita, making herself a few notes. "I have to find somewhere to live first and also organise some kind of office. But in the meantime I have decided that it would good to inject a few new ideas into the show when it reaches the North Pier in Blackpool. Perhaps some fresh routines from the dancers, moving the programme around a little so that it doesn't look the same as the show we have running here. Don can do as he pleases and I am sure he will be open to suggestions. Since Elsie has been back on board he sees things differently."

Jill and Doreen were very excited about the prospect of changing some of the routines for Blackpool and mentioned one or two things they had been working on. And it was good to know that they had the green light to include more boys in the line-up. Jenny requested that, as a tribute to Ted, they put in a Tiller Girl routine. She knew that Ted had always loved the Tiller Girls and Rita nodded in agreement. Doreen and Jill headed back to their dancing school leaving Jenny and Rita to chat some more.

"You are full of surprises Rita," said Jenny. "I can't tell you how great it is to know that you will be moving here. If you need someone to look over property with you I would be more than happy to help you."

"There is one thing you can do for me Jenny," said Rita. "Can you suggest anywhere I might be able to find an office to work from. It needn't be very big, but it would have to be functional. And I expect I would need to have an assistant to cover me when I wasn't there."

Jenny beamed, it all sounded very exciting and she intended to begin looking for an office for her friend that very morning.

* * *

That evening, with Ricky at her side, and both wearing wigs, sunglasses and beach wear, Derinda made her way safely past the few remaining reporters and on to the pier. Taking their time so as not to arouse suspicion they went to the ice cream stand and purchased a cornet apiece. Sauntering along they stopped to admire the sea view and walked right round the back of the theatre building and to the safety of the stage door on the other side. They both burst out laughing and said hello to Jack.

"There have been several people trying to get hold of you Miss Daniels," said Jack, "and one left you a note." He handed Derinda the envelope.

"Thanks Jack," replied Derinda, with a smile. "I am sorry about all of this."

"No problem Miss," said Jack, "I read the papers. At least you haven't committed a murder."

Not yet, Derinda thought to herself, recognising the handwriting on the envelope, not yet.

Thursday 20th August

Throughout the days that followed the headlines kept coming. An article from the secretary of the private members clubs said that their venues were being mismanaged by the new owners – the Boureme family. Members were dissatisfied with the quality of entertainment on offer and wanted to know why Miss Daniels was no longer appearing. Just when Sasha believed things could not escalate further, there was a statement from the representative of Lorna Bright which said his client had been duped by Sasha Boureme and made to believe he could make her an overnight singing sensation. He had changed her name to Dupree, gave her a French singing coach and used her to ensure that his ex-wife, Derinda Daniels, was prevented from appearing at the clubs where she had had a faithful following for years. It went on to say that Sasha planned to bankrupt his ex-wife in the hope of keeping control of his daughter Jeanie, who was disabled and receiving special care in his native France.

Derinda had read the articles in disbelief each day as they appeared, and far from making it more difficult for her to attend the theatre every evening she allowed photographers to take pictures, shrugged her shoulders and, with Ricky beside her, always gave them the same reply, "No comment."

Derinda knew that she had the support of the company behind her, but even so she did not speak of either her marriage or her daughter. The less she said, the less anyone could comment if approached.

Saturday 22nd August

Petra again read and watched with interest. Maybe she could get a story out of this. She ran the idea by her husband Mario and went and spoke to one of the reporters who were now permanently camped outside the pier entrance. And within a couple of days The Olanzos were also news. Petra told the reporter all about her life with Mario, and how together they formed a poodle act touring European circuses. They had changed their names from Pam and Mike Denham from Birmingham and adopted Italian personas to launch their singing and spinning act to Great Britain audiences. The story touched on the fact that they had never been able to have children, the problems they had had financing their original idea, the loss of their beloved poodle act and the new lease of life the new act had given them.

It seemed that local lad Jonny Adams was also jumping on the bandwagon when he paid homage to Ted Ricer, saying that without his help he wouldn't have been able to overcome his stutter. He emphasised that Ted had taken him under his wing and given him confidence and for that he would always be grateful.

The newspapers articles and the reports appeared nationally and locally across all media and in turn began to generate public interest in the show at the end of the pier. People were queuing for tickets at the box office or getting friends to do it on their behalf. Maud and Barbara found themselves working non-stop as, show by show, first and second house began to sell out.

In his London office Don Stevens smiled at his wife rubbing his hands with glee. A sell-out at the *Golden Sands* could only mean repeat business at the North Pier Blackpool, what could be better?

* * *

When Freda read the revelations that just kept coming, in her usual fashion she folded her arms, raised her eyes to the heavens and proclaimed to anyone within earshot that there was no need to watch *Crossroads*, it was all happening down at *The Golden Sands Theatre*. And many secretly thought she may well have a point.

Muriel kept her own counsel believing it to be a big publicity stunt.

Monday 24th August

With all the news that was coming out concerning the Boureme family, it was evident that one way or another Sasha and Derinda were going to have to talk to each other face to face. So in the presence of a solicitor the two thrashed out their differences, both trying to salvage what they could from the mess they found themselves in. Sasha's offer for Derinda to return to her billing at the *Mayfair Club*, fell on deaf ears. She flatly refused to have anything to do with any business that was connected with the Boureme family. Sasha said that his mother had been behind the business ventures and when she learned that Derinda was one of their regular resident summer attractions had ordered that Sasha deal with it immediately. Lorna Bright had come onto the scene quite by chance. Sasha knew a little of Lorna's connections in the world of variety from what he had read when the stories of the dysfunctional Ashby sisters had been revealed the previous year. Failing to find an artiste that could take over the mantle from Derinda he had clutched at the lifeline Lorna offered and embarked on a path that had been a disaster from the word go. Now, facing his ex-wife, he felt some shame and remorse about his actions. Derinda, flanked by Ricky, remained unmoved and demanded that all monies be repaid to her with interest and she wanted access to her daughter on a more regular basis. It was going to be a long day for all concerned and would probably end up in the courtrooms if all else failed.

* * *

Don Stevens made an unannounced visit to see Rita. He wanted to go over some details with her about the possibility of her becoming an agent. He was happy to have some of the acts he had represented move across to her and was pleased to tell her that Mystic Brian was among those who would like Rita to manage him. Rita laughed; if only Ted were here to witness this conversation. Elsie had drawn up a list of requirements Rita would have to adopt, with some suggestions concerning how she could best set up her agency. The two chatted over all things business and the talk naturally turned to

Ted. Rita told Don about the plans to rename the theatre bar after him, which in turn brought Don on to a subject he thought Rita would embrace.

"Elsie and I were wondering if a midnight matinee in memory of Ted would be appropriate with the takings going to a charity that Ted supported." Don waited for Rita's reaction.

She was clearly taking the suggestion seriously. "It's a lovely idea Don," she said finally, "but quite impossible at such short notice. Our show closes soon and we're getting prepared to move to Blackpool; the thought of trying to organise a midnight matinee fills me with dread. It would need advertising and then there's the theatre to consider. Who would appear on the bill? It would need more than the artistes we have here, otherwise no one would come. It's too much pressure me old lover."

"Which is why I have been doing a little bit of work behind the scenes," replied Don, warming to his theme. "The date we had in mind was Friday 4th September; Bob says the theatre is ours and his crew will work free of charge. The entire company are on board, plus I have secured the services of a few acts Ted worked with over the years. And Elsie thought it would be a nice idea if you sang at least one number. The whole thing need be no more than two and a half hours long. Petra Olanzo has a slightly longer puppet act she can use, Jonny has a new set of tricks he has been rehearsing and is keen to show off. Doreen and Jill have put together a team of eight male dancers they are calling *Teddy's Boys* for the evening, and Mystic Brian is willing to make an appearance providing he doesn't go on until two in the morning to give him time to drive down. Of course, it will include those beloved doves of his, Lottie, Enid and Caroline. Oh, and the advertising is all set to go to press – tickets will cost thirty and twenty pounds which includes a free drink at the bar in the interval, courtesy of the theatre management. All I need is the name of the charity. What do you say?"

Rita took hold of Don's hand and gripped it tightly. "What can I say me old lover?" she said, with tears in her eyes, "Yes please, and thank you very much."

And so with one phone call the advertisements for the show were to be seen in *the Eastern Daily Press* and *Great Yarmouth Mercury*, and Don had even managed to get a secure a deal with *The Stage*. The show was to be called *Ted Ricer's Midnight Matinee* and was to be in aid of *Heart Research UK* and *Barnardo's*.

* * *

Some days the theatre seemed busier during the day than it was in the evening. In the early mornings Doreen and Jill were working with the dancers on new routines for the Blackpool show, then with the all-male dancers in mid-morning, and rehearsals for the midnight matinee took place in the afternoon.

Rita secured the help of Jenny and together they worked out a running order for the midnight matinee, using timings supplied by the various acts that Don had secured. The printers were putting together a programme featuring photographs of Ted and many of the acts, bulked out by the generous advertising of local businesses including *Palmers*, *Arnolds*, *Jarrold's*, *Matthes*, *The Growler*, *Henrys* and *The Star Hotel* to name a few.

But while things on the show front continued, the real drama was being played out off stage. Derinda and Sasha were finding it difficult to compromise; Audrey Audley was trying to get herself back on top of things; Jim wrestled with the idea of selling the family home; Dave and Dan looked at literature that the estate agents sent them, while Madge and Josie viewed possibilities on their behalf; Rita continued to plan her move to

Great Yarmouth, while Freda and Muriel disagreed on who was responsible for keeping the pavement at the front of their guest houses clean and the subject of guests paying upfront.

* * *

In a clinic back in London, where she had been many times before, Lorna Bright sat on her bed stabbing newspaper photographs of Sasha Boureme with a pencil point, cursing him and thinking of ways she could make him pay for her downfall.

Friday 4th September

The curtain had fallen on the second house of *Summertime Sunshine* and the company were getting ready for the midnight matinee. The acts Don had secured were at the stage door by ten-forty-five and shown in to the Green Room by Roger, awaiting further instruction. Once the theatre had been emptied of the audience they would all be able to assemble on the stage to take direction from Rita and Jenny. Mystic Brian was not expected until about one-thirty and Rita couldn't help but feel a little nervous. Having been at the mercy of Brian and his 'girls' on more than one occasion she hoped that just this once everything would run smoothly. That the girls, his beloved turtle doves, behaved themselves and that Brian didn't trip over one of his many streams of colourful handkerchiefs and end up in the orchestra pit.

* * *

Jim, with Stella, Dave and Dan, walked slowly along the pier and joined the queue already beginning to form. Lilly Brockett accompanied by Enid, Muriel with her husband Barry, and Freda with her Dick, as she often referred to him, Don and Elsie Stevens and Lucinda Haines were just ahead of them. The doors opened and the crowd began to shuffle in. Programmes at one pound were being offered and no one refused. Even Freda managed not to tut at the price and nudged her husband to buy a programme as well. The usherettes, wearing badges supporting the two named charities, showed people to their seats and the arrival of the mayor, his lady wife and one or two local councillors caused a bit of a stir. Representatives from *Barnardo's* and *Heart Research UK* were shown to the reserved fourth row.

The audience was dressed in its evening finery, with Freda Boggis in a new creation she had run up on her sewing machine three days ago. Roses had been replaced by poppies, material that she had got cheap on the market. In fact, when other members of the audience looked more closely at the design they were sure they could make out faces staring back at them in a crooked sort of way. As Freda had entered her row, few would ever forget the smell of her perfume, *Love in a Mist*, coupled with mothballs and *Dettol*. Muriel had a handkerchief sprinkled with lavender in her handbag, which always came in handy when on an evening out with her neighbour.

The audience settled down as Maurice Beeney and his boys struck up an overture from the musical *South Pacific*. The curtain rose on eight male dancers, billed as *Teddy's Boys*, attired in sailor outfits singing *There is nothing like a Dame* and welcoming on to the stage a very nervous and slightly emotional Rita. Dressed in a crimson gown that had been a favourite of Ted's she walked down to the centre microphone, took a deep breath and made a short welcoming speech and as the applause rang out she walked down the side steps off the stage to join Jenny in the audience.

The stage became a fast-moving revue of everything variety could offer. The JB Dancers recreating the high kicking Tiller Girls, jugglers, comedians, speciality acts and the company of the current show. Mystic Brian pulled out all the stops with his twelve-minute act and quite a few of the audience were pleased to note that Brian's 'girls' were behaving impeccably. Derinda Daniels, with Ricky at the piano, sang a new selection of songs they had rehearsed and as the hands of the clock approached two-forty, Rita walked on to the stage and sang *Hello Young Lovers*, dedicated to her late husband and, as Ted would have so aptly put it, there wasn't a dry seat in the house.

As the audience filed slowly out of the theatre, they dropped loose change in to the charity boxes the usherettes were holding. All agreed it had been a cavalcade of entertainment. Rita, with Jenny, Don and Elsie at her side, thanked all of the artistes who had taken part and introduced them to the charity representatives and local dignitaries. Rita was especially pleased to see that Ronald and his wife Janice were there and went over to speak to them. Janice was quite a shy woman. Smartly attired, she wore glasses, had a shock of wavy red hair and was wearing what Ted would have said were 'sensible shoes'.

"I'm so pleased you came along Ronald," Rita said, warmly. "And this must be Janice, how do you do?" Janice took Rita's hand and as her eyes peered over the top of her glasses she smiled in acknowledgement.

"It was a lovely show," said Ronald, making up for his wife's lack of conversation. "We both enjoyed it didn't we Janice?" Janice nodded and smiled again. "You did my father proud Rita. I hope you manage to raise lots of money for the two charities."

Rita smiled gratefully. "The ticket price alone will be a big part of that. All of the artistes gave up their time freely and I know that several of them have made their own donations. I'm so pleased that the theatre was full. It's a lot to ask of people to come out so late at night but, as you can see, they did."

"Well, we better head off," said Ronald, "we have a bit of a drive ahead of us. Thanks again Rita."

"You have nothing to thank me for old lover," she said, giving Ronald a hug. "I am very pleased that we all have met at long last and please keep in touch. I'm moving down here after our Blackpool stint, that's if I have got a property to move in to. But in the meantime you will find me at Lucinda's guest house. Perhaps we can all meet up one day and have lunch together."

Ronald nodded and, taking his wife's arm, walked out of the theatre.

Sitting in the back of the taxi that had come to take her and Lucinda home, Rita gazed out onto the now deserted promenade feeling elated that they had done Ted proud. Just as the car was about to turn off the parade, Rita asked the driver to stop and motioned for Lucinda to wait for her in the car. She walked slowly to the end of the jetty and looked up. There in the night sky was the brightest star she had ever seen. She gazed at it knowingly, blew it a kiss and smiled.

Chapter Thirteen   *Travel a New Highway*

Monday 7ʰ September

W hen Rita pulled back the bedroom curtains she could hardly believe that *Summertime Sunshine* was entering its final week. The plans were in place to transport the show to Blackpool ready for the opening on Monday 21ˢᵗ September, which was a week earlier than had originally been planned. Dave Grant was going to take control of the operation to ensure that all the sets, costumes and props made it to the North Pier and were in place to start dress rehearsals on Thursday 17ᵗʰ September. Most of the company had either booked in to bed and breakfast accommodation or were staying with friends in the business. Rita was going to be at a small guest house which Ted had favoured on many of his visits to the resort. The proprietors were a retired husband and wife duo who had been known in the business as Greg and Peg and had performed a knife-throwing act until Greg sustained an injury and they both decided it was time to put the knives away and find something else to do. Rita liked the pair and was looking forward to seeing them both again.

* * *

Dave reported to the *Golden Sands* later that morning to take a look backstage and to be briefed by Roger Norris concerning the lie of the land. Dave knew how to execute such a job as he had done it many times at the *Wellington Pier*

Theatre, but he wasn't one for treading on people's toes. Roger had proven no match for Jim, as Bob Scott had realised early on in the proceedings. Roger confided to Dave that since Jim hadn't been around the theatre hadn't been the same and he had no intention of returning the next season and was on the lookout for something else. Seeing a solution to a problem, Dave said he would suggest Roger to his cousin at *Sparkles* as he was now looking for someone to replace him and hadn't found anyone so far that he could trust. This cemented a friendlier approach from Roger and the rest of the morning passed smoothly.

* * *

The press continued to publish occasional updates about Derinda, Sasha and the Mayfair nightclub scene. The local press followed suit but their readers were getting fed up reading about it and where pleased when they read reports from the two charities that had prospered from the midnight matinee performance. There was also news from the *Golden Sands* that the theatre was going to have a makeover when the season ended and that the theatre bar was to be renamed. Many locals nodded in approval saying that the theatre needed redecorating.

* * *

With hardly a single ticket to be had for *Summertime Sunshine*, Maud was able to settle down and finish the bed jacket she had started some weeks before.

* * *

In *Henry's Bar*, Dan was chatting with Stella and saying how sorry he was that he would be leaving at the end of the month. He had enjoyed working with Stella and the two had become firm friends. Dave, he explained, was going to be staying with his parents in Preston and would drive to and from Blackpool or stay over the odd night. Dan was planning to join him at the end of September and then the two could get stuck in on the two-bedroomed property they had found which was in Lytham St Anne's, not too far from Marie Jenner and Graham Pettingale.

Madge and Josie had been going in to the house when time allowed, rubbing down the paintwork and generally having it prepped for the boys to make their mark on it. Marie had been to the house and measured for curtains and had offered to make them once they had decided on material. It would be her house-warming present to them both. Graham had promised to tidy the back garden and to trim an overgrown bush that was taking over the front wall. Dan was getting quite excited by the thought of moving nearer to home; Dave was, as usual, in two minds but knew it was for the best and time to move on.

* * *

Audrey Audley sat in her office and read again the letter from Derinda informing her she would no longer require her services. Audrey had looked after Derinda for some years but, on reflection, she admitted to herself that in recent years she had taken her eye off the ball and let things slip. She walked round the office and looked at some of the photographs of the acts she represented that hung in their mock-gilt frames on the walls. The Pearl Twins – Singing and Swinging, Lenny Williamson – Comedy with Heart, The Gypsy Creams – Latin American Guitars, The Dean Sisters – International Roller Ball Stars, Cornelia Winklenut – Contortionist with a Twist, Rory Royce – Music and Magic and many others. Only a handful worked regularly. Derinda had been her biggest success and certainly her biggest earner.

Audrey sat down and made herself a list. She would need to go out in to the cabaret and show world across the country and, if necessary, further afield and get some more acts on her books or suffer the consequences. She pressed the button beneath her desk and waited. How stupid, she thought to herself, there is no Margaret, Julie or anyone, there is just me. And as she splayed her manicured hands on her desk she suddenly felt terribly alone.

* * *

Jenny Benjamin was excited, as Lucinda showed her into the lounge to wait for Rita.

"Where's the fire?" said Rita. "Lucinda said you had some news."

"I think I may have found you the perfect location for your agency," said Jenny, who was fit to bursting. "I've got the keys here. I've been to look it over twice; the estate agent thinks I'm barmy. It's on Northgate Street, opposite the church and I viewed it last week. I wanted to tell you then, but I thought, what with all that was going on, I'd hold off. It's above an antiques shop. It has two large rooms, a reception area, small kitchenette and a separate toilet with washbasin. The main entrance is a door at the side of the shop with a flight of stairs which leads on to a small landing. It's been empty for some time and it would be on lease. You won't believe the price they are asking, it's a snip. I had this marvellous idea, but you would have to consider it first. How would you feel about combining the office with the *JB Dancing School*. The girls keep going on about needing an office to work from. If they were able to share the office facilities we could put in a secretary who would look after both. The cost could be shared across the board. What do you think Rita?"

"I think you need a drink," said Rita, throwing her bag over her shoulder. "Now let's go in to town, look over this find of yours, have some lunch, chat about it some more, go back and give the office another look then take it from there." Rita had never seen Jenny so animated. The idea sounded a good one, but it needed to be looked at more carefully. "Off out Lucinda, see you later," she called, grabbing Jenny by the arm and heading her out of the front door.

Lucinda was feeling a bit down. She would miss having Rita around and although she had had reservations about her when they first met. But Lucinda had to admit she had become very fond of them both. Lucinda wasn't a person who did fond, as she readily admitted; she put it down to getting older. She had enjoyed the midnight matinee and couldn't help but shed a tear or two when Rita had sung that lovely song at the end of the show. It had summed up things in both their worlds. When she had first got to know Ted she knew it was love at first sight, but she could never have come between a man and his wife. She sighed, picked up her tin of *Pledge* and went to tackle the dusting.

* * *

Freda sat herself down and Muriel came over with two cups of coffee. *Palmers'* coffee shop wasn't too busy, which made a nice change.

"I was thinking," said Freda. She had Muriel's attention immediately, who was of the opinion that her neighbour never thought very often. "I am going ask my Dick to put locks on all of the bedrooms and an alarm on the front door, so that when someone is going out I will be able to clock them in case they are making off with anything. I had two bedspreads go last week, cerise with gold thread tassels, got them off the market, they went a treat with them curtains you gave me."

Muriel stirred her coffee. "Don't you think putting an alarm on the front door is going to cause a few problems, especially if people are coming in late?. You might be in bed and you and your Dick will be up and down all night, and him with his dodgy elbow."

Freda huffed. "There has got to be a way of stopping people nicking things. And why it's always from my house I don't know. It's as if I have a sign on the front door saying 'Come in and help yourself'."

"If I were you, I would go have a word with that nice young man Raymond in *Hammonds* and see if he can offer you a solution. Perhaps you need to have a desk at the front door and have someone sitting there all day like they do on *Crossroads*."

Freda huffed again. "And they would want paying and my name is not Meg Richardson."

"No," said Muriel, taking a sip of her beverage, "but you do have a passing resemblance to Amy Turtle."

* * *

Jenny and Rita decided to have lunch in *The Star Hotel*. Rita helped herself to more vegetables. The steak and kidney pie was especially tasty and Jenny seemed to be making fast work of her gammon steak.

"The office is quite brilliant," said Rita, "I really like it. The only problem I have at the moment is getting the house sold in Hull and finding somewhere to live down here."

"Dave and Dan will be vacating the flat over Enid's shop quite soon, had you thought of that as a possibility?"

"Now you come to mention it, it did cross my mind. If I could have had the shop as well as my agency with the flat above, it may have been the perfect solution," said Rita. "But I think I would be happier with my own front door and maybe a little garden. I can stay on at Lucinda's until I'm fixed up. I have one or two things to put in to storage and then the house can go on the market."

"I'm pleased you like the idea of Northgate Street. It is quite central and not far from Vauxhall station as the wind blows. Have you any idea what you are going to call the agency?"

Rita put down her knife and fork. "Now that is the big question. To be honest Jenny I haven't a bloody clue. Perhaps if we have a discussion with Jill and Doreen about sharing the offices, they might have a suggestion."

"Oh, it's all very exciting," said Jenny. "It's like starting up all over again. I remember when I first opened the dancing school, I felt so proud. Of course, the offices will want decorating and some new carpets."

"Jenny, if we are able to come to some arrangement with the girls, I wonder if I might leave decoration in your hands. I can give you some idea of how I would like my office to look and the girls will no doubt have their own ideas for theirs. I won't be able to give the project much thought, what with Blackpool on the horizon, and it would help me greatly if I knew I had you to rely on."

"Of course, of course," said Jenny, "nothing I would enjoy more. Leave it to me Rita."

When the idea was put to Doreen and Jill the deal was sealed. Rita decided on a colour scheme she thought she could live with and the agency was to be called *Rita's Angels*, incorporating the office of the *JB Dancing School*.

Rita gave Elsie a call to let her in on the latest news and Elsie in turn informed Rita that she had been in touch with Wally Barrett. She had told him about the situation with Lorna Bright and Sasha Boureme and wondered if he might be able to track down June. Wally had said he would do his best, though June's whereabouts remained something of a mystery.

Since she had supposedly left France, no one in the circles that she moved in had heard anything of her.

"And any news on Lorna?" asked Rita

Elsie sighed. "Well, I've done my best. I visited her a few times as I promised. She is out of the clinic now and back in her old flat. To my mind Rita she really shouldn't be on her own, the girl is clearly unbalanced and there is no telling what she might do. The article she gave the press didn't go down well with Mr Boureme, but she said there hadn't been any contact between them. She did let me in on the fact that they had been having an affair. The flat looked a mess when I visited a couple of days ago. To be honest I feel totally out of my depth with her."

"Look Elsie." said Rita. "you've done all you can do. We both have enough on our plates at the moment. It really isn't our concern, though I do feel sorry for her. What a mess."

There was silence between them for a moment and then Elsie continued, "So Rita, tell me again about this office Jenny found. It all sounds exciting and Don will be over the moon when I tell him. He has a couple of acts he would like to put your way, so you will have something to keep you busy. And if you need a hand setting up I can come down any time, I've relented and told Don to get in a temp, but I've insisted on a man. The agency he was in touch with said it may take a few days but were hopeful of finding someone."

* * *

Jim put the crossword to one side and went to wash his cup and saucer. He felt he needed some fresh air and grabbing his car keys and jacket he headed out. Stopping off to buy some flowers at *White's* florist in Gorleston High Street he continued his journey to the cemetery. He parked alongside the cemetery walls and walked slowly to Karen's grave. The distance seemed longer than usual and he put it down to not sleeping well the night before. He hadn't visited the grave for some weeks and the flowers in the urn were brown and withered. He removed them, refreshed the water and set about arranging the ones he had purchased. He whispered a prayer and put his hand to his head, the headaches were coming back again and he cursed himself for not bringing any medication with him. He steadied himself on the headstone as he pushed himself to his feet. He felt slightly dizzy and blinked his eyes trying to focus. He stood quite still for a few minutes until he felt he had composed himself then, with a steady gait, he made his way back to the car and started the engine. He headed towards the crossroads of Crab Lane and went straight across onto Shrublands Way toward the railway bridge. His headache worsened and he screwed up his eyes, desperately trying his best to focus. Unable to bear the pain any longer he put both his hands to his head, losing control of the wheel and went straight in to the side of the bridge, just missing an oncoming car. His head hit the steering wheel and he blacked out.

Tuesday 8ᵗʰ September

Dave answered the shrill ring of the telephone. "Hello Debbie, how lovely to hear from you." Dave listened and he felt his blood run cold. He replaced the receiver just as Dan came out of the bathroom.

"Are you okay, you've gone as white as a sheet?"

"It's Jim," said Dave, doing his best to control himself. "There's been an accident."

Dan pulled Dave close to him. "What do you want me to do; shall I drive you to the hospital?"

Dave shook his head. "I need to let Maud know and I would sooner do that face to face. I will probably catch her at the box office, she is usually there by ten. Rita will need to be informed, she's staying with Lucinda Haines, I think Stella will know the address. Could you go and see her for me please?"

"Of course I can mate," said Dan, "but first you need a cup of tea and some breakfast inside you and I am not taking no for an answer."

As soon as Maud saw Dave standing at the door to the box office, her heart sank. "It's Jim isn't it? Oh my God whatever has happened? Come inside."

Dave told Maud all that Debbie had said. "Poor kid," said Maud, "Jim knew dam well he shouldn't be driving that car of his. He must have been coming from the cemetery, that's the only reason he ever goes over to Gorleston these days."

"We aren't allowed at the hospital," said Dave, "Debbie is going to keep me informed. I can't go to Blackpool now and leave my best mate in hospital."

Maud took hold of Dave and spoke firmly. "Now you see here David Grant, Jim wouldn't want you changing your plans on account of him. You have a lot riding on your move and you cannot disappoint Dan. Besides, you are going to be Rita's right-hand man and you really cannot let her down. Jim will pull through this, I know he will." But Maud was unsure who she was trying to convince. "Lilly will need to be told," she continued. "We don't see much of her these days but she is very fond of Jim and I know he is of her." She caught her breath and Dave gave her a hug. "Oh Dave, I thought we had seen the end of this. If only he hadn't driven that bloody car, he does make me angry sometimes."

Beverley, who had spoken with Maud, told Bob Scott the news and, as the office door was ajar, she was overheard by Mona. Mona moved herself slowly along the corridor and into the theatre preparing her *Brasso* and dusters, meaning to give the brass rail a clean. "I said there was sadness here," she mumbled to herself and gave a sniff as her eye watered. "The spirits never lie." Then with all the energy she could muster, and steadying herself on the brass rail, she knelt.

Roger was just coming up the theatre aisle and spotted her. "Hello Mrs Buckle," he said cheerily. "Is everything okay?"

Mona looked up. "I dropped the top off my *Brasso*," she said, wiping her eyes and then she began to hum *The Old Rugged Cross* softly to herself.

Rita was shocked when she heard the news, she thought Jim was looking more like his old self when she last saw him and there had been a glimmer of the old spark in him. She sat with heavy heart and looked out of the window. What was life all about? The backstage staff would be upset and she must do what she could to soften the blow. She picked up her jacket and handbag and went out into the autumn sunshine. She walked along the promenade and purchased an ice cream. She did her best to take her mind off all that was going on hoping that these final few days in Great Yarmouth would be without further incident. She was very grateful that Dave had been able to take charge of things and he, like Jim, would have everything in place.

The wardrobe staff had also agreed to accompany the show which was a great weight off Rita's mind. Most acts were used to managing their own costumes, but it was always good to have some extra pairs of hands when alterations, repairs and ironing needed to be done. There were also the wigs to be taken care of. The dancers wore two wigs apiece during the show and heavily jewelled headdresses for the finale. The Tiller Girl routine especially choreographed for Ted's midnight matinee was staying in the show as a new opening and the extra male dancers had also been retained. Don had given the go-ahead, seeing it as a step in the right direction. This was great news for Jill and Doreen who intended to incorporate more male dancers in future productions, and for the following year they already had four summer shows on their books.

Rita's mind was a jumble of things, the house in Hull, the office, the agency, the move, she sat herself down on a bench and allowed herself the time to file these things in her head. She took a notebook from her handbag, something she always had to hand. Initially she had used one to make notes for Ted's act, now it was proving a useful tool for everything else. Making an orderly list, she smiled to herself. She could concentrate on the things that needed doing now and tick the others off when the time came. Feeling better she continued her walk to the theatre.

Chapter Fourteen   *Every Cloud*

G reat Yarmouth continued to enjoy the fruits of its labours and the holidaymakers continued to arrive in cars and by train or coach. The town bustled with the newcomers as they jostled with the locals going about their business. By day the families flocked to the sandy beaches, enjoyed ice creams, candy floss, chips and hotdogs. While the less discerning customer enjoyed meals in the many restaurants in Regent Road, others who had sampled what *Matthes* restaurant and *Palmers* coffee shop had to offer in previous holidays at the resort returned to reacquaint themselves with familiar surroundings and good quality fare.

The Hippodrome Circus and its twice daily performances of daredevil acts, clowns and animals were a hit with all ages. With the Old Time Music Hall at the *Gorleston*, the twice nightly performances at the theatres in Great Yarmouth and the late night cabaret bars, discos and dance halls, there was something for everyone to enjoy.

Landladies turned their vacancy signs to *No Vacancies* and the local papers reported that Great Yarmouth was enjoying a successful season despite the current stress of preparing to move to decimal currency, which was proving something of a headache for the older ones.

Wednesday 9ᵗʰ September

The Sister smiled at Debbie. "Your father had a reasonable night but I do have reports from the night Sister that he was shouting out the name Karen. Isn't that the name of your baby daughter?"

Debbie nodded. "Yes it is," she said, "but it would be my mum he was calling out to. Her name was also Karen, and he misses her."

"At least it shows that his brain is active," said the Sister, laying a folder on her desk. "I think it best if only family were to visit for the present time."

"That makes it difficult," said Debbie, "there is only me and my husband and he is in Norwich working. My daughter is with her grandparents. Dad knows so many people and I am certain his best friend Dave would like to come in and one or two others."

"We mustn't overtire patient," said the Sister in a commanding yet friendly tone. "Too much excitement will not help his recovery and we do want to see him back on his feet and home again don't we?"

Debbie, feeling she was in the presence of her old headmistress, nodded, thanked the Sister and went to her father's bedside. Jim was asleep and he didn't move or react to his daughter's visit. She sat quietly looking at him for any sign that he might open his eyes, but an hour later she kissed her father's cheek and left unrewarded.

Her phone call to Dave was brief. There was little or no change at the moment and she repeated what the Sister had said about visiting. But, as Dave pointed out, the Sister wasn't there all the time and he would go with Debbie on Friday evening. He was determined to see his old friend before he had to set off to Preston and no Sister was going to stop him.

Debbie made a quick call to her in-laws to make sure that young Karen was okay. She would have to call Peter when she got back from the hospital that evening, when she hoped her father would be awake. She tried to keep busy around the house, but her father had proved to be such a good housekeeper that there was little for her to do. She decided that a walk into the town might be a good idea. She could say hello to Enid at the shop and maybe walk down to theatre and see Auntie Maud.

She walked over Haven Bridge and along the quayside; the pleasure boats were still doing some late summer business. Walking up through Market Row she arrived at Enid's gift emporium and went in to pass the time of day. Enid was pleased to see her and passed on her best wishes for her dad. After admiring some of the stock and buying a trinket for her mother-in-law, Debbie headed across the market. There were a lot of holidaymakers about the town. Queues for the buses at the side of the *ABC Regal* theatre were plenty and she noted people were still trying to get tickets to see Peter Noone before it, too, closed. Trying to take her mind off things she wandered around *Martyns'* gift shop, which had everything that Enid stocked and a lot more besides, cuckoo clocks, jewellery, ornaments, party hats and all manner of novelties.

Back on Regent Road she fought her way through the crowds and arrived at the *Golden Sands* box office feeling she had walked for miles. Barbara was at the box office window and alerted Maud who came out of the office and put her arms around the girl.

"Debs, you look done in my love," she said. "Come with your Auntie Maud and we'll go and have a nice cup of tea, a cake and chat."

She waved at Barbara and taking Debbie by the arm took her to the Italian ice-cream parlour at the bottom of Regent Road. The colour had drained from Debbie's face and Maud felt quite concerned and wondered if she should take her along to her doctor's surgery. After a few minutes and a few sips of tea, Debbie began to get some colour back in her cheeks. But as she spoke about her father she began to sob and Maud feared the dark days ahead.

* * *

At the *House of Doris*, Muriel was having her hair done. She had tickets for the final performance of *Summertime Sunshine* and wanted her hair to look nice. Doris always gave her a tighter perm, which was easily managed.

"Been a while since you were in," said Doris. "You are going to need some of this cut, it's got very long. You must have had a busy summer."

"Been rushed off my feet," said Muriel. "I haven't had a moment to call my own. Barry's off today so he's holding the fort for me. We have been lucky to have been full most of the season, unlike my neighbour."

Doris, who didn't entertain idle gossip, changed the subject. "I was sorry to hear that Jim Donnell was back in hospital, his mother and I were good friends way back. I used to cut her hair. I must put a card in the post, he's a good sort is old Jim."

Muriel nodded. "I was just about to tell you about my neighbour." But before she could utter another word, Doris had Muriel's head under a shower of water and began giving her a good shampoo.

As was the norm in Doris's, as Muriel's perm was taking hold, Doris was shampooing another customer and then attending one from under the dryer ready to comb her hair out.

Muriel came out of the salon after two and a half hours, her neck the colour of a radish and with a bouffant that Elsie Tanner would have been proud of. Taking a chance that one would stop, Muriel waited on Lowestoft Bridge for the Number One red bus back to town. Luck was on her side and the driver of the *Eastern Counties* service pulled up to allow her to get on. The bus would go all the way to the bus station just off the promenade and she wouldn't have so far to walk home. She sat herself on the upper deck and looked out of the window. It wasn't often she had the chance to get over to Gorleston and she promised herself that once the season was over, she would make a trip to Gorleston High Street to do some shopping. She would also be able to go into the wool shop to stock up on some skeins of wool. Muriel intended to try her hand at knitting Barry a jumper for Christmas and, if she found she enjoyed the pastime, a couple of woolly hats for Freda and Dick in matching colours. She smiled to herself, popped a sugared almond in her mouth and continued to enjoy her journey.

* * *

Dave continued to prepare for the transportation of the sets to Blackpool and had drawn up a plan that everyone could follow. He would be on hand to supervise on Sunday 13th September and then make his own move to Preston the following day where he would be met at the station by Josie and Madge. Roger, who had secured Dave's old job at *Sparkles* nightclub, was now more than eager to see that he did a good job for Dave and gathered the backstage boys to look over the proposed ideas.

Meanwhile, in the main office, Bob Scott had invited Mona Buckle in for a chat. "Mrs Buckle, as you will be aware, the show closes on Saturday evening and your work with us will end on Wednesday 16th September. Firstly, I wanted to personally thank you for the sterling work you have done here this season."

Mona nodded. "That is very nice of you to say Mr Scott. I have enjoyed working here. I wasn't sure at first, but that Mr Donnell put me right, told me what was what."

"I'm pleased you have enjoyed working here and I wondered how you would feel about coming back next season?"

Mona sat upright on the chair and, placing her hands firmly on her knees, leaned forward and looked Bob Scott directly in the eye. "I am most humbled to be asked Mr Scott," she said, her left eye beginning to squint and water. "I would be most happy to return here. The spirits and I have unfinished business. As you know, I've got the gift and not many have." She picked up Bob's teacup, placed it on top of the saucer, turned it three times and then gazed inside. "I'm pleased that secretary of yours uses proper tea. I can see things in this cup Mr Scott, oh yes, the leaves are telling me you are coming in to some money and going on a long journey."

Yes, Bob thought, I get my wage packet at the end of the week and then I'm off to Scotland for a holiday. "How very canny Mrs Buckle," he said, with a smile. "And you can see all of that in my teacup?"

"And more besides," said Mona, warming to her theme. "Have you got a dog?" Bob shook his head. "Well you are going to have one Mr Scott. Oh yes, it's as clear as day, the tealeaves never lie."

Bob hoped it wouldn't be the greyhound he had backed at the stadium the previous evening. For all he knew it had never left the trap.

* * *

Petra and Mario were enjoying an unexpected day of relaxation. It wasn't often they donned sunhats and sat in deckchairs watching the tide come in. Gorleston beach had the tranquillity that Great Yarmouth sometimes lacked. They had found a quiet spot at the far end of the beach where not many holidaymakers ventured and enjoyed the sunshine. Petra had received news that once the Blackpool show was done, there was a chance to work abroad in the New Year. It all depended on the agent who was coming to see them at the North Pier. Biting into a lettuce and salad cream roll, Petra decided that working abroad wasn't such a big deal after all. Their poodle act would have long since been forgotten and if it meant a warmer climate it beat shivering in the winter of Great Britain.

A dog barking distracted her attention and she saw a familiar figure coming towards her. With Bingo dancing and running about, Ricky came into view and waved.

"Not often I see you two out and about," he said with a smile, his Hollywood-white teeth gleaming in the sunlight. "Mind if I join you?"

Petra smiled. "Of course not Ricky, though you'll have to make do with the sand, unless you go and get a deckchair."

Mario nodded and smiled, continuing to eat his sandwich. Ricky sat down beside Petra's deckchair. "I often bring Bingo down here, he loves running along the shore and chasing the waves."

"It is a lovely spot," said Petra, pleased to have some company; Mario was in one of his silent moods. "I wish I had ventured over here before. Mario favours going to Norwich and looking round the castle and cathedral. We did make a trip to Cromer one day but the wind was that keen it nearly blew me away."

"I love Cromer," said Ricky. "But I know what you mean about the wind. They have a great little show on the end of their pier, I went to see it one year and it was brilliant. No big names, just good old-fashioned entertainment, a bit like we do I suppose."

"I'd like to go and see the music hall here," said Petra, "but working every night I haven't had the opportunity."

"You could go on Monday evening. Their show doesn't close until the next weekend. Mind you, it would mean you delaying your journey to Blackpool. Tell you what, if you're keen I'll come along with you, if you don't mind that is, I could do with a night out."

Petra smiled; she couldn't remember the last time that she and Mario had actually been in the company of others. They had always kept themselves to themselves. "That sounds like a great idea Ricky. Is there anyone you can bring with you?"

"I could ask Derinda, she could do with some light relief, she hasn't been having a good time of it lately."

"I don't really know her very well," said Petra. "In fact, I am ashamed to admit that I don't know any of the company that well, only to say hello. Of course, I read what was written in the papers, but I didn't feel it was my place to comment."

"Derinda has a great sense of humour," Ricky replied, running his fingers through the warm grains of sand. "On my walk back I'll buy four tickets at the box office and if she can't come I'll sound out one of the others."

"Oh, I'm really looking forward to it. Thanks Ricky."

They chatted a while longer, Mario had fallen asleep, and then Ricky got up to leave. "See you back at the theatre tonight, thanks for your company. Come on Bingo old boy, time to head for the heather."

Petra watched them go and then turned to Mario. "We are silly Mario, all these years we've kept away from others when we could have been having fun."

* * *

Freda was sweeping her front pathway when Muriel returned from her outing. "See you had your hair done," said Freda, leaning on her broom. "Been over to Doris?"

"I always go to Doris as well you know Freda Boggis, she does a very good style," said Muriel, touching the side of her stiff hair and giving a token sniff.

"Fancy," said Freda. "I went there once, but I couldn't stand all those ablutions she put on your hair, the smell made my eyes water."

"You mean the perming *solutions*," said Muriel. "I've been going there for so long, it doesn't bother me."

"My mate Beryl trims mine every now and then. I won't let her anywhere near me if she's suggesting a *Twink*, unless it's for a special occasion, the smell of that could knock your socks off, too much pneumonia."

"Beryl isn't a trained hairdresser though is she?" said Muriel, taking her door key from her handbag.

"No, but she worked at the poodle parlour in Gorleston for years, so she knows her way around with clippers."

"Well, that says a lot," said Muriel, opening her front door. "I'm surprised she didn't enter you at *Crufts*."

* * *

Derinda was not surprised when she opened her front door and found Audrey on the doorstep. She stepped aside and invited her in.

"I won't beat about the bush," said Audrey, throwing her shoulder bag on to the settee and sitting herself down. "You can't desert me darling. Look, I know I haven't been the greatest agent in the world, but I have always had your best interests at heart. You wouldn't have had all those London engagements without my influence. I know a lot of people in the business. I just took my eye off the ball that was all. I should have been paying more attention. I work hard, I go along to clubs I would rather not be seen in and for what? To try and find talent I can nurture and put on the road to fame. I have little time to enjoy myself, I'm in that office most of the time taking calls and negotiating contracts. It's not easy darling, a slave had better work rules than I do. It's dog eat dog in this world and you have to be up with the lark and down with the cock, or something like that. It's a treadmill, no sooner have you signed one deal than you are on to the next. My world should be parties, banquets and balls. Not this nine-to-five drudgery. I am always thinking of others first, so what am I to do?"

Derinda looked at Audrey dressed in purples and blacks, a wide choker sporting jewels around her neck, a Robin Hood hat with a feather and heels that could be mistaken for running shoe spikes. "You could begin by taking a deep breath and then you should think long and hard about giving up the business."

Audrey looked at Derinda, startled. "Give up the business darling? It's my world, it's my life."

Derinda moved to the other side of the lounge and turned to face Audrey. "You have just said yourself that you don't have a life, so find one Audrey. I reckon you have enough money to do anything you like and don't tell me otherwise. You see this agency as a plaything, a toy, something to amuse yourself with. Look at some of the naff acts you have on your books. Who in their right mind would book the Gypsy Creams? Have you ever heard Pedro and Joao sing? Joao is slightly deaf, falls behind on the melody and then speeds things up to try and catch up with Pedro. Cornelia, that contortionist, I watched her work at *Batley's* once. She entangled herself around the microphone stand and it took two fireman and the whole of the local St John Ambulance to put her right again.

"When you took me on your books, you knew that I was your meal ticket. I turned down the attention of the *Grade Organisation* to give a local agent a chance. It was my choice, no one made me do it. I came along for the ride, but this latest chapter has made me realise that the ride is well and truly over. I need an agent that is going to fight for me, not sit back and take all the glory. I am sorry Audrey but there you have it.

"Now, I have to get ready to go over to Great Yarmouth, I have two shows to do in case you'd forgotten. You'll find the exit where you found the entrance. Goodbye Audrey."

Derinda left the room and hurried up the stairs leaving Audrey hurt, deflated and feeling very sorry for herself. She picked up her bag and walked out of the front door closing it gently behind her. Grateful that she had sensibly arrived by cab, she got back into the waiting vehicle.

Back at her office she dialled Rueben's number. "Darling, the most dreadful thing has happened."

Rueben listened. "Now my dear, remember what we talked about all those years ago, well let's do it. Get rid of the shackles that have kept us both confined. Let us throw caution to the wind, pack some bags, book a cruise liner and go off to all those foreign shores we always talked about. Spend some time in Australia, anywhere, but let's live!"

"But Rueben, what shall I do about the agency? How will I tell my staff?"

"Give Don Stevens a call and ask him to take the acts off your hands. You can worry about the office another time, you hold the lease. Let the cottage out to some of your friends, and as for the staff, Audrey dear one, this is me Rueben you are talking to, there are no staff. You must owe Beryl Reid loads of money in royalties. Hush now, don't say another word. Go to your task and let's aim to sail by the end of the month. Look out world, here we come!"

Chapter Fifteen   *Touching Bases*

Friday 11th September

"I'll leave you two to chat," said Debbie, squeezing her father's hand gently.

"It's great to see you mate," said Dave, looking at Jim. "You had us all worried there for a moment."

Jim smiled and replied slowly, "I was too. Debs said I crashed the car, but I don't remember that."

"It will come back," said Dave, "it's early days yet. You'll be back on your feet in no time. Dan sends his best and so does Stella. Oh, and the backstage boys asked me to give you this." Dave laid an envelope on the bed.

"Thank you," said Jim. "I'll look at it later. I've still got all the cards that people sent me before, I must be costing them a fortune."

"You're worth it mate," said Dave, doing his best to control his emotions. He had never had another friend like Jim before and through all the years they had known each other, whatever life had thrown at either of them, they had always been there for each other. "Peter is coming down tonight and bringing young Karen with him. I expect Debs will bring her in to see you."

"I don't think Sister allows children on the ward," Jim replied, his eyes beginning to close. "I don't think she likes..."

Dave stood up and took Jim's hand. "I'll let you rest my old mate. I'll come in again on Sunday." He stood and looked at his friend for a few moments. Then outside the ward he gave Debbie a hug and whispered goodbye.

* * *

Rita was pleased to let the staff and company know that Jim seemed to be improving. Dave had given her the low-down on his brief visit and she had learned more from Maud who had had a call at the box office from Debbie. Everyone was delighted to hear the news. The heaviness they had felt lifted and their moods lightened. Jack was so pleased to hear the news that he promised everyone he would bring in a couple of bottles of Scotch for the closing night that he had been keeping for a special occasion.

Rita had also spoken with Wally earlier and he reported that he had not been lucky in his search for June Ashby but that if he heard anything she would be the first to know. She told him about her decision to move to Great Yarmouth and to open her own agency and he applauded her, saying she would make a great agent. He also promised to come and see the show once it was up and running in Blackpool. He hadn't been up North for some years so the idea of seeing the illuminations excited him. Rita gave Wally the telephone number of the guest house she would be staying at and also of a couple of hotels that had been recommended.

* * *

Don and Elsie Stevens were due to arrive in Great Yarmouth later that evening and would come to see the final performance on Saturday. They were both keen to see the offices that Jenny had found for Rita's agency and also to ask Rita if she fancied taking on a contortionist and a guitar act, plus one or two others. Don had taken a call from Audrey Audley the day before and had to stop her halfway through because she had been talking so fast and he couldn't understand all she was saying.

* * *

Jenny Benjamin watched the first house from the back of the auditorium and reacquainted herself with the routines that Jill and Doreen had choreographed for the show. The two boys certainly did pull their weight. She took from her handbag the dog-eared notebook in which she had, over the years, written all of her routines for shows, cabarets and pantomimes. Though parts of a few of her routines were evident in what the girls had put together, they had done so in a way that only enhanced the overall dance. Only last year she had been fearful that something awful was going to happen to her dance school, but the evidence was before her. Jill and Doreen had worked round the clock to turn out performances that would not be out of place on the London stage and Jenny felt a great sense of pride. As the interval brought the first half to a close, she decided to treat herself to a large gin and French.

She found Rita sitting at the bar deep in thought. "Penny for them."

"Hello Jenny, I was just going over the preparations for the final night. I have bought everyone a small gift to thank them and I was making sure I hadn't left anyone out." She handed Jenny her list.

"Mona Buckle isn't on there."

"Oh my goodness," said Rita, "how on earth did I forget Mona? I hear Bob has asked her back for the next season, she seems to have earned her stripes despite her funny little ways. Now, do I address the gift tag as Mona or as Mrs Buckle, and what can I buy her?"

"Mrs Buckle to be on the safe side," said Jenny, "and I would suggest something to do with moons and stars. *Martyns* have some brooches. I don't think she's a flowers and chocolates sort of woman. What did you buy the backstage boys?"

"I got them three bottles of *Lacons Legacy* each and a tankard with their names on; I thought it would be a keepsake. They've worked hard behind the scenes, and for wardrobe a scarf each with a scarf ring. I'm giving Jack some record tokens, as I know from Jim that he collects classical records and I wouldn't know what to select, unless it was Beethoven or Mozart on it. You would never think of Jack as a classical music lover would you?"

"He always struck me as a Bing Crosby kind of man," said Jenny, sipping her gin and enjoying it. "Any more news on Jim, do you think he will be here tomorrow?"

Rita shook her head. "Debbie is not expecting him back home until Monday at the earliest. The doctors think he's making good progress but according to Maud, who went to visit and got past the ward Sister, he really didn't look good and was struggling to remember things. Poor Dave is really upset by all accounts. He's off to Preston on Monday and would have liked nothing more than to take Jim for a pint. Sadly that isn't going to happen."

"Oh look," said Jenny, "the cavalry have arrived," as Don and Elsie Stevens walked into the bar. "I'll get some more drinks in. I won't go back for the second half. Are you having the same Rita? Hello Don, Elsie, what can I get you both?"

The party of four settled themselves at a corner table looking out on to the pier. When Don revealed the news from Audrey, Rita shook with laughter.

"How the hell do you manage a contortionist?" she said, as Jenny began to giggle. "And the guitar duo sound a hoot, I can't wait to see them in action."

"Well you'll be in luck there," said Don, "according to Audrey they are playing the *Palm Court* in Blackpool for one night. I need to check on the date."

"You wait until you see some of the other acts she's trying to unload," said Elsie. "I made a couple of phone calls to enquire about one or two of them at venues Audrey said they had played. The feedback was hilarious, everything from awful to bloody awful."

"Why is she giving up the agency anyway?" said Jenny, doing her best to control her titters. "I always thought she was one of the better agents."

"Not according to my source," said Don. "She used to be on the ball, but has let things slide over the years. You know what this business is like, you have to keep an eye on the quality of your acts. You don't just send them out in the hope they are going to perform as they did on the day you auditioned them. It doesn't work like that. Mystic Brian wouldn't be half as good as he is now if it hadn't been for some intervention on my part, I'm sure you can back that up Rita."

Rita nodded. "I couldn't agree more. Even old Ted, God Rest His Soul, needed careful handling. You have to turn up when the acts least expect you to. That way you see them as the venue sees them. Watching them in rehearsal studios is all very well, but it doesn't give you a proper idea of what they are like in front of a live audience."

"By all accounts," said Elsie, "Audrey is off on a world cruise with some friend of hers from the Smoke, Rueben Roberts. There is more to Audrey than perhaps we know."

"Well, good luck to her," said Rita. "I'll take a look at these acts. Jenny, perhaps you would like to accompany me, Elsie too if your stomach can stand it. What's happening with Derinda?"

Don smiled. "Well, I think she could be yours my friend," he said. "I don't think I could take her on at the moment and as she lives in Norwich she will be on much the same footing as she was with Audrey. Though how you will go about securing her the London engagements she craves I'm not sure. All that stuff in the papers didn't make comfortable reading."

"The little girl lives in France," said Jenny, "I think I could get her some work there. I still have a lot of contacts in Paris. And besides, she may want to get away from the entire hullabaloo once the Blackpool season is over."

"Jenny, you are full of surprises," said Rita, smiling at her friend. "There's room for a second desk in my office if you're interested?"

Jenny laughed. "You must have read my mind Rita. I was hoping you were going to ask me. I think you and I would make a great team."

And without hesitation they all raised their glasses to the new union.

* * *

Backstage the company prepared for the curtain to go up on the second half of the show. Bingo had once again run off with his master's hairpiece and, with a towel firmly tied on his head, Ricky had chased the little dog until he dropped it just in front of Jack's window.

Jack looked over his glasses. "Everything all right Ricky?" he called, looking at Bingo who sat looking up with such an angelic look it made Jack smile. "We had a dog when I was young. He was always turning over our dustbin and taking out all the tins and putting them in the back of his kennel. My mother was forever emptying it. There was a time when Paddy had so many tins in his kennel there was barely room for him."

Ricky rescued his hairpiece and smiled at Jack. "He can be a little rascal at times, but he's the best companion I have ever had." Bingo barked and followed his master back to the dressing room where Ricky hurriedly began to get ready to go on stage.

*   *   *

The foursome in the bar had a couple more drinks then decided to go and have something to eat and headed for the *Steak House* in Regent Road. Rita was pleased to be in the company of others. The last time she had eaten in the *Steak House* was when Ted had taken her one Sunday evening as a treat.

There was plenty to chat about and Don began to see a very different side to Jenny. They had often been at loggerheads over the years, but since Jenny had hung up her dancing shoes and handed the reins over to Jill and Doreen, she had blossomed and come into her own. He and Elsie had both been concerned about Rita since Ted's death, but Rita appeared to be coping, but it was comforting to see that Rita had found a good friend in Jenny who could keep an eye on things.

At the end of a very pleasant meal the four walked along the promenade and enjoyed the balmy evening air. Jenny departed in a taxi when they reached the Pleasure Beach, Don and Elsie walked Rita back to Lucinda's and then headed towards the *Carlton Hotel* where they had secured a sea view room for the weekend.

*   *   *

"Mr Boureme, I think you should know that Miss Dupree is in the dressing room. She arrived earlier this evening and says she is going to perform here tonight."

"Thanks Malcolm," said Sasha, somewhat taken aback by the news. He walked through the club; there were a few people at the bar and one or two others dotted around the tabled area, but the club was nowhere near as busy as it should have been for a Friday evening. He went through the rear door to the backstage corridor. He opened the door of Room One and there seated at the dressing room table with her makeup laid out in front of her was Lorna.

"Lorna, why are you here?" he asked, not moving from the doorway. "I think you should leave."

Lorna turned round with a makeup brush in her hand. "But my darling Sasha, I am here to sing. I cannot pay my bills if I don't work and you employed me to sing at your clubs. You promised me bright lights, adulation, fame, fortune and all so that you could prevent your ex-wife from performing. You wanted to hurt her and make her pay for abandoning your daughter and following her dream. You whispered sweet nothings in my ear and made love to me with all the passion that you possessed, and now you are telling me to leave when all I want to do is sing."

There was a strange fire in her eyes when she spoke that Sasha had never seen before. She spoke calmly and with such clarity that the hairs on the back of his neck stood on end. She turned back to face the mirror and continued to apply her makeup with all the skills of a fine artist. It was something she had learned from her sisters all those years ago. After a few moments she stopped and turned to face him again.

"Sasha, please make sure Mikael is ready to play for me at twelve. I left him the sheet music on the top of the piano. I will sing of unrequited love, of heartache and tragedy and finish with the anthem to end all anthems, *Non, Je Ne Regrette Rien*."

"I am asking you nicely to leave Lorna, or I shall remove you forcefully from the club."

Lorna stood up, walked towards him and stared him straight in the eye. "I don't think you understand Mr Boureme, I will sing here tonight. I have invited journalists to report on my triumphant return and I think you know how powerful the press can be, especially when they are fed a story."

"I will not allow them to come in here, now do as I ask and leave," said Sasha, feeling slightly alarmed by Lorna's attitude. She had guts he had to admit.

Lorna raised her right hand and put it to his throat and as he moved to stop her he felt the strong arms of someone behind him pull his arms back. He gasped at the pressure that had been applied.

"My friend Lars will look after you Mr Boureme if you cannot behave yourself. He will escort you to Mikael who you will instruct to announce me at midnight. I shall perform and then, my darling man, you will write me a cheque for ten thousand pounds and you can then consider our contract to be ended. I should warn you, Lars has a great strength and he will not be afraid to use it. No one messes with Laure Dupree."

At midnight Lorna sang, with a helpless Sasha looking on as Lars kept him company. The audience responded with polite applause. When the set was finished, Sasha returned to his office and Lorna came in smiling.

"That went very well, *mon chéri*," she oozed, sitting herself on the edge of the desk. "Now my darling, as much money as you have in cash and the rest I shall accept as a cheque. Lars, Mr Boureme will need some help and then you can pour us both a celebratory drink."

Lorna sat and watched as Sasha counted money. "Thank you my love," she said. "You may write a cheque for the remainder. Lars, help Mr Boureme find a pen."

"What more do you want from me?" said Sasha, doing his best not to lose his temper. "You have what you came for, now please go."

Lars placed two glasses on the desk.

"But we must drink together my sweet and cement this new understanding we have reached. Please don't even consider contacting the authorities when I leave, I have given a friend of mine access to all those lovely photographs we had taken. Far more interesting than those tame images you were trying to blackmail Derinda with. You see, my dear Sasha, I have been one step ahead of you all the way." She laughed gaily. "Let's drink to us."

As Lorna raised her glass, reluctantly Sasha raised his and drank the brandy. Lorna lent over the desk and kissed his cheek. "Our business is over my darling."

Smiling broadly she walked out of the office with Lars following. Closing the door Lars turned back, smiled and nodded at Sasha who winked in reply.

Sasha rinsed the two glasses and longed for the phone to ring. He tried to busy himself with some paperwork but he couldn't concentrate. He paced the office like a caged animal. He opened the door and looked along the corridor. Thirty minutes had passed and he felt beads of sweat on his brow. He banged his fist on the desk causing a barman who was passing to put his head round the door and ask if everything was okay. Just when he thought he couldn't stand it any more the phone rang. He grabbed the receiver and listened.

"She is sleeping like a baby."

Sasha replaced the receiver. feeling relief sweep over him and he smiled. "No one messes with Sasha Boureme," he whispered. "No one!"

Saturday 12th September

Enid passed Maud a cup of tea. "Bread is under the grill, won't be long." Maud thanked her sister and busied herself with the contents of her bag; somewhere in there she was sure she put the box office keys. She got up and went through to her own part of the shared property. Moving the book she was currently reading on the coffee table revealed the missing keys. Tutting as only Maud could, she picked them up and re-joined Enid who was now buttering toast at the kitchen table.

"Found the key then, that's good," she said. "Marmalade or damson jam? The damson is what Lilly made. She dropped a jar off at the shop after she had been to visit Jim yesterday. I think she finds living over Gorleston a bit cut off, with all of her friends dotted about the town."

"Lilly Brockett is a bloody marvel," said Maud. "That latest book of hers is an eye-opener. You would never know she had it in her. There are things that are going on in the bedroom that I didn't think were possible. I was trying to work it out last night in bed."

"I'll borrow it when you're done," said Enid, chomping on a bit of overdone toast. "I've just finished reading an Agatha Christie. I do love a Miss Marple."

"You might find Lilly's latest a bit racy for your tastes Enid. I should read it with caution. Now, I have got to pop in to *Middleton's* on my way to the theatre. My magazine didn't arrive again this week and there was a free packet of seeds with it."

"If you remember, Maud dear, you could see if they still have a copy of *Woman's Realm*, Lilly told me they had a couple of knitting patterns in there. Be right up your street. I'll be pleased when you've finished that bed jacket, those needles clicking away night after night is enough to drive me to drink."

Maud sighed heavily. "Then stay in your own side of the house Enid, that's why we had it divided up in the first place. If you will venture into my living room in the evening, then you will just have to put up with my knitting."

* * *

Rita returned from an early morning walk to the smell of bacon and eggs and was tempted to bypass her usual cereal and toast in favour of one of Lucinda's fry-ups. Ted had also enjoyed them. The dining room was relatively quiet and she acknowledged the two single gentlemen who had arrived two days earlier. She sat down at her usual table and glanced at the morning paper.

A familiar voice rang out in the hallway and in walked Dinah and George Sergeant. "I said, George, it was a rip-off, you can't go around charging that kind of money for cream teas." Dinah walked straight over to Rita and laid her hand on Rita's arm. "Mrs Ricer, George and I were both very sorry to hear of your loss. Your husband was a good turn."

Rita smiled gratefully. "That's very kind of you to say so. I didn't expect to see you both again this summer."

"Well," said Dinah, "I said to George, didn't I say to you George, why don't we go and spend a few days down at Lucinda's and we can catch the last night of the show at the *Sands*. We arrived last night and, as luck would have it, that nice lady at the box office had two tickets, even though the board outside said sold out."

"They will be house seats," said Rita, "we always hold one or two back for each performance in case we have special guests."

"Did you hear that George, they're special seats," said Dinah. "We are really looking forward to seeing the show again, aren't we George? Though it won't be the same without your husband, may he rest in peace! He was very good Mrs Ricer, he made my George laugh and, believe me, that is a feat in itself. Well, mustn't detain you any longer, here's Mrs Haines with your breakfast." Dinah sat down opposite her husband and continued to chat away happily with George nodding and smiling in the right places.

* * *

Debbie had been up most of the night with a very overtired Karen. Peter was still asleep as she put a mug of tea on the bedside cabinet and opened the curtains. Her thoughts went to her father and she wondered if he had had a good night and was feeling any better. A photograph of her mother caught her eye, it was one that she had had since her schooldays and there it was still on the chest of drawers, the silver frame kept bright by her father's keen polishing. She picked it up and stared at it.

"Are you okay love?" said the sleepy voice of her husband and she turned and nodded.

"Just thinking," she replied and put the frame back in its place.

* * *

There was a buzz of excitement about the theatre that night, talk of the Blackpool opening to come and what plans they all had when *Summertime Sunshine* approached its final curtain that evening. An end of the season party had been planned and all were expected to attend. Jonny Adams had been continually rehearsing his act in the Green Room. He was excited that his parents were going to the in the audience and would accompany him to the gathering afterwards when he would be able to introduce them to all the friends he had made. Petra and Mario were checking plate stock to make sure they had enough for the two final performances. The dancers were making use of the vacant stage to limber up and Bingo was running up and down backstage clutching a rag doll that Derinda had bought him firmly between his teeth, leaving Ricky secure in the knowledge that his two wigs were at least safe that evening.

As the audience filed in for the second house, there were several people missing. Lilly Brockett had taken to her bed with a cold, Maud was looking after baby Karen so that

Debbie and Peter could visit Jim and then have an evening out. Freda was putting her feet up with a box of *Weekend* and a film on the telly, while her husband Dick made his regular appearance at the *Legion*. Lucinda, who was feeling somewhat exhausted from a very busy week, was enjoying some peace in the separate apartment that she called her haven and Dave was having a couple of drinks with Dan and Stella on a rare night off for both of them. Ken was coping behind the bar with two temporary bar staff on what turned out to be one of Henry's Bar's busiest summer seasons.

Muriel duly arrived at the theatre on the arm of her husband Barry and they took their seats just behind those reserved for Don and Elsie Stevens. Rita, who decided that there was little she could do now, avoided going backstage and joined Jenny for a quick drink at the bar before they both went into the auditorium.

The lights dimmed and for the final time that summer, Maurice Beeney raised his baton and the show began just as it had done since it opened all those weeks before. Whether the dancers had an extra spring in their step that evening, or Tommy told one of Ted's old jokes, or Jonny did an extra trick, or The Olanzos' plates spun faster, or if Derinda sang a ballad with more tenderness in her voice than she had ever done while Ricky lightly touched the piano keys, was for them to know. But the audience showed their appreciation with loud applause and cheers as everyone took their final bows.

* * *

The following day Dave went to see Jim one final time and was pleased to see that his friend seemed a little more like his old self. Dave chatted away nervously, knowing that the time was drawing near when he would be on his way to Preston, not knowing when they would see each other again. Jim listened to his friend and he too felt the sadness that only a close friendship can bring when paths must lead in different directions.

"You promise me you'll make a go of it in Blackpool," said Jim. "You have a good mate in Dan."

Dave nodded. "I intend to do my best by him," he said. "This is something I thought would never happen. I just wish I didn't have to move away, I have so many friends here."

"And you'll make new ones in Blackpool," said Jim, reassuringly, "but that doesn't mean the old ones will be forgotten, they will still be there. Where will you stay overnight in Blackpool until the house is ready?"

"Marie and Graham have offered me a bed. Most nights I will probably go back to Preston, Dan's parents Mary and John are looking forward to me being there. They say we will be able to get to know each other better before Dan moves up. They've been giving Josie and Madge a hand with the house and Marie and Graham have been chipping in too."

"I am really pleased for you Dave," said Jim, smiling. "Now do me a favour and pass me some water. The heat in this hospital is unbearable."

* * *

Rita packed her suitcase and loaded it in to the back of the car. Lucinda waved her off and said she looked forward to seeing her when she returned later that year. By that time Rita hoped to have her house on the market and in the meantime Jenny was looking out for suitable properties that Rita might make her home.

* * *

Don and Elsie Stevens took one final walk along the promenade, stopping by *The Golden Sands Theatre* and watched as the sets were being loaded on to the trucks ready for their northbound journey. They looked up at the show hoardings and both agreed that their summer season show had been a great success, mainly thanks to its director Moira (Rita Ricer) Clarence.

Chapter Sixteen *And the World Goes Round*

S *ummertime Sunshine* continued to be successful and
brought new life to the *North Pier Theatre* during the
illuminations season. As many of the company commented, as
they walked the pier to the theatre, maybe the show should
now be called *Autumn Winds* as the earlier warmer days of late
September had turned to the chillier and more colder days of
October.

The seafront was a hive of activity at night, with many
coming for the lights and staying on to see a show. The
atmosphere was totally different to the calmer Great
Yarmouth promenade. The trams rattled along on their
journeys between Lytham St Anne's and Fleetwood.
Blackpool, known for its kiss-me-quick hats and fun
atmosphere, lived up to its name and there were plenty of
nightclubs that the company could visit if the fancy took them
after the show.

Dan had taken a temporary job in a pub in Preston until
the house in Lytham St Anne's was completed. Dave had
settled into a routine at the North Pier and now that Dan was
home, he only spent a couple of nights a week staying over
with Marie and Graham. Dave visited the house almost every
day and did what he could. Graham Pettingale had made a
wonderful job of the garden and Dave was hopeful that he and
Dan could move in by mid-November. He had had a couple of
interviews for jobs, one at Blackpool Tower and another at a
nightclub in the centre of town. On recommendation, Dan had
been interviewed for a bar job at a four-star hotel at the north

end of the town and would be able to start the first week of December.

* * *

Back in Great Yarmouth, Debbie and Peter had moved in to the Southtown house, with Peter staying in Norwich most nights but driving over on a Friday evening to spend the weekend with his family. Jim continued to sleep downstairs in the front lounge and enjoyed having his family around him. He could escape the activity of nappy changing and the cries of his granddaughter and enjoy the tranquillity of his own room. Maud visited every other day and Lilly Brockett popped in whenever she was in town to do her shopping, regaling Jim with details of the latest book she was working on. The odd phone call from Dave kept him abreast of what was happening up North, though Jim longed to have his friend sitting opposite him so they could enjoy a drink and a chat together. Now he realised how much he missed his best friend.

* * *

Jenny had kept her promise and with input from Jill and Doreen the office over the antiques shop in Northgate Street had been decorated, carpeted and curtained. Though in Rita's agency office, Jenny had decided upon wooden blinds which she thought were more befitting a business operation. A sign was duly erected above the one for the shop below and *Rita's Angels*, in bold blue italic lettering, incorporating the office of the *JB Dancing School* became a reality.

In a telephone conversation with Rita, Jenny arranged for the acts that they were putting on their books to audition for them both, with Jenny joining Rita in Blackpool for three days. They both agreed there was work to be done, especially with a couple of the turns, who needed stage presence drummed into them and Jenny was itching to give them further direction.

* * *

Enid turned her attention from current stock to reintroducing one or two things in readiness for Christmas. With Maud able to spend more time with her in the shop, now that the box office was closed, they continued their usual banter and disagreements as had become the normal routine for them both.

* * *

Stella mourned the loss of Dan and thought that whoever Ken employed as a replacement in *Henry's Bar*, they would never match up to the person she now regarded as a close friend and confidant.

* * *

Lucinda said farewell to her regular summer guests and welcomed back the winter ones of lorry drivers and offshore workers, well used to Lucinda and her funny little ways.

Muriel and Barry decided to take a holiday away from the guest house and with no bed occupancy they closed up for three weeks and went in search of sunshine abroad.

Freda, who never understood why people would want to travel abroad, made do with a wet weekend in Margate at an ageing aunt's leaving Dick to his own devices, which she knew she may later regret.

Mona Buckle was now back at home and the ritual of the silent breakfasts before her husband Bertie left for work were back in operation. Still receiving news and money from his two sons, he longed for the day when he could kiss his wife goodbye for the last time. Her mood had improved while she had been working at the *Golden Sands* he freely admitted to his fishing friends as they dangled their rods off the pier. But it didn't take her long to settle back in the old ways that had been the blight of his married life.

Saturday 7th November

The club was very busy and Sasha was pleased to see that some familiar faces had returned to his favourite of the four clubs his family ran. He had visited the other three venues earlier in the evening and business had also picked up. A decision had been made to feature cabaret at these venues two evenings a week, making it more of an event and meaning that the money being saved from having a nightly show could be used to attract the top stars of the day. Negotiations were taking place with some of the top agents in the business. The clubs were only open for business from Wednesday to Saturday and the membership had increased because of it. No one wanted to sit in a half-empty venue at the early part of the week.

Saying good night to the staff as they left the venue shortly after 2am, he told his security guard not to wait. He would lock up as he had some things he needed to attend to before leaving. He poured himself a Scotch and retreated to his office to go over some paperwork his mother had sent. Figures were not his strong point and he struggled to understand what he was reading. His mother had attached some notes written in French and instructed him that they needed his urgent attention. The overhead light was causing a shadow and so he switched on his desk lamp and turned the other off. Pouring another Scotch as he did so, he went into the staff toilet and cursed that the roller towel had not been replaced as per his instruction earlier. What was the point of employing a manager when it was necessary to do everything himself? He cursed the English. He pulled some paper from the cubicle and dried his hands as best he could. He had overdone the Scotch and wished he had taken more water with it. How he longed to be back in France instead of marking time in London. The sooner the family got rid of this stone around his neck the better as far as he was concerned. He walked back in to the office and froze in the doorway, not believing what he saw. It had to be too much Scotch, and his eyes were deceiving him.

"Did you think I had gone to heaven?" said the familiar voice speaking from behind his desk. "You *are* a naughty boy Sasha to try and double cross me."

Sasha was aware of someone standing closely behind him and he knew that he was trapped.

* * *

It wasn't until the following Wednesday that Sasha's body was discovered, with a suicide note beside it, by a shocked employee. The news of his death was headlines the following day in the national papers which Derinda read in disbelief. With Ricky at her side she walked the rain-sodden promenade trying to get things straight in her head. To her mind Sasha had never been the suicide type and she knew that there would be questions that would need answering.

That evening as she sat at her dressing room table applying her makeup she was interrupted by the arrival of two policemen. She invited them in and closed the door.

In an interview to the press, Derinda explained how, through solicitors, a new agreement had been reached with her ex-husband and that once she had finished her season in Blackpool a meeting was being arranged between them to iron out the final details.

* * *

Rita made a phone call to Elsie and both were of the same opinion; Lorna Bright had to be found. The police had found her London flat empty of any personal belongings. The only indication that anyone had been there were two unwashed mugs gathering mould in the kitchen sink and a discarded toothbrush in the bathroom. There were no clothes, no bed linen, no towels; even the curtains at the windows had been removed. A few days later the headlines were now reading that the police wanted to question Lorna Bright in connection with the suicide of Sasha Boureme.

Derinda seemed totally unfazed as the stories unfolded and although the media attention was unwelcome, she behaved with dignity, answered any questions and cooperated with the police. The publicity again acted in her favour and the North Pier box office was bombarded with requests for tickets. The papers were read back in Great Yarmouth with many an eye raised to the ceiling and the odd tut was heard. Rita gave Lucinda a call to let her know that everything was well and not to believe all she read in the papers.

As the search for Lorna widened, the name June Ashby was mentioned. Wally, who had still had no luck in tracing her, went voluntarily to the police to give a statement. It seemed to everyone that the Ashby legacy from the season of 1969 lived on.

* * *

The illumination season came to a close and the company of *Summertime Sunshine* said goodbye for the final time, each returning to their homes for the forthcoming pantomime season or to take stock before moving on to their next engagement. Derinda considered the offer from the Paris club which Jenny had set up, with the agreement that Ricky could accompany her as part of the package. She would begin her engagement in January. Derinda would then be able to see her daughter on a more regular basis. Jeannie was now in a special boarding school away from the clutches of her overbearing grandmother and since the death of Sasha all ties had been broken. It wasn't any easy decision to make, but one that Derinda thought was best for her Jeannie.

Rita returned to Great Yarmouth and was shown the property that Jennie thought would best suit her. The three-bedroomed house was in Gorleston, had a small garden and was situated in one of the quieter roads near the Parish Church. Rita didn't need much convincing and put in an offer, much to Lucinda's disappointment who hoped Rita would remain with her for a while yet.

The agency was up and running and Rita was able to take command of her new ship and help all those wishing to tread the boards and make names for themselves.

* * *

It was on the very cold morning of the 4th December that Dave, with the help of a hospital nurse and Peter, wheeled Jim through the cemetery grounds and placed him in front of his wife's grave. Debbie stood a few feet away with Karen wrapped in her arms, and with Peter and Dave by her side she watched. Jim was barely able to keep his eyes open because of all the drugs that had been pumped into him. He sat in quiet contemplation looking at the headstone. The words written there he had read so many times and were etched for ever on his mind and in his heart. In his gloved hand he held a single red rose which, with some effort, he tossed onto the grave where it fell against the headstone and stood proudly on its thorny stem. And then, as he had done many times before, Jim recited the Lord's Prayer in his head and then aloud he said, "Hello my darling Karen, I have missed you every day we have been apart. I have taken care of everything, just as we planned and now I can leave and be with you again." Despite the chill in the air Jim felt a warm glow come over him and something like the texture of a feather touched his cheek and he closed his eyes for the final time.

* * *

The days that followed were of quiet contemplation by all those who knew and loved Jim. All thoughts of the forthcoming festive season were cast aside as more important duties took priority. There were flowers and wreaths to be ordered and an obituary to be written for the papers. There was a wake to organise and family and friends to be contacted.

Hidden within the pages of the newspapers that few were finding time to read was the news that a woman's body had been found washed up in the River Thames and was believed to be that of Lorna Bright. Jenny spotted it and pointed it out to Rita. Rita, whose head was awash with so many things and now the news of Jim's death, dismissed the report and said it was for others to deal with now. Jenny, making them both a cup of tea, wholeheartedly agreed.

Ricky read the article to Derinda whose only comment was, "Well, that's that then."

The storm clouds gathered and the heavy rain that had been forecast did its worst. For two days the town was bombarded with rods of steel and few ventured out if they could possibly avoid it.

* * *

The weather had settled and become much calmer when the cortège left the Southtown house on the 14th December and made its way slowly over Haven Bridge. There was even the glimmer of sunshine trying to break through the clouds. The procession rode slowly in to the town centre where it made its way slowly down Regent Road and stopped outside the pier where the name Jim Donnell had been placed on the hoarding above the entrance. Outside, a local crowd of employees from cafés, shops and amusement arcades had gathered to pay their respects. Maud Bennett with Bob Scott, Roger Norris, Mona Buckle, Jack, Barbara, Beverley and all the backstage crew walked slowly out of the pier entrance and into the waiting cars. Continuing along the full length of promenade the cortège turned back towards the town for the service at St Nicholas church opposite the newly christened offices for *Rita's Angels*.

With Dan at his side, Dave spoke on behalf of every one of the friend that they had lost, and Bob Scott, not one for public speaking, echoed the sentiment and told of the wonderful work Jim had done at the *Golden Sands* and why he would never be forgotten. A tearful Debbie sent her father on his way with a passage from the Bible that he had read at her mother's funeral.

Derinda Daniels stepped forward and, as Maurice Beeney played the organ, she sang Jim's favourite hymn *The Old Rugged Cross*.

Mona turned to Lilly who sat beside her. "I sang that one day at the theatre when I was cleaning. I sensed that Mr Donnell liked that hymn, the spirits never lie."

The wake was held at *Henry's Bar* at the expense of Ken the proprietor who had insisted on doing so, much to the surprise of Stella. Memories and stories were shared and some taped music provided by Peter played some of the tunes that Jim had loved.

Dan could only partly feel the pain he knew Dave was going through. Over the months they had been together, not a day had passed when Dave hadn't mentioned Jim. Dave excused himself from the circle of friends and went outside. His head was so full of many things that he wanted to share and he broke down in tears. Like Debbie and all those who loved Jim, he wondered how he was going to cope with the pain he felt banging inside his chest and manage to get through life without his best friend.

Chapter Seventeen   Over the Rainbow

June Ashby looked out of her dressing room window on a beautiful vista. She felt alive again and her appearances were proving to be a great success. The television stations were forever pestering her to do interviews and the offers of more work flooded in. Her new agent, Alfonso DuBrette, was doing sterling work promoting his star across the land. New Zealand was going to be the next port of call for a short season, but for now *The Theatre Royal* in Sydney would do nicely. She loved the old building which had originally started out as *The Prince of Wales* in 1855. The theatre had retained all of its original features with the wonderful proscenium arch that reminded June of the theatres she had played back in Great Britain.

She turned her attention to the postcard that lay on her dressing table and finished writing to Rita and Ted in the hope that it would find them both well and would also surprise them to learn that she had made a new life for herself. She had long decided that when Wally and she had parted she could no longer stay in contact with the past. Lorna and Robin appeared to have got themselves sorted out and she felt she had done all she could for her sister. She knew that Lorna had improved both in singing and her own wellbeing and no longer needed the pills and potions to get her through the day. June had, with no announcement, made a visit to Norfolk in the hope of sourcing clubs where Lorna could play, but had decided that it was for her sister to decide without further help from her.

When Robin and Lorna had taken off for the day in Paris, June had made her final preparations to move on. Leaving only a note that she would be in touch some time, she gave the two the full run of the chateau, but informed them that the agents would be putting it on the market within six months and they would have to find themselves somewhere else to live. At first she had felt guilty about keeping the secret from them, but she needed to make a new life away from all the dramas that had ensued. Making a clean break of it was the only way she knew how.

She signed the postcard *With fondest love, June* and left it for her personal assistant to arrange posting. The following day she would see the final rushes of the film she had made and which she hoped would broaden her appeal when released. Alfonso had made things happen for her, something she had never experienced in England. Unlike the old days she no longer had to rely on musicals and revues to see her through. Here in Australia there was more on offer and she intended to make the most of every opportunity that was given to her.

* * *

Some weeks later, relaxing in their rented Sydney apartment, Audrey kicked off her shoes and rubbed her aching legs. Walking about in the heat in heels was not the thing to do. Rueben handed her a drink and began to plan their sightseeing for the following day. They were both enjoying Australia so much that they had decided to stay on for a few weeks and then book another cruise liner to New York. With the shackles of the agency firmly shaken off, Audrey was embracing her new life and Rueben had proved to be the perfect companion.

After an early evening meal they walked back to the city and, on a whim, decided to go and see a film. Not paying any attention to what was showing, Rueben paid the cashier and they went in to the air-conditioned movie house. As back in England, the adverts came thick and fast and then they settled down for the main feature. Audrey sat bolt upright when the name June Ashby flashed before her eyes. The title was *To Catch a Falling Star* and the film concluded with the following scene...

The reflection in the mirror looked back and for a few moments flashbacks from memories flooded back. The lights around the mirror illuminated her face as she looked at the array of makeup that lay on the dressing room table. Leaning forward she studied her complexion carefully. Taking the foundation container in her left hand she applied the base with her right in firm sweeping strokes. With a deft hand and attention to detail she applied her eyeshadow with the soft brush, the one she treasured. The wand of mascara provided lift to her eyelashes and the black eyeliner made her eyes appear wider. Picking up the false eyelashes she applied a thin streak of glue to each and laid them to one side in order that they would become tacky. Adding more colour to the base foundation her face came alive as if it had been kissed by rays of sunshine. The rouge highlighted her strong cheekbones creating her other persona. She applied the thick top false eyelashes and the less heavy bottom ones. Her eyes looked wider and ready for the strong stage lights that would dazzle them. Her lipstick added a final touch of colour to the collage and the thin black pencil outlined her lips with definition. She sat back from the mirror to study the finished product. With fingernails freshly painted, she clipped the diamond earrings to her ears, fastened the matching necklace about her slender neck and slipped into the stage gown. She placed her feet firmly in the silver stilettos and prepared to face her public. Her white teeth dazzled as she smiled at her reflection, her transformation was complete.

"Are you ready now?" She turned and looked at the person who stood in the doorway and nodded. She got up from the dressing room table and, after the handcuffs were applied to her wrists, she was led away in complete silence knowing that her fate was sealed.

As the final scene concluded, the slamming of a cell door was heard followed by an image of June hearing the applause of an adoring public. She turned to face the applause and, with a chilling smile, she took her final bow.

As the credits rolled, Audrey relaxed her breath. She had been mesmerised by the film from start to finish; even Rueben, not usually a lover of films, commented on how much he had enjoyed it.

* * *

It was many months later when in the *Great Yarmouth Mercury* the advertisement appeared for the *ABC Regent Cinema*.

The New Hollywood Sensation *To Catch a Falling Star*. starring Ronald DeWynter, Carrie Graham and introducing June Ashby.

Critics called it – 'Breathtaking', 'A Story of Love, Passion and Betrayal', 'A Fusion of Hollywood Glamour and Sexual Longing', 'Newcomer - June Ashby - lights up the screen', 'Ronald DeWynter and Carrie Graham sizzle'.

And as Enid was wont to say over the breakfast table to Maud, who was finishing some ribbing, "I much prefer a Bing."

The End

A Word from the Author and Acknowledgements

W ith the exception of the references to the stars of the day, Leslie Crowther, Ted Rogers, Kathy Kirby etc. all other characters in this story are fictitious and do not represent any person either living or dead.

At the time of going to print - The Britannia Pier Theatre continues to present one-night attractions during summer months. The newly refurbished St Georges Theatre is back in business with a varied programme of concerts and plays that will delight audiences. The Gorleston Pavilion is the heart of entertainment with shows, pantomimes, visiting theatre companies and variety acts throughout the year. The Hippodrome Circus continues circus tradition with a varied bill throughout the year with Peter Jay and son Jack overseeing productions.

Palmers Department Store in the Market Place remains Great Yarmouth's prestigious store and a restaurant that is bound to please the hungry shopper.

Details have emerged that a much needed overhaul of Yarmouth Vauxhall Railway Station is imminent.

Matthes - In my debut novel *Twice Nightly* I referred to the Bakery Matthes as Mathews. Matthes were the producers of the local *Sunshine Loaf* and had a much-loved coffee shop and first floor restaurant in King Street Great Yarmouth at the rear of their Bakery Shop. Another shop/restaurant was situated in England's Lane, Gorleston almost opposite the Matthes factory where workers could be seen riding their bicycles to work every morning. I am happy to put the record straight and apologise for the error.

Lacons New Brews

Lacons Brewery, famous for its Falcon emblem, landed back in Great Yarmouth after a 45-year hiatus with the launch of three new permanent beers — ENCORE, LEGACY and AFFINTY. I would like to thank the brewery for giving me permission to use the new beers in *TCAFS*, and take this opportunity to wish them every success.

A Selection of what Readers said about *Twice Nightly*

"I enjoyed the book – it really had the feel of an early sixties seaside. I had a couple of family holidays in Great Yarmouth at the time and remember the on-the-pier shows and the circus. You have a very good memory!"

"Really did enjoy your book, brought back memories of a happier time. Love the twists and turns. Amazing description of the times. When is the next one?"

"Looking forward to the *Twice Nightly* sequel."

"Read your book, could hear you telling the story in my head – very impressed! Keep going… you have talent."

"Thank you for your encouragement re: my creative writing this year. And big congratulations on publishing your book this year."

The comments are taken from letters and cards I received. Other comments can be viewed on Amazon and my website: http://www.twicenightly.net
You can email me at tonygarethsmith@twicenightly.net

My Thanks to

Marika, Simon, Pauline, Jodi and all at Fast-Print Publishing for bringing this sequel to fruition.

David McDermott, my Norfolk agent. David works so hard on my behalf to bring my writing to the attention of others.

To the Staff at
The Prom Hotel, 77 Marine Parade, Great Yarmouth www.promhotel.co.uk for always making me feel welcome, and also to their sister hotel The Pier Hotel, Harbour Mouth, Gorleston on sea www.pierhotelgorleston.co.uk
The Prom Hotel – 01493 842308
The Pier Hotel – 01493 662631

To my friend and fellow author David Wailing who has had his ear bent on more than one occasion when I have needed advice. www.davidwailing.com

And finally to my family and friends for their continued support and belief in me.

A Note to my Readers

Authors, proof readers and editors are human and while every endeavour has been made to ensure that text and punctuation are correct at the time of going to print, please forgive any slight error. When my first novel was published one of the first comments made to me was "did you know there was a comma missing on page...."

I sincerely hope you will enjoy this sequel and if you do please tell your friends and ask them to purchase a copy for themselves or as a gift. I am always happy to send a signed compliment slip if you supply me with a name and address and the dedication you would like. Please email me. See my website for details.

The Landladies Convention
A Short Tale from Great Yarmouth

By Tony Gareth Smith
Author of the novel *Twice Nightly* and *To Catch a Falling Star*
set in the world of seaside variety entertainment.

Website - http://www.twicenightly.net

I dedicate this story to Ian my favourite nephew-in-law —
who gave me the idea for one of the characters.

Copyright ©Tony Gareth Smith 2014

The Landladies' Convention

The Great Yarmouth and Gorleston Guest House Association, affectionately known as GAGGA, had served old and new landladies for a number of years. It supported those that had opened their doors to the throng of holiday makers that made their way to the East Coast's premier seaside resorts of Great Yarmouth and Gorleston on Sea.

To become a member of this elite club, you had to be nominated by a member who had been with the association for at least two years. Lucinda Haines, who had been a guest house proprietor for most of her life, had nominated rival Muriel Evans and had never let her forget it. Lucinda held quite a clout with the committee, and even though Muriel and she didn't always see eye to eye, this was business and Lucinda did her best to keep the peace for the sake of the association.

Muriel in turn had nominated her less than well heeled neighbour Freda Boggis, and over the years had tried to encourage Freda in the world of guest house accommodation. Although this had often fallen on deaf ears, Muriel nevertheless soldiered on, true to the cause.

The summer season of 1969 had come to an end and it was time for GAGGA to meet and arrange what they termed as 'The Landladies Convention', an evening of social intercourse with a meal and dance to follow. It was a time to celebrate and congratulate each other on a job well done and for prizes to be awarded to the top three guest houses of the season. The judging of these differed from year to year. Sometimes each guest house was visited by a panel of three members of the public randomly chosen to inspect all the houses, while other times actual guests were asked about their stay, and rewarded with a voucher for a tea and cake at Matthes coffee shop, More often than not, secret guests stayed one or two nights and reported back to the committee. Due to the number of guest houses involved, not all houses were visited and it was never revealed which ones had been omitted.

Winning any of the top prizes had eluded Lucinda, Muriel and Freda over the years. But ever hopeful of succeeding, they all had their eye on the coveted silver cup and blue sash of excellence.

At the head of the proceedings was Shirley Llewellyn, who had been Chair of the Committee for 15 years and ran a guest house that was known around the town as second to none. She had been the first to have wash basins installed in all of her 10 bedrooms.

Shirley was ably assisted by Secretary Fenella Wright and Treasurer Agnes Brown. All three had won the top prize respectively and were regarded in high esteem and some jealousy by many of the other members.

In the meeting room of the Masonic Lodge, Shirley Llewellyn called the gathering to order and noted that not all members were present, something she frowned upon. Her blonde hair had been styled by Mr Adrian, a salon she favoured in the town, and she was dressed in a black two-piece trouser suit which flattered her slim form. The white blouse highlighted the red beads that hung round her neck, matching the lipstick and nail polish she had used for some years.

She tapped her gavel lightly and beamed her toothy smile to the assembled gathering, keeping a weather eye on her secretary to ensure that all discussion was duly noted.

"Ladies, we are here once again to discuss what has been a busy season for us all. The reports of holiday makers to our resort have been much covered by the Mercury with some rather lovely snaps of people enjoying themselves. Fenella has been busy sourcing a venue for this year's dinner dance, and following a less than favourable time at the Caravan Park's event hall last season, we are going to be catered for at The Cliff Hotel."

Murmurs of approval sounded and Fenella gave a nervous giggle and blushed.

Shirley gave a light cough and continued. "A three-course meal will be followed by dancing to Maurice Beeney and his All Rounders..."

But before she could finish, Freda raised her hand. "Can I ask if we can bring our husbands like last year, only my Dick likes a night out?"

Shirley gave Freda a steely look, she disliked being interrupted. "As I was about to say before Mrs Boggis pre-empted, your husbands will be most welcome. The ticket price has been set at three pounds which will include a complimentary sherry on arrival."

Agnes Brown, who had been trying to clip her unruly hair in place, looked up at Shirley. "There is also a raffle and books of tickets are on sale should anyone wish to get the ball rolling."

Agnes received the steely look and Shirley continued. "As Agnes so rightly points out, there will be a prize raffle...."

Before she could continue, Agnes - who was totally oblivious to anything that was going on around her - said, "Mathees are offering a cream tea for two, Jarrolds are giving ten pounds of book tokens and Palmers are donating a pair of silver candle sticks, some bed linen and a picnic hamper. There are lots of other things to be won and the tickets are two and six a book."

"Thank you Agnes," said Shirley who was doing her best to remain calm and focused. "The date set for this event is Friday 31st October."

"That's the Legion dinner and dance," said Freda to Muriel, who was making notes of her own. "My Dick won't like to choose."

Muriel raised her eyebrows and shook her head. "The way your Dick is attached to the Legion, I'm surprised he never thought of joining the foreign years ago."

Freda gave her friend a quizzical look. "Dick doesn't speak any other languages, only English."

"And he doesn't do that particularly well," Muriel replied.

Another steely look from the Chair rendered the two silent.

"We are also delighted to tell you that we have lined up a first rate act to entertain you for part of the evening. Agnes has secured the services of Rick O'Shea and the Ramblers," said Shirley, who had had a crush on Rick for some years.

"My Dick loves them" said Freda quite elated by the news. "That will put pay to the Legion; he'll be rocking and a rolling with the best of them."

Muriel shuddered at the thought, she could hardly wait!

"I did try to get the Beverley Sisters," said Agnes, wrinkling her nose.

"Well I am sure Rick and his boys will do just nicely," said Shirley as she felt a bead of perspiration run down her forehead. "It's rather hot in here; shall we have a window open?"

"Isn't it him that wears that silver llama suit?" said Freda, playing with the clasp of her handbag and clicking it.

Aware of a reprimand from Shirley, Muriel did her best to answer quietly. "I am sure they played the Sands one Sunday evening supporting Dandy Cole, that singer comedian who looked like he had fell in to a dressing up box by what he had on, and there was that dreadful trumpet playing duo who couldn't have carried a tune in a bucket."

"My Dick would know, I think he rather fancied himself in a llama suit," said Freda who was getting a bit bored and fancied a nice cup of tea and a cream horn. "Oh look out; Shirley is going to bang that toffee hammer again."

Shirley had composed herself and smiled warmly. "Now I think we can move on to any other business."

Agnes spoke up. "The subs are due."

"Thank you Agnes dear. Yes ladies, it is that time of the year again and I am pleased to say that we haven't raised these in two years thanks to the generous legacy from Wilma Hewitt who sadly fell under a double decker when on busman's holiday in Margate."

There was silence in the room as they all remembered Wilma who had for many years been one of the top guest house landladies.

Freda felt a tear roll down her cheek. "She gave me a lovely blue china bowl."

Muriel looked at her friend. "It was a chamber pot, Freda, I told you not to put it in the dining room."

"But it did look lovely when the bulbs came up" said Freda wiping her eyes. "It had little pink and blue flowers on it."

"Where is it now?"

"Dick uses it to keep his maggots in for fishing and then one of the handles broke off, he is so clumsy. But whenever I see that bowl I think of Wilma."

Shirley coughed loudly causing several of the ladies to awake from their forty winks. "Now for some forthcoming events which I hope you ladies will be making note of in your Landladies Diary which we gave you last Christmas."

There was a rustle of handbags as people tried to locate the gilt edged slim line diary much loved by the committee. Many had mislaid their treasures or given them to grandchildren to crayon in.

"Both Agnes and Fenella have been busy and I am pleased to say that our coffee mornings through the winter period will be held every other Wednesday morning at 10.30 in Matthes function room. The gals have lined up some suppliers to come and show us their wares of table and bed linen. We will also have a rep from Crockett, Crockett and Crockett who will be showing us some lovely lines in cutlery, crockery and kitchen wares. Fenella will give you all the dates in her newsletter which I think is proving quite popular among you all. Now I think that is about everything."

"Typical!" said Freda. "Trust them to choose market day, why couldn't we have it on a Thursday when it's half day closing?"

The sound of Shirley's gavel stopped the conversation and drew the meeting to a close. Freda heaved herself up from the chair, still thinking of her much missed piece of china.

Lucinda Haines had sat at the back of the hall to make a quick exit, she didn't want to get caught up with Freda and Muriel who no doubt would be heading off somewhere for a natter.

As Lucinda walked along the now deserted promenade, the chilly breeze blowing in off the North Sea made her wish she had put on her heavier coat. Thinking of clothes, her mind went through the few items that hung in her wardrobe and she knew that she would have to purchase something new for the forthcoming dinner and dance. The thought of going on her own didn't appeal, but with no spouse she would have to brave it as she had done other years. Now if that nice Ted Ricer, the comedian who had played at the Golden Sands Theatre had been single, he would have been a most suitable escort.

The noisy chatter of Freda and Muriel could be heard coming up behind her and before they caught up with her, she turned off the promenade and headed down St Peter's Road.

"Now where is she going I wonder?" said Freda.

"Probably visiting Ruby Hamilton, she never turns up for these meetings, always claiming she is too busy running her guest house, yet she'll be first in line when it comes to a free drink at the bar."

"She's like Judas in a chariot that one," Freda huffed knowingly. "And she never dips her nets."

Muriel raised her eyebrows. 'Pot, kettle' she thought, deciding not to comment. It was Freda's turn to pay for coffee and cake and she wasn't going to let that slip by.

Standing at her gate, Lettice Webb saw Lucinda approaching, "No doubt off to visit that Hamilton woman," she thought to herself. Lettice had only been a guest house proprietor in Great Yarmouth for three years after moving away from a guest house she ran near Land's End. Lettice was of medium height and slim build. Her features were soft and gentle. She dressed in high buttoned collar blouses, long skirts and low court shoes. Her hair was dark auburn and quite curly. Her attention to make-up was immaculate considering the image the rest of her portrayed, a little eye shadow coloured her lids and her heavily powered face was highlighted by the red lipstick she favoured. Lettice had an unusual voice and it was of the general opinion that she must have had throat problems as a child and it had left her with a gravelly sound. Her manner was pleasant but hid a deep suspicion of anyone who tried to get too close.

Lucinda stopped at the gate and smiled at Lettice. "Hello Lettice, I had hoped to see you at the meeting today, you did get the invitation I take it?"

Lettice smiled. "Yes thank you I did, Lucinda, but I really don't think I would have much to offer GAGGA."

"It's a shame," said Lucinda, who was always keen to get someone on her side. She never had much luck making friends and when Lettice Webb had come on the scene, Lucinda had been the first to offer the hand of friendship having known the previous owner of 'Gull House'.

Lucinda had an idea. "Look I wonder if you would be interested in coming along to our dinner dance on the 31st of October. It will be at the Cliff Hotel this year and it would be an opportunity for you to meet some of the other landladies and perhaps reconsider joining the convention."

Lettice, who didn't wish to offend but would prefer to be left alone to run her business, considered the idea. What would be the harm? One evening out and it would be a change from staying in on her own.

"I think I will join you, Lucinda," said Lettice surprising not only Lucinda but also herself. "It would, as you say, give me a chance to meet other landladies and I don't really get out very much. You must tell me how much the tickets are and I will settle with you now."

Lucinda held up her hand. "I won't hear of it, please come along as my guest."

Lettice nodded gratefully. "That is most hospitable of you. Would you like to come in for a cup of tea?"

Lucinda was somewhat taken aback, Lettice Webb never entertained and all invitations to her were gently rebuffed. "I can't stop," said Lucinda looking at her watch. "I promised Ruby Hamilton I would call in with the news from the meeting and I am running slightly late."

"Then I mustn't detain you further," said Lettice who was secretly itching to get back inside to remove her corset.

Lucinda said she would drop off the details of the dinner dance and arrange a time and place for them both to meet and went on her way.

Lettice closed her front door, heaved a sigh of relief and went up to her bedroom to disrobe.

* * *

Freda Boggis had just come out of her front door and witnessed Barry Evans washing down the paintwork of the immaculate painted frontage. Looking back at her own, she knew it would take some persuading to get her Dick up a ladder doing likewise, but maybe a suggestion of a few drinks in the local would sweeten the request.

As she reached the end of the road, Muriel came around the corner humming a tune.

Freda put her shopping bag down and greeted her neighbour with a smile noticing the Palmers carrier swinging from Muriel's arm. "Bought something nice?" she asked.

Muriel nodded "I have just purchased a lovely gown for the dinner dance. It was greatly reduced and will look lovely with the fur cape Barry gave me last Christmas."

"Fancy!" said Freda, pulling a handkerchief from her coat pocket and blowing her nose loudly.

"And what will you be wearing, Freda?" asked Muriel, "and please don't mention your old faithful, that has had more outings than the over-sixties club in Hopton."

Freda huffed. "Well it's all very well for you Muriel Evans, being able to afford Palmers prices. I shall probably run something up on my treadle; I have some material I got at the jumble – black velvet and some chiffon with orange and yellow spots."

Muriel winced; the thought of her slightly overweight neighbour in anything with spots didn't bear thinking about. "Why don't you see if Arnolds have something on their rails, they often have a few bargains."

Freda picked up her bag. "I'm just off to the market for some chips, I'll see if Danny has anything on his dress stall if not I might do as you suggest."

Muriel watched as her neighbour walked away, and sighed.

* * *

Lettice had been surveying her own wardrobe; most of the items of clothing were for running the guest house or lounging around in. She really didn't have anything that could be termed as suitable evening wear, especially where a dinner and dance was concerned.

Lettice had led a quiet life and liked to keep herself to herself, but this invitation from Lucinda had got her thinking. She was tired of moving around the country when things got 'difficult' and maybe this time she would be able to settle in the seaside town and become one of the locals. She looked around the sparse room and sighed, there wasn't much here that constituted a life. The house was functional with all the things that it needed to make it so. But of her own life, there were no trinkets, no photograph frames, nothing to suggest that she had ever done anything exciting.

She gazed at the locked brown suitcase on top of the wardrobe and hoped it would be a long time before she had to use the contents of that again. Maybe this invitation to the dinner was an omen, maybe this time it would all work out and she could finally relax.

* * *

Shirley had decided that a new gown was in order and went in Palmers department store to see what she could find. She had shopped there for some years and was well known to the store staff.

Looking through the selection of evening wear, she couldn't decide whether to go plain or sparkly, but one of the trusty assistants came to her aid and encouraged her to try on four gowns. One was a stunning peacock blue with chiffon sleeves and a diamante collar, another was black velvet with a fishtail, the crimson gown sparkled and was heavy weight due to the amount of bugle beading and sequins, and the final gown was a floaty lemon chiffon affair with bell sleeves.

The sales girl made simpering noises of approval as Shirley came out of the dressing room and offered accessories to complete the look. Each gown came with a hefty price tag but Shirley knew what she liked and what she looked good in. Her figure was the envy of many and she could carry off any outfit without effort. Finally deciding on the peacock blue, she charged it to her account and then went to find some suitable evening shoes and bag. The dutiful assistant followed behind carrying the gown to ensure that madam was completely satisfied with her purchases which would be delivered.

Giving up on what the market stall and Arnolds had to offer, Freda had settled on making her own dress from material she had procured from the jumble. She had a pattern she had used before and set about her task with aplomb. She intended to be the belle of the ball, providing she wasn't let down by the suit Dick would be wearing. She hoped the dry cleaners would be able to get the beer stains out as all her own scrubbing had not been successful.

Muriel was pleased that Barry had decided to buy a new suit, though there had been nothing wrong with the one he had. It always pleased her that her husband made the effort to look his best with no words of encouragement needed. With the outfit she had purchased they would make a very handsome couple indeed.

Lucinda had taken the bus to Tuttles department store in Lowestoft and found herself a bargain in the shape of a black cocktail dress with matching jacket. It was the last one in her size and had been greatly reduced. Her black court shoes would do nicely with the black evening bag, a gift from Rita Ricer. A string of pearls and matching earrings she had inherited would complete her look. Though not usually one for social events, she was quite looking forward to a night out.

* * *

Friday 31st October came round all too quickly for some, while most landladies were ahead of the game, some had given little or no thought to the evening and they were madly dashing around the town in search of something suitable to wear.

A majority had made appointments with their hairdressers, but in the case of Freda Boggis, she caught her reflection in the bathroom mirror and wondered whether allowing herself to have a Twink home perm had been the most sensible thing to do. She knew that Muriel would be having her hair styled at The House of Doris in Gorleston and wondered if she too might have preferred the deft hand of Doris Banbury to sort her out. But ever the optimist, Freda was sure that with a little gentle teasing and a brush she would be able to pass muster, and with the trio of feathers she planned to wear in her hair thought she would look the business.

Dick's suit had come back from the cleaners in a much better condition than when it had been deposited. Because of the time it had taken to remove the stains, Dick was none too pleased to be charged extra and grumbled about it to Freda. Freda, who knew he was already smarting because of the clash with the Legion dinner and dance, did her best to calm him and said she would treat them both to a couple of bottles of Lacon's Affinity, which seemed to do the trick. Unfortunately during the course of the day, Dick had managed to hit himself in the eye while attempting to erect a new shelf in one of the bedrooms and Freda had the job of bathing it and obtaining an eye patch for him to wear from the chemist, for fear someone might think she had given her husband a black eye.

Lettice, who would never have won an award for snappiest dresser, had managed to find a very nice frock in Arnolds. It was a long floaty style with a high neck and long sleeves in lilac and black. She had also managed to pick up some gold evening sandals at a greatly reduced price and a small evening bag that had also been on offer.

Lucinda arrived outside Lettice's house in the taxi she had ordered and was pleased to see Lettice coming out of her front door. Obviously punctuality was high on her friend's list, which secretly pleased Lucinda who hated anyone who was not on time. The ladies greeted each other and both commented on the other's outfits, which were barely visible beneath the coats they had both donned in order to keep out the easterly wind that had taken hold.

They were greeted at the door of the Cliff Hotel ballroom by Shirley, who welcomed them and pointed them both in the direction of the waiters who were hovering with schooners of sherry on silver trays. Shirley noted Lettice and wondered why she hadn't joined her happy band of landladies and made a mental note to have a chat with her sometime during the evening. She might even use her authority as chair to wave the nomination process, she needed to keep the GAGGA numbers up as they had been dwindling over the last couple of years.

Muriel and Barry Evans were enjoying their sherry as Lucinda and Lettice approached. Pleasantries were exchanged and then Lucinda guided Lettice to meet Fenella and Agnes, keen that her friend should meet as many of the GAGGA members as possible and thought it best to start at the top.

Muriel was just taking another sip of sherry when she spotted the arrival of Freda and Dick Boggis; she nearly choked on her drink.

"Oh my goodness!" she exclaimed gaining the attention of her husband who had been admiring the scene. "Look what the wind has just blown in, it's the Lone Ranger and Tonto."

There was no doubt about it; the eye patch which was slightly larger than it should have been was covering part of Dick's good eye and the feathers, that were prominent in what

Muriel was later heard to describe as a birds' nest, did give Freda the look of the Lone Ranger's sidekick. The velvet gown had been very well executed but this was overshadowed by the orange and yellow dotted chiffon sleeves, which were doing nothing for the overall effect. Freda had also overdone her makeup and the two red circles on her cheeks matched the diameter of the circles on the chiffon.

As Shirley greeted them both, she was clearly lost for words and could only point to the waiters. Taking two schooners of sherry, Freda and Dick went to join Muriel and Barry who had downed his sherry in shock and made his excuses to go to the bar to get a stiff brandy leaving his wife to entertain their neighbours.

"Hello Freda, good evening Dick," said Muriel. "Barry has just rushed off to the bar, why don't you join him Dick."

No further word was needed; Dick detached himself from the arm of his wife and went in search of a decent pint.

"I bumped in to Gladys Morrison yesterday," said Freda, "she told me her Jenny was expecting her second child."

Muriel smiled, "That's nice, and Gladys loves her grandchildren. Let's hope they don't have the problem they had last time when her first was born."

Freda shook her head and sipped her sherry.

"You must remember," said Muriel warming to her theme. "Gladys wanted Jenny to call the baby Polly after her great aunt, but Jenny and David wanted to call her Esther."

"So what did they settle on?" asked Freda who wasn't good with names.

"Esther Polly in the end," Muriel replied.

The ballroom had been laid out with round tables of 12 edging the dance floor. The stage at the far end had Maurice Beeney playing background music on the piano before being joined by his boys later in the evening for the dance.

At 7.30, Shirley sounded the dinner gong and everyone was seated according to the plan that Fenella had spent hours perfecting. Muriel and Barry were at the same table as Lucinda and Lettice and Freda and Dick were sat at the table next to them. The promise from Muriel of afternoon tea in Palmers had persuaded Fenella to alter her seating arrangements some days before. Freda found herself beside Ruby Hamilton who she wasn't particularly fond of. Dick had Tom Danger and his wife Petunia who giggled at every given opportunity, causing Dick to make free with the carafes of wine.

Ruby, who was none too pleased to be sat beside Freda, tried to make the most of it. She turned to Freda who was just about to tuck into her melon and smiled sweetly. "Are you religious, Mrs Boggis?" she asked.

"My mother was brought up chapel," said Freda.

"And Mr Boggis, does he partake of religious beliefs?"

"My Dick is C of E, his father was always in Church of a Sunday, and he had a lovely singing voice. His 'He who would true valiant be' brought tears to my eyes. Are you religious then, Mrs Hamilton?"

"My family were Quakers," said Ruby with a sniff.

"So you all liked your oats then," said Freda, "that's nice."

The three-course meal had met with murmurs of approval from the gathering, and came to an end at 8.45 when Shirley, with Agnes and Fenella in tow, took their places on the stage to award the top three prizes.

Shirley, who loved this part of the evening, made the most of the spotlight that had been shone on her and spoke clearly in to the microphone. Announcing the results in reverse order – Petunia Danger was third, Fenella Wright came second and the first prize was awarded to Ruby Hamilton who practically snatched the silver cup out of Shirley's hands and took several bows complete with blue sash before being escorted back to her table by her husband.

This should have ended the formal proceedings, but Shirley tapped the microphone to gain attention.

"I think you will agree we have three worthy winners, ladies and gentleman." Polite applause followed. "Breaking with tradition, I have one further prize to award. This prize, a bottle of champagne, is given to the newest landlady to join GAGGA. Please give a hearty round of applause to Lettice Webb."

Agnes was confused by this announcement and racked her brains to think when this had been decided, it certainly hadn't been run by her.

A rather surprised Lettice approached the stage with caution and as Shirley handed her the bottle Shirley whispered in her ear.

"Welcome to GAGGA, my dear, I hope to see you at our next committee meeting. I think you will be a valuable addition to our cause."

Lucinda sat in shock, never before had Shirley Llewellyn strayed from the formalities. She could see that she now had a new nemesis to contend with, and the winning cup seemed to be even further from her reach.

Shirley then announced the cabaret for the evening and with trembling hand she gave the microphone to Ricky O'Shea who winked at her. Blushing and with her legs shaking, she left the stage and headed towards the bar with Fenella and Agnes in hot pursuit.

"Where is the money coming from for that bottle of bubbly?" said Agnes "I certainly haven't accounted for it. However much did it cost?"

"Well I do not recall it being discussed at the meeting, I shall check my notes when I get home," Fenella added, feeling somewhat aggrieved that as secretary she hadn't been consulted.

Shirley had attracted the attention of one of the barmen and ordered a large gin and tonic. "Now what would you ladies like to drink? Fenella, a gin and French perhaps, and what about a sherry for you Agnes?"

"I don't think I should" said Agnes. "I have had two already."

"Then let's make it an uneven three" said Shirley nodding at the barman. "Now then you have no need to worry your heads about the champagne; I have paid for it out of my own purse."

"But why?" asked Fenella. "We never give bottles, only certificates, cups and sashes."

"And since when did Lettice Webb become a member of GAGGA, who nominated her?" said Agnes in a rather challenging voice that was far removed from her usual less forceful approach to things.

"I nominated her," said Shirley handing over the drinks. "I spoke with her earlier and asked her if she would be interested in joining us, she said she would think about it, so I acted on impulse. This nomination idea is a bit old hat. We need to encourage fresh blood to GAGGA otherwise the whole cause will fold in a few years time."

Agnes wrinkled her nose. "The whole thing needs looking at if you ask me. People are very suspicious about how these awards are given out."

The bar was beginning to get busy. "Let's talk about this next week," said Shirley. "Tonight is about enjoying ourselves, and if I play my cards right I might just be able to get a dance with Rick."

"Rick who?" asked Agnes.

Fenella raised her eyes "The one up there in the silver lamé that's wriggling his hips and fancies himself as another Elvis."

Shirley smiled at the two and went to get a closer look at the action on stage. Another couple of gins and who knows where she might end up.

The cabaret went down very well with the crowd and Shirley regretted that she hadn't had the insight to book Rick and his boys for the whole evening. Maurice Beeney and his All Rounders had now taken to the stage and were banging out waltzes, foxtrots and sambas. No doubt they would end the evening with the Gay Gordons, a conga and the hokey cokey. During a short break for the band – it was Shirley's duty to call out the raffle and true to form several familiar names appeared to have won prizes, but the surprise of the evening was Freda winning the hamper from Palmers and the look on Muriel's face was a picture as Freda went to collect her bounty. Freda was beside herself with joy as she carried the wicker basket back to her table. Ruby Hamilton, who had not won anything in the raffle, couldn't contain her displeasure.

"Why Mrs Boggis, the contents in there may not agree with your delicate palate. Have you ever eaten cod roe or truffles before?"

Freda glared back with a smile. "I am sure my Dick and I will manage quite well, thank you very much Mrs Hamilton. Perhaps we'll invite the neighbours in. I was going to offer you and your husband a lift back home in the cab we have booked; I noticed your car was off the road again."

Ruby faltered in her reply. "A problem with the engine I believe."

"Never mind," said Freda settling herself down. "I expect you will use your usual mode of transport tonight."

"I don't think I understand."

"Well I always thought it was the custom for witches to use a broomstick on Halloween."

Ruby blushed. "You and your little jokes, Mrs Boggis." But the look on Freda's face told a different story.

When Maurice and his boys struck up the band, couples went to the dance floor to see if they could remember all the steps to the waltz. Freda let herself go when the twist was played and very nearly fell over when she tried to raise herself up again. Muriel and Barry did a rather elegant foxtrot which cocked a snook at Ruby Hamilton's attempts with her husband who had been blessed with two left feet. Shirley had persuaded Rick to spin her round the dance floor before he and his band went off to another venue to perform. Everyone joined in the conga, and the hokey cokey had people in fits of laughter as they remembered parties and dances of years gone by. Maurice Beeney raised his baton for the last time as everyone stood for 'The Queen' and applause and calls for "More!" brought the evening to a close.

And so the Landladies Convention of 1969 passed for another year, and while there had been surprises for some, others had been left wanting. For Lettice Webb, who reflected on her integration with GAGGA, things were definitely looking up. She took down the brown suitcase from the top of the wardrobe and unlocked it. Looking at the contents she sighed, perhaps she could now do away with this baggage?

Little did she realise at the time that the battered and trusty brown suitcase would one day be her passport again, to escape!